OUTER BANKS

Three Early Novels

RUSSELL BANKS

AN ecco BOOK

HARPER  PERENNIAL

NEW YORK • LONDON • TORONTO • SYDNEY • NEW DELHI • AUCKLAND

HARPER ● PERENNIAL

Portions of *Family Life* have appeared in the following periodicals: *Tri-Quarterly*, *Z-Z*, and *Extreme Unctions and Other Last Rites* (Latitudes Press).

"By Way of an Introduction to the Novel, This or Any," of *Hamilton Stark* was originally published in slightly different form in the anthology *Statements I*, Jonathan Baumbach and Peter Speilberg, eds., Fiction Collective/Braziller, New York, 1977.

Portions of *The Relation of My Imprisonment* was previously published in *United Artists* magazine.

P.S.™ is a trademark of HarperCollins Publishers.

FIRST EDITION

Designed by Justin Dodd

Library of Congress Cataloging-in-Publication Data is available upon request.

ISBN 978-0-06-154452-1

08 09 10 11 12   ID/RRD   10 9 8 7 6 5 4 3 2 1

OUTER BANKS

ALSO BY RUSSELL BANKS

To my granddaughter, Sarah

CONTENTS

PREFACE

IT'S DIFFICULT FOR me to speak as the author of *Family Life, Hamilton Stark*, and *The Relation of My Imprisonment*, even though I did indeed write them and eventually published them under my own name. But it was so long ago, and I was such a different person then, that they seem to have been written by someone else. It's as if the books were written, not merely by a younger version of my present self, but by a different writer altogether. He's a man in his mid-thirties, which makes him thirty to thirty-five years younger than I am now. He's not I, but he's someone I happen to know rather well, almost intimately, the way one knows a much younger first cousin or a favorite godson. It's nice that we share the same name, since I'm not ashamed of the young man, and he seems to have launched a promising career as a novelist on his own. We don't look much alike (although there is a noticeable family resemblance around the eyes, nose, and mouth), in spite of the fact that I am bearded and have thinning white hair, and that other, much younger Russell Banks has a drooping moustache and long brown hair and wears those silly seventies-style sideburns. We're approximately the same height, but I'm about twenty pounds heavier than he. No one today would confuse either one of us with the other.

The titles of the three separate works of fiction in this book are his. The title of the book itself is mine. I chose it, not for the pun on our shared surname, but because in the life and career of their author they are like low-lying offshore islands, barrier-islands, perhaps—a half-submerged archipelago marking where once, way back in the 1970s, the continent met the sea. A young or beginning writer spends a great deal of time mapping the extensions and limits of his imagination. Some finish the job in a matter of weeks or months and, having quickly charted their personally owned territory and its coastline, are able to commence their life's work. The young man who wrote these three novels (two of which might better be counted as novellas), took a bit longer than most before getting his map made. He took about twenty years. From his late teens to his late thirties. These works represent an essential part of that process.

Banks came to writing, to the idea of being a fiction writer, hesitantly at best and in a tentative, indirect way. It was not something he felt born or even inclined to do. He did know by the age of eighteen that he wanted to be an artist, a visual artist, even though he had never visited a museum or gallery and had never actually met an artist of any kind. He and I back then had not yet come to know each other, naturally, so he had no one in the family to model himself on, no template against which to measure his nascent ambitions and fears. As a child he had displayed a talent for painting and drawing, and had received attention and praise for his pictures from family, teachers, and other adults. It was as if he had a gift for walking on his hands, however, or juggling—a remarkable thing, yes, but not something a smart boy would make his life's work. Certainly not a boy from a working class family in rural New England in the 1940s. Still, he persisted in dreaming of becoming an artist—whatever *that* was. He did know that making pictures was more like play than work, which was good. He did not want to spend his life doing work, certainly not the kind of work done by his father, uncles, and grandfathers and their friends—plumbers, carpenters, laborers, loggers. Their work seemed mostly to leave them exhausted and angry and resentful of men who sat in offices all day. They growled about their work and at the same time worried that someone would take it away from them.

At eighteen, with his family already busted apart by alcoholism, violence, and divorce, Banks packed a duffle and left home, hitchhiking south, intending somehow to learn how to be an artist and hoping along the way to join Fidel Castro and his men in the mountains of Cuba. It was January 1959. He had a copy of Jack Kerouac's recently published *On the Road* in his duffle and an issue of *Life* magazine containing an article by a reporter named Herbert Matthews that glorified the young Cuban revolutionaries' effort to overthrow the brutal dictator, Fulgencio Batista. At that age, Russell Banks was a late-arriving beatnik with an adolescent boy's romantic, self-defining affection for the underdog, which he mistook for politics. In a rented room in Miami he drew pictures and made small paintings and tried to figure out how to get across to Cuba and up into the Sierra Maestra Mountains without Batista's people noticing. He had not begun to write yet. He had not really begun to *read* yet.

In early February 1959, Fidel Castro and Che Guevara and their merry men rode into Havana in triumph and no longer needed the help of a skinny artistic kid from New England who couldn't speak Spanish anyhow. So he got a job moving furniture in a hotel. Fell in love with a girl named Darlene. Married Darlene at nineteen and became a father at twenty. Worked as a display artist and sign-painter at Webb's City, an early box-store in St. Petersburg, Florida. Divorced at twenty-one. Then Boston, New York, Los Angeles, New Hampshire, and Islamorada Key. On the run in a stolen car in Mexico with an ex-con and an AWOL sailor he'd met in a card game in a brothel in Key West. By now, however, he had begun to read. Recklessly, randomly, omnivorously—with an appetite that fed on itself. And where before he had spent his free hours painting pictures, Banks was now writing poems and making up stories. Thanks to public libraries and the bookmobiles that cruised once a week down the Florida Keys, he had fallen in love this time with literature and like a clever monkey was trying to imitate what he loved.

His first writings aped the modernist poets, Eliot, Pound, and Stevens, whose work was impenetrable to him and thus seemed easy to imitate. Wider reading gradually aided penetration, but made imitation rather more difficult. He tried Joyce, Faulkner, Dos Passos, and Hemingway. Same thing—as long as he hadn't a clue as to what he was imitating, it was easy. As soon as he began to comprehend the source of the greatness of these works, they became sui generis. So he went to their sources: Yeats, Whitman, and Baudelaire for the poets; Melville, Flaubert, Ibsen, and Dostoevsky for the novelists. And so on, working backward in time, like an archeologist excavating an ancient, layered city with only a whisk broom and tin spoon for tools.

What I'm making here is a portrait of the artist as a young autodidact. Untutored, without guidance or even a freshman English syllabus, the literary-minded autodidact tends to seat everyone he reads at the same table, with Edgar Lee Masters placed next to Sappho, Edgar Rice Burroughs alongside Tolstoy, and Will and Ariel Durant cheek by jowl with Herodotus. Randomness in reading has its rewards and advantages, to be sure, but it brings with it a nagging suspicion that along the way many of the essential texts—those that every properly educated man or woman has studied—have been missed. And often with that suspicion comes an insecurity that generates a desire, expressed by a tell-tale intellectual and literary strut, to show off what one has *not* missed. I sense in these early works of Russell Banks a bit of that. He seems to want to alert us to the breadth of his reading and its high level of literary sophistication. We can see that he's read his Laurence Sterne, his Gertrude Stein, and his John Bunyan and Robert Burton. We can see that he enjoys fable and allegory as much as self-referential metafiction. We are invited to believe that he is, above all, a *literary man*.

That's not all he is, however, and we are grateful for that. For these are not merely apprentice works. In a carefully round-about way, Banks is edging up on the themes that will probably preoccupy him as a writer of fiction for the rest of his life. *Family Life* is aptly titled. Perhaps the only way he could contend with and come to an understanding of the pain and confusion of his childhood was by forcing its materials through the grid of fable. Later, having reconciled with his parents, he'll no longer need that grid and will write *Rule of the Bone*, also about family life, but told from the point of view of the abandoned child. *Hamilton Stark*, for all its formal elaborations, is an exploration of the mysterious charisma that surrounds domestic violence and the godlike power held by fathers over their children. We will see Banks explore these themes further in the late 1980s in his novels *Affliction* and *The Sweet Hereafter*. And *The Relation of My Imprisonment*, ostensibly a parody of the allegorical accounts of spiritual testing written by John Bunyan and seventeenth-century New England puritan divines for the voyeuristic delectation of their religious brethren, is as much about the theme of redemption through suffering as novels Banks will write in his late-middle age, *Cloudsplitter* and *The Darling*.

It's interesting, as well as anxiety-producing, that with each novel or collection of short stories that he publishes, the young Russell Banks comes ever more closely to resemble me. It has become increasingly difficult for me to stay ahead of him. It's hard to find a genre or narrative mode that he hasn't already turned to, to come up with a theme or conflict or character that he hasn't found first, or to generate a plot that he hasn't thought of yet. I don't know what he'll write next, but it scares me to think that I may end up chasing *him*, and he may end up writing an introduction to *my* early novels. Or worse, to my late novels.

FAMILY LIFE

A poor prince who is weak in cavalry, and whose whole infantry does not exceed a single man, had best quit the field; and signalize himself in the cabinet, if he can get up into it—I say up into it—for there is no descending perpendicular amongst 'em with a "Me voici! mes infants"—here I am—whatever many may think.

—LAURENCE STERNE,
A Sentimental Journey

1

1.

To go back to the beginning would be fruitless, timewasting, pretentious. It's much more productive, faster and more sincere to commence *in medias res* with the king squealing angrily, the princes, all three of them, lolling through their extended adolescences, the queen quietly comforting herself in her chambers, and the several secondary characters gathered together in small groups scattered variously about the palace—the Green Man (so-called), the Loon, the Twit, Genghis, *etc., etc.*

This, then, is not unlike the opening scene of a favorite opera, *The Trojans,* by Hector Berlioz (after *The Aeneid,* by Virgil), part 1, "The Sacking of Troy." That is, one thinks of that narrator, and of Cassandra, Coroebus, Andromache, Astyanax, Aeneas, Priam, Hecuba, Panthus, Helenus, Ascanius, Polyxena, Hector's Ghost, and others (in order of appearance), and one thinks of Troy or Carthage or of a castle-like citadel inside a ravaged city, of city walls and a vast plain beyond, and one recalls that particular narrative line and obtains thereby a pretty fair idea of how it all begins.

2.

This is intended, actually, to be a family story, after the Greeks. But after Thomas Wolfe, too. And Gertrude Stein. Certain late nineteenth-century Russian novelists. William Faulkner. Marcel

Proust. Thomas Hardy. Henry James. D. H. Lawrence. New England poets of the mid-twentieth century. André Gide. The Scandinavian playwrights. Truman Capote. Wright Morris. Nathaniel Hawthorne. Vladimir Nabokov. John Milton. Philip Roth. George Bernard Shaw. Washington Irving. James Agee and Walker Evans. Charles Dickens. Harriet Beecher Stowe. Sigmund Freud. Eudora Welty. William Burroughs, Jr. Laurence Sterne. Thorstein Veblen. William Carlos Williams. Edna Ferber. The Grimm Brothers. William Saroyan. Anton Chekhov. William of Occam. James Branch Cabell. John Steinbeck. Ellen Glasgow. Sarah Orne Jewett. Frank Norris. Katherine Anne Porter. J. D. Salinger. Franz Kafka. Anne Frank. Sinclair Lewis. Bede. Erskine Caldwell. Charles Addams. Tennessee Williams. James T. Farrell. Rollo May. Giovanni Boccaccio. Theodore Dreiser. Elia Kazan. Sherwood Anderson. Henry Fielding. Louisa May Alcott. Zelda Fitzgerald. Oscar Handlin. Thornton Wilder. Flannery O'Connor. The King James Version of the Old Testament. William Makepeace Thackeray. Ed Sanders. Jane Austen. Ignazio Silone. Isaac Bashevis Singer. Ernest Jones. And Ford Madox Ford. —After these, too.

After them in *time,* of course, if not in manner. Yet also, and perhaps more important than either time or manner, after them in a subtler way, and suggesting through that a previously unrecognized, yet ancient tradition, the nature of which should be apparent as soon as one has considered which authors, insofar as their names are absent above, cannot be said to participate in that tradition: The Tradition of the Bloody Orange.

3.

THE TRADITION OF THE BLOODY ORANGE—A PARADIGM

Someone appears on the horizon as a black speck, a fly stuck against the lavender sky. He draws closer and closer, at first slowly and then more rapidly, until he has drawn face-to-face with the viewer, whereat he is repelled. He tries not to reveal the depth and extent of his revulsion, nausea, disgust, boredom, by describing himself, his family, his friends and lovers, and the enemies of all. At last, unable to conceal his true feelings any longer, he draws from the leather pouch at his waist a large Florida orange (of the hybrid type, called "navel"). He brings the perfect sphere slowly up to his mouth, which is ample, and chomps suddenly into it, splattering billows of blood over his face, hands, green lamé shirt and tan suede boots. Then, continuing to eat at the orange, he turns and withdraws quickly to the horizon again, where he remains, a speck of changing color from black to red to orange and sometimes (to the naked eye) appearing cadmium yellow or even, as he should, green. From such a distance, he is quite beautiful to observe, changing color like that, especially against the lavender sky!

4.

This is the start of the action. A handsome youth who wore slick green suits and strangely decorated hats went to the king with three sons and expressed in public a passionate desire to have one of the sons for his lover.

—I don't care which one, he cried. —Any of them will satisfy me. I have this thing about princes, he said.

5.

For two days and nights, the king ambled down the many-tapestried corridors of the palace, laughing and murmuring to himself. —A thing about princes, indeed. That's rich!

6.

It was a late, amber-colored afternoon. In the gymnasium the three princes practiced the sports. Naked and oiled, they ran and kicked and threw. Soft light from the windows above drifted down and shimmered over their sleek bodies.

One of the ballboys attending them, a cripple desperately

seeking favor and possible advancement, told them about the young man in the slick green suit and his strange request. The way the ballboy told it, the man's request was actually a demand, ominously put.

—He gave your father, His Royal Highness the King, just three days to decide which one it would be, the ballboy told the athletes.

They laughed and called the ballboy a twit. —Far out, twit! they teased.

7.

In defense of himself, the ballboy changed his story and said that he'd made up the part about the funny-looking hat with the geraniums in it and the tan suede boots and the moustache and even the accent with all the flat As. But it availed him nothing. The princes pelted him with handballs, badminton birdies, medicine balls, and basketballs. They even fell to rolling a shot put at his feet, aiming for the arches. They were disturbed.

8.

The king fucked the queen on two successive nights, keeping the lights on throughout copulation on both occasions. He was obviously disturbed.

9.

—I like a plucky faggot, he breathlessly confided to the queen after each of her orgasms. After his own, however, he remained silent.

10.

The queen, pondering both his remark and the timing of his silences, had difficulty sleeping. At breakfast following their second night of love, she asked her husband, —Have you ever performed a sex act with a man? Or with a boy?

—My dear, he answered. —I once caught and screwed a loon. Unforgettable! Jesus, I had an appetite! he bellowed, heading swiftly for court.

11.

The three princes were already there, waiting nervously for him to arrive. They wanted to know beforehand how the king was going to handle this one. In this matter, they each had a private ambition for the king's policy. The oldest son was named Orgone. He was a well-known wrestler and bachelor. The second son, Dread, drove sports cars and was a big-game hunter. The third prince was named Egress (the Wild), a bad drunk, melancholy, a favorite of those fallen from grace of any kind. He was rumored to be dying of consumption. He kept a brace of fighting cocks and a kennel of Staffordshire pit bull terriers and wrote very successful, leather-rock song lyrics.

12.

The story is about all these people, then: the queen, of course, and the king, the youth in the slick green suit, Orgone, Dread, young Egress, and the loon. The queen's name was Naomi Ruth, the king's name was Egress (the Hearty, sometimes the Bluff). The youth in the slick green suit had many names, all, as it will later turn out, aliases. And the loon was called Loon, sometimes Lone, Lon, Lonnie, l'Ange, Lawn, Lune.

2

1.

Naomi Ruth languished alone among the gin-and-tonics afternoon after afternoon. Oh, she knew she was a card, but who was there to enjoy it? Besides, she never hit her stride till after three P.M. and her fourth gin-and-tonic, and by then everyone else was at court. Except, of course, for the servants, whose rapt attention had thankfully been guaranteed by their station.

2.

She told the slender, hard-muscled wine steward everything she could recall of her childhood—gazebos, cupolas, domesticated animals with names like Donkey, Fru-fru, Fluff, and Jingle, her friendly father's ruddy face as he swung her over his white-haloed head, brushing her back against the cloudless sky, meadows strewn with dipping daisies, golden twilights, lemonade, Mamma, Dilsey, Bubber. . . .

—Jesus, Your Majesty, you're a card! the steward laughed, wiping away tears. —I mean it, he said, suddenly serious.

—Do you? Do you *really*? she queried intently. —I mean, do you *really* think that?

—Yeah. You're a right-on queen. Want another drink?

—Why the hell not? she answered throatily. —Pour.

3.

Sprawled naked across the wine steward, her white body splayed like a fallen birch, she asked him, in a detached, impersonal way, as if she were asking herself —What if you were afraid that your husband was gay? Assuming you had a husband, of course. What would you *do*? What would you *feel*? she asked herself.

—Well, the steward answered. —You just never know about these things. I mean, I once knew this rabbi who surprised everyone by going into his father's business. A coat manufacturer. It's like that.

4.

The wine steward, lighting both their cigarettes with a single match, to Naomi Ruth, the two of them lying on their backs on the llama skins that covered the floor, —Lots of men switch careers in mid-career, as it were. A lot depends on the man's P-factor, the amount of pain he can endure, if you know what I mean. The important thing is that he discuss it with his family and loved ones, even though his decision ultimately may be autocratic. I mean, in the end, it's how you present these things that counts. I say this, Your Highness, because I know you are capable of great forgiveness. For instance, I once knew a priest who became a psychiatrist. Turned out he was happy as a priest, when a priest, and he was happy as a psychiatrist, too, when a psychiatrist, if you know what I mean. So you really never know. Take me, for instance. I may be nothing but a wine steward now, and I'm happy being one, believe me, but I know, if my P-factor is high enough, that I could be happy as, for instance, court chamberlain, say. That doesn't mean I'm not happy as a wine steward, however. No, ma'am, not at all. That's the important part of my notion, but the other part's important, too, of course. . . .

5.

Naomi Ruth wasn't very interested in the wine steward's observations. She was interested in his sexual organ. —What do you think is the meaning of life? she demanded.

He shrugged helplessly, as if to say, What can a poor wine steward know?

The queen wept bitter, angry tears. She pounded the pillows with her tiny fists.

He kept shrugging helplessly, trying to look stupid. What a drag, he thought. A fucking drag.

6.

Finally, the queen got the wine steward's rather large and fortunately erect cock loosened and into her, and she rode him like a log, whooping and slapping him loudly on his hairy, white thighs. For most of the afternoon, they bumped and shoved each other wildly about the room, knocking over furniture, tipping bottles of liquor and perfume, spilling the contents onto the thickly carpeted floor, and sliding with slick rumps across magazines, satin sheets, candy boxes shaped like hearts, velvet-covered love-seats, taffeta gowns, crinolines, silk underwear, a closet floor cobbled with dancing slippers, Turkish towels, talcum, facial greases, squirts of urine, bits of feces, scents, daubs and smears until, eventually, she passed out and he, exhausted and fearful, slipped out and quickly away to the servants' quarters.

7.

Naomi Ruth felt no guilt. Anger. Only anger. Mainly at the king, but also at the Loon, whoever that one was. Some kind of freak, she thought. Some kind of sicko freak. Her heart aching with loathing and revulsion, she broke her thumbs with a small instrument of torture.

—Ai-yee! she cried.

8.

What the hell's going on down there? she wondered, meaning the court.

—Today's the big day! the king had informed her that morning at breakfast.

Sensing a significance in the remark, she put her coffee cup onto the saucer noisily and said, —Big day for what? What's going on? Why am I being left out of things all the time? I never find out about anything until after it's happened or been decided. What's going on today? What's the occasion? Who's coming? Why don't you tell me what happens down there before it has already happened? Do you think that I'm stupid or something? A child? Do you think that all I can do is ask questions? Is that why you leave me out of the only life around here that's worth living? Is it? Is it? she asked.

He looked up from his newspaper and grinned. —What was the question? he asked.

—*Bastid!* she hissed to no one in particular. That was when she asked him whether or not he had ever performed a sex act with a man, or a boy.

9.

—Maybe I should try writing a novel, she suggested. A love story, like *Cinderella* or *The Song of Solomon*.

10.

In a cold room in the tower above her chambers she wrote, facing an oval mirror on the wall. Whenever she stopped writing, she looked up and stared at her own face and long, white neck and smooth shoulders, her panther-black hair tumbling down in cascades, her delicate, plum-shaped breasts, her meticulous, ivory-skinned hands, the single lily in the vase on her desk, the gold pen, vellum sheets of paper bound in brocade, her intelligence, passion, imagination, craft. She wondered what it was going to be like as a famous lady novelist. Then she would go back to her writing. Scratch, scratch, scratch.

11.

Naomi Ruth, like most normal persons, slept, and when she slept, she had a dream. It's possible, therefore, that one would wonder about Naomi Ruth's dream. What can be the dream of a *queen*? one would humbly, especially if one were a man, wonder.

12.

She rang for the wine steward, and rang, and rang, and rang.

3

1.

While making his morning toilet, Egress the Hearty thought aloud (so as to better remember his thought): Reality unperceived is form without content . . . and thus the hedonist becomes metaphysician, the mere student of consciousness becomes epistemologist, whilst the phenomenologist ends divided against himself, a self-willed irrelevance for a state of mind. . . .

His broad face covered with a thin film of sweat, the king lapsed momentarily into a deep and intense silence. Then he finished his toilet, washed his hands carefully, and strolled downstairs to the veranda for breakfast with the queen.

2.

Egress the Hearty (sometimes the Bluff), Duke of Sunder: son of Donald the Flailer, son of Jack the Boor, son of Moran the Tick-minded, son of Orgone the Tree, son of Hannigan the Pus-filled, son of Bob the Boy-killer, son of Vlad the Sad, son of Roger the Lodger, son of Sigmund the Camera, son of Sabu the Dwarf, son of Egress the Obvious, son of Dread the Courteous, son of Norman the Shopper, son of Grendel the Theorist, son of Warren the Fist-faced, son of Arthur of the Direct Vision, son of Ray the Innovative, son of Ralph the Meatpacker, son of William the Roadbreaker, son of Harry the Hat . . . and so on . . . to the beginning, the word.

3.

In any Kingdom, the most important person is the king. Period. Everyone should know that, but if someone does not, it doesn't matter. That's how true it is.

4.

In a hurry, the king took a shortcut to the office, crossing the great yard to a cut stone walkway that bordered the head-high hedge that surrounded the queen's own knot garden. The hedge had been shaped by gardeners, sculptors, actually, into the form of a mountain range, and as he walked hurriedly along the side of the range, he suddenly stopped, for, from the far side of the mountains, he heard the queen weeping. He listened for a moment, and then he thought: The worst thing about being a king is that you're still a man, goddamnit. And a man has *feelings*!

He thumped himself on his broad and thick chest and walked swiftly on, and quoting to himself a poem by Robert Frost, he sang, —. . . and miles to go before *I* weep, *miles* to go before I weep. . . . O!

5.

As soon as he reached the carpeted, air-conditioned privacy of his inner office, the king picked up his telephone and, bypassing his secretary, personally put through a call to the Loon.

> KING: Loon? This is Egress. . . .
> LOON: Oh. What do *you* want? *More?*
> KING: No, no, no! I . . . I was just . . . thinking about you, and . . . just wanted to hear your voice, I guess. That's all. . . .

LOON: Well . . . you've heard it.

KING: Yes, I have. So, how are you, Loon? Well, I hope?

LOON: Yes. I'm well.

KING: Good, good, good. And . . . so'm I. Well.

LOON: Oh.

KING: I know I wasn't going to call you anymore, but . . . as I said, I was thinking about you and just wanted to hear your voice. Actually, I had a very vivid dream last night, a dream in which you figured rather prominently . . . and you know how it is. I had this tremendous urge to hear your voice. . . .

LOON: Okay.

KING: Yes. Well, good-bye, Lon. Loon.

6.

When a king is ashamed of his weakness, to whom can he speak of it? Any mention would precipitate a political crisis. Egress kept silent, except when he could be hearty. He was, before all else, a good and faithful ruler, in the Victorian mold. —That's got to be worth something, he said to no one but himself.

7.

Full of melancholy, he left his office by a hidden door and strolled the parapet adjoining, walking along it to a watchtower at the far end, which he entered. Secreted there, he stood for some time peering into himself near a window that opened onto the great yard and quarters below, when he glanced up from himself and saw a figure he recognized as belonging to the wine steward, saw it exit somewhat furtively, though staggering, from the queen's apartment, slip through her knot garden, cut through the hedge, and limp down the walkway to the servants' quarters, where it ducked into the door that led to the PX.

The king clapped the palm of his hand against his forehead. —Oh, Jesus! he groaned. —Oh, sweet Jesus, what now? I need an unfaithful wife like I need a wine steward!

8.

This story is not about what the king will tell the Robin Hood figure, the youth in the slick green suit. It's about what happens while everyone waits for him to show up in court after the three days are up and face *down* that brassy bastard of a green-suited youth. So one needn't worry, one is missing nothing, nothing important; for it's all right here in black and white like a series of svelte bruises laid along a frail lady's lovely arm.

9.

The king was reminded of his father, Donald the Flailer, who, for no apparent reasons, had beat his eldest son mercilessly, constantly, while never touching the boy's five brothers, except to caress them affectionately. Once, after a particularly bad beating, Egress, then twelve years old, cried out, —Why, Papa? *Why? Why?*

—What do you think should be done with a man who beats women and children? the then-king demanded.

—He should get to a doctor, Egress blubbered. —He's *sick*!

—*Wrong!* the king screamed, flailing his son about the head and shoulders. —You're going to be *king,* goddamnit, and a king has to know that a man like that must be *killed*! When you know that, I'll stop beating you, he promised his son.

10.

Egress the Hearty loved his sons no less than his own father had loved his. It was a family tradition. So many things simply cannot be helped.

11.

—I want the wine steward killed immediately, the king said to the Sergeant of the Guard, who ran to the servants' quarters as fast as he could and fragged the PX with a hand grenade, blowing the wine steward to pieces.

12.

The king reasoned with himself thusly: The meanings of most things lie in our descriptions of them. . . . Explanations, the good ones, are always reenactments. . . . The man with the greatest access to reality is the man possessing the most comprehensive mode of perception. . . . And that man will end up not merely wise and useful, but also sated, glutted with meaning. . . .

He picked up the intercom and called to his secretary in the outer office. —Miss Phlegmming, come in here, will you? I have a few thoughts I want you to take down for posterity, for The Library.

—Certainly, Your Majesty, she murmured slavishly.

4

1.

There were three sons, and at this time the eldest of the three was Orgone (the Wrestler). He was the best athlete in the kingdom. Twenty-six years old, his supremacy had been recognized for a decade, and though there were a fair number of athletes whose skills in particular sports or events were greater than his, every athlete nonetheless honored Orgone as foremost among them. This was because no athlete was superior to him in two important areas of bodily endeavor: wrestling and copulation.

2.

For instance, once, three years ago, young Ralph Bunn foolishly beat Orgone (by two-tenths of a second) in the 100-meter run. Orgone immediately threw a double hammerlock on Ralph and fractured both his arms. Then he took Ralph's wife, Pearl, for a walk under the grandstands, where he screwed her three quick times in a row, dog-fashion, while the excited fans in the bleachers peered down through the slats and, with a frightening ferocity, cheered.

Ralph, lying at the end of the 100-meter runway, unattended, writhing in pain, was full of praise for Orgone's marvelous running ability. —I jumped the gun! he kept insisting.

3.

Because of his reputation, Orgone was desired even by women who had only heard of him. Naturally, this added to his reputation. Who is more respected as a copulator than the man desired by women who have never even seen him? One defines respect here, however, as a careful form of envy, which is not true respect. Thus it was that a survey taken four years ago revealed that no fewer than 36,312 young men were traveling about the kingdom saying they were Orgone the Wrestler. Shrewdly, Orgone publicized a claim which he hitherto had made only in private, that he could satisfy anyone, male or female, he fucked, and the number of false Orgones quickly fell off.

4.

Orgone thought well of his father, the king, and treated him with deference. His younger brothers, men perhaps a shade more complex than he, he treated with derisive tolerance. He loved to snap their naked buttocks with a wet towel. *Crr-r-ack!* —Gettin' much pussy? he demanded.

—Fuck off, they snarled in unison.

—Hah! 'Course you're not gettin' any! Little ol' puds like yours, who'd want to get stuffed with weenies like those, when they could have a goddamn *sequoia*! he roared, thrusting his enormous organ out in front of him, letting the warm waters of the shower splash over it.

5.

Later, serious, he said to Dread, —I *like* to work out. It's as simple as that. To work myself right out of the world. If I push myself hard enough, to extremities that can be reached only if one is already in superb shape and is physically gifted, the only noise I can hear is that of my breath and blood, I see nothing except through a film, I am aware only of my body—and of that I am totally, almost religiously, aware. The intensity is exquisite.

The same thing happens when I'm fucking someone. I become the world. All of it. I probably could accomplish the same thing with yoga, but how would it look for a dauphin to be a yogi? It's more *politique* for me to get off on sports and balling.

6.

—Yeah, Dread mumbled. He cracked open his Belgian 10-gauge and peered down the barrels at the twin circles of light at the end. —That's *one* way to deal with death. But it seems a bit of an avoidance, wouldn't you say? I mean, why sublimate the inevitable?

He jammed a wad of oil-soaked cotton into one barrel and ran it to the end with a long, steel rod, catching it with his tobacco-stained fingertips.

7.

The youngest of the three, Egress, who had been feigning sleep, rolled over in his bunk and faced the others. —It occurs to me, he announced in his usual, pontifical manner, —that you're both in your own ways protecting yourselves against the proper and necessary expressions of yourselves as the typical sons of a typical king and queen in a typical, middle-sized kingdom.

—And just exactly what "expression" would that be, Mister Wiseass? Orgone inquired.

—Violence, Egress said, smiling warmly. —Talk about sublimation, he added. —You two might as well be alcoholics. Or why not drugs? Sports, sex, death—*hah!* You guys make me laugh. You two run your egos as if they were government agencies and you meek bureaucrats, he laughed, pitching a handful of eight-penny finish nails at them.

8.

—Hey, knock it off, Egress, or I'll pound the shit out of you! Orgone yelled, ducking the nails. Egress turned back to face the simulated-log wall next to his bunk. Dread continued cleaning his shotgun, as if nothing had happened, and after a few moments, Orgone resumed reading his pornographic magazine, chuckling loudly at the cartoons, trying occasionally, but vainly, to interest his brothers in ogling the photographs of the young women's bodies. —Son of a *bitch*! he would cry. —How'd you like to get into *that*! After a while, unable to share his excitement with them, he lapsed into a leering silence and flipped through the pages with one hand, rubbing his lumpy crotch with the other.

9.

When Orgone had finished looking at the magazine, he put it down on the floor beside his Morris chair and said, —Listen, guys, I've been meaning to ask you something. What did you think of that creep in the green suit who was at court yesterday, the one Twit told us about? You two move in funnier circles than I do, so what do you think? Is he some kind of suicidal fairy? I mean, is the guy *political*?

He jumped up and started to crank out deep knee bends, his tight double-knit pants bulging hugely at the calf and thigh as he descended and ascended, one-two-three-*four*, one-two-three-*four*! He was able to finish fifty quick ones before either of his brothers could answer him.

10.

Dread responded with a cynical, weary laugh. Then he said, —Aren't you really worried about how political the old man is?

Crown Prince Orgone leaped to the carpeted floor and snapped off a hundred perfect pushups. —One trouble with being in my kind of perfect condition, he said as he finished, —you have to work harder and harder just to get a little exercise. I mean, *look* at me! I'm not even breathing hard!

11.

—What the old man *should* do, Egress said, facing the wall, —is turn all three of us over to the guy. Then the question would be whether he had given us to *him* or him to *us*. Now that's what you call "political," he said pointedly. —He won't, though. The old man's not able to think abstractly, never mind act abstractly, for Christ's sake, he snorted.

Orgone grabbed his sneakers from the closet and made for the door. —I'm going down to shoot a few baskets, maybe run some laps. Is that ballboy on duty today, the crippled one?

—You mean Twit? Dread asked.

—Yeah, the slimy one.

—You like that humpbacked, slimy stuff, eh? Dread teased good-naturedly.

—Try dope, Egress mumbled.

—Fuck you guys, Orgone said, slamming the door.

12.

On his way to the gymnasium, Orgone passed through his mother's knot garden and, glancing up, saw his father staring down at him from the tower adjacent to his private office. To the left of his father, Orgone saw two black rooks fly into the sun. As he entered the gymnasium, a black cat scurried across his path. He shot, and missed, fourteen easy set-shots in a row, and then, ominously, made the fifteenth. After missing seven more, he gave up and ran a dozen laps on the track with Twit, who, later, in the shower, ejaculated prematurely and burst into tears, running from the room when Orgone began to curse. All the towels in Orgone's locker had large rust-stains on them, and he dropped a bottle of body cologne on the tile floor and cut his left foot on a piece of the broken glass. These were omens, and Orgone knew it.

5

1.

Feeling, in an odd way, hurt by the goings-on at the court, wounded somehow, and certainly feeling needlessly distracted by it all (for, really, what of it concerned *him*?), Dread decided to pack in his gear and head for Blue Job, where, in recent weeks, there had been three cougar-sightings of the same, steel-gray, male cat.

It would be good to kill that beast, he thought, for he had not killed anything in almost a month, and he felt the hunger and the deprivation snarling in his belly like tangled ropes. Besides, the cougar was a big one. It was a fast one and it was strong, and a very wise and very dangerous one, he thought.

2.

He knew the tough, high country around Blue Job as well as any white man did and better than most Indians. He had hunted up there along the wind-shattered sides of the blue, nose-shaped rock for seven summers, night and day, from his thirteenth year to his twentieth. For the first five summers he had hunted with the guides, Abenakis, most of them, and then he had spent a couple of summers up there alone. For five years now—though he had traveled to, and hunted on, every continent in the world—he had not been back to Blue Job. It was almost as if he had become afraid of the mountain, he thought, lacing up his L.L. Bean hunting boots.

3.

He took no more gear than what he could carry on his own back: a one-man Greenland mountain tent, his down-filled sleeping bag, one pot, one skillet, a Svea gas stove, his Norm Thompson fold-away flycasting outfit, one change of clothes, and the Ten Essentials: maps (Geological Survey maps of the Blue Job quadrangle), a compass, a flashlight, sunglasses, emergency rations (raisins, chickpeas, and powdered eggs), waterproofed matches, a candle for starting fires in dampness, a U.S. Army blanket, a Swiss Army pocketknife, and a small first aid kit. Also, a skinning knife, which he wore on his belt, one hundred rounds of ammunition, and his trusted Remington 30.06 rifle with the special Howard Hughes scope and sight that he had used to such miraculous advantage in Tanzania. —This one helps you kill the big ones, he had written to Hughes.

4.

Egress rolled over in his bunk and watched his brother finish packing. —Where you going? he asked idly.

—Goin' to the high country, the far outback, headin' for the deep piny woods, lightin' out for the territory.

—Alone, I suppose.

—Alone, Dread said.

—Coming back soon?

—Cain't say, Dread opined. Seated cross-legged on the floor, shoving his gear into the Kelty, he looked like a young, rawboned lieutenant in the U.S. Cavalry, a noble fool preparing to leave on a dangerous mission behind enemy lines, a secret mission that he, and no one else, had volunteered for. He had covered his pale, freckled face with lampblack and his long, blond hair with a watch cap.

—Why're you done up like that?

—So no one will see me, Dread told him.

—Right, Egress said.

5.

By dawn he had reached the shadow of Blue Job. Standing in a clearing, he watched the sun inch heavily over the mountain's knobby profile, and he guessed he was now inside the cougar's territory, about eight miles in a line from the top of the mountain.

He began looking for signs, cougar shit, tracks, or a fresh kill, as he walked headlong toward Blue Job. The sun rose higher, and he began to sweat. He could smell his woolen clothing, and he knew the cougar could, too, and it excited him. He shoved three bullets into his rifle and took off the safety and kept on walking, his head facing the mountain, his eyes darting from side to side and down, searching for signs. This was how the Abenaki had taught him, but he did not remember that, for he'd learned it truly.

6.

Suddenly he knew he was being watched. Turning around, slowly, like a sleepy cat, he saw the steel-gray cougar crouched about twenty yards away in a short, shallow crevasse between two high, moss-covered rocks. He and the animal stared at each other for nearly a full minute, when, in a single move, the cougar sprang to the top of one of the large rocks and disappeared into the dense underbrush behind it.

Dread felt a chill wipe his entire body. Next time I'll get closer before I look at him, he decided. Then he sat down on the sun-warmed ground for a moment; his legs felt watery, and he was afraid he would fall.

7.

Walking on, he unaccountably remembered watching an Indian woman have her baby in a pine grove, mingling the blood and afterbirth with the warm, sweet-smelling pine needles on the ground. But then he couldn't remember if he'd actually seen that or had only dreamed it and was remembering a dream. He finally decided that it didn't matter: whichever, he had been mightily impressed.

8.

He stopped for lunch—tea and beef jerky—on the side of a large, granite outcropping. This time the cougar walked out of an aspen grove at the far end of the outcropping, and, leaping onto the rock, sat there and waited, watching him while he chewed on the dried beef and sipped his tea. They seemed to be studying each other's eyes. Finally, the cougar turned and loped back into the forest, headed east, toward Blue Job.

Dread started to feel a little crazy. —My god, he thought, —who needs to race automobiles at 160 miles an hour, when you can have *this*! He named the cougar Merlin, after his favorite car, a Merlin Lotus Rue.

9.

As he got to his feet, moving slightly off-balance and too quickly, he reached for his rifle, which he had leaned against the chunk of rock he had been sitting on, and he knocked the gun off the rock to the grassy ground about ten or twelve feet below, where it fired, sending a bullet into the young man's right ear and out the top of his head, hurling him off the rock into the blackberry brambles on the other side, where he had three quick visions, and died.

10.

DREAD'S FIRST VISION

A hot wind roaring, a tilt to the landscape, which is quickly righted, and then he is flying through the air a few feet above the ground, when suddenly the flight ceases, and he seems to hover, bodiless; looking down, he sees gray paws and legs, and he lets his tongue loll, and he pants, and for a second realizes that he is becoming the cougar; and then he forgets this, for he has in fact become the cougar, which immediately pisses on a blackberry bush and commences hunting.

11.

Dread's Second Vision

His battered, hurt body is washed and anointed with oils and laid out in a white gown and left on a redwood bier in a dimly lit room heavy with the smell of burning incense; he is conscious, sort of, but is unable to speak or move, until a man enters the room, a man wearing an exotically cut, glistening green suit with flowers, daisies, apple blossoms, black-eyed Susans, in his curly hair; and when the man takes Dread's hand, Dread is able to speak and move, as if by magic; sitting up, he steps lightly from the bier and, his hand still held by the green man, says, —Am I the one? —Yes, is the answer, uttered in a melodic voice full of sweetness and light and delicate caring. —The others? Dread asks. —The others are where they have always been. You were chosen to leave because you alone were thought to be the angelic one, the green man informs him; and together, holding hands, they leave the darkening room for the sun-drenched meadows outside.

12.

The Vision of Too Bad: Dread's Third Vision

The first two visions are categorically denied.

1.

Meanwhile, back at the palace, Prince Egress, alone in the Bunkhouse (the name given to the apartment years ago by the press, when the boys' rooms had been redecorated with plastic, simulated-log walls, false fireplaces, electrified kerosene lanterns, stuffed heads of mountain sheep, elk, and bear, and for each prince, his own bunk bed), was "getting in touch with his anger."

He strolled through the five rooms of the apartment, tipping over all the furniture, pitching lamps and wall hangings and draperies onto the floor, smashing every piece of glass he could see—windows, mirrors, dishes, liquor bottles. Then, finally, emptying the contents of the closets and dresser drawers onto the floors, he splashed kerosene from one of the lanterns that had not been converted across the heaps of cloth and flipped lit matches into each room, one after the other, and worked his way toward the hall exit. With the rooms blazing behind him, he ran out, passing the just-arriving bucket brigade in the hallway.

2.

He rapped on the door of his mother's chamber and, without waiting for an answer, walked in. She quickly covered her breasts with a satin sheet; she had been brushing her soft, ebony-colored hair. Smiling easily, she said, —Egress, how nice to see you. Will you wait outside for a second, honey, while I dress?

He coughed, wiping his mouth with a lace cuff, smearing it with sputum and blood. —I want to talk with you about something important, Mother, he announced. He could hear the shouts and cries of the firemen and the volunteer bucket brigade in the distance as they doused the flames in the Bunkhouse.

—What's all that sound and fury? asked Naomi Ruth.

Egress coughed again. —It's coming from the Bunkhouse. I just wrecked the place and set it on fire. Vandalized it, sort of.

—Oh-h-h, Egress, not again! she said in a low voice, pulling him to her, pressing his cheek against her soft, white, plum-shaped breasts.

—I'm sorry, Mamma, he said.

—I know, dear, she replied.

3.

Feeling superficially refreshed, young Egress left his mother's chamber. But the old heaviness swiftly returned.

—Good god! he exclaimed to himself. —Is there no outrage outrageous enough to lift these dead spirits of mine? Am I doomed, he soliloquized, to an existence of dull eeks and melancholic squeals with naught but long intervals of sodden thought between? Oh, daily, daily diminishes the possibility for suddenness; hourly shrinks the spontaneous! The hot squirts and jacks of ecstatic youth are in manhood mere dribbles, and what ere remains of that rough ecstasy now flatly lies upon the frozen turf before me. I can but prod and poke the memories as if they were the drained entrails of a goat! Would a future could be divined there as sharply as a past! He kicked the loam of his mother's knot garden with a booted toe. —Shit! he decided. —Guess I'll snort some coke and go to London and jam. This crap with the Green Man will blow over in a few days anyhow. It won't amount to shit. Nothing ever does.

4.

He smoked hash and snorted some coke in the library and, rubbing a couple of drops of hash oil into each ear, went up to the east-facing parapet to watch the landscape darken before him while the sun set behind him. Pretending he was the sun setting was a favorite fantasy.

This time, however, just as he was getting off, he heard a ghost. —Eee-gress! the voice called. It was not an unpleasant voice. —Eee-gress! He looked all around him but could see no one. The guards were in the watchtowers. He was alone on the parapet. —Eee-gress!

Well, he'd had bad trips before and had learned the hard way to "go with it," so he sat down well out of the bitterly snapping wind and said, —Okay, I'm listening. Go ahead. There was a pause; then he said, —I suppose this has to do with the green man. He's been on my mind a lot today.

—Righto, said the ghost.

—Before we go on, said Egress, —do you mind telling me who you are?

—You can call me Bob or Jack, whichever you prefer. It doesn't matter, because I'm only a messenger. We've never met before and I rather doubt if we'll ever meet again.

—Okay, Bob or Jack, shoot, Egress said.

5.

After Bob or Jack had given Egress the message, which, he told him, was a "plan" from a "source" whose identity he "could not reveal," Egress went down from the parapet, caught a car for the airport, and flew to London, where it was morning. The sun shone and birds sang. For the first time in months, young Egress was elated.

Inside the cab from the airport, he snorted more coke and went straight to where his friends lived, in an elegant, brick townhouse near Grosvenor Square. They were all members of a world-famous rock band from California called The Sons of the

Pioneers. In the last few years their most popular songs had been written by Egress.

—Hey, man! they all cried when they saw him. —What's happening? they sang.

—Hey, man! he answered.

—Far out! they exclaimed. Then they all sat down on the floor in the middle of the classically proportioned drawing room designed by Sir Christopher Wren and snorted some coke together.

—Good dope, they agreed.

6.

Egress showed them the lyrics to the song that he wanted The Sons to record and release as a single as soon as possible. He told them it was part of a "plan" he had. Then he hummed the melody. —What do you think? he asked.

—Far out, said Mick. He was the spokesman for the group. The others nodded enthusiastic approval.

Together, they went upstairs to the recording studio and prepared their instruments. Egress stood in a corner and coughed on his sleeve, which by now was covered with a thick crust of dried phlegm and blood.

—Hey, man, you gotta do somethin' about that cough, Mick called to him.

—I guess so, Egress said. —Anybody got a clean shirt I can borrow? he yelled. Then he laughed long and loud, which made The Sons of the Pioneers very nervous.

7.

BALLAD OF THE GREEN MAN

(to the tune of "Battle Hymn of the Republic")

Mine eyes have seen the glory
of the coming of the Lord;

He is trampling out the vintage
where the grapes of wrath are stored;
He hath loos'd the fateful lightning
of His terrible swift sword,
His truth is marching on.

I have seen Him in the watchfires
of a hundred circling camps;
They have builded Him an altar
in the ev'ning dews and damps;
I can read His righteous sentence
by the dim and flaring lamps,
His day is marching on.

I have read a fiery gospel
writ in burnish'd rows of steel;
'As ye deal with my contemners,
so with you My grace shall deal';
Let the Hero, born of woman,
crush the serpent with his heel,
since God is marching on.

Chorus:

Glory, glory Hallelujah!
Glory, glory Hallelujah!
Glory, glory Hallelujah!
His truth is marching on.

8.

The group sang and performed the song well, but the experience left them shaken, Egress included. It was an aggressively antisocial song, and they knew it.

One by one, they put down their instruments and drifted

down the stairs and left the house. As Egress went out the door to the crowded street, he called back to Mick, —Be sure the record gets distributed worldwide by nightfall. I'll take care of any extra expenses.

—Righto, man! Mick replied. Then, to the drummer, Hadley, —Oh, wow, man, that cat is into some heavy shit. Can you dig it? he said.

—Good dope? Hadley asked.

9.

Egress immediately caught a cab for the airport and flew home, where it was morning. As he entered the courtyard, he noticed ahead of him a group of Indians in breechcloths, moccasins, and war paint. They carried their Stone Age weapons. He could tell from their facial tattoos and scars that they were Abenakis, "Friendlies."

—What's up? Why the war paint? Egress asked one of the savages, a rotund man whom, because of his slightly arrogant manner, Egress took to be the leader. The others seemed slightly intimidated by the palace and all, which was natural, considering what the wretches were used to.

—We just got paid for cutting trees for the lumber barons, so we kind of decided to drift into town to spend all our money in a few hours of hysteria, the red man said. —Know of any bars that'll serve Injuns? he asked.

—There's always the Tam, Egress said. —They'll serve *anyone* at the Tam.

—What we really want is white wimmen, the Indian added.

—Oh, Egress said. —Mind if I tag along?

—Not at all, please do, said the Indian.

10.

One thing about Indians attracted Egress more than any other: They were in touch with their anger. He used to talk about his attraction with his analyst. —They're so damned self-*entitled*! he would exclaim. —You can take everything away from them, their land, their history, their whole culture, for god's sake, and they still come back at you with that wonderful drunken Indian thing! It's incredible!

And sure enough, when they got to the Tam, all the Indians started ordering double boilermakers three at a time, and in fifteen minutes they were fighting with each other and anyone else who'd hung around. They broke all the furniture and glass in the place and, with Egress joining in, paid for the damage and moved on to the next place, a hotel bar called Lulu's, where, Egress had assured them, there would be "plenty white wimmen."

It was at Lulu's that Egress told the head Indian, whose name was Horse, about the plan he had received from the ghost on the parapet. Horse thought it ridiculous. —You white-eyes really go for that apocalyptic crap, don't you?

11.

—I'll tell you the one thing you white-eyes can't seem to learn from us, no matter how well-intentioned, disciplined, and sensitive you are. It's the distinction between the impulse to anger and the impulse to destroy. Too bad. Some of you make pretty good drunks, and except for that destruction impulse, your suicides are downright attractive, Horse said.

Egress unfortunately didn't hear him. He was eating his glass, and all he could hear was the snap and crunch of a mouthful of shards.

—For example, Horse went on, —an Indian would never break his glass with his mouth, because, for an Indian, the impulse would never be to destroy, not the glass and certainly not his mouth. Rather, the impulse would be to hurl the glass, to create a missile, and if, as a result, the glass were shattered, it would not matter, for it would already have been converted, by anger, into something else. To illustrate his point, Horse threw his own glass into the mirror over the bar and created a beautiful silver explosion. —Intentionality is everything, he said. —Everything.

12.

Egress fell off his chair, gagging and choking on his own blood. He had coughed unexpectedly and had torn open his throat with a sliver of glass, and in a short time he had strangled. The white people in the room were horrified and, looking for officials, ran out of the bar into the streets. The Indians knew it was an accident, so they continued to drink and brawl. They only got to town once a month and they wanted to make the most of it. They had liked young Egress, though, and, to honor that fact, they played "The Ballad of the Green Man" on the jukebox over and over, all night long, until dawn, when Horse hallucinated and thought the jukebox was a bear and attacked it with his hatchet. He made a beautiful robe of the skin and wore it proudly for the rest of his days.

7

1.

The Green Man was not the real name of the Youth in the Green Suit. Prince Egress had first called him that, rather publicly, and consequently most people took it to be his real name. But, as one may recall, the truth is that he had many names, none of them legal. He was, in all respects, an *alias,* a true underground man. It's not even clear that he was a *man;* he may have been a woman, as well. Thus he was the definitive guerrilla, a person with absolutely no past.

All this, but nothing more than this, was known to the king within hours of the youth's arrival in court and his presentation there of his odd request, or, as some said, his demand. The king, after the youth had spoken, had leaned over to his chief of intelligence, the well-known Grand Inquisitor, and had said to him, —I want that kid's past on my desk this afternoon!

But all he got was an empty manila envelope.

—All right, the king had said, after his rage had fled, —then watch him. The bastard's got to have a *present!*

2.

The youth is extremely attractive, to men as to women, although it's not exactly sexual. They stare at him unabashedly wherever he goes. Of medium height and build, he moves with extraordinary grace and purposefulness and seems thus to be both a taller and a stronger person than he probably is. His "costume," upon close examination, turns out to be hand-tailored, somewhat conservatively designed, of a lightweight, finely woven fabric imported either from the Middle East or North Africa, possibly from Greece. The youth himself, however, is a Nordic type. The color of his suit is forest green and is not "slick" or "shiny," as was thought, a mere illusion caused by the way in which the finely woven cloth reflects light. The general impression given to strangers by the youth is that of a person with immense, unquestioned authority. It is not yet clear, however, what exactly his authority is over, for he seems to disdain exerting it.

3.

After completing his address to the king, immediately the youth, hereinafter referred to as the Subject, departs from the court. The crowd eagerly backs off to make way for him. Outside, in the great yard, he is seen talking with Genghis, the Royal Dwarf. A fragment of their conversation luckily is overheard and taken down:

> SUBJECT: You're treated *kindly*?
>
> GENGHIS: Ya, except for all da time ven dey are laffink at me.
>
> SUBJECT: They think you are *funny,* then?
>
> GENGHIS: Ya! Dey like da vey I am so short in da body und so big in da head. I tink it's kinda fonny myself!
>
> SUBJECT: It must be painful for you, to be treated as other than human.
>
> GENGHIS: It's a job. I got a family.
>
> SUBJECT: Personally, I think you're disgusting. You should try telling jokes. Make them laugh at your jokes.

At this point, the Subject departs from the dwarf, heading downtown.

4.

At a busy, downtown intersection, the Subject seems bewildered, as if he is not familiar with the plan of the city. He notices an adolescent girl standing near him, waiting for the light to change. She is wearing a short red skirt, a football player's sweater many sizes too large for her with a huge, red A sewn onto the front, and saddleshoes. She is a schoolgirl.

—Can you tell me where the gymnasium is located? the Subject asks her.

—Hi! she replies. —I'm 37-24-37! Terrific, huh?

—I'm trying to locate the gymnasium. I want to see the famous Prince Orgone run and jump and throw.

—Jeepers, my daddy says I've got the body of Raquel Welch, the personality of Marie Wilson, and the brains of a quail! I *love* the prince! I've got all his records! Do you *know* the prince? Jessum, how em-barrassing! I'm 34-27-34! I mean, 37-24-37! How em-barrassing! I can't even remember my own name!

—Are you all right? he asks.

—I'm dying! she cries, and noticing the light has turned green, she scampers across the street, scattering books and papers behind her as she runs. The Subject speaks to no one else and succeeds in getting to the gymnasium on his own.

5.

The Subject wears his hair in current fashion. He has little or no facial hair and no distinguishing facial marks, scars, moles, warts, or tattoos. He is quite harmless-looking. Except for his obvious intensity and the fact that none of his graces appear to have been learned (the final grace), he looks like a young man or woman in the diplomatic service. Thus, even though he does not present the proper identification papers, he is waved into the gymnasium area by the guard, is issued a "Distinguished Visitor" pass, and is given the run of the place.

It should be noted that everywhere he goes, the Subject inadvertently reveals flaws, oversights, and malfunctions in the various systems. It is not clear whether this is intentional. If not, he might be of immense use to the systems.

Conclusion: The Subject warrants further study.

6.

He leans against the chain link fence that encloses the playground behind the gymnasium proper and watches the Crown Prince run, jump, and throw. When the prince has completed his exercises and has gone into the showers, the Subject departs, and, as he departs, he drops, or perhaps throws, to the ground the small piece of paper on which he earlier was observed writing:

Right-handed, favors left knee and hip slightly (chondromalacia, probably). Will doubtless move to his right when threatened. Large muscles are overdeveloped, small ones underdeveloped: not as much endurance as he probably thinks he can rely on if threatened. Could be dangerous, if threatened, especially because of martial skills, but can be overcome by almost any opponent using disciplined, intelligent force.

On the strength of this note, the Subject is arrested and imprisoned, where he presently languishes unafraid.

7.

First Interrogation

INQUISITOR: Are you working alone?
SUBJECT: Alone?

INQUISITOR: Do you have co-conspirators?
SUBJECT: No. Of course not.
INQUISITOR: Then you *are* working alone!
SUBJECT: Well, yes.

SUMMATION: Subject insists no one else involved in his assassination plot.

8.
SECOND INTERROGATION

INQUISITOR: Did you realize, when you hatched your insidious plot, that in this country assassination is a capital offense? Did you know that we execute assassins?
SUBJECT: I surmised it.
INQUISITOR: Aha!

SUMMATION: Subject is not insane, as was formerly thought, and must be judged responsible for his actions.

9.
THIRD INTERROGATION

INQUISITOR: What is your real name? Your *legal* name.
SUBJECT: Steve Katz.
INQUISITOR: Don't fuck with me, wiseass, or I'll break your fingers. What's your real name? We have ways . . .
SUBJECT: Ronald Sukenick.
INQUISITOR: Cut the funny stuff. This is serious! You are in no position to be funny.
SUBJECT: Artemas Ward. Laurence Sterne. Lamar Sabacthani.

INQUISITOR: One last time, before we break all your limbs. What's your real name?

SUBJECT: John Doe.

SUMMATION: Subject is hereinafter to be referred to as John Doe.

10.

FOURTH INTERROGATION

INQUISITOR: Why were you in the vicinity of Blue Job mountain when Prince Dread was shot and killed?

JOHN DOE: I went there to watch him hunt a cougar. I wanted to know if he was the hunter he thought he was.

INQUISITOR: And was he?

JOHN DOE: No. Obviously not.

SUMMATION: John Doe freely admits to having tracked down Prince Dread on the ill-fated "Blue Job Cougar Hunt."

11.

FIFTH INTERROGATION

INQUISITOR: What were you doing at Lulu's the night Prince Egress was killed by the Indian band?

JOHN DOE: I wanted to see if he was as in touch with his anger as he seemed to think he was.

INQUISITOR: And was he? No, never mind. Disregard that last question.

SUMMATION: John Doe freely admits to having goaded the child-like band of Abenaki "Friendlies" into attacking Prince Egress at Lulu's.

12.

Sixth Interrogation

Inquisitor: Do you know a schoolgirl named 37-24-37? She claims that you are her father and that you made obscene sexual overtures toward her.

John Doe: I know her only slightly. But I'm not her father, a man who insults and reviles her and who, therefore, is probably the person who made a pass at her. Thus, she's only half-right. *Someone* made a pass at her. But I would never do such a thing. I'm virtually a stranger to her.

Inquisitor: Do you know the dwarf Genghis? He claims you are responsible for his having been fired from his job.

John Doe: I do know him, and I'm glad he's being treated more fairly, but no, I can't claim responsibility.

Inquisitor: Okay, answer this one correctly and you get all the prizes. How did you kill Prince Orgone?

John Doe (proudly): Blood poisoning. You'll recall that he broke a bottle of body cologne in the shower a few days ago and stepped on a piece of the broken glass, cutting his left foot slightly. He should have stayed away from those public showers until after the cut had healed, but he knew he'd go crazy if he skipped a workout. He was trapped by himself, like the others.

Inquisitor: Well said, Mr. Doe. But just for the hell of it, why these three young princes, each in the prime of his life? Why these young fellows? Why not the king?

John Doe: I've got a thing about princes, I guess.

Summation: We've got our man. We've got his plot.

8

1.

The Loon, because of his job as janitor, or custodian, for the Star Chamber, a position obtained for him by the king, had no difficulty in keeping abreast of developments. He knew more about what was going on than did the king himself. Unlike the king, however, he didn't care about what was going on, which is why the king had appointed him to this somewhat delicate post in the first place. The king had many faults, but he knew how to maintain security. He knew that every morning, after a night of cleaning up the inquisition rooms, the Loon would go home to his tree house in Central Park and forget practically everything he had seen, heard, or smelled. The Loon was much too self-absorbed to be a busybody.

2.

The Loon was like a bat. He slept all day long, from sunrise to sunset, regardless of where he was or what was expected of him. He would, as the sun rose, simply fold whatever piece of cloth there was at hand, a drapery, a rug, a coat, around him like a shroud and drop off to sleep, usually positioning himself in a foetal heap in a corner. The only thing that could wake him was the sunset. In many ways, the habit was inconvenient and some-times embarrassing to others, but it was a habit he had formed early in childhood and thus he was devoted to it. Actually, all his habits were formed early in childhood, and he was devoted to all his habits. He had not formed a new habit or broken an old one since his fourth birthday.

3.

People in positions of power seemed to fall in love with the Loon, through no design or effort of the Loon himself. There were the director of the nursery school he had attended, the cop on the block, the mayor of the small town in the South where he had spent his middle childhood, the president of the University of Virginia where he had matriculated, the governor of a large industrial state in the northeast, the head of a television network, a Latin-American dictator, a Greek shipping magnate, a U.S. Secretary of the Interior, and, most recently, Egress the Hearty, a king. Only coincidentally were all these powerful persons men, but as a result of that coincidence, most people thought the Loon was a homosexual. They did not, of course, think it of his lovers.

4.

Often, on late-night TV talk shows, he was asked by the host to talk about whether or not he was, as the host put it, a "homosexual." —Are you, Mr. Loon, a "homosexual"?

—Way-yell, Dick, the Loon would drawl (he had a pronounced southern accent, especially on TV), —since you put it "that way," ah, not *really*.

The audience and Dick the host would roar with laughter, winking and elbowing each other fiercely.

5.

When the Loon learned, one by one, of the deaths of the three princes, he was surprised but not particularly saddened. He had never thought of them as high-quality persons. All three of them had, at one time or another, jerked off on him while he was waiting, naked, in the anteroom for the king. They hated him, and even if they didn't know it, he did. It was their ignorance, more than the semen on his hairless chest, that had bothered him. The king, on the other hand, had always known he hated the Loon, and thus he never once had jerked off on him. He simply would come into the anteroom and go right to work, buggering the Loon once or twice, and then lie back and tell him his troubles all night long. You had to respect the king.

6.

Because of his sleeping habits, the Loon ate breakfast at night and dinner in the morning. He usually took a light lunch around midnight. Although, as mentioned, he lived in an excellent and completely outfitted tree house, designed by Michael Graves, he rarely ate at home. Rich and exciting people were always calling him up and inviting him over for breakfast or dinner. Eggs Benedict at nine in the evening with the Loon was regarded as a social event of no mean proportions. This was partially because of the Loon's physical attractiveness (resembling, however, a young Marcel Marceau, he clearly was not "handsome"), partially because of his well-known proximity to power, and partially because of the brilliance of his conversation: He disagreed with everything everyone said, but only by pretending purposefully to misunderstand what was said. He was therefore regarded as an accomplished and dangerous wit.

7.

The king learned of Dread's death at three in the morning, when a group of Abenakis, led by the one called Horse, came in with the body. At four-thirty, he called the Loon, who had just got home from work. —Oh, Loon! The queen is mad with grief! She blames *me*! he cried.

—Why not? the Loon asked. —You're supposed to be in charge of everything, aren't you?

—This is no time to be funny, the king said sadly. —She's blaming me because I'm the one who taught him to use a gun.

—Oh, said the Loon. —I see. And you didn't teach him very well.

—Oh, I taught him well, all right, groaned the king.

—No, you didn't, the Loon said sympathetically. —You can't take all the blame for this onto yourself, Egress. You taught the boy as badly as you could.

—Oh, no, I didn't.

—Yes, you did.

—No, Loon, I didn't.

—Sure you did.

—I did?

—Of course.

—Thanks, Lone, you've been a sweetheart. I wish I could talk to my wife this way.

8.

Basically, the Loon was a gentle soul and tried always to hurt no one. But to avoid exploitation, to keep from becoming "passive," as they say, he was forced to develop certain stratagems. He developed these early in childhood, and because they worked, kept them into adulthood. As can no doubt be observed, one thing he was very good at was "Changing the Subject." He was also good at "Non Sequitur" and "Petitio Principii." If none of these worked and it looked like he was going to be forced into a choice between hurting someone and being exploited by him, he still had two, somewhat extreme, stratagems left: "Fawning," and, if that failed, "Total Surrender." Social scientists have called this last stratagem "Self-objectification," turning one's self into something else, in Loon's case, the exploiter's self. This didn't matter to the Loon, however, because, for him, it was a question of survival.

9.

That afternoon, the king learned of the barbarous death of Prince Egress. He first called the Loon at four, but wasn't able to rouse him until six-fifteen, when the sun's setting set off a gong inside the Loon's head. Still drowsy, he answered the phone. — H'lo?

—Oh, Lone, Lone! They've killed my baby! Egress, the wild and woolly one, gone, gone, gone! cried the king.

—Who did it? the Loon asked.

—I did it, l'Ange! *I'm* the guilty one! the king hissed into the receiver. —Ask my wife, he added. —She'll tell you.

—Have you asked her?

—No! God, no! These deaths of our children have riven us as a wedge splits a fallen tree. Just when we were really getting it together, too, he said wistfully. —Comfort me, Loon! the king commanded. —Comfort me! My wife doesn't understand me!

—I once knew a man in Oregon who hadn't any teeth, not a tooth in his head. Yet that man could play on the bass drum better than any man I ever met, the Loon said soothingly.

—Do you think so? the king asked.

—Of course.

—You know, I should have connected this to that kinky green-suited guy in the first place! You're a genius, Loon! I'll have him arrested immediately!

10.

—H'lo, Egress. The Loon knew who was calling even before he had picked up the phone. He was getting ready to go to bed and was sleepy and cross.

—Oh, Loon, my Lawn, my angel! Doom, doom, doom! the king bellowed.

—He got Orgone, eh?

—Yes, Orgone, my pride, my joy, my Crown Prince, my dauphin! *Dead!*

—And it's your fault, I imagine.

—Yes, yes, yes. My fault, the king cried excitedly. —Comfort me, Loon! I need you to comfort me. I need you.

—You *need* me? the Loon asked, incredulous, and wary, too.

—Oh, yes, yes, yes. I used to think of you as my weakness, but now that it's clear to me how much I am hated by my wife, I think of you as my strength.

—That doesn't follow, the Loon said.

—No matter, it's *true*! asserted the king.

—Okay, then. It's not your fault because you did everything you could, the Loon reasoned.

—Yes, you're right, you're right. I did everything I could, the king said.

—Listen, Egress, it's early, so I've got to get some sleep.

—Of course, of course. I'm sorry, I forgot.

—G'bye.

—'Bye. And, Loon, kiss-kiss.

—Kiss-kiss-kiss, the Loon answered. Then he hung up, and, feeling a bit antic, wrapped himself in a flag and went to sleep in a corner of the bathroom.

11.

—Oh, Your Majesty, your puissance, I'm deeply flattered by your proposal that I accompany you on your pilgrimage to the Empire State Building, but, really, no one so kingly, so majestic, so all-puissant, so inspiring, so inspired, so chosen, so exalted, so with-it, so hip, so heavy, so together, so tough, so mean, so fancy, so witty, so refined, so sensitive, so enlightened, so manly, so kind, so sunny, so benign, so wise, so benevolent, so flexible, so awesome, so handsome, so clean, so sexy, so potent, so resourceful, so brave, so balanced, so sane, so stable, so innovative, so talented, so considerate, so disciplined, so skilled, so patient, so independent, so deliberative, so wealthy, so restrained, so young . . . needs *me*!

—I don't know, maybe you're right, the king said. Kiss-kiss.

—Kiss-kiss-kiss, the Loon answered, letting out a long sigh of relief. If the king's taking off on a guilt trip, let him travel alone, he thought.

12.

—Loon! I've changed my mind. I need you. Either you accompany me on my pilgrimage to the Empire State Building or I'll kill you.

—I'm yours! the Loon cried.

9

1.

The king showed up at the Loon's tree house just before dawn, and if the Loon hadn't been expecting him, he probably wouldn't have recognized him. He had shaved off his bushy beard and had cut his hair short, rather clumsily, it appeared, with a knife. He looked a little psychotic. He was dressed in a burlap grain bag with holes cut in it for his head and arms and a length of half-inch rope tied around his waist for a belt. He was barefoot. In a small bundle, he had a wooden begging bowl, a string hammock, and a brick-sized bar of solid gold which he said was his Atonement Gift. Evidently, he intended to present it at the Empire State Building.

—Jesus, you're really dressing down for this, aren't you? the Loon observed. —Is it okay if I wear something a bit fancier?

—Whatever, was the dour reply, so the Loon put on a powder-blue, wet-look jumpsuit with a long gold scarf tied at the throat.

2.

It was already evident, from the king's appearance, that the journey was going to be arduous. —Maybe I'd better bring my credit cards, the Loon suggested hopefully.

—Whatever, the king replied.

After taking a quick peek into the king's bundle, the Loon packed one for himself—begging bowl, string hammock, offering (a thumb-sized block of Moroccan hash), plus a few extras: the Ten Essentials (see p. 25), and his packet of internationally honored credit cards. —Well, he announced, —I'm ready.

The king murmured, —Whatever, and they started out across the park, heading in an easterly direction, toward Fifth Avenue. They hadn't traveled more than thirty or forty yards, however, when the sun came up. Immediately, the Loon hung his hammock from two small maples, wrapped himself in his U.S. Army blanket, and dropped off to sleep.

The king looked at his companion, shrugged and said, —Whatever, to himself and sat down on the ground to meditate. He certainly was a Changed Man, and no one was more aware of this fact or more impressed by its significance than he himself, he meditated.

3.

The first obstacle they encountered was the jungle. It was a dark and moonless night. They could hear the roars of the hunting beasts and the high-pitched wails of the hunted. A small, magenta bird with its head torn off fell at their feet. —I think we're in the jungle, the Loon said.

A large, dark jaguar crossed the path a few feet in front of them, dragging with its mouth the broken, bleeding carcass of a spotted fawn, while a pair of hyenas, delirious with barking laughter, followed after. The heavy, moist air was filled with feathers, fur, and the smell of blood. At the river, crocodiles were catching unwary drinkers, peccaries, small deer, armadillos, yanking them into the slow, muddy waters, tearing them apart and devouring them. Snakes fell to the ground with rubbery thumps and rushed slithering after lizards, rodents, small apes, to crush and swallow them.

At last, the sky began to silver at the eastern edge, and they saw a trading post, where they quickly went in and enjoyed a sumptuous Polynesian meal. —Good old American Express! toasted the Loon, raising his rum-filled coconut.

4.

They were crossing the desert. In the moonlight, the sand was like a sea of silver grain. The king, plodding through the sand, silently beat his breast.

—You know, Egress, the Loon said to him, —I was wondering. After you've paid this penance, what then?

—Whatever.

—Jesus Christ! the Loon exclaimed petulantly. —You haven't said anything but "Whatever" since we left! I suppose that's part of the penance, too!

—Whatever, repeated the king, and, in heavy silence, slogged on.

5.

Scaling and crossing the Great Snowy Mountains was neither easy nor painless, especially the way they were dressed. At the Divide, they were hit by a blizzard and for three days huddled in a snow-cave, waiting out the storm. They surely would have frozen to death or starved, had they not, on the second day, been joined by a small band of Abenakis. The Indians were fleeing the genocidal persecution of Abenakis that had followed the deaths of Princes Egress, Dread, and Orgone, violent deaths in which the tribe was slightly implicated. Their leader, named Horse, was wearing a jukebox. The others were dressed in the usual flashy, slightly tacky, Indian costumes. They had corn, venison, maple syrup, bread, birch beer, quail, baked potatoes, raisins, apples, and some good New Mexico grass—plenty for all, though the king accepted only a few crusts of bread, which he washed down with snow-melt.

—He's trying to get tight with God, the Loon explained to them.

Ah, the redmen nodded, understanding. They, of course, did not recognize the king, and the Loon wisely thought it best not to tell them.

6.

Horse and the Abenakis led them down the eastern slope of the Great Snowy Mountains to the plain, where they parted company. The Indians headed south to New Mexico; the Pilgrims headed north to the Empire State Building, the prime shrine in the religious life of every believer in the Empire State. At one time or another during their lifetimes, most true believers managed to make it to the great, stone spire, to worship there in awed silence, perhaps even to join in the traditional penny-dropping ceremony afterward. The king's all-consuming passion was the dropping of his gold brick. He pictured himself standing humbly at the top, head bowed, dropping his fifty-pound offering over the edge into the windy, abysmal space below, and at that precise instant, the very hand of God Himself would reach down from His perch to touch him on the nape of his neck, forgiving him, freeing him to return home in a 747 jumbo jet, King Egress the Hearty, home again, victorious, self-transcendent, a truly enlightened despot! A grateful people; a gracious ruler: It would be his finest hour!

7.

On and on they walked. Until they came to the sea, and here they had to stop. The Loon stripped and ran into the foaming surf, delighted with the chance for a moonlit swim. He laughed and splashed and called to the king, but got no response. The king sat down on the beach and waited. Finally, the Loon came out of the water, giggling and rubbing his body to warm it. —Terrific ocean, Egress! You ought to try it. Wash some of that roadfilm off.

Nothing. What a drag, the Loon thought. If he weren't such a good walker, I'd think he had tired blood. —Okay, ol' buddy, he said to the king, —how're we going to get across? This is your trip, so navigate, please.

Just as the king was about to say —Whatever, a large, silent boat appeared out of the shadows. The boat was of Egyptian design, constructed entirely of papyrus reeds, and was being poled along in the shallow water by a dwarf-like gondolier singing Wagner at the top of his voice. He saw the pilgrims and pushed his sturdy craft in to the beach. —Gif a lift? he queried.

—Do you take credit cards for payment? the Loon asked back.

—Ya, all kinds! Ve got da cross-now-pay-later plans for effrey-buddy! Climb aboard! he sang, and they did, the Loon somewhat apprehensively.

8.

On the crossing; which took a little over fourteen weeks, the king began to come out of his grim withdrawal. The first break came early the first night out. The dwarf, who seemed an excellent sailor, was whistling aft, busying himself with knots and scrimshaw. The king and the Loon lay on the foredeck, watching the full moon rise out of the ink-dark sea. —This afternoon I dreamed of disaster, the king informed his companion.

—No kidding, the Loon said.

—I saw a bloody moon hanging in a white sky. I saw a museum sculpture garden with all the statues carefully beheaded. I saw four sets of bloody handprints upon a white wall, and every hand was missing the middle finger. I saw two rooks fly into the sun, and only one returned. The king lapsed into a thoughtful silence.

—So what are you going to do? the Loon asked, studying the moon with affection.

—I don't know yet, but I'm beginning to think that my wife had something to do with the deaths of my sons. It's still only a feeling, but a strong one.

—Can you *dig* that moon! the Loon said rapturously.

9.

The third night out, the king walked onto the foredeck and saw the Loon lying on his belly, watching the moon rise out of the sea again. The king crept up behind his friend, dropped to his knees, undid the Loon's blue jumpsuit, spread his buttocks, and silently sodomized him.

Finishing, he uncoupled and fell away. He leaned against the mast and began to talk about his childhood, which, to the Loon, sounded awful. The king, however, was speaking with fondness and the kind of hazy nostalgia that often comes over a man on a long sea voyage.

10.

After ten days at sea, the king talked constantly of his wife, the queen, and her nefarious plots against him and his sons. Also, he screwed the Loon at least once a night, much to the erotic delight of the boatman.

—I guess you don't feel so guilt-ridden anymore, eh? the Loon panted.

—Not really, the king said, zipping up the Loon's jumpsuit. —But after all, isn't that what a pilgrimage is *for*?

11.

One night on the foredeck, the king, leaning exhausted against the mast, waxed slightly philosophical: —I think that guilt, once perceived, *i.e.*, experienced, is a passion, to be spent, like other passions. The meanings of most things, of passions, certainly, lie wholly in their enactments or in analytical description, *i.e.*, reenactment of those things. The point of human life, when it comes right down to it, is simply to provide content for the otherwise empty forms of reality. The basic difficulty of human life is in knowing when a particular form has been sufficiently filled, or perceived, experienced—knowing when an experience has become redundant. Thus, most of the "good" life is an exercise in good taste, and I do mean ethically.

—Is it safe to assume, then, that you no longer feel guilty? the Loon asked wearily.

—Right! the king said, surprised. —You know, Lon, for a kid with no college degree, you certainly can think abstractly.

—Thanks, said the Loon.

12.

After one hundred days at sea, they docked in Liverpool, where they caught a train to London, a cab to the airport, and a jumbo jet for home, first-class.

—Good old American Express! the king said, raising his champagne glass in a toast.

—Yay, said the Loon quietly. He was thinking of the block of Moroccan hash he had brought as an offering for the Empire State and how much he was going to enjoy smoking it when he got back to the tree house. —Yay, he said, clinking the king's glass with his own.

—Kiss-kiss, you little devil, said the king happily.

—Kiss-kiss-kiss, answered the Loon.

The king lit a large Cuban cigar. —"Yay," huh? Heh, heh, heh. God, Loon, that's rich! You're such a disgusting faggot, the king said chuckling.

10

REMEMBER ME TO CAMELOT
A Novel
by Naomi Ruth Sunder

1.

"Be good to Kay," Rex instructed his eldest son, Bif. "Your mother's never been on her own before, she doesn't know how to take care of herself, son," he explained to the boy.

I stood somberly in the center of the living room with Hunter and Rory, fighting back the tears, proud of our three little boys, our little men, but proudest of Rex, my husband, because I understood the deep pain he was feeling at this, the moment of his departure. He was leaving us—perhaps forever.

Our country in her need had called him from the side of his loved ones, and he had no choice but to go. Rex was a major in the Air Force Reserve, and his unit had been activated for combat duty in Vietnam, which at that time I couldn't even have located on a map. They needed all the veteran pilots they could get, and Rex, in Korea more than a decade earlier, before Bif was born, had been one of the best in the skies. He had been almost legendary, and, as he leaned down to kiss me good-bye, I saw him wink away a tear with a brave grin, and I knew that he was still one of the best.

We kissed, long and joyously, and then he patted each of us on the top of the head and walked out the door to the waiting car.

2.

It *was* true, what Rex had said to Bif—I had never been on my own before, and I didn't know how to take care of myself. I had been the only child of protective parents, raised in Sarasota, Florida, where, as a fifteen-year-old girl trying out for the cheerleading squad, I had met Rex. He was two years older than I, a junior and the captain of the football team.

We fell in love that autumn, the season I made the cheerleading squad and the football team went undefeated, and from the first, ours was a love that never wavered or wandered off center. Rex was everything I wasn't, and thus it was only with him and through him that I felt completed. He was stern and disciplined, sophisticated yet rough-hewn, gentle but at the same time demandingly straightforward.

And there was a sense in which I completed him, too, for I allowed him to be tender and naive, shy and insecure—character traits he otherwise would have been ashamed of and would have denied himself.

3.

As soon as Rex graduated from Sarasota High, we got married. It was the summer of 1950 and the second half of the twentieth century had just begun. How were we to know that war with the Orientals would break out and, within a year, with me pregnant, would separate us?

Rex went to Texas as an Air Force cadet and earned his wings in record time. I closed up our little apartment, put our wedding gifts and furniture in storage, and went home to live with my mother and father. Three weeks after Rex had left Texas for Korea, I gave birth to our first son, Rex, Jr., whom Rex in his letters instructed me to call "Bif," the name by which he had been known when he played fullback for Sarasota High.

Even from that great a distance, Rex was a doting father. My parents and I would laugh gaily over his long letters filled with careful instructions as to how we should care for his namesake and how my parents should care for me. In some ways, Rex was able to make it seem that he had never left. In my heart, though, I knew how far away he really was.

4.

But now it was twelve years later, and just as the Vietnam War was different from the Korean, Rex's absence from his family was different. Over a decade had passed between the wars, and our life together and our lives separately had changed in many subtle ways.

When Rex had come back from Korea, taller, leaner and, yes, harder than when he had left, we had been able to resume our life almost as if there had been no interruption at all. And in a real way, for, when he had been drafted, our life together had not yet had a chance to begin, there *was* no interruption. As if his absence had never existed, and as if we had not begun at all, we were able to begin anew.

We bought a new, three-bedroom mobile home with a cathedral ceiling in a mobile home park over by the Bay, and Rex went back to work for his father's plumbing company, a journeyman plumber, as before, starting at the bottom, as before. But, "The sky's the limit!" he used to say to me, late at night as we talked in bed of our plans and hopes for the future.

I was newly pregnant with Hunter, and touching my swelling womb, feeling the life stir there, knew how right he was. "Oh, Rex, not even the *sky* can limit *us*!" I would tell him, as he drifted peacefully off to sleep.

5.

Hunter was born, a healthy, bright child, serious and intense from birth, just as Bif had been boisterous and cheerfully gregarious from birth. Hunter's personality brought out another side of Rex, a side I hadn't seen before. With his second son, Rex was somber, morbid almost, encouraging in the boy, and thus in himself, activities that were solitary, physically strenuous, and somewhat dangerous—such as hunting and deep-sea fishing, rock-climbing, scuba diving. Was this a result of his war experiences, things he wouldn't talk about, couldn't talk about, even to me? I wondered helplessly.

"What else are you going to do with a boy named Hunter?" Rex would tease me whenever I asked him why, for example, he was encouraging his son to hunt alligators in the swamps with Negroes.

"But he's only a *boy*," I would plead.

"A boy's only a small man," he would explain to me.

I was no less concerned over Rex's enthusiasm for Bif's adventures in sports—Little League baseball, Pop Warner football, playing for two or three different teams at a time, day and night, throwing, batting, and kicking balls, sobbing exhausted and disconsolate whenever his team had failed to humiliate the other.

6.

When our third son was born, I named him Rory, after Rex's father, and determined to protect him, if possible, from the several influences of his father that I was fast learning to be frightened of.

As aspects of his whole personality, Rex's fierce competitive pride, his love of sports and danger, and his occasional, dark fascination with solitude did not in any way alarm me. But in our sons, one or another and sometimes several of these aspects became dominant, intimidating, and, eventually, I feared, killing the milder, sweeter traits which, in Rex, made me love him—his tenderness, his shyness, his naiveté, and his insecurity.

Immediately, it seemed, Rex sensed my protectiveness toward Rory, and he subtly undermined me, encouraging and thereby instilling in his youngest son yet another negative aspect of his own personality.

"You're like your mother," he would tell him. "All emotions. Now, your mother is a wonderful woman, and I'm pleased that *one* of my sons is like her, so don't go thinking I'm putting you down, son."

But of course poor Rory thought his father was rejecting him, so the only emotion he allowed himself to feel with passion was anger, raging, explosive anger, even as a child.

7.

Thus it was with deeply mixed emotions that I watched my husband in his Air Force major's uniform stride down the steps of our blue mobile home, cross the pebbled driveway to the white convertible waiting for him at the curb, pausing a second at the sidewalk to give Bif's soccer ball a friendly boot into the goal in the side yard. And then, flinging his flight bag into the back seat, he jumped into the low-slung car without opening the door and signaled to the lieutenant to take off, which, with a great roar of exhausts and squealing of tires, the lieutenant did.

Little did I know that I would never see my husband, my beloved Rex, again. If I had known it, or even had suspected it (I was so enthralled with the man that I imagined him winning the war quickly and returning home in a season), I never would have allowed myself to feel the wave of relief that swept over me as he drove away. I did not then understand that feeling, and naturally I felt terrible for having it, as if I were an *evil* woman. Rex had made my life possible. Without him, I had no reason for living. I knew that I loved him deeply. Why, then, did I feel this hatred for him?

8.

Happily, the feeling swiftly went away, and I began to miss Rex awfully. I stayed up late night after night writing long, amorous letters to him (one thing about my Rex, he was a marvelous lover). My days were busier than ever, taken up completely with the boys and my housekeeping.

Then, one night late that summer, I was startled from my letter-writing by a telephone call from the Tampa hospital. There had been a terrible accident, the doctor told me, on the causeway between St. Petersburg and Tampa, and my mother and father, who had driven over to look at a new Golden Age planned community, had been killed. I quickly got my friend Judy from the trailer next door to baby-sit and took a bus to Tampa, as the doctor had suggested, to identify my poor mother and father.

"Yes," I sobbed, "it's they!"

The doctor, a kind, handsome, young man with a blond moustache, comforted me by holding me in his arms. "There, there," he said, "you'll be all right. They went together," he reminded me. "Think how much that would have meant to them."

I wiped away my tears, blew my nose, thanked him for all his trouble, and walked slowly out of the hospital into the cool, palmy night, terrified.

9.

Now I was truly on my own—in spite of what Rex had said to Bif. He had known as well as I that a twelve-year-old boy can't take care of a twenty-eight-year-old woman. He had said it mainly for Bif's benefit, not mine—so the boy would feel the proper responsibility, regardless of whether or not he could act on it.

At first, I had felt sorry for Bif, who was trying hard to live up to the terms of his charge, but then, as increasingly he began to order me around, I began to feel anger toward him. As long as my mother and father were still alive, I was able to get Bif to stop worrying over me simply by assuring him that Grandpa was taking care of us all while Daddy was away in Vietnam. But after the accident, even that assurance was no longer possible.

Then, finally, one evening about six months after my parents' death, all my anger flooded over. I served the boys a supper of turkey hash on toast, leftovers from the roast turkey of the night before, and Bif slammed his little fists down on the table and said loudly, "We never had to eat this crap when *Dad* was at home! What makes you think it's any different now?"

I slapped him across the mouth with my open hand as hard as I could, sending him spinning off his chair to the floor. After calling Judy over to baby-sit, I stomped out and caught the bus to Tampa.

10.

I arrived home again just before dawn (the doctor, Ben, insisted on driving me in his new Buick sedan), exhausted, slightly woozy from the gin-and-tonics, and in spite of the endless shame I felt, still raging. The combination of guilt and anger was almost too much to bear, and I was afraid I was going mad, though Ben assured me that I was not, that it was perfectly normal for the wife of a man away in the service to feel this way.

I sent Judy home, and while I waited for the boys to get up for their breakfast, I sat down and tried to write a letter to Rex. I began the letter many times, tearing each new attempt to shreds just as I got to the place where I had to tell him I had let Ben make love to me. I couldn't do it. I just couldn't make that man's life any more painful than it already was. I remembered his last letter to me, received the day before.

> Kay, honey, even though I'm 9000 miles away from you and
> the boys, my heart and mind are there with you, believe me.
> I still feel that I'm the king in that little kingdom. I feel like a
> government-in-exile or something, waiting for the signal from
> you, or from somebody, that it's okay to return. (Hey, I'd bet-
> ter be careful or the military censors will think I'm talking
> politics, eh? Ha ha!)

At last, I heard the boys happily slamming each other with pillows, and wearily I got up and started setting the table for breakfast.

11.

That very afternoon, I received the letter from Washington, D.C., the Department of Defense, informing me that Rex's plane had been shot down by the enemy while on a mission over North Vietnam, and he had been taken prisoner. He was now a POW, and, as far as they knew, he was not injured.

In that one brief moment, as I read the letter, I felt my life turn over and go back to zero and start anew, the opposite of drowning. I still loved Rex, of course, but deep inside, I said a prayer of thanks to the North Vietnamese gunners who had shot him down. I would never be able to explain that gratitude to anyone, I was sure, and I probably could not explain it even to myself, but I could not deny to myself that I felt it, no matter how hard I tried. And though I was not especially proud of the feeling, neither was I ashamed of it.

I joined a group of POW wives from central Florida, and for a while went around with them, speaking to groups of men who were said to have influence in Washington in ways that would somehow benefit the POWs. But I could never quite understand how POWs or their wives could benefit from a more aggressive war policy, so I dropped out of the group. I took good care of my sons and our home, saw Ben about once a month, and just sort of cooled my heels for a while.

12.

Gradually, I became used to the idea that I was on my own and, therefore, had no choice but to take care of myself. I enrolled in night school and got my high school diploma with an ease that astounded me. I went on a diet and exercise program and studied yoga at the Sarasota YWCA. I started sending Rory to a reading clinic, because of his disability, and no longer insisted that the boys get their haircuts where their father had always gotten his. I started trying new foods, exotic dishes, and occasionally took in an X-rated movie with Ben. I took driving lessons, got my license and borrowed the money from a bank to buy a Japanese station wagon.

Rex would have forbidden me to do all these things, if he'd been here, and when the war is finally over and he has been repatriated, he will come home again, and I hope we both can sit down and cry for what has been lost. If he can't do that, I will leave him.

THE END

1.

It was morning when their jumbo jet was ready to descend, and by then Egress and the Loon were both quite drunk. —Boy, oh boy, Loon, I feel like havin' a party! Le's take some speed an' stay up four days 'n' nights in a row! It ain't every day y'get back from a goddamn pilgrimage, y'know! the king cried to his diminutive friend.

—Hoo haw! Hoo haw! Hoo haw! the Loon carefully responded. He knew how wild the king could get when he was drunk.

Champagne glasses in hand, the two staggered out the door of the aircraft and walked unsteadily through the arrival gate. —They ain't no one here t'*meet* us, the king observed, surprised.

—And it's a good thing, too, the way you're dressed, the Loon said, pointing at the king's grain bag, which was spattered with caked mud, champagne, salt spray, dried semen.

—Yeah, I guess you're right, the king agreed, and they walked to the taxi stand, got into a cab, and instructed the driver to take them to the palace. —Toot sweet! the king said flirtatiously.

—Going to see the queen? the driver impertinently asked. He was a bent-over, long-haired hippie type who closely resembled a ballboy who'd once worked at the gymnasium.

—You betcha! Egress said heartily. He loved the fact that the driver didn't recognize him. —I'm gonna *fuck* 'er, he confided.

—Yeh. You and everybody else, the driver said, winking.

2.

When the cab pulled up at the palace gate, the Loon saw the handwriting on the wall and decided to seek cover. —Say, Egress, I'm going to split for my place, okay?

—Yeah, yeah, sure, sure, Egress said, thinking only of Naomi Ruth and how happy she would be to see him again.

As soon as he reached his tree house, the Loon made a few quick phone calls and confirmed his suspicions. Just as I suspected, he thought. The queen has taken over. He made one more call, found out when the next bus left for his small, southern hometown, and packed a large suitcase with most of his belongings, his simpler, lightweight clothes, his chambered nautilus, his five favorite records, three favorite books, four favorite autographed photographs of movie stars, and his thumb-sized lump of hash.

The Loon was not a prophet, actually, but with regard to political matters, he was practically clairvoyant. This was doubtless because he himself was as apolitical as a four-year-old child. With his talent, he ought to have been made the premier political advisor in the state. But, ironically, the very thing that gave rise to his talent disqualified him as a councillor: he had no loyalties whatsoever to anyone, except as he himself was personally threatened or rewarded. His politics were based entirely on what he saw as necessary for his own continued survival. This did not, however, make him amoral, for, in all his personal dealings with people, he remained both generous and kind.

3.

Egress the Hearty strode manfully into the Great Hall and roared, —Honey, I'm home!

The tapestry-covered walls soaked up his noise and left him standing alone in silence. —I like the way she's decorated the place, he mused, fingering one of the thick tapestries. —French. Then he saw her, standing on the dais at the far end of the enormous room, and he ran, arms spread wide, to her. —*Baa-a-a-bee-e-e!* he bellowed.

After he had kissed, hugged, and fondled her awhile, he began to realize that she had not responded, that she had stood still throughout, as if she were made of alabaster, silent and motionless and cold to the touch. —What's the matter? Aren't you thrilled to see me? he asked her. —Hey, baby, he growled in his sexy voice, —you really turn me on when you hold it back like this. He started to paw her breasts.

But still there was no reaction. —What the fuck . . . ? he exclaimed, drawing back to look at her. Maybe she had the rag on or something. You never can tell.

Finally, she spoke to him in a low, calm voice. —Egress, you've been gone for more than seven years, and in that time I've acted in your place. . . .

—Fantastic, terrific, he said. —That's why you're the *queen.*

—And in those years, she went on, —I've made a number of decisions, executive decisions. Foremost among these is the decision that I am to remain the chief executive, even after your return. I am, to put it simply and crudely, taking *my* turn, she declared.

—If you were a fucking man, he hissed, —I'd kill you. But you're not. You're a woman. My woman. Now, c'mere and give me some ass.

4.

A troop of Abenakis emerged from behind the arras next to the queen, and at a signal from their chief, the one called Horse, they surrounded Egress and tied him with deerhide thongs and pitched him onto the floor in a heap at the queen's feet. Egress was beginning to feel a little frightened. —You're *serious*! he exclaimed to her.

Not answering him, she turned and regally left the hall.

—Horse! Don't you recognize me, man? I'm your king! It's *me*, Egress the Hearty, for Christ's sake!

—Yeah, I know who you are, the red man answered. —Or rather, I know who you *think* you are. The fact that you think you're still in charge, though, just because you're who you are, doesn't mean goatshit around here anymore. It's hard to run around claiming Divine Right when you ain't got no Enforcer! Horse joked, leading his band over to one of the far corners of the room. He was still wearing his jukebox, and one of the warriors punched E-5, a Buffy Sainte-Marie tune, and the group formed a small circle and started to dance.

—For god's sake, don't you guys have any loyalty to your own *kind*??? the king shrieked at them. —Where are your *balls!!!* Egress was beginning to comprehend what was happening, and his fear had turned to rage. Trussed up like a pig in a market, he roared, thrashing and rolling himself about the room.

Sadly, while the other Indians danced, Horse watched him. —The only good king is probably a dead king, he murmured to himself.

5.

This is how Egress escaped: The Abenakis, as redmen often will, took to drinking, and after having exhausted themselves with brawling, singing, and dancing, fell asleep in a pile in the corner. At dawn, a young girl, coming from one of the barracks rooms where, apparently, she had been visiting her boyfriend or her brother, stole across the Great Hall in the half-light and almost stumbled over the fuming body of Egress.

—Watch it, for Christ's sake! he snapped.

—Oh, golly, I didn't see you there! I'm *terribly* sorry, she said sincerely. She was wearing a high school cheerleader's uniform and had large, pointed breasts. —Are you all right? she asked the king.

—Listen, I was captured by some Indians working for my wife, the queen, because she hates men. Do *you* hate men, too? he asked kindly.

—Oh-h-h, gosh, *no*! I just *love* them! I mean, I have too much *respect* for men. I'm 37-24-37, you know, she said proudly.

—That right? Well, then, why don't you just untie me, honey, so I can stand up and get a good look at your body?

—Oh, I'm so em-barrassed! she giggled, bending down to untie him, brushing his nose with her naked thigh as she worked.

When she had freed him, he stood up, grabbed her by her left breast, and together they ran from the room to the court-yard outside. There he leaned her against the wall, yanked down her panties, and stuffed his stiff cock into her. He pumped half a dozen times, came, and quickly withdrew, saying as he left, —I'll be in touch.

—'Bye, she said weakly.

—Don't forget to douche, he warned her.

6.

Egress decided swiftly that the best way for him to get his throne back was to go underground, at least until he could size up the situation. He called the Loon, but there was no answer. —The little bastard's probably hiding out in Biloxi, he cursed.

The streets were filled with Indians carrying weapons and wearing makeup on their faces. —Goddamn faggots, he said to himself. —They'll work for anyone who'll let them paint them-selves up.

With his back to the street, the door of the phone booth closed, he made one more call, to a number his security chief had given him years ago. —H'lo, he said when the party answered. —Is this the Underground?

—Ya.

—Good. I need to drop out of sight for a while. You know what I mean. Can you arrange it?

—Ya, I tink so. How many iss dere in your party? the man asked.

—One, Egress said.

—Und vat time may ve expect you?

—In about fifteen minutes.

—Ya, dot's fine. Und vat iss da name, pleese?

—Sunder.

—Tank you for callink us, Mister Soonder. Ve vill be expectink you, den.

Hanging up the receiver, Egress darted out of the phone booth and leaped into a cab that had just pulled up to the curb. The driver was a tiny man, so short he could barely see over the steering wheel. —Vere to? he asked.

—Underground, Egress commanded.

—You iss da Soonder party?

—Yeah, that's right.

—You are early, Mister Soonder.

—Yeah, sorry about that. I got away earlier than I expected, he explained as the cab sped away.

7.

The drive took him to the clubhouse of a long-abandoned golf course in one of the suburbs. Inside the shuttered building, a low, ranch-style, log structure covered with vines and moss, a group of men and women, mostly young, long-haired, and filthy, were making bombs and various incendiary devices. They greeted him with silent, agreeable nods and continued with their work.

Egress admired their discipline and decided to tell them who he was. When he had finished speaking and the laughter had died down, one of the group, a slender youth with flowers tangled into his hair, took Egress aside and said to him, —You may not remember me, but we've met. I know who you are, who you *were*, he said in a confidential voice. —These kids, they're rather heavily into revolution, so they're not going to be of much help to you, except to hide you out for a while—but they'll do that only so long as they think you're a little crazy and are wanted by the State. That grain bag you're wearing helps, also that psychotic-looking hair cut. You look like Richard Speck, he said with a snicker. —But you're going to have to be more careful, he went on. —They're serious about this revolution thing. . . .

—Wait a minute, Egress said, interrupting him. —Aren't you . . . ?

—Yes.

—But I thought I ordered you executed!

—Yes, you did, but your wife countermanded your order and had me freed right after you left on your famous pilgrimage. She thought I was gay, and there was an amnesty offered, and so. . .

—I thought you were gay, too. Aren't you? the king asked, incredulous.

—Not *really*. But never mind all that. If you want to hide out here, you better start acting crazy, and you better start helping make the bombs. You'll find that your family problems won't count for very much here, not with this group, he chuckled, leading the king back to the young men and women at work on the floor among the wires, fuses, gasoline, and dynamite caps.

8.

Late that night, while the others slept, the king rolled over on his pallet and whispered to the Green Man, who was lying on the pallet next to him. —Are there any others left, besides you, who have remained loyal to me?

—A few, I imagine, the Green Man answered, yawning. —And you really can't count on me for much more than company.

—How many are left? the king persisted.

—Ten, maybe.

—*Ten!* Ten men! Ten loyal men. Ten stout-hearted men! he whispered with growing excitement. —Okay, Greenie, you and I are getting out of here now, he announced.

—What for? I like it here. I mean, hiding out isn't a bad way for a man to spend his life.

—Not this man, fella. We're getting out of here, and we're going to contact those ten stout-hearted men and get them together as fast as we can, tonight, if possible. And by tomorrow night, we'll have ten thousand *more!* he almost exclaimed.

Once outside the house, the king asked him, —Which of the ten is closest to where we are now?

The Green Man told him of Twit, who used to work at the gymnasium and now was a student of Oriental religions and a part-time cab driver in the city. —He's kind of wacky, though. Childhood traumas, asthma as a kid, that sort of thing. He's very big on exploring personal power potentials—mysticism, karate, scientology, peyote, Sufi rites, etc. But he's still very loyal to you. I think he's Jewish, he added.

—No matter. He sounds okay to me. Extremism in the defense of liberty means a man like that can be trusted. You'll see. I wasn't king for all those years for nothing, y'know. I'll make him a general. I know the type, he said as the two of them set out in the dark for the city, where Twit maintained a flat.

9.

After Twit was appointed First General of the Loyalist Army, the king, the Green Man, and the new General set up their head-quarters in a hidden canyon far in the countryside west of the city. They pitched a high, conical tent and ate free-ranging prai-rie chickens shot on the wing while they waited for the army to gather, as they knew it would, once word of Egress's return leaked out.

The first volunteers showed up around noon—the world-famous rock band, The Sons of the Pioneers. They came roaring into the canyon on matching, ruby-flecked, Harley Davidson motorcycles. —Hey, man, what's happening? the leader of the band said to the king, and the king quickly explained.

—Far out, the musician said. —You want us to do a fund-raiser or somethin', man? he offered.

Introducing the group to General Twit, Egress agreed that a fund-raiser would be fine, but not till after the war. Meanwhile, he wanted them just to let the fact of their endorsement of his project get around, maybe hold a press conference or two, that sort of thing.

—When this thing hits the media, he said to the Green Man as they strolled out to the dusty plain to hunt prairie chicken, —we'll be in! Every mother's son in the fucking country will be fighting on our side! Let Naomi Ruth *have* her minorities. *I'll* have the rest. Don't forget, these kids have never had a chance to fight for something they *believe* in! he reminded his cohort.

10.

That night, lying on his cot in his tent, the king had a dream which confused and troubled him. He dreamed he was the pilot of a fighter-bomber on a bombing mission over North Vietnam. Sweeping down on his target, a Standard Oil refinery operated by the enemy, he released his bombs and then suddenly realized he had overshot his target by about five miles. As he pulled the nose of the plane skyward, he glanced out the canopy to see what in fact he was bombing, and he saw three little boys standing in the middle of a clearing in the jungle. For an instant he saw their faces, recognizing them, and then they were gone. And then he heard the sickening sound of the bombs exploding in the clearing in the jungle. All the way back to the base in Laos, he roared with incoherent pain.

The Green Man, mercifully, woke him, but when he told the king that the army was ready to march on the city, the king began to sob uncontrollably. —No, no, this is *insane!* What are we *doing?* We're *killing* each other!

The Green Man gave him a couple of ten-milligram Librium capsules and got him calmed down again, so that, by sunrise, Egress was once more his hearty, unshakable self.

—I always have a nightmare the night before a big battle, he explained to the Green Man as they rode toward the city at the head of the motorcycle corps.

11.

Behind Egress, General Twit, the Green Man, and The Sons of the Pioneers, the Loyalist Army spread out like a gigantic cape all the way to the horizon. Most of the police and military, practically all professional groups, athletes, clergymen of all the more popular faiths, many clerk-typists and petty bureaucrats from the civil service, members of all the building trades unions, motorcycle gangs, automobile mechanics, miners, realistic novelists, coaches, and all the youth of the land who had been about to apprentice themselves to members of these groups (but who were, in actuality, probably attracted to the Loyalist cause by the presence of The Sons of the Pioneers) turned out to have remained loyal to the king. They seemed to have been waiting only for the proper opportunity to express that loyalty. There were, of course, legions of older men who had wanted to join the battle on the side of the king, but, because of their age, had been put to better use as medics, service personnel, councillors, etc. Stationed with them at the rear of the marching army and at the canyon headquarters, the numerous women who had joined the army had been put to good use making uniforms, bullets, tents, and victory banners.

12.

On the way into the city, there were a few isolated skirmishes, quick forays by small search-and-destroy units into farmhouses and crossroads hamlets where the inhabitants had tried to resist the king's army, not so much because they were loyal to his wife, but rather because they were out of touch with the conflict and thus had no loyalties at all. The sheer mass of the Loyalist Army overwhelmed them, and the raping, looting, and slaughter that followed barely delayed the army in its march. Like pebbles in the path of a river that has burst its dam, they were swallowed whole and caused not even a ripple of hesitation. But when the river reached its destination, the city, it created, then swirled, eddied, slowed, and finally ceased movement altogether, as if, blocked by a second dam, it had emptied into a new, unexpected basin, creating in a short time a huge, motionless lake of bewildered men.

The city was deserted, empty, and all the major buildings had been destroyed. The streets were filled with rubble, concrete, wrecked automobiles, buses, trains, mattresses, broken cases of food, furniture, clothing, and glass, as if there had been an earthquake and it had occurred at the one moment when everyone was out of town. Egress was at first astonished, and then, when he had begun to piece together what had happened, a process in which he was aided by the Green Man, he was deeply depressed. One might say broken.

12

1.

He recognized her by the nape of her neck and his powerful attraction to it. She stood motionless in front of him, like Leda before the swan or Europa before the bull, waiting her turn to purchase a ticket, presumably for the next flight out. There were no longer any arriving flights; departing flights had been doubled.

Hungrily, he stared at the tendons on her neck, the fine strands of hair lifting like an Elizabethan tune toward the high, severe tail of her haircut. It was in the new style, he noticed, the one called the "French Barricade." She curled her head forward as she drew a credit card from her purse and, handing it to the harried clerk, paid for her ticket. Egress ached to strum the taut muscles of her neck, the braid of tendons and sinews that ran like Greek bread from under her earlobes to her shoulders. He felt his hands open out, reaching like morning glories at dawn, his fingertips swarming with impatience for heat.

She accepted her ticket from the clerk, turned brusquely and saw him standing there behind her. —Oh! she said, clearly startled. —Surprise, eh?

—Ah . . . yes! Surprise-surprise-surprise-surprise-surprise, he said mockingly, cursing himself for it as he spoke: —Goddamn you, goddamn you, goddamn you . . . , he cursed.

—It's your turn, I believe. The man is waiting, Egress, she reminded him, inclining her head in the direction of the uniformed clerk at the counter. She seemed to have a sarcastic smile on her thin lips, as if she felt superior to her husband.

A short and exceedingly fat woman with a pair of long-legged, unhappy, teenaged sons stood in line as a group behind Egress. She kicked one of her large suitcases along the floor until it crashed into his heel, battering his Achilles tendon with it as she kept on kicking. Her arms, like meat-filled pillows, were folded pugnaciously across her huge breasts, and, while swinging at her suitcase with one stubby foot, she glared intolerantly at Egress and Naomi Ruth.

—*Next!* the clerk pointedly called out.

—They think they're in a movie, the fat woman muttered to her sons.

—Okay, okay, I'm next, Egress said, turning for a second to the clerk, saying to him, —One way, please, and when, a second later, he looked back, Naomi Ruth was gone.

—One way . . . to where, mister? the clerk impatiently asked him.

—Oh. Ah . . . Nevada. Reno, Nevada.

—First-class or tourist?

—Ah, tourist, tourist. Yes . . . tourist. He placed his credit card onto the counter in front of him and the clerk ran it through the machine and handed it, with the ticket, back to him.

Egress deftly stepped away and slipped into the crowd as if slipping into a broad, slow river, and let the current carry him. He said to himself, I've never felt so tired, so bone-weary. I feel a thousand years old. I wish I'd been born a member of a different race, one with more of a future. I almost wish I'd been born a woman.

Oh, but just the same, thinking that one over, he thought, I'm glad I don't have to be born again as *anything*. The risk isn't worth taking, he observed shrewdly. Maybe everything's only as decently worked out as possible. It's hard to run off and turn your back on the fact of your own manhood, when you are a man and have been one all your life. I mean, what the hell, an ego's an ego, and you sort of have to take it as it comes from where you get it. Right? he humbly asked himself.

Right, he declared with confidence, sliding forthrightly along with the crowd and keeping a sharp lookout for the proper boarding gate and any possibilities of Naomi Ruth.

2.
(ON THE BEACH)

Egress sat atop the smooth, sow-sized boulder, looking out to sea, diddling idly with memories of his childhood. The harsh cry of a gull caused him to look to his right, along the gray beach, and though he could see little more of the figure walking toward him than that it was a woman's, he knew immediately that it was Naomi Ruth's. The languorous yet sporty walk, that slow movement of muscles hardened leisurely by tennis, could belong to no other woman, certainly to no other woman in *his* life, which, at that exact moment, he realized, in terms of the number and kinds of women he had studied closely, had been rather oddly narrow. Was that *usual*? he wondered. Was he, then, therefore, lonelier than other men of similar means and abilities? Was this, the catastrophe of his middle age, his *own* fault?

She didn't give any sign of recognition until she had drawn near enough for her to speak to him, when she said simply, —I never thought of you as a sun-worshipper, Egress. She was wearing a tiny, cerise, two-piece bathing suit. He had on a rust-colored tanksuit made of wet-look nylon. They both had good tans, leathery brown and evenly distributed.

—Having a good time? he asked.

—Yes! And you? She sat down lightly beside him on the rock and looked out to sea.

Egress looked out to sea also. —Yes, I guess one *could* call it that.

—What?

—A "good" time.

—Oh.

—I mean, I've been "good" lately. Travel and most other forms of inactivity, as you know, produce in me a certain . . . "morality," he said carefully.

—That's pretty decadent-sounding, Egress, she said, laughing. —You were many things, but I don't remember you as particularly decadent.

—I don't know. No, I don't think I was, not at all. Nowadays, though, well, maybe I am. After all, life has to go on, *n'est-ce pas?* "The old biological imperative," as the Loon used to call it. . . .

—The *Loon!* she sneered.

—Oh, you can't blame *him*, Naomi. Not for this. He was weak, that's all, and he knew it. For him, everything had to come down to that old biological imperative. His one ethic, his only possible morality, was survival, for god's sake. We shouldn't go off projecting our own alternatives onto him, not now. That's just too easy. . . .

—I know, I know. It's just the associations. They're still very strong, you know. And painful.

—Sure, I understand. It's the same for me—though of course I'm temperamentally slightly more existential than you.

—That makes it easier, probably.

—Aw, please, Naomi, I happen to treasure this moment, so please, don't indulge in sarcasm. Not now.

—Sorry.

—As a matter of fact, just as you came walking up, I was sitting here wondering whether or not this whole thing was my fault completely. I mean, *completely.*

—Completely?

—Yeah. Except for a few things, of course. All that destruction at the end, for instance. I mean, Jesus, Naomi, you could
have just "left" me, you know. All those innocent people! he
exclaimed compassionately.

—Nobody's "innocent," she said grimly. —It's Greek, and
that means everything's interlocked. When the House of Atreus
finally collapses, the entire city has to collapse around it. *I* had
nothing to do with all that destruction at the end, not personally, any more than you did. Not as much as you did, if you ask
me, from what I heard. What were you doing when you went
underground, anyhow? Working as some kind of secret double
agent? No, I'm sorry, I don't mean that. I know you had nothing
personally to do with all that violence and destruction of property at the end. It was just coincidence. Fate.

Egress sighed with evident relief. —If that's true, then maybe
the whole thing wasn't my fault, not entirely. Right?

—Who cares about "right" now? she asked rhetorically,
leaving the rock. —Good-bye, Egress. I'm glad you are having a
good time, however decadent. I don't miss you, but I wonder lots
of times how you are now.

—Same here, he said. —Are you "lonely"?

—Yes. But as I said, I don't miss you.

—Right. Same here, he said to her lithe back as she walked
athletically away.

3.

(IN THE MUSEUM)

He had stepped into the museum to get out of the rain, a sudden, unexpected shower that probably would not last. I never
seem to have an umbrella when I need one, he thought, as he
glanced into the adjacent roomful of midnight blue, very abstract
paintings. The paintings, recent acquisitions, evidently, were all

about six feet square, covered completely with a smooth coat of midnight blue paint. The surface was so smooth that it seemed to have been applied with a large roller or spray gun. There were between twenty-five and thirty of the paintings hanging in the large room, distributed evenly along the walls and hung at exactly the same height. Egress found himself moved invitingly by the sight and went into the room for a closer look at them.

They were by an artist whose name he did not recognize, and they were entitled, "Composition A," "Composition B," and so on, in sequence, all the way, he discovered, to "Composition Z," which brought him back to the door again. The exhibit gave him considerable peace of mind, and it was with pleasure and a kind of relief that he noticed, after having gone through the exhibit a second time to study each individual painting closely, that he was the only person in the room—until the moment when Naomi Ruth, in a lemon yellow dress and carrying a matching yellow umbrella, entered the room.

—Oh, she said, seeing him. —Well, we meet again. We can't go on meeting like this, she laughed, shaking her small, dark head provocatively. —Are you enjoying the paintings? she queried.

—Oh, yes, immensely. As a matter of fact, they have given me a great peace, a deep spiritual equilibrium which lately I seem to have lacked to a considerable degree. They've offered an order to my chaos.

—The artist is my present lover, she said in a flat voice.

—Ah? Ah, well . . . ahem, how shall I say it, then? How nice? Or, perhaps, congratulations? Or would it be more polite to admit a personal relation and hope he's like his paintings—that is, lucid, totally consistent, witty, and well-hung. He smiled coldly at her, pushed past and out the door, broke into a flagrant run and exited from the museum to the downpour outside.

4.

(AT THE CAFÉ)

—Actually, I'm all right now. Things are much better for me, he assured her.

—Are they? Good. I was worried, she said, motioning with one hand for the waiter. The waiter arrived, and Naomi Ruth ordered their drinks, in French, which impressed him, for her accent was quite good.

—Yes, I have a girl friend, a good woman who loves me well, he lied. —We share a nice little flat in a charming quarter of the city. Very comfortable place. A lot of Russian émigrés live in the district. We're very happy. She's a dancer. Quite young. Lovely. Smokes those Russian cigarettes. Young. A sparkling beauty. Tanya. She's Russian. A dancer. Quite young. She loves me.

—Ah, good. And you? Do you love her as well? The waiter brought their drinks, a martini for Naomi Ruth, Campari and soda for Egress.

—Oh, well, you know. As I said, she's quite young. Let's just say that I'm "fond" of her, and grateful. She's a marvelous dancer. Flying feet.

—How nice, said Naomi Ruth, nipping at her martini with pursed lips. Though she didn't believe a word he said, she judged him as she would if she had believed everything. The man's still a cad, she decided. Even his lies betray him. It's no use. —It's no use, she informed him.

—No?

—No, she said, getting up from the table.

—Must you rush off?

—Oh, I left long ago, Egress. If only I could get *you* to leave, I'd be a free woman, she declared, and she picked up her coat and walked hurriedly away.

He finished his drink slowly, thoughtfully, then, brightening, drained hers. He suddenly felt like celebrating. —*Garcon!* he called. —Bring me a double martini, *s'il vous plait*!

5.

(In the Hansom Cab)

—Where *my* money comes from, said Egress to Naomi Ruth, is not of much importance, you know that. After all, it doesn't matter to *me* where it comes from, so why should it matter to anyone else? Most of my economic theories are of the type used to describe other people's financial situations, not one's own, which happily places me in the grand tradition of modern economic theorists, and also leaves me free to take whatever I can get from wherever I can get it without offending the glorious abstract—letting the general principles freely transcend the particularities of my usually very complex finances. So, the answer to your question, What am I doing for money these days? is, casually, I get by. What about *you*, however? Since you happen to be a woman and thus have spent most of your life locked by the abstract into a very particularized and personal dependence on other individuals (first your father and then me) for your money—to the degree that your most important personal relations have been, as they must be, with whomever you have economic relations—What are *you* doing for money these days? Asking a woman about her financial life is not much different from asking her whom she's sleeping with, I know, and if you had not slept with me for twenty-five years or more, believe me, I would not feel entitled, as I do, to pry.

—I get by.

—We're quite a pair, Egress laughed, aren't we? It's a damned good thing nobody's counting on us to play big historical roles, to lead his revolution or put one down.

Naomi Ruth responded with a chuckle. Egress, leaning forward in the seat, called to the driver and instructed him to stop at the next corner, in front of the American Express office. Then, to Naomi Ruth, he said, —Well, I'll leave you here. It's been kind of you to share your ride with a walking-man, a member of the walking class, heh-heh. Seriously, though, thanks for the lift. I might've had to stand there for hours before convincing a cab to stop. The hansom cab stopped in front of the American Express office. —Well, here we are! Good old American Express, eh? By the way, if you're going to be here in the city for a few days, maybe we can get together for lunch . . . ?

—No.

—Right, right. 'Bye, then.

—'Bye.

Exit Egress cheerily. Naomi Ruth signaled for the driver to go on. Exit hansom cab.

6.

(AT THE PLAZA)

—Ah, you breakfast at the Green Tulip Room? I didn't realize. . . .

—Well, yes, I've been coming here on Sundays for several months, all winter, in fact. It's a bit ornate, but quiet, peaceful, and of course there is the food, and the service. . . .

—Yes, the Plaza. . . .

—What about you, is this your first time, I mean, for breakfast?

—No, not really. I mean, not that I haven't dined here before, as you must remember. . . . We stopped here many times together, for lunch, remember? Never on Sundays, though. Oh, will you listen to me, making jokes like that! It's so difficult, though, when you reach a certain age, I guess, to avoid references either to the past or to the popular culture . . . so difficult just to be personal and immediate. I'm sorry about that.

—You think it's *age*? That we've gotten so old, or so tired, that now our lives are either in the past or "public" . . . ? I wish *I* believed that. I'd give up fighting it, if I thought it was an impossible fight to win. I'd let myself go, either into the past or into the public life, you know, that fantasy of one's life as a movie, or a TV series, or maybe a *Time* magazine cover story. . . .

—Which appeals to you more?

—I don't know, to be honest about it. Today, seeing you, here, on an early spring morning, with all this hushed, tasteful luxury around us, I think I prefer the past. But any other time, when the associations aren't so strong and aren't especially pleasant anyhow, well, then I prefer the other.

—But never this, this life now, here, the real one . . . ?

—No, I suppose not. But I can't *imagine* it any different from the way it is—I can only *fantasy* a different life, my old life, with you, or as someone else altogether, someone created by the public, as a kind of community effort, you know . . . ? That's how bitter *I* am.

(Both Egress and Naomi Ruth break into nervous laughter.)

—Well, I don't suppose we should have breakfast together, do you? The pain. . .

—We might be seen by a columnist, you know. The Green Tulip Room is not exactly your cozy, little, out-of-the-way café. We don't need any more gossip than we've already endured, do we, now? As it is, by the time you get back to your apartment, or wherever you're living now, you'll flip on the radio or TV, only to hear that Egress and Naomi Ruth "accidentally" met in the lobby of the Plaza outside the Green Tulip Room, spoke quietly together for a few moments, and then went their separate ways, etc. Where *are* you living now, incidentally? In the city?

—Yes. As a matter of fact, I've been staying right here at the Plaza—all winter.

—Amazing.

—Yes.

—Yes, well, good-bye, now. . . . It's been . . . *odd.*

—*Hasn't* it! But pleasant, too. We'll have to do it again, sometime. . . .

—Yes. Well, good-bye.

—Good-bye.

—Good-bye.

—Yes. 'Bye.

—'Bye.

—So long.

—*Ciao.*

—*Ciao.*

—Tra.

—La.

7.
(AT THE PARTY)

They spotted each other at the same instant on opposite sides of the crowded, smoke-draped room and made their respective ways through the crowd, holding their cocktail glasses over their heads so as not to spill, excusing themselves with careful graciousness as they stepped on toes, crunched corsages, bumped breasts, kicked canes, until they finally were together, breathless, in the center of the room, light peck on the cheek, sip from the drink as eyes appraise each other's bodies, faces, clothes, cigarettes lit, puffing, smiling nod to acquaintance nearby, appreciative and only slightly critical analysis of the posh apartment's décor, and, at last,

—Well, I didn't expect to run into *you* here! Naomi Ruth said in a hard but gay voice.

—And I didn't expect to run into you *here*! Egress countered.

—Jesus, Egress, we can't seem to say anything new to one another, can we?

—Not at this level, m'love. There's lots we could say if we weren't so obsessively intent on discussing our failed marriage every time we happened to meet.

—I know, she said sadly.

—Too bad we can't fuck, he said. —By God, *then* we'd have something new to talk about!

—Yes.

—I know.

—Yes.

—Um. Well, it's been "real," as they say. . . .

—Yes. Did you come alone? she asked him.

—Oh, no, no, no. No, I came with a "friend."

—Yes, she said, believing him. —The dancer. The young Russian girl. I remember.

—You alone? he queried idly.

—No, no. No, I'm not. Well, good-bye, Egress, she said hurriedly, and started to pull away from the center of the room.

—Good-bye! he called after her.

A friend, a man obviously attracted to Naomi Ruth's not inconsiderable beauty, happened to be standing just behind Egress, and, recognizing his bluff voice, punched him affectionately on the shoulder, and said to him, —Hey, ol' buddy, who's that fine-looking woman you were just propositioning?

—Oh, that's just . . . that's my ex-wife.

—You sound regretful, ol' buddy.

—Naw. Not regretful. The wages of sin, you know. Wistful, though . . . and something else. But not regretful.

8.

(At the Casino)

—Stay close, m'love. I started winning the second you entered the room, and I'll have to quit if you leave.

—Do you think there are some sort of house rules against . . . ?

—Against what? Luck?

—I thought it was slightly more than that, luck. I mean, the way you carried on. . . .

—Well, it is more than luck, of course, but we don't want *them* to know it, because, yes, there is a house rule against magic, another against divine intervention, a third against astral projection, and so on. Your usual house rules.

—Which one are *we* breaking, confidentially? Whisper it.

He whispered into her diamond-encrusted ear. She shuddered down into her furs. He turned back to the table and continued winning.

It was quite a night, for both of them. They had such a good time together that on several occasions, half a dozen, at least, the pain brought one or the other of them to his knees. They were almost relieved when it was over and they could go back to their respective hotels along the Strip.

9.

(AT THE BANK)

—Making a deposit or withdrawal? she asked him.

—Oh! I almost didn't recognize you in that business suit. A withdrawal, as it happens. What about you?

—Deposit.

—Neat, he said appreciatively.

—What?

—Oh, you know, the balance of payments, as it were. It's almost cosmic. I *love* analogies, as you well know, he reminded her gently.

—I don't need to be reminded, she informed him.

—Yes, I remember your telling me that, too. And just about everything else we say to each other as well.

—It's not exactly an opportunity for adventure, is it, being one of a pair of parallel lines? We stayed together too long, Egress; she reminded him again.

—Yes, I know, I know. I've been thinking about that a lot lately. Remembering it, I mean.

—What's the solution?

—Infinity, he laughed.

—No, be serious, Egress.

—I am, I am. We're a pair of parallel lines, you said it yourself, and if that's become a problem, as it most evidently has, then the only solution is "infinity," which is where they meet, finally.

—Or diverge.

—Right, or diverge. Of course. But we're not Greeks, nor were we meant to be, so we ought to be careful not to get our ethics mixed up with our mathematics. We're neither of us skilled enough a mathematician to accomplish it with anything like grace or good feeling.

—Don't worry about me, she said. —You're the one who loves analogy, remember?

—Yes, yes, of course. But you're the one who brought the parallel lines into this, which I've merely accepted as an indication of how you perceive our lives, past, present, and, presumably, future.

—I can't stand this quarreling. It's all so familiar to me, she exclaimed. —So *déjà-vu*. Good-bye, she said to him, and hurried from the bank.

He finished his transaction with the teller and left also, feeling no stranger to his anger with himself, even taking perverse pleasure from the familiarity.

10.
(IN THE COCKTAIL LOUNGE)

—H'lo again.

—Again. And again. And again. And again. And again. And

again. And again. And again. And again. And again. And again.

—Been here awhile, eh?

—The better part of a season, I'd say. I thought I'd found a place you'd not found and wouldn't. But here you are. I see I should've kept moving, should've kept taking those chances instead of this one. . . .

—I'm sorry.

—*Don't* be! No, it's not *your* fault! None of it. Not a bit.

—I've changed.

—I know it. I can tell that. I know you've changed. Trouble is, I've changed too. And you know where that puts us? I'll tell you where it puts us! It puts us right back where we started. What we've got to do is change, all right, but only one of us at a time!

—Right. Well, don't let me interrupt you. 'Bye.

—Yeah. G'bye. Too bad for the bartender, though.

—Why?

—Wal, y'see, he just lost *two* customers. A "regular" and a "potential."

—Oh, I know. Well, don't worry, someone else will take our places, I'm sure.

—Yeah, sure, the world is full of people running away from each other.

—Right. 'Bye.

—G'bye.

11.

(At the Hospital)

—Are you a patient?

—Here for tests.

—Really? Anything wrong?

—No, I'm sure it's nothing at all. A little innocuous bleeding. A lump or two, shortness of breath. But still, one has to treat these things as if they were serious. . . .

—I know.

—What about you?

—The same. Tests, X-rays.

—Nothing serious, I hope?

—Not really. A cough, occasional pain, a cut on my wrist that won't heal properly . . . Probably coincidence.

—Of course. Like our checking in here at the same time, eh?

—Yes, sure. Just like that.

12.
(AT THE OPERA)

—No?

—No.

—Right.

—Right?

HAMILTON STARK

*The individual has a host of shadows, all of which resemble
him and for the moment have an equal claim to authenticity.*

—Kierkegaard, Repetition

CONTENTS

Chapter 1

By Way of an Introduction to the Novel, This or Any

IT DIDN'T OCCUR to me to write a novel with A. As the prototype for its hero, Hamilton Stark, until fairly recently, a year ago this spring, when I drove the forty miles from my home in Northwood across New Hampshire to his home outside the town of B. Upon written invitation (via post card, as was his habit), I was on my way to visit him for the afternoon and possibly the evening. The post card read:

> 4/12/74. If you don't show up here Sat. with a fifth of CC and a case of Molson I'll stop up your plumbing with my toe. Number 5 has gone back to Mother and I've gone back to my old habits. Bring me a box of 30.06 rifle shells too. We'll do some shooting. A.

Typically, he had typed his message, and the four-color photograph printed on the reverse side was of a building he had helped construct, in this case a Tampax factory in the southwestern part of the state. A. was a pipefitter with a wide range of

practical engineering skills, and on that job he had been the foreman for all the plumbing, heating and air-conditioning systems.

After leaving my home around noon, I stopped in Concord,
the state capital, and as instructed, purchased a fifth of Canadian
Club whiskey and a case of Molson ale, which also happens to be
Canadian. A. loved practically everything Canadian and thought
Canada a truly "civilized" country, especially its far northern
regions, where no one lives. "Up there," he once told me, "there's
so many rocks and so few people, the people act like rocks. There
aren't even any goddamn trees up there, once you get far enough
north! Now that's *class*," he pronounced.

I had nodded my head in agreement, as was my habit, but
I wasn't actually sure—wasn't sure that I agreed with him, of
course, but also was not sure that he had meant what he had
said, that he hadn't been criticizing the Canadian landscape and
people rather than praising them. I didn't bother to pursue the
subject; I knew my confusion at his ambiguous tone would only
have been compounded by the further, inclusive, ambiguously
hostile pronouncements that he would have heaped upon my
head. He was like that. Once he perceived a crack in his listener's
confidence in the meaning and intent of his remarks, he gleefully
hurled himself like a boulder against the crack until he had split
the egg of assured understanding wide open and had it lying
in pieces like Humpty Dumpty at the bottom of the wall. And
like a fallen Humpty Dumpty, the listener always felt foolish and
guilty, as if the fall and the consequent shattering were all his
own fault, a just punishment for his exceeding pride.

In many ways, A. was a peculiar man.

I was saying, though, that I had left Concord, and a half-
hour later, as I was driving past the pink and aqua house trailers
along the road, the two-room shacks with rusted stovepipes poking through the roofs, the old farmhouses boarded up or half-
covered against the winter with flapping sheets of polyethylene,
the fields compulsively cleared by long-dead generations of Yan-

kee farmers gone now in this generation to scrubby choke-cherry and gnarled stunted birch, saw the gap-toothed children with matted hair and dirty rashes on their round faces playing by the side of the road, glimpsed in windows the blank, gray faces of young women and the old men's and old women's faces collapsing like rotted fruit, the broken toys and tools and ravaged carcasses of old cars lying randomly in the packed-dirt yards, the scrawny yellow mongrels nastily barking from the doorsteps at my passing car—as I drove through this melancholy scene and thus neared the home of A., it occurred to me for the first time that I might write a novel with A. as the prototype for its hero.

I will tell you how I arrived at such a notion.

It fascinated and amazed me that a person born into squalor such as this could grow to his adulthood in that same neighborhood and yet could possess qualities which, upon close examination, could be seen as both wisdom and passion.

How was that possible? I asked myself.

And then I asked myself if A. possessed these qualities (wisdom and passion), in fact, or if he were merely peculiarly mad. But on the other hand, I countered, even if he *were* peculiarly mad, and if his peculiar madness, which sometimes took forms that could be construed as wisdom and passion, happened to be a condition necessary for the man's mere survival—after having been born and raised in social circumstances that ordinarily dun a human being to death, turning him wormy with passive, quiet desperation long before he reaches adolescence—why, then madness was indeed wisdom, and to cling to such madness was passion!

That way, spiritual survival became, in my eyes, self-transcendence, practically an evolutionary move on the part of the organism. The question of love, its mere possibility, a question that had haunted me in my long consideration of A.'s character, thereby became wholly irrelevant. He was beyond offering love, above it and superior to it—at least the kind of love that I, from my indulgent background, had learned long ago to value in myself and seek from others.

This was, for me, a welcome series of insights, and I felt greatly relieved, as if from a dreaded, demeaning chore, like cleaning out a septic tank. I thought: Any person whose life provides us with that particular relief is worth writing a novel about. For who among us has not wished to be freed of his need to love and be loved?

IT WAS WITH considerable excitement, then, that I approached the turnoff from the paved to a dirt road, practically a trail, that led through a quarter-mile of approximately flat and unkempt fields to A.'s home. The fields on both sides of the deeply rutted road, lined with slowly collapsing stone walls, had retreated to furzy bushes and scrambling tangles of wild blackberries, sumac, and poison ivy. Scattered over the fields in no discernible pattern were ten or twelve rusting shells of windowless cars and trucks, some of them further decomposed and more nearly destroyed than others, also several farm vehicles—harrows, plows, cultiva-tors—a one-handled wheelbarrow, an outhouse lying awkwardly on its side, rusty bedsprings and swollen mattresses spitting yel-lowish stuffing onto the ground, a pile of fifty-gallon oil drums, an engine block and a transmission housing, both lying atop a child's crushed red wagon which lay atop an American Flyer sled in splinters, next to a refrigerator (with the door invitingly open, I noticed), and a red, overstuffed couch which had been par-tially destroyed by fire. None of this wreckage was new to me. I had observed, enumerated, and reflected on all of it many times, both alone and with friends, especially with my friend C. (about whom more later).

The fields and the road were all part of A.'s property, but a stranger, noting the broad, carefully maintained lawns, gardens, house and outbuildings which spread out from the closed gate at the end of the cluttered fields, would surely infer two separate and probably quarreling owners, one for the fields and badly maintained roadway, another for the house and grounds. But that was not the case. A. was fastidious and energetic, even compulsive, about the maintenance of the house and the yards, gardens and outbuildings that surrounded it. The region that lay beyond the white, iron rail fence, however, he cared for not at all, even though some seven hundred acres of that region was his private property, had been deeded to him with the houses and outbuildings by his parents.

Actually, it was fortunate that so much of the world beyond the fence was A.'s private property, because for years he had been tossing his garbage over that fence, throwing his rubbish, all his used-up tools, vehicles, furniture, even his old newspapers, over the fence and into the field. Every now and then, perhaps once a year, depending on domestic changes, he rolled out his bulldozer, took down a section of the fence, and shoved the rotting garbage and trash roughly toward the main road and away from the house, to make more room near the fence. It was a casual operation. The vehicles stayed pretty much where he had left them, and he usually left them where they had got stopped, either because of running aground on a huge boulder, of which the field had an abundance, stalling or coughing out of gas, getting stuck in the mucky, tangled ground, or ramming into another car or truck from a previous year's trash. He used his vehicles until they were too weary and broken to drive any farther than to this odd burial ground, and he always tried to make that last drive as exciting as possible. Then he would hitchhike twenty miles to Concord, where there were half a dozen automobile dealers, and buy a new vehicle, usually a different type from the one he had just interred—a pickup truck if last year's had been a sedan, a station wagon if a convertible. Because of the intense way he drove them, his new vehicles rarely lasted longer than a year.

Similarly, whenever he disposed of furniture, tools, garden implements, waste or rubbish of any kind, he took from the act whatever last pleasure he could wring from it—making bets, and usually winning them, that he could lift and throw a sofa over the fence, or hurl a transmission housing from his pickup bed onto a pile of old toys, and then an engine block onto the transmission housing; or that he could carry a refrigerator in a broken wheelbarrow for a quarter of a mile over a rough surface under a hot August sun. Afterward, to complete the act, he liked to sit up on his porch, usually in the admiring company of a friend or one of the local adolescent boys he permitted to hang around him, and while guzzling Canadian whiskey and ale, fire his rifle at the new trash. He shot his rifle at many things, animate and inanimate, but he always seemed to enjoy it most when he was shooting at the things he had used up and thrown out.

On this particular day, a blotchy, glutinous gray afternoon with a cold rain lightly falling, as I neared the gate where the road ended and A.'s wide, paved driveway began, I noticed a high, wobbling stack of what appeared to be new furniture—a Formica-topped kitchen table and four chairs, a double bed with bookcase headboard and matching dresser, several table lamps, and two or three cardboard cartons filled with pastel articles of clothing and possibly curtains and bedding. This carefully constructed stack, with all the articles balanced and counter-balanced, was located a few feet from the fence and about twenty feet from the roadway, and I had never seen it before. I assumed, therefore, that these were his fifth wife's leavings, her effects, an assumption which later proved correct.

I got out of my car, walked up to the gate, unlatched it, and swung it open. I could see A. in the distance, sitting on the porch of the house at the far side, swinging slowly in the wood glider. Neither of us waved or signaled to the other. That was customary. I returned to my car, drove it through the gate, got out again, and closed the gate behind me, as I knew I was supposed to do, and then drove up the long, curving driveway past the smooth, freshly greening lawns to the house, and parked next to the house on the side opposite the porch, where the driveway ended, facing the entrance to the small barn, which under A.'s care had been converted after his father's death into a modern garage and workshop. Behind the house loomed the humpbacked profile of the mountain, Blue Job, adding its shadow to the day's gray light and casting the darker light like a negating sun across the house and onto the fields in front.

IT OCCURS TO me that I really needn't bother with all this. Certainly not at this point. Perhaps later in the narrative such descriptions will be of significance, but here, now, I'm merely attempting to explain how I came to write a novel with a hero whose real-life prototype is my friend, my own "hero," as a matter of fact. And though that notion had *occurred* to me barely moments before, by the time I had parked my car and had started walking around the front of the house to greet A. at the porch, I had already completely forgotten the idea. I was worrying over whether or not I had properly secured the gate at the end of the driveway.

We spent the remainder of the day and most of the evening cheerfully drinking, first out on the porch, where until dark we sat and took turns shooting at the furniture A. and his fifth wife had bought as newlyweds the previous November. After dark, we lurched into the house and sprawled on the floor of the kitchen (the chairs and table were all in the field, ripped apart by high-powered rifle slugs), finishing the bottle of whiskey and the case of ale. I remember that A. had recently installed a central vacuum-cleaning system in the house, so that one could simply plug the hose into outlets located in the baseboard of every room without having to drag a heavy cannister or tank along from room to room, and he was quite proud of the system. He said to me, "I've got a dishwasher, a clothes washer and dryer, and a microwave oven that bakes a potato in forty-six seconds. And now I've got this vac' system. Now, you tell me, what the hell do I need a *woman* for?"

I said nothing. I was too drunk to speak clearly, and also, his question had seemed rhetorical.

Then he said, "I can get laid when I want to get laid. And if the day ever comes when I can't get it, it'll only be because I don't want it enough."

This last statement seemed wise to me then, and it does now, too.

I was quite drunk, naturally, but I somehow got myself safely home, and that was the end of the day last spring when it first occurred to me to write a novel about A., or rather, about someone very much like A., so much like him that I would have to give him the name of Hamilton Stark, or A. would know that the novel was about him, a thing he would hate me for. I did not want A. to hate me. Luckily, he is no longer alive, or naturally, I would not be writing this introduction.

(I SHOULD SAY that I *believe* he is no longer alive, and although technically he does not exist, that is, his body has never been located, it would certainly be strange and ironic if the publication of this novel brought him out of a hiding place. I can imagine the letter I would receive, postmarked in some tiny, far-northern Canadian village where he is thought of as a hermit:

> The only reason I'm not suing you is that a lawyer would cost me more than you could make from such a piece of crap as your so-called novel. Just know that if I ever run into you I'll run right over you. You are an asshole. And a lousy writer too. You're going to get everything you deserve, you faggot.

AND THEN, FOR the rest of my life, silence. Cold, stony silence. It would be a hard thing to bear.)

• • •

IT WASN'T UNTIL almost a full year later, a Sunday early in February of this year, that I again thought of writing about him. This is how it happened.

I was in the neighborhood, as they say in New Hampshire when you are within ten miles of a place, photographing birds in winter scenery at a state park not far from A.'s home, and as it was still early in the afternoon when I finished, I decided to stop by for a brief visit. I rarely visited him unannounced or uninvited, but for reasons too vague and smokily intuitive to go into here, I decided that this time it would be permitted and perhaps even welcomed.

When I arrived, I noticed immediately that he had parked his car in the driveway outside the garage, which was not his habit. At that time he was driving a pale green Chrysler. It was an airport limousine, an unusually long vehicle that he took considerable pride in being able to park wholly inside his garage. Swinging open the garage door, raising it like the curtain at a stage play and revealing the blunt green tail of an automobile that, like a dragon, seemed to go on forever, disappearing into the far, cavernous darkness of the converted barn, was an exquisite pleasure for him. As a matter of fact, on several occasions I myself, as the audience, had found the experience oddly satisfying and had broken spontaneously into applause.

But on this day the car was parked outside the garage, and the garage door was locked. I walked quickly around to the side door at the porch, knocked, and then called. That door, too, when I tried it, was locked. It was a cold, diamond-clear day, with about eight inches of dry, week-old snow on the ground, and there were hundreds of footprints in the snow, most of them probably A.'s. But fresh prints could not be distinguished from week-old ones. A narrow path had been tramped from the porch down to the fence in front of the house, and on the other side of the fence was a waist-high pyramid of the last week's garbage and trash, most of it frozen solid. Across the snow-covered, bumpy fields in front and into the woods behind the house and on either side were numerous chains of footprints—but it was impossible to tell when in the previous week any of the chains had been laid down. Beyond the woods hunched the mountain, mute, seeming almost smug.

It wasn't so much that I couldn't understand A.'s absence as that I could not understand both his absence and the car's presence. Except under severe duress or drunkenness, he never rode in anyone else's vehicle. I knew he must still be on the premises. On the other hand, if he were just out for a walk in the woods, a normal activity on such a crisp, clear afternoon, why did he leave his car parked outside the garage? That was not normal. (Rather, it was not *usual*. Nothing about A. was normal.)

I decided to examine the car more closely. Perhaps there was a note, or a clue. After circling the enormous green Chrysler twice, I finally noticed the three holes in the front window on the driver's side, holes surrounded by interconnected cracks, like spider webs, holes that could have been made only by high-powered rifle bullets.

This was certainly a curious, if not ominous, development.

I called out his name several times, doubtless with fear in my voice and surely with urgency. No answer. Silence—except for the whisper of the cold wind riffling through the pines and the distant, harsh cries of a pair of crows from somewhere in the woods behind the house.

What could I do? I couldn't ask any of A.'s neighbors, those folks in the trailers and shacks back along the road, if they had seen him recently. The mere mention of his name and myself as a concerned friend would have invited any of those folks to slam his door in my face, or worse. Years of living in A.'s proximity had aroused in his neighbors a certain amount of anger. I couldn't call the police. To a stranger, especially to a law enforcement official, the circumstances simply weren't that ominous. The police chief,

A.'s brother-in-law, but no help for that, doubtless would have advised me to drop by again in a day or two, and if A. still hadn't moved his car, then perhaps an inquiry could begin. And though at this time his divorce from "Number Five," as he called her, had been legally consummated, A. nevertheless was still living alone, so there was as yet no new spouse, no proper "next-of-kin" to alert and interrogate.

Feeling puzzled, helpless and, increasingly, alarmed, I got back into my car and started the long drive home to Northwood. I had not gone many miles when I imagined, successively, three separate events, or eventualities, which, successively, I believed true—that is, I believed in turn that each event sufficiently explained the peculiar circumstances surrounding A.'s absence.

Event #1: Upon arriving at my home in Northwood, I built a fire in the library and was about to fix myself a cognac and soda when the phone rang. It was A. His voice was sharp, harsh, annoyed with me, as if he had been trying to reach me for several hours.

I tried to explain that I had spent most of the day photographing jays and chickadees in the snow and had stopped by his house on the way home, but he interrupted me, barking that he didn't give a damn where I'd been; he'd been arrested by his own brother-in-law, Chub Blount, and had been charged with the murder of Dora, his fifth wife. He told me that he'd been permitted one call, and he'd called me, and then, when I hadn't answered the phone, he'd decided I was probably in on the arrest somehow, so now he was calling to let me know what he thought of that kind of betrayal.

I was shocked. I assured him that I was shocked. "I didn't even know Dora was *dead,* for God's sake! And you know what I think of your brother-in-law," I reminded him. "If I had known that Dora was dead, murdered, I mean, and if for whatever reason I had thought you were responsible, you *know* I'd never have called Chub in. I probably would have called the state police, not *that* idiot," I reassured him. "Assuming, of course, that I would've called anyone. I mean, what the hell, A., you know what I thought of Dora," I said.

Apparently my words soothed him, as good sense inevitably did. Above all else, even in distress, A. was a reasonable man. In a calm voice now, he said that he wanted me to hire a lawyer for him.

"Did you do it? I mean, you know, kill her?" I asked. Perhaps he'd shot her with his 30.06 while she was sitting in his car— though I could not imagine any circumstance under which Dora might have ended up sitting in the driver's seat of A.'s Chrysler while he stood outside with his rifle. But I did want those bullet holes explained.

For several uncomfortable seconds A. snarled at me, literally snarled, like a bobcat or cougar interrupted at a meal. Then he shouted that he hadn't called me so he could confess to me, and he hadn't called to protest innocently that he was being framed by his brother-in-law. He'd called, first, to tell me what he thought of me if I had been a party to his arrest, and then to instruct me to hire a lawyer for him. Not a shyster, a *lawyer,* he bellowed. He figured it was a job that fitted my natural and acquired skills rather well. (A.'s sarcasm rarely failed to make a point, though often an obscure one.) As to whether or not he had in fact mur-dered his ex-wife, A. told me that if the lawyer I hired was able to convince a jury that he didn't do it, that would be the truth. If he failed, that would be the truth too, A. explained. That was why he wanted the best lawyer in the state of New Hampshire, he shouted. Did I understand?

"Yes, I understand. How do you think it happened, though? I mean, how do you think Dora was killed? How does Chub, the police, explain those bullet holes in the Chrysler?"

A. uttered a low, sneaky-sounding giggle, almost a cackle, except that he was genuinely amused. He was intrigued, he said, by my knowledge of those holes. Until now, until I had asked about them, he himself had wondered who killed Dora. But now . . . and his voice drifted back into that low, sneaky giggle.

"Now, look, A., you don't think that *I* . . ."

He assured me that he thought nothing of the kind. Besides, he pointed out, it didn't matter *what* he thought, *who* he thought had killed her. All that mattered to him was getting his case presented to a jury by the best damned lawyer in New Hampshire, and if I could find him the best damned lawyer in New Hampshire, he'd forget all about my knowledge of the three bullet holes in the Chrysler.

I agreed to the terms. I had no choice. But who could such a marvelous attorney be? I wondered. In a backward state like New Hampshire, how could there be a barrister sufficiently gifted to create the kind of awful truth A. had defined? The task of locating and hiring such a person frightened me. I am an ordinary man. I felt alone, young, inadequate.

Event #2: I departed from A.'s house, driving carefully along the rutted, rock-snared path to the main road, where I turned left, and in a moment I was beyond A.'s property and was passing the battered house trailers, tarpaper-covered shanties, and those all but deserted farmhouses. Then there was a stretch of road where for about a half-mile there were no dwellings and the dark spruce and Scotch pine woods came scruffily up to the edge of the road, darkening it, creating the effect of a shaggy tunnel or a narrow pass through a range of craggy mountains. As I entered this stretch of road, I saw a young woman standing by the side and was about to pass her when I realized who she was and what she was carrying in her arms.

It was Rochelle, A.'s twenty-six-year-old daughter, his only child and at that the child of his own late childhood. A lovely red-haired girl with long thin arms and legs, dressed in a forest green wool parka, hatless, with the hood laid back beneath her dark, tumbling, red river of hair—she was a startling figure to behold, especially when she was the last person in the world one expected to see out here, and even more especially when one realized that she was carrying a rifle, which, because of the telescopic sight attached to it, I instantly recognized as A.'s own Winchester 30.06. She had the rifle cradled under her right arm and across the front of her flat belly, with her left hand gripping the bolt as if she had just fired off a round, or was about to. She seemed distraught, shaking, green eyes darting wildly, roughly, and in the direction of the woods on the left side of the road. She did not seem to notice my car as I slowed, crossed over, and stopped beside her.

Leaning out the open window so she could recognize me, I cried, "*Rochelle!* What's the matter? What are you doing out here?"

"I'll *kill* him!" she screamed into the woods, as if I were located in that darkness rather than behind her in my car. "I'll *kill* the bastard! I'll *kill* him!"

"Where is he?"

"In there someplace," she said in a hoarse voice, as if she had been screaming for hours and had exhausted all her vocal resources but the roar. All she had left was her maximum effort; anything less collapsed of its own weight. "I know he's in there," she croaked, motioning toward the woods with the tip of the bar- rel. "I think I hit him once, maybe twice, at the house when he drove up. When I chased him down here, I could see he was bleed- ing, his face was bleeding, all over his lousy face, the bastard!"

Her own face was gathered up like a fist, her green eyes agate-hard. Her fine, even teeth were clenched, and the muscles of her long jaw worked ferociously in and out. Her delicately freckled hands had turned chalk white from the force of her grip on the rifle.

Though she had acknowledged my question by shouting her answer into the woods, she had not acknowledged my presence yet and continued to stare searchingly into the tangled darkness.

With extreme care, moving slowly yet smoothly and, I hoped, gently, I got out of my car. She seemed not to notice so I took a single step toward her; then she wheeled about on her heels and swung the gun up, slapped the butt against her right shoulder, and pointed the tip at my heart. She sighted down the barrel with care, focusing the telescope with her left hand as if she were tuning in a distant radio station.

"*Don't!*" she ordered.

I froze, one foot held delicately off the ground, both hands palm down and off to my sides, as if quieting an orchestra. "Rochelle," I said in a calm voice, "give me the gun. C'mon, honey, let me have the gun now, you don't want to kill your dad. I know you're mad at him, I know he's upset you, but you don't want to *kill* him for it, now do you, honey? C'mon, honey, let your ol' buddy have the gun, then we can sit down and talk about it." I had slowly let my foot descend to the ground and had taken a second step.

I was terrified—the sight of one of the most stable creatures I had ever known, one of the most admirably predictable and rational women I had ever met, standing wild-eyed before me with a high-powered rifle zeroed in on my thundering heart, so upset my notion of the real and expected world that anything could have happened, anything, and it would have seemed appropriate. Rochelle could have broken into a Cole Porter song and started tap-dancing her way down the road, using the rifle as a cane, waving over her shoulder at me as she pranced out of sight, the end of a musical comedy based on the exciting life of a girl revolutionary. Or she could have suddenly opened her mouth wide, as if to eat a pear, and shoving the tip of the barrel in, jammed her thumb against the trigger and blown the top of her lovely head away. Or she could have simply squeezed one finger, nothing more than that, just wrinkled her trigger finger one-sixteenth of an inch, and I would have heard the explosion, possibly would have smelled the fire and smoke, seen a shred of the narrow belt of the blue sky fall into my face as I was blown back against the side of my car, my chest an erupting volcano for no more than a split second, and then Nothing, unimaginable Nothing.

With a shudder, I decided it didn't matter what happened so long as anything could happen. I took another step, then yet another, and gradually, as I neared her, she lowered the barrel of the gun until, by the time I could reach out and touch her shoulder, it was pointing at the ground. With my left hand I took the gun from her, and with my right I reached around her shoulders and drew her to me.

Suddenly she was sobbing, her bony, fragile shoulders hunched and twitching with the sobs. And then it all came out, what he had said in his answer to her letter, what her letter had said about her mother, A.'s first wife, until finally she was blubbering wetly against my chest. "Oh, I don't understand, I just don't *understand!* Why does he have to be that way, why is he so *awful? Why?*"

I sighed. It was not going to be easy for me to explain. After all, she was his daughter, his only child. And she loved him.

Event #3: (From the *New York Times,* Wednesday, May 1, 19————.)

ABERDEEN LAKE, Dist. of Keewatin (AP)—On and off for the last twenty-four years a man with a long gray beard has lived in an empty tomb in a little used cemetery in this tiny (pop. 49) village one hundred miles below the Arctic Circle. He says, "It's nice and peaceful.

"Well, it's waterproof and nobody is going to trouble a fella living in a tomb," says the sixty-five-year-old man, who goes only by the name of Ham.

"They call it a receiving tomb. They put the bodies in there until the ground thaws and they can bury them. But they haven't used it in a long time," says the old-timer, an American who refuses to talk about his past.

He considers himself a retiree and draws a $62.50 monthly Social Security check. Does it bother him living in a cemetery?

"No, I kind of like it," he says. "You know, we all got to die sometime, and this just helps a fella get used to the idea. Besides, it's kind of nice here."

Where did he come from? What kind of life did he lead that brought him to this end? "I'm luckier than most," he says. "I got what I wanted, not what I deserved."

I read the article with slight, barely conscious interest, prodded by my daily habit of reading every article in the newspaper from beginning to end diligently, regardless of the content, but perhaps also prodded by the vaguely familiar tone of the somewhat cryptic remarks attributed to the old man, an assertiveness tempered by a strangely familiar form of personal humility, a kind of matter-of-fact pride and wisdom that I had not heard in many years. There was a small wirephoto of the graybeard above the article, and when I studied the blurred face, I recognized, in spite of the long beard, the hair, the stooped posture and the obvious aging that had taken place, my friend of long, long ago. It was A.

And thus, once again, after a lapse of what seemed an entire lifetime, I began thinking obsessively about the man. "*Where did he come from? What kind of life did he lead that brought him to this end?*" I chuckled to myself at the poor, befuddled reporter's questions and imagined A. frustrating the fellow with half-truths and outright lies, flattery and aggression. The reporter should not have been talking to A., I snorted, but *me*! He'd never learn the truth from A., not in a million years.

BELIEVING AS I did that each of the above three events, taken separately, could explain A.'s peculiar (to me) absence that Sunday afternoon in February 1975, I had reached a point in my relation to him where almost anything could happen and where whatever did happen would be believable. It would seem "natural," "right," consistent with all I had known of him before. In other words, the man had become sufficiently real to me that I could, and therefore should, write a novel about him.

IT WAS ALMOST four o'clock by the time I arrived at my home in Northwood. The sun was setting coldly behind the low hills, dragging a darkening gray blanket across the snowy fields and woods while the temperature tumbled fast toward zero and below. Then, as the sun dropped wholly behind the farthest hill, leaving only a sky fading from red to peach to sooty gray to deep, starry blue, a low cold wind cruised across the snow, from the colder, eastern horizon to the slightly less cold western, as if following the waning light. Then the wind was gone, like a pack of silent dogs, and the night settled motionlessly down to its business of making the icy lakes creak and boom, of making the trees snap, the streams whimper, the hibernating animals underground turn worriedly in their sleep, of making the rocks beneath the snow concentrate their mass.

Inside my house, as soon as I had built the fire to blazing in the library, I sat down at my desk, plucked my pen from the holder, and, opening a blank notebook before me, wrote in large letters on the first page, HAMILTON STARK, A NOVEL. I turned the page, and continued to write.

CHAPTER 2

The Matrix: In Which Certain Geographic, Historic, Economic, and Ethnic Factors Get Described and Thence Enter the Drama; Also Flora, and Fauna, and Other Environmental Marginalia; Some Local Traditions; a Fabled Place and an Early Murder There

matrix (mā´triks, ma´), n., pl. **ma-tri-ces (mā´-tri-sēz´, ma´), ma-trix-es. 1.** that which gives origin or form to a thing, or which serves to enclose it: *Rome was the matrix of Western civilization.* **2.** *Anat.* a formative part, as the corium beneath the nail. **3.** *Biol.* the intercellular substance of a tissue. **4.** the fine-grained portion of a rock in which coarser crystals or rock fragments are embedded. **5.** fine material, as cement, in which coarser material in lumps, as of an aggregate, are embedded. **6.** *Mining.* gangue. **7.** *Metall.* a crystalline phase in an alloy in which other phases are embedded. **8.** *Print.* a model for casting faces. **9.** master (def. 18). **10.** (in a press or stamping machine) a multiple die or perforated block on which the material to be formed is placed. **11.** *Math.* the rectangular arrangement into rows and columns of the elements of a set or sets. **12.** a mold made by electro-forming from a disc recording, from which other discs may be pressed. 13. (on the circuitry of an electronic computer) an array of components, diodes, magnetic storage cores, etc., for translating from one code to another. 14. *Archaic.* the womb. [<L: female breast kept for breeding (LL:. register, orig. of such breasts), womb, parent system (of plants) deriv. of *mâter* mother]

—from *The Random House Dictionary of the English Language, The Unabridged Edition* (New York, 1967)

1

How far back in time is it reasonable to push, before one detaches himself from the near bank and poles himself, guiding the drift back downstream, home again, by straddling the current at midstream, stroke over stroke down to the present? Eh? Back there the stream had narrowed, had run with a swiftness that increased geometrically with each mile as one returned to the source. There were rapids, low overhanging trees with dangerous strange beasts residing among the dark foliage; there were hidden shoals, sudden waterfalls, mythical creatures drinking at the edges of eddies and pools, caves along the banks, dawns savagely bright and silent, dusks that fell in seconds and released at their fall the cacophony of nighttime hunts. And the farther back one poled his fragile craft, the closer one came to the source (that high clear spring where a mountain toad bejeweled by sunlight squats upon a thick pelt of moss and sleeps), the more trivial seemed whatever quandary, shame, or project that characterized one's present.

How, then, to justify the well-known practice of understanding one's present by going into the past, when the farther into the past one travels, the more trivial seems the present? For if such understanding is available there, its nature at bottom would seem to be that the present is of no special significance. Why stay down there, it (the past) asks you, in that mucky, mosquito-infested, broad delta region where the muddied waters mix turgidly with the green and blue of the sea? Why indeed, when you have seen the flumed waterfalls here inland, the crystalline streambed glittering in noontime sunlight, the exotic beasts and highland orchids where the stream curls farther and farther into the mountains, through the mists to the mossy crags and the lichen-covered high plateaus?

For just look at where we, reader and writer of this book, stand now. Look at our quandary, our shame, our project. A mere crank, questions of his intentionality, of the quality of our love for him and possibilities of his love for us—that's what's got us down! A rube! A citizen of the provinces, a man whose life may well be incapable of offering posterity a single slice of cheese more than his particular sociology! How mere. Especially when to speak of love, or of cruelty, or of "demons" and the possession thereby (as indeed we must and shall), we are in all probability speaking solely from our private and peculiar, narrow versions of our very own lives. Worse, of our lives as *children*! Brats, puling, polymorphously demanding dependencies, social and genetic accidents dropped into an inappropriate time and place. We are so used to our own whining about how we never *asked* for our parents, their limitations and friends, that we forget how little our parents and their friends had to do with requesting *us*. We weren't exactly what was wanted—unteethed, limp-limbed, blind, bawling, caul-wrapped, hungry and without gratitude. What would any poor people, poor and therefore leisureless, in bad health and nasty-tempered, want with children? Or at least with children such as we were? A poor people, if, as a consequence of the quick and cheap pleasure of copulation with sick and tense bodies, it must produce children, wants them to be born fully grown, strong, intelligent, useful and filled with abiding gratitude. No people is in such dire need of a healthy slave population as a poor people in a poor land. But one of life's great ironies is that all these people get are children, and more of them than anyone else. If the reader does not yet agree, let him read some population statistics. It's enough to make a sensitive man weep and think longingly of infanticide.

But despite the irrelevance and the triviality of the place where we are standing now, it does have historical background. This poor mongrel has a pedigree. Several of them, in fact. We might prefer running with a blooded hound, but we cannot have one; perhaps we'll accept the run with our own mangy cur, even learn to admire him, if we can know something of his ancestry. For it is true that—though he may seem it and though we sometimes despise him for seeming it—he does not come wholly from nowhere out of nothing.

HE SPRINGS FROM the Valley of the Suncook, so named for the ululating river meandering gently southerly and westerly to the Merrimack, which is, in turn, a larger, coarser stream that poles the region south of the granitic mountains and widens and fills across bumpy flatlands all the way to the sea of Massachusetts, where at last it empties its finely ground contents onto the outflowing tide and adds yet another petulant lip to the North American continental shelf. To speak solely of the Suncook River, however, is to speak, at its head, of a man-stride-wide rill that breaks across boulders thrown in springtime thaws and by snowmelt from the sides of glacial morraines. It is to speak then of a confluence of brooks, streams, creeks—the Webster, the Perry, the Crooked Run—all of them southern outlets of muskegs, ponds, small lakes, with names like Halfmoon and Brindle, Huntress, Upper Suncook and Lower Suncook. Thus, in referring to the Valley of the Suncook, and specifically to its northern terminus, one is referring to the beginning of a system, if he follow nature's path, and the end of a system, if he follow a manmade map, which inevitably traces the path of white settlement. These two paths, that of nature and that of white human settlement and the particularities thereof, are what determine the affective history of a people springing from that region, or any region, for hundreds of years afterward, long after the paths have been worn smooth and straightened with machinery, widened and bridged, overpassed, clover-leafed and median-stripped.

It is tempting to make much of the observation that the essential movements of nature here have been from north to south, while those of white neo-European society have been from south to north. Regard the prevailing wind and water systems, the tendency of erosion to flow inevitably to the sea. What are now called the White Mountains were then ten-thousand-foot-high upthrust blocks of granite, stocky mountains in the prime of life, the craggy head of the robust Appalachian chain. In the blond valleys and sun-warmed plains below the peaks, herds of gigantic bison with horns like barrel hoops grazed peacefully, while lions the size of modern horses loped lazily along behind, keeping to the shadows of the briars and the low nut trees, waiting hungrily for a straggler or a fat calf to wander from the herd's protection. So far as is now known, this was a region without bipeds, human beings.

Then the first signs of the glaciers—lingering winter snows, each summer shorter than the one before, streams and lakes that fail one spring to boom and break from ice to water and thus they complete a full year icebound, and winds, high, relentlessly cold winds, carting across the mountain barrier moisture-laden clouds from the snow blanket of the farther north, blotting out the sun for month after month, then year after year. The herds shift the loci of their grazing circles farther south, on to the Carolinas, and even through the gaps and west into the Valley of the Mississippi. Until there comes a time when the hard icy tongue of the glacier has carved a notch in the mountain wall and has extruded enough of its body through that notch into the soft valleys beyond to drag with it a never-melting pelt, finally covering even the very peaks with a mantle of ice, accelerating its march now by making its own weather unimpededly. And as the glacier, conjoined with several separate glacial forays from the two far sides of the mountains, crunches its way across those upthrust blocks of granite and the bumpy flats beyond, great wads of earth are scraped away, huge chunks of stone are ripped free of the mountain wall, deep trenches are gouged through the effluvial plain, and all the matter, stone, till, boulders, billions of tons of black earth, all of it, is plowed ahead or is eaten by the ice and as if being digested is passed along and ground finer and finer as the head moves southward and is at last spat out at the sides or lodged deeply beneath the grinding white belly. What escapes being eaten by the glacier gets shoved ahead of it, all the way to the sea, where great blocks of ice laden with soil and rock torn from the continent hundreds of miles away crack and break of their own weight and fall tremendously into the storm-tossed sea, where as icebergs they bob and float southerly, gradually diminishing in size, eventually melting, crumbling apart like saturated lumps of sugar somewhere off Hatteras.

The glaciers are not driven back from the south. No, under the influences of forces centered deeply behind them in the arctic thermal systems, they retreat. This is not the nice distinction employed by military strategists trying to save face with an angry and hurt civilian population from which future infantries must be drawn, but rather, in the case of glacial movement, "retreat" is a scientifically descriptive term. For, truly, what could stop a glacier's scourging march across a whole continent if it did not entirely of itself slow its march, hold, and then begin to withdraw? So, too, with the glaciers that covered what is now known as New England. Simply, they began to retreat, and as they did so the skies began to clear, for weeks, then whole months at a time, while below, dark patches of wet ground showed, and then whole soggy regions, vast swamps near the coast, huge deltas, and above the deltas, gradually rising fields stuffed and swollen with smoothly ground boulders, stones, streams of gravel and

sand. In the low places, there were deep cold lakes filling rapidly
with fresh icemelt, spilling over the till deposited like dams at
the ends, making streams that gushed with clear waters toward
the plains and the sea. And as the sullen glacier moved still
farther back, beyond Massachusetts, deep furrows and mile-high
moraines were revealed, here and there an isolated monadnock,
dripping wetly in the sunlight as if just disgorged, too tough to
chew and too bulky to swallow whole. Until, finally, the White
Mountains themselves stood revealed, humbler now, lower,
scraped clean and smoothed, gouged with new deep valleys and
notches, yet still obdurate, still planted deeply below the earth's
crust, altered, yes, but not moved. While beyond the mountains,
its noise daily diminishing, the glacier still retreats, leaving
behind long lakes, swamps, rivers, a tough-skinned corrugation
of hills and low mountains, a topsoil of gravelly land and a subsoil of boulders, clay, sand and shale. The winds die down, and
for the first time in ten thousand years there are low and warm
winds for a full half-year. And then the grasses appear, the low
berry bushes, the fruit and nut trees, and the taller, straighter
conifers. Come the forests, come the birds and beasts of the forests, for now there is plenty again—the fruits and the sorrels,
the produce of the yamboo, the blooms of the yulan, all the bear-
loved blood-gutted berries and wrinkled cresses, whole heavy
branches of juice-slimed sloes and ferns, whortles and plums,
the speckled eggs of daws, the roe of the dee, the milk of the
dameen. Thickly mottled with dark shapes are the skies, for now
have arrived the crested cormorant, the heron, the melancholic
loon, the sharp-eyed hawk and the eagle, the sun-blotting geese,
the grackle, the starling, the lowly wren, the jay, and the chicka-
dee. Chuming silver are the waters of the lakes and the streams,
for now spawn the salmon, the blood-flecked pike, the turgid
bass, the muscular trout. Great-bodied shad surge upstream from
the low warm waters near the sea, followed by waves of alewives,
bream and pout. Flushed are the dark new forests with the foot-

fall, bark and cough of the brawny bear, the roar of the urinating cougar of the claws and fangs that rend, the pad and nighttime howl of the timber wolf, the scowl of the badger, the sneak of the lynx. Add to these the fox who deceitfully reasons and stays forever hungry, the dutiful beaver, the martin, otter, muskrat and mouse—all the wee new beasties of the wood. Add to these the white-tailed deer, the rabbit, the moose with gobs of saturated moss dripping from its great jaws. Add to these the names of the hundreds not named, and fill the air with the buzz of bees, hornets, deerflies, blackflies, butterflies, the nighttime moths, dragonflies, and below, all the newts, toads, grackles, salamanders, snakes and centipedes that populate the ground beneath the great trees and the grasses, stones, logs and sweetly moldering leaves.

Now, curl a pair of great, god-sized arms and lift these names of creatures great and small, finny and fur-warmed, feathered and scaled; hold and heft all the names of the mast-high pines and spruce, the straight and the gnarled sword-hard woods, the fruit-laden, the briary, even unto the lacy ferns and maplike lichens; and cart in the god-arms all the names to the ovoid valley bisected by the stream later to be named the Suncook, barred on the south by the morain later to be named the Blue Hills, on the north the Belknap; and here, scattering them as if sowing seeds, set the names upon the ground. Now, standing back a few leagues, see what you have made.

This is what it is: a good place for creatures capable of hunting game year-round. And a good place for creatures that are at least capable, if they cannot hunt year-round, of gathering nuts and berries and fruits and storing them against the barren winter. Creatures that must graze on long or even short grasses cannot live here, nor can creatures unable to endure long cold winters. Hummocky, rock-laden, tree-covered land bound by steep hills and potted with small shallow lakes and narrow, rapidly coursing streams, with a thin, swiftly eroded topsoil and a subsoil of sand, clay and yellow shale—this place is good only for tough, heavy-coated, pugnacious, stubborn animals, and also for birds that travel south in winter, and too, all hibernating creatures. No others can prosper and multiply under such harsh conditions. They might try it for a few generations, but sensing the approach of species-wide depletion, they inevitably drift to the south and west.

THIS IS THE pattern followed by the first bipeds, the first human beings, to appear in the region. They were, of course, Indians, coming, like the glaciers, from the north, walking down from what is now called Quebec and New Brunswick, first in small foraging bands following deer herds and moose, then in larger groups, families, groups of families, and finally whole tribes. They were from the Algonquin nation of Indians, these first arrivals— Penacooks, Pemaquids, Sasquatches, Deemolays, Awtuckits, Ogunquits, Kanvasbaks, Katshermits, Merrimacks, and so forth, one band after another, passing into the Suncook Valley from the north, usually following the valleys southward from the large lakes in the north, the Winnepesaukee, the Squam, the Ossipee, along the banks of the rivers that drain them.

But all these people, one following upon the moccasined heel of the other, after entering the Suncook Valley, soon departed for the broader, more bountiful valleys to the south, saving this region up north where the streams narrow for when, late each summer, the alewives run or a week in spring when the salmon spawn and can be easily snared in wicker weirs set into the shallow cold waters or even speared from the shore by boys. For the rest of the year, these tribes, the Narragansett, the Penacook, the Pemaquid, and so forth, lived in relative peace and ease, cultivating corn and tobacco, fishing from the rocks along the bays and estuaries, hunting deer and other sweet-tasting game like turkey and rabbit, along the coast of what later came to be known to the English as Massachusetts and Rhode Island.

The only tribe that made do with life year-round in the small northern valleys like the Suncook was the Abenooki, late arrivals from New Brunswick, a short, slightly bent, flat-nosed people who spoke an Algonquin dialect. They, unlike their neighbors to the south, were strictly hunters and gatherers. They did not make any attempt to cultivate the soil, which is just as well, given the poor quality of the soil and their lack of modern farm implements.

The Abenooki, because they were the first group of human beings to make a more or less permanent settlement in the Valley of the Suncook, are of interest here. As their economy was essentially that of hunting and gathering, with no trade for leaven, their existence was what has been called "marginal." They lived in huts constructed from birchbark, moss, leaves, and muddied grasses tied with thongs to a frame of saplings which they had broken and beaten down with stones. Their clothing was not woven but rather made from the tanned hides of animals, deer mostly, laced loosely together with tendons and ligaments torn from the animals. They were not potters nor even weavers in any sense, nor did they possess the skills one usually associates with eastern woodland Indians, such as canoe-making, weir-weaving, tobacco-growing (though they seem to have participated in the custom of *smoking* tobacco, apparently acquiring the substance by stealing it in the summer from wandering members of the more agrarian tribes to the south and west of them), body decoration, and organized warfare. Their religious life seems to have been an extremely simple one, based on a belief in the Great Spirit as the Creator and first principle of both the visible and invisible worlds (between which worlds they made awkwardly few distinctions). Additionally, they believed in the existence of numberless woodland gnomes and minor good spirits, evidently guardians of places thought to be especially beautiful and, therefore, lucky. Similarly, places thought to be especially ugly and, therefore, unlucky were watched over by "devils," minor evil spirits. Except for these devils, there does not seem to be any larger dark spirit, or negative principle, to oppose and thus define their belief in a Creator, their so-called Great Spirit (elsewhere named Mannitoo). It does not seem that any rites were associated with the minor deities, whether to propitiate, charm, or merely to honor them, nor, surprisingly, were there even any rites associated with their belief in the Creator. Therefore, though they certainly believed in the existence and power of these several deities, the Abenooki cannot be said to have worshiped them. And while it can be said that they had numerous *customs* associated with religious life, because of the absence of ritual they cannot be said to have had a religious life as such.

Their social structure was extremely loose, based as it was on a male-dominated family unit and sexual promiscuity. Although incest was a taboo, it was nevertheless practiced extensively, especially in winter. There seems to have been no established rite for selecting leaders, no council of elders, no father-to-son descent of authority. Simply, the largest and strongest male was usually accepted as leader until such time as he was replaced, in hand-to-hand combat or through manipulation and deceit or by simple assassination, by a younger male. The old, when they became ill or infirm, were allowed to freeze to death, usually by the others' refusal to allow them to come into the huts when the weather turned cold in mid-October. With a like tough-mindedness, sickly infants or badly injured children were drowned by their own parents. Cross-eyed children, especially females, were highly prized for their beauty, and female obesity, when limited to the lower trunk and legs, was regarded as sexually provocative. Large breasts were also praised.

Most of this information, incidentally, comes to us by way of a small body of chants or song poems, for the Abenooki, as much as they loved hunting and torture, also loved singing. Consequently, we have (from the first white explorers in the area) a number of songs, and while most are concerned exclusively with hunting and torture, a few reveal homely details of the day-to-day existence of the Abenooki. For instance, a "Hunger Chant":

> *Wa-wa-wa-wa-wa-wa! Wa-wa-wa!*
> *A belly full of smoke*
> *Turns to stone.*
> *Ribs try to cut it*
> *But keep on breaking off.*
> *Wa-wa-wa-wa-wa-wa! Wa-wa-wa!*
> *I'd chew my hands off*
> *If I knew how to grab and hold them.*
> *I'd eat my dog and baby boy*
> *If they weren't so scabbed and thin.*
> *Wa-wa-wa-wa-wa-wa! Wa-wa-wa!*
> *(repeat)*

The entire corpus of the Abenooki chants and song poems were transcribed phonetically by a pair of Jesuit missionaries, Fathers Michel LaFamme and Bruce Brôlet, who traveled in the region in the late seventeenth century, investigating reports then circulating among the Canadian Algonquin residing along the Saint Lawrence River that there were in the forests to the south of them small bands of "angry people who know nothing of a life." From the name, the Jesuit fathers had speculated that these might possibly be remnants from the voyages of the Irish monks, meditative men who supposedly had sailed across "the northern mists" in the eleventh and twelfth centuries. Naturally, when they discovered only the scattered tribes of the Abenooki scratching a living from these valleys, the fathers were disappointed, for they had hoped to locate a native brethren in Christ. Nevertheless, the two priests lived for a winter among the Abenooki in the Valley of the Suncook, studying their customs and manners, such as they were, learning their language, such as it was, and taking down, as well as they could, the Abenooki literature. This was made difficult because Abenooki, although an Algonquin dialect, is a wholly uninflected language spoken in a low, nasal monotone. There is no sound for *R* and none for *W* or *L*—so that, for instance, the phrase "drifting over the waters in a sloop" would come out: "difftingovathatazinna-soup" (which is one of the reasons that so few Abenookis ever learned English, French or Latin). It is, of course, not a written language in any sense of the word. To complicate matters further, there are no obvious rules of syntax, and though a sharp distinction between nouns and verbs is held, none is held between adjectives and adverbs, nor are verbs declined beyond the present tense. But since verbal communication between the Abenookis surely took place, one must assume that there are whole phonemes that simply are not heard by the non-Abenooki auditor.

Against such formidable obstacles as these, LaFamme and Brôlet nevertheless were able to notate and eventually translate into Latin seventy-three entire songs, plus one hundred and forty staves from what appears to be a half-forgotten epic of creation, certain elements of which suggest a linear kinship from ancient times with the Indians of the Labrador flatlands, the so-called Graelings of the early-arriving Norsemen. A few typical selections from that long poem (called by the Abenooki "Stone-People-Long-Song") might be of interest:

Stave 12

Seal mother, take from me the sharp-toothed cold!
Take from me the deep-chest cough!
Take from me the ice-toed feet that bleed!
Take from me the banging-hard fingertips!
Let me lie here in the snowfield and die warm!

Stave 37

Ninnomakee chews on the ear of Gan the Wolf,
And Gan cries out, "Let go, Tooth-faced One!

My father is your father's only son!"
But Ninnomakee does not stop his biting mouth
Because of his far-sung thunder-like rage,
Which covers his eyes like a bloody hide,
Which stops up his ears like a lump of mar row,
Which fills his throat like a gob of seal-fat.
And when he has chewed off the ear of Gan the Wolf,
Ninnomakee of the Terrible Teeth bites
Gan's face twelve times.

Stave 114

Ninnomakee's fat wife gives him the
bear-coat and the grease,
And he slaps her twice and smiles the big love-smile.
"You are twice the wife the thin girl-woman makes,"
He tells her, "I slap her one time and she breaks!"

Stave 122

The time for drinking the honey has arrived again!
Ho-h-ho-h-ho-h-ho-h-hee-hee-hee!
We cook it and wait, full of jokes and wrestling.
Then we open our big mouths and pour it down,
And for five nights and days we are crazy.
Ninnomakee breaks more big trees than anyone else.
That is why the women love him and are so afraid again.

As mentioned earlier, the Abenooki, because they were the first group of humans to make a more or less permanent settlement in the Valley of the Suncook, are of interest here. One should not make too much of it, but nevertheless it does seem that, as a society, they were preeminently well adapted to the harsh and selfish environment, its parsimony and the cruelty with which it protected itself against human exploitation. It would be a long wait before a second group of human beings would appear who were so well adapted. And as the reader has doubtless guessed by now, foremost among this second group of humans (anthropologically speaking) would be the pipefitter A., or Hamilton Stark. As a matter of fact, one might properly think of him as the single most evolved instance of a type or class of human beings which, as type or class, had made an astoundingly successful adaptation to an environment that had successfully been turning other groups away for well over a thousand years.

ONE ADDITIONAL PECULIARITY of the Abenooki. They were the only people to have resided in the several hinterland valleys north of the coastal plain of Massachusetts, west of the coastal plain of Maine, south of the great barrier range of mountains that crosses from Vermont through New Hampshire well into Maine and terminates at Mount Katahdin, who were willing to defend their valleys against incursion. They defended them against the remnants of the southern tribes when these tribes began to be pushed northward by the English; they defended them against the Algonquins who, in the employ of the French, ranged southward and attempted to set up bases from which they could harass English settlements farther south; and they defended them against English and later Irish Protestant colonists who came tramping northward looking for cheap land to speculate with and sometimes even to farm. No one else, before or after, bothered to defend these lands against newcomers. It's almost as if the Abenooki knew that, because of the subtlety and the peculiar extremity of their adaptation, they were unable to live at anything approaching their present low state anywhere else. They were like duck-billed platypuses, or giraffes, or strange top-eyed fish able to survive only in extremely cold waters at great depths with very high atmospheric pressures against their bodies. Remove them from what had become a "natural" state and they would gasp for air, their eyes would bulge, their skin would dry and crack open, fissures and large warts would appear, and flopping pathetically in the mud of a truly foreign shore, they would slowly, painfully, die.

Their violence, then, their pugnaciousness and witless recalcitrance, when, for example, they were offered the alternative of removing themselves to the rich forestlands of Nova Scotia, seem to have been deeply instinctual responses to their real situation, responses prompted by a sense of themselves more subtle and perhaps more profound than any native history, oral or otherwise, would have permitted expression. They were called "irrational," "savage," "suicidal," even, by the chroniclers attached to the military forces sent out from the large coastal settlements to pacify and, if possible, remove them from their valleys—lands which, according to royal grants, charters, contracts and deeds, now belonged to companies of white Englishmen. One studies the response of the Abenooki to this particular stimulus, hoping to learn from it, and one more or less successfully draws several generalizations from that response. The difficulty is in knowing what those generalizations should be applied to. To Hamilton Stark? His family, friends, neighbors?

Perhaps, perhaps—but if so, one must also remember that there is more to explaining a single human being than the ancient history of his region allows.

Ergo: SOME OBSERVATIONS less anthropological, less geographic, less distant from the true object of our study than the foregoing; by the same token, however, observations, now following, which are as wholly from outside the conscious life of the true object of our study as have been all foregoing observations.

2

Moving northward now, from the third, fourth, and fifth generations of families of Europeans who had settled in Boston, Newburyport, Salem, Gloucester, Charlestown, Cambridge, Belmont, Concord, and on and on—the small, yet crowded, cities and villages clustered close to the coast, bays and estuaries—all those seventeenth-century business communities with theological interests and connections, whose interests and connections, of a business as well as of a theological nature, had begun to jam harshly against one another by the end of the century. Second sons often went unemployed, and third sons came up landless, too. And there seemed to be an excess of ministers and schoolmasters. What to do? What to do? One of the nicest things about being an American in that century (or in the two centuries that followed, for that matter) was the liberal plenitude of land not yet populated by white people. This, of course, is an old story, well known. The second sons and their younger brothers pack up wife, ax, gun and bag of seed, and they head out for the back country, the far outback, the territory, the hinterland, the boonies.

LEMUEL STARK, AET. twenty-four, out of Newburyport, Massachusetts, in 1703, with his wife, Eliza, and son, Josiah, in a company of thirteen men and twelve women and seventeen children of various ages, went forth from Newburyport on 22 April to clear and establish residence upon certain lands near the headwaters of the Suncook River which had been properly surveyed and marked the previous year by a party of engineers sent out for the Newburyport Northern Regional Development Association.

There they met the resident Abenookis, who, innocently, the previous summer had traded forty freshly speared salmon and twelve maple-cured cougar skins for a knife and hand mirror offered by members of the surveying party. The leader of the Indians in 1703 was a tall (for an Abenooki), muscular man named Horse. His name had been given him by a wandering Cree from the far northwest, a man who enjoyed the luxury of having actually seen horses and so knew what they looked like, which of course the Abenooki did not. It was rumored among the Abenooki that sometimes the white people stood upon and even had sex with enormous, long-tailed, big-nosed beasts, but the Abenooki word for the animal was Kiyoosee-hi-yi-ho-yo ("enormous, long-tailed, big-nosed beast that gets screwed by the white man"). When the wandering Cree had told them, first, that the animal was called by his people a "horse," and second, that the white people were in many ways dependent upon the "horse's" good nature and great strength, and third, that the tall (for an Abenooki), muscular, big-nosed boy before him looked something like a horse, the boy's family immediately changed his name from Water Lily to Horse. When later, after having passed many trials of strength and courage, he became the leader of the Abenookis residing in the Valley of the Suncook, Horse was very proud of his name, for among the Abenooki, while there were many who were named Water Lily, there was but one named Horse.

Horse, as noted above, was a physically gifted man, but he was also known to be shrewd and inventive, and among his people he was regarded as a driver of hard bargains. For instance, to their endless wonder and admiration, it was he who had succeeded in convincing the surveying party to give up the mirror and knife for a bunch of fish and furs. This is leading up to the moment, probably anticipated by now, when it can be announced that Horse was a proper match for the similarly gifted, shrewd, inventive and careful man Lemuel Stark. A classic confrontation.

It was atop Blue Job Mountain, supposedly, that the two finally met, at the end of a long chase, a foot race with a bloody dying for the loser that had begun at sunrise on the mist-blanketed bank of the Suncook. Lemuel had left the safety of the camp for an early morning leak in the bushes, and Horse, with three comrades, had surprised him at it. Lemuel ran, stuffing himself frantically back into his trousers. Horse gave chase. The others, as Abenooki are wont to do, melted back into the forest to await the outcome of the chase. If Horse lost and were slain by the white man, one of his three comrades would be able to take his place as leader of the Suncook Valley Abenooki. If, on the other hand, Horse either captured or killed the white man, all Abenookis would benefit alike, although obviously Horse would benefit the most. Even so, the Indians reasoned, it wasn't a bad idea to melt into the forest and meet back at camp and sit around all day beneath the balsams, drinking fermented honey and waiting for the race results to come in.

Lemuel ran armed with his unloaded musket. Horse was armed with the knife and mirror he had obtained the previous summer by smart swapping. Lemuel had the advantage of height and probably good speed. Horse had the advantage of knowing the country, especially the Indian paths that followed the meandering shore of the river. Both men were in excellent physical condition. The race was a toss-up.

They ran along the river, following the narrow pathway through what is now called Center Barnstead. Here Lemuel stumbled and fell, skinning his knee. Horse, not believing his good luck, hesitated, just long enough for Lemuel to scramble to his feet and speed away southward, running slightly downhill, to what's now called Barnstead Parade. Lemuel was beginning to enjoy the race, was gaining slightly on his pursuer, and was probably reaching that point of exhaustion where lightheadedness and exhilaration replace fatigue and anxiety. Horse, on the other hand, having finally realized that he was alone in his pursuit of the white man, was beginning to understand the political implications of the chase. He had to catch the white man now. If he did not, he would be humiliated in front of his people and would lose his position of leadership, probably to someone named Water Lily. Horse had a fairly well developed sense of irony.

What the author would like to do here, but because of his respect for historical truth cannot, is to describe the awful death of Lemuel Stark, suggesting, through metaphor, symbol, and literal utterance, the effect of that death on Lemuel's son, Josiah, who, under the understandably careful care of his mother, Eliza Stark, grew up (1) to hate "Injuns" (and all other non-Caucasian racial groups, whether minorities or not), (2) to resolve personal conflicts by the use of personal violence, and (3) to adore his mother, mainly because it was through her that he received first-person testimony as to the heroic stature of his lost and long-grieved-for father. Thus her testimony:

"YOUR FATHER, MY son, loved you. He loved you perhaps too well, and as it turned out, not wisely enough, though that, of course, is not for me to judge, Heaven forgive me for presuming, I was not presuming, Father, it was a figure of speech, and it's just that you, Josiah, and I, my son and I, Father, it's just that we both have lived here so long, except for Thee and Thy everlasting comfort, that sometimes in our frailty we wonder and ask, Where has he gone, my husband and my son's father, why did he not come back to us, why did he leave in the first place? . . . when of course, Father, we know all the answers to those questions, don't we, Josiah? it's not easy for us, the weak and fragile vessels of Thy everlasting love, to keep ourselves from crying out in the long night of our solitude, is it, Josiah, my son, my dear sweet boy, my beloved boy, you do so resemble your father, Josiah, his black hair, and his eyes, eyes the color of Irish peat, the clear white skin, the smile, the teeth, the tiny ears . . . thank Heaven I have you, my son, else my grief for your lost father would surely break me, I fear it, I'm ashamed for it, but I am a weak woman, my son, your mother is weak, son, but you shall be strong, I know it, as your father was strong, a tall, muscular, energetic man, who loved you, my son, oh, yes, he surely loved you, and if I say he did not love you wisely but too well, I say it only because his love for you, his *love*, was what made him run from that pitiless Indian chief, that Beast of the Forest, the one they call

Horse—the ugly one you have seen in the village, the same who now claims he is Christian, yes, but who cannot be, or he would confess publicly what he did to my husband, your father, and be hanged for it or thrown in a pit and slowly pressed by stones until he is crushed beneath them, forgive me, Father, for the force of my anger, I know that revenge is Thine, yet I cannot bear that the savage who slew my husband, the father of my son, I cannot *endure* that the murderer is allowed to walk easily about the village and forest like any Christian and loyal subject of the king, and if I cannot have revenge, and I know, Lord, that to continue lusting after it would only lead me sinfully to envy what power is rightfully Thine, but if I cannot have revenge, if I cannot see that savage pressed to death by stones, cannot throw the final, crushing, bone-snapping stone upon him myself, then I shall at least make sure that you, my son, know the truth, that you know your father loved you and was no coward, that you know he was not afraid, no, and that you know he now resides in the bosom of the Lord and is looking down on us, surely, and weeping at our plight and the way his good name has been smeared with mud and filth by that savage, the one called Horse, yes, my son, he would weep to see us now, his good wife and baby boy living alone on the land below the very mountain where he was cruelly slain, here on the plot of land he purchased with his honest toil the year before you were even born and a full year and a half before I myself even saw this place, this bleak and ungiving plot of earth, this scab, this mountain-shaded rockpile where the winds come all year long and bring us disease, chills, agues, where we must wake every gray morning and look out onto the mountain where your father ended his all too brief life in courageous defense of your life and my honor, for that is how it truly happened, my son, not as the savage, the heathen, Horse, would have it, no, and not as those in the village would have it, those who wish to believe that the heathen is converted so they can gain credit for it in Heaven, we both know who they are, my son, and why they choose to believe the Animal instead of the knowledge that God Himself has placed into their darkened hearts. They choose Satan, and God will surely loose His rage upon them for it, my son, just as surely as He will protect and comfort thee and me in our distress and despair, here in this tiny cabin where every morning we must wake to shade, winter and summer, shade cast by the heathen as much as by that mountain. You must not cry, Josiah, for the Lord is our shepherd, He will comfort us, the Lord and His truth, and the truth of your father's love for us, his bravery, and the treachery that followed, what we should expect from Savages but not what we should have expected from our neighbors, our friends, *Christians*, men and women who knew your father from his childhood and who chose to believe a heathen Indian chief, an Animal, a Dusky Beast of the Forest, one of Satan's own henchmen, before they would believe the Lord Himself, before they would believe even the wife of the slain man, for I told them, Josiah, just as I am telling you, have told you, will go on telling you, for I must strengthen you against the burden you will have to bear in this village as you grow into your boyhood and young manhood, strengthen you with the truth, so that someday when you are grown you will be able to redeem your poor father's stained memory and return his name to its rightful place of respect and honor among Christians, and though the people of this village choose not to believe me, I know that you will believe me, and thereby will come to know the truth of your father's life and the grandeur of his death, for I am the only one who saw it, I and the Beast who slew him, we two are the only ones who know what happened that morning, yet people have chosen to believe him because they wish to believe him converted, they wish to obtain credit for his conversion, when in fact it's *he* who has converted *them*, and they know it, they must, they cannot truly believe your father would leave his wife and son, his infant son, alone in the wilderness, just disappear into the woods, like a fox, the Indian said, that's how he said it when they asked him, What happened to Lemuel Stark? they asked when the Heathen had learned to speak a few words of English in that *awful* way of theirs, enough to pretend he had converted to Christ, and he told them, Like a fox, into the woods, we talk and him go like fox into woods, gone, big smile on face, smile like fox, Horse told them, and they all looked at each other and nodded, yes, how true, how sad for his wife and son, to desert them at their hour of greatest need and dependency, but they *forgot, they forgot that I saw your father leave*, Josiah, that morning, the dawning of our second day in this wilderness, for we were all camped out on the shore of the river, near where Dame Edna now lives, very early in the morning, just at sunrise, and the mist was floating low over the dark, nearly still water, and I opened my eyes and saw your father rise from his pallet beside me, and before he left my side, he whispered that he wanted to look at the mist and the still water and watch the light change as the sun rose, for your father was a tender man, not a coward, a deeply tender and God-fearing man, though he was not a man who talked easily of his Love of God, not like these others who now surround us, he was a *true* Christian, a quiet man tender enough to wish to see the sunrise his second day in the wilderness, in the valley where he had chosen to build his home and live out a peaceful God-fearing life in the comfort and love of his family, and so eager was he to watch the light change as the sun rose over the river that he walked away from the camp alone, carrying only his musket, doubtless in the event that he saw some game, a deer or rabbit, that he could bring back to share in camp with the company of people he thought were his friends, all of them people from the town he had been born and raised in, people he had known all his life and with whom he had joined in this venture into the wilderness, and I lay there next to his pallet with you at my breast, and I smiled up into his broad face, and surely, as surely as God is in His Heaven, as surely as anything on this earth exists, I would have known if that man was going to leave us, was going to walk off and disappear into the forests, leaving behind his wife and baby, alone, without money or possessions, with nothing but a seven-hundred-acre plot of rock- and tree-covered land in the wilderness, I would have known that, such things cannot be hidden, they are too horrible, too inhuman, for me not to have known that, a man's wife knows certain things about him that no one else may ever know, and oh, Josiah, oh, my son, I would have known if your father, that early morning when he stepped into the bushes at the edge of the clearing by the river, were deserting us, were leaving us here to choose between scratching pitifully in desolate and deprived isolation on this land or enslaving ourselves to the charity of a village that would sooner believe an Indian's version of a tale than a man's own true wife's version, and I saw his face as he left my side, Josiah, *I saw his face,* remember that, for that's how I know the true story of what actually happened once his square-shouldered form had disappeared into the tangle of bushes at the edge of the clearing, I know what happened then, I know that he was set upon in cunning silence by Horse and a band of bloodthirsty Abenooki, and I know that your father, instantly deciding that the Indians would be able to overcome and slay the party of sleeping Christians, chose to run instead of fight, chose to lead that pack of savages as far as he could from the place where his friends, his young wife, and most important, his baby son, lay sleeping, and so, indeed, he ran, a strong young man who, you may enjoy knowing, was a well-known runner, once said to be the best long-distance runner in the entire colony of Massachusetts, a man who could run all day long, from Hopkinton Green all the way to Boston Common once in only a little over two hours, thought by some to be a miracle, thus when your father decided to run from those savages, he was not behaving in a cowardly manner, oh, no, he was instead choosing to employ against them the strongest weapon he owned, his ability as a runner, which he was to use so effectively that no one would ever know of his decision, of his great bravery and love, so that the very people he saved from death, and worse, were later to deride your father's memory and to pity me, *pity*, pity a woman and child they should *honor* instead, as the wife and son of a hero, the only hero this village has so far produced and probably the only one it ever will produce, unless it be a son of Lemuel Stark or a son destined to spring from that seed in some future time, a hero who will know the truth of Lemuel Stark's life and death and therefore will not believe the fiction, who will know instead that Lemuel Stark courageously led the ravening pack of Abenookis along the river and away from the camp all the way to Blue Job Mountain, where, tireless, he ran ahead of the savages, who, like hounds with one replacing the other as the lead hound grew tired, pursued screaming behind with axes and knives and other murderous devices brandished above their heads, led that pack up the side of the mountain that towered above the very plot of land he had chosen for a homesite, led them up the tortuously brambled and tangled path to the craggy top, where no trees grew, where the cold winds scraped every living thing away, scourging it, leaving only boulders, crags, and the sky above—and there, at last, he turned and faced his pursuers, for there was nowhere farther to run unless he could leap into the sky, and to accomplish that, he needed his murderers' aid, which they eagerly provided, first the brutal, sly Horse, then each of his followers, like Brutus and the vicious Romans, one after the other sinking his dagger into your father's body, a dozen, a hundred blows, each of them mortal, so that after the first blow your father's soul had flown away to Heaven, releasing him from his torn and bleeding body, leaving behind, atop the mountain, a pack of satanic savages tearing at a mere chunk of flesh, while far below, by the river, a gathering of Christians were beginning to wonder where their friend had gone, and a wife was beginning to worry that something terrible had happened to him, and an infant son was beginning to wake hungrily from his peaceful-sleep . . ."

CHAPTER 3

Three Tales from His Childhood

TRUTHFULLY, I PLANNED from the beginning to bring into the narrative at precisely this point Rochelle's version of three tales told to her by her father when she was a child. Or at least that is what she claims. It's quite possible that she invented them herself (quite unlike her, however; her methods of composition depend heavily on observation and memory; she leaves formalism, fantasy, hallucination, meditation, etc., to others).

Let us think of this sequence of tales as coming from Rochelle's own novel about her father, a project I will describe and speculate on in some detail later. At this moment I am concerned with her lovely, fragile ambivalence toward her father, a man she believes is either a demon himself or is merely possessed by one. I am also concerned that she believes it was not always true that her father either is a demon or is possessed by one. She believes that when she was a child, a young child, but one of indeterminate age, it seemed to her that her father loved her. That's very important. It may be the hinge of her ambivalence. These tales are important to her (important to me for other reasons, which doubtless will soon become apparent) because it seemed to her that her father never loved her as much again as when he would take her like a flower into the curl of his huge arm and, at her urging, tell her tales from his childhood. Or so she believes.

Only three of those tales from the many that he told her remain with her today, perhaps because, above all his other stories, it was these three that bore significance for him, telling them, as he apparently did, three and four times over, when he never repeated any other tale even once. And too, it may be only that these three bore significance, later, for Rochelle herself, when, as emblems of an as-yet-unrevealed future, they foretold either the name of the demon he would become or the name of the demon who became him. Regardless, it was with stories such as these, tales from his childhood, that she first learned to perceive her father's present perfected state (her very words), and that is the context in which, in her attempt at a novel, she offered them to others. It is not, of course, the context provided here, in spite of the fact that the prose style and narrative form are strictly Rochelle's. The context offered here, my personal contribution, is merely the frame.

The Fighting Cocks

Every morning Hamilton Stark [in Rochelle's ms., this character is named Alvin Stock; for obvious reasons, I have substituted the name of the person she was really writing about. More on this later. The author.] fed and watered his father's fighting cocks. His father had told him that it was his "job," and for doing it Ham received every Sunday a small amount of money, which his father told him was called an "allowance."

Ham also had to feed and water the chickens, but because he enjoyed doing that, he didn't consider it part of his "job." He had chosen a name for each of the ten hens, and whenever he discovered a gravel-colored egg in one of the nests, he thanked whichever bird had laid it, saying quietly in the dusty light of the henhouse, "Thank you, Amy. Thank you, Jane. Thank you, Harriet."

Living in the henhouse with the hens was a fat old rooster named Henry. He was a Rhode Island red, like the hens. To Ham, Henry seemed shy, especially compared to the fighting cocks, because he only crowed twice a day, at sunrise and sunset, and quietly at that (unlike the fighting cocks, who crowed loudly and constantly). Ham liked Henry, and in spite of his shyness, Henry seemed pretty friendly toward Ham too. Not as friendly as the hens, maybe, but surely more friendly than those fighting cocks.

They were bantam fighting cocks, half the size of Henry and the other Rhode Island reds, but so fierce they had to be kept inside wire mesh cages in their own special corner of the henhouse. Also, they had their own caged sections of the henyard, which they got to in warm weather by way of their own little doorways. There were only two of them, and Ham's father had named them Jack and Gene, after two famous boxers. "All these guys know is fighting," he had said. "You wouldn't want me to name them after a couple of violin players, would you?"

The fighting cocks made Ham's father happy. He had brought them home with him, their cages stashed in the back of his pickup truck, early one summer evening, after having spent several hours in Pittsfield at the Bonnie Aire Café with some friends. He had bought them from a man he had met there, a lumberman from Canada who was going out west by train and couldn't take them with him.

That first night Ham's father had talked excitedly about staging cockfights with Jack and Gene. Even though he'd never actually seen a cockfight, he figured there wasn't much to it once you had a pair of fighting cocks. Ham's mother said that she really wasn't interested in anything that had to do with animals such as that, and she had gone into the kitchen to wash the supper dishes. Then Ham's father had fallen asleep in his chair by the radio.

As soon as he realized that his father had fallen asleep, Ham crept over to the cages, which his father had placed on the floor next to his easy chair, and he studied the strange-looking birds. The one named Jack was red, the one named Gene was yellow, and they both looked fiery—fast, sharp, sudden little birds with wildly round eyes, short orange combs, beaks like the points of scissors, and long knifelike spurs attached to the backs of their legs. They reminded Ham of snakes—their cold, unblinking eyes, the way they held their bodies motionless while they watched him, always from the side, turning only their wedge-shaped heads as Ham moved in a careful circle around their cages.

Finally he sat down on the floor next to the cages. His father was snoring. Reaching out one hand, Ham brushed the top of Jack's cage and quickly yanked his hand back. The bird didn't move. Trying the same thing with Gene, he joggled the cage a bit, knocking the bird off-balance for a second, but getting no other response from it. Moving back to Jack's cage, he once again reached toward the mesh, and just as he felt the touch of the cold wire against his fingertips, he realized that the bird had lanced the palm of his hand with its beak, and a hot flower of pain filled his hand and shot up the length of his arm.

He screamed, and his father woke up, and his mother came running in from the kitchen. Blood was pouring from a small hole in the palm of his hand all over his flannel pajamas and bare feet. Ham kept screaming and slapping his hand against himself as if a tiny spot of fire were stuck to it.

Wrapping his hand with the dishcloth she had been carrying, his mother hurried him upstairs to the bathroom, where, after a while, she was able to calm him and wash and dress his wound. Then she took him into his room and helped him put on a clean pair of pajamas and tucked him into bed.

Kissing him good-night, she said, "Don't be afraid," in a voice that helped him not to be afraid, because it was a voice that told him she was not afraid.

Then she went downstairs, and he could hear her talking to his father, though he could not hear the words. Several times his father interrupted her, but she quickly resumed talking.

After a few minutes his father started talking, and his mother began to interrupt, but he kept on talking in his low, steady voice. And when he finished, he left the living room and came into the hall and started up the stairs.

He came into Ham's room and sat down at the foot of the bed. "Let me see your hand, son."

Ham extended his gauze-wrapped hand to his father, who examined the dressing for a second, then returned it. "Still hurt?"

"A little," Ham said somberly.

"A lot, I bet."

"Yes, a lot."

"Did you learn something?"

"Yes. I guess so."

"What?"

"To stay away from your fighting cocks?" he tried.

"No, not exactly," his father said to him. "I don't want you to be *afraid* of them, boy. And if you just stayed away from them, that's all you'd be. Afraid. I want you to *respect* them. Do you understand the difference?" his father asked. "Respecting something that can hurt you is different from just being afraid of it. And to respect the fighting cocks you're going to have to deal with them face to face. Maybe that way you'll get over being afraid of them," he promised. "Do you understand?"

"No . . . not really. Maybe I do."

"Well, it doesn't matter. You will," his father told him. And then he told him that he had a "job" for him. Every morning from then on Ham would have to feed and water the hens and roosters, including the fighting cocks. He would start the next morning, when they would do it together, so he'd know how much corn to give them and how to handle the fighting cocks so they wouldn't hurt him or escape from their cages. But after that he would have to do it alone. It was a "job," his father explained, because he was going to be paid for it—fifteen cents a week, every Sunday morning before church.

But Ham could not stop being afraid of the fighting cocks. He might have if one morning early that first week Gene, the yellow one, had not nipped off a piece of the meat of his hand between thumb and forefinger. After pitching corn into Gene's cage, Ham simply had not been fast enough in pulling his hand away, and the bird had got him.

His father had showed him how to do it, but true safety depended on speed, so he was not sorry for Ham. "If you'd done it the way I showed you, he never would have got you. You've still got to learn how to respect those birds. It's not *fear* that'll get your hand out of that cage in time. It's respect."

So Ham had concentrated on speed that he believed was derived from respect rather than from fear. He practiced on old Henry, the Rhode Island red, whom he knew he respected and of whom he had no fear whatsoever. He would walk into the henhouse carrying a can of corn, and extending a handful of it, he would call, "Here, Henry! Here, Henry! Corn, Henry!" and the bird, head cocked to one side like a partially deaf old man, would stalk somewhat wobbly toward the boy, and when his beak was a few inches from Ham's hand, the boy would throw the corn onto the cold, bare ground, and Henry would dive for it.

If that's what respect feels like, Ham thought, I like it. I especially like it better than being frightened.

Nevertheless, when it came time to feed the fighting cocks, the only speed Ham developed seemed to depend on fear. He was terrified of the birds—their endless anger, their suddenness, the weapons they carried. Whenever he neared their twin cages in the corner of the henhouse, his hands started to throb, his arms grew weak, and his back and shoulder muscles stiffened. One night he dreamed that as he opened the sliding door to feed Jack, both cocks had flown out and had furiously attacked his face, hunting madly for his eyes, and he had awakened screaming. When his mother tried to get him to tell her about the dream that had frightened him, he had refused to tell her. "I can't remember," he had lied.

Throughout the fall, Ham struggled to overcome his fear of the fighting cocks. The birds had grown used to his feeding and watering them every morning, so they no longer treated his arrival as a chance to attack or escape but instead waited patiently for their food, which, as soon as Ham had slid back the door to their cage, they greedily devoured, swinging their heads like short hatchets swiftly chopping the corn to bits.

In spite of this change in the birds' expectations regarding Ham's arrival, a change that in some sense gave them a measure of reliability and even a type of kindness toward him, he was still frightened of them, and he continued to move his hand with the food or water dish in and out of their cages as if he were plucking hot coals from a fire. He tried to respect them for their new restraint, but he couldn't. He knew that the reason they were no longer flying at him was merely because they were hungry and had realized that it was his job to feed them.

They didn't like their cages, especially when every day the hens and old Henry left the henhouse to scratch in the fenced-in yard outside. Also, the daytime proximity of Henry and his harem amiably socializing together seemed to enrage the fighting cocks, and every hour or so the pair would crow angrily at the other birds. As always, Henry continued to crow only at sunrise and sunset.

Ham's father no longer talked about arranging cockfights and making lots of money from Jack and Gene. Ham's mother explained that it was illegal anyhow. "And with good reason," she had said angrily, but that was as much as she would say.

Every Sunday morning, before Ham and his mother got into the pickup truck and drove to the church in the Center, his father, who never went to church except at Christmas and Easter, paid Ham his fifteen cents—a dime and a nickel. "Put the nickel in the collection plate. Save the dime," he told his son each time he paid him.

And Ham did save the dimes. The first Sunday he had been paid, he had taken the calendar down from the kitchen wall, and studying it a while, had calculated that by Christmas he would have saved almost two dollars, which, he decided, he would use to buy Christmas presents—for his parents and his cousins. Until then, he had been too young to have any money of his own, and he had not been able to buy any presents for anyone. Like a baby, he had been forced only to accept. But now that he had a job, he was not a baby anymore.

Then one Sunday morning in early December, after it had snowed heavily all night long, the milky, overcast sky in the morning and the dense silence of the first snow caused everyone in the family to sleep a few minutes later than usual. Even old Henry overslept and didn't crow until almost eight o'clock—a half-hour late at that time of the year.

In a rush to feed and water the birds, Ham neglected to close the door to Jack's cage with the snap that locked it. He hurried back through the foot-deep snow to the house, and while his father shoveled out the long driveway to the road, he gulped down his breakfast and got dressed for church. Before he and his mother left, his father paid him.

Later, when they returned from church and walked into the kitchen, his father said somberly to Ham, "Leave your coat on, boy. I want you to come out to the henhouse and see something." He got up from his chair, put on his own coat and hat, and led his son outside and along the narrow path he had shoveled to the henhouse.

At the door to the henhouse, his father stopped and lit a cigarette. Then he said, "Go on in," and Ham swung open the door and stepped inside.

The cold-eyed fighting cocks, locked inside their cages, were striding rapidly back and forth. Across from them, in the farthest dark corner of the henhouse, the hens were huddled silently together in a rippling mass, all of them facing the wall. And in the center of the packed dirt floor lay the body of old Henry, shredded at the breast and head, with a flurry of blood-tipped feathers scattered about it on the floor.

Ham turned around and stepped back outside to where his father stood smoking and waiting for him. The sky had begun to clear, and the snow glared brightly in the sunlight, so that for several seconds Ham could not see.

He heard his father say, "You know what happened, don't you?"

Ham tried not to cry and finally succeeded and answered, "The fighting cocks killed Henry."

"You forgot to close Jack's cage this morning, and after you and your mother left, all hell broke loose. By the time I got out here, Jack had killed the rooster and scared the hens so bad they probably won't lay till spring."

Ham said that he was sorry. He said it several times because it felt strange to him when he said it, almost as if he didn't mean it, as if somehow he were glad that Henry was dead and the hens wouldn't lay.

His father told him that being sorry never changed anything in this world. Never. "So the first thing you're going to do is buy a new rooster for those hens. If we're lucky we'll get them laying again. It'll probably help if we put the fighting cocks out in the barn right away, so this afternoon I'll build a couple of coops for them out there. Up to now I kept them in here because it was easier for you to feed them all at once. Now it'll be harder for you," he said grimly.

"How much will a new rooster cost?" Ham asked, knowing the answer even before he heard it.

"Two or three dollars," his father said, flicking his cigarette butt into the snowbank and heading for the house.

Ham stood there alone for a few seconds and then started running to catch up to his father, who had almost reached the house.

The Drunken Pigs

In certain years the family raised a pig. Always Poland China pigs. But there was a period of about five years when they were raising two pigs, every spring butchering the older of the two and replacing it immediately with a young one. In two years that pig would weigh one hundred and fifty pounds or more, and its turn, as the older of the pair, would have arrived.

By that time Ham, whose responsibility it was to feed them, would've grown attached to the bristly, pinkish white beast, so he was grateful that every time his father and Archie Carr, the butcher, packed one of the pigs into the back of Archie's truck and drove off with it, they left behind a football-shaped and sized piglet, so small it had to be fenced separately for a while to protect it from the clumsy, thrashing bulk of the remaining adult pig.

"Pigs don't get along until they're about the same size," Ham's father had explained. "Like people." Then he had laughed down lightly at his son, and touching the boy's coal black hair with his enormous fingertips he said, "Naw, not like people."

Ham knew that they raised the pigs to kill and eat and that it saved them a lot of money. It was wartime, and even though his father worked hard every day as a plumber, Ham knew that they were poor, so he tried to think about the pigs the way he thought about the vegetable garden.

It wasn't easy. The pigs themselves made it difficult for him. They had too much character for it. Certainly they rooted like potatoes in the dark ground of the pigpen, but sometimes Ham would stand on the rough board fencing of the pen and watch them snuffle through the dirt, and when the pigs realized that he was there, they'd stare up at him and wrinkle the loamy surface of the dirt with their buried noses, as if signaling to him. Besides, the pigs *ate* potatoes—or at least they ate the peelings, whole buckets of them, left over from Ham's mother's cooking at the end of each week.

And yes, it was true that the pigs were in fact shaped more like a summer squash than anything else—they surely weren't shaped like animals, or people. Rounded at the ends, long and smooth-sided, so fat their tiny legs in soft ground were almost invisible, with a tendril-like tail at one end and leafy ears at the other, it should have been easy to think of them as nothing more than gigantic pinkish summer squashes. Except of course that they ate squashes, ate greedily the seedy cores that Ham's mother scraped away when she was canning for the winter.

Another thing that made it hard for Ham to think of the pigs in the same way he thought of the vegetables from the garden was that the pigs made noises, grunts and loud, high squeals, which Ham thought he understood. One time the pigs broke loose from the pen and were very hard to find and catch because, once loose, they remained silent and out of sight. But when Ham's mother discovered one of them rummaging noiselessly through her geranium bed over on the shady side of the house, the pig had started squealing loudly and had headed straight for the pigpen. The other pig, the older one, had wandered out behind the barn and had fallen through the wooden platform that covered an old unused well back there. Twelve foot down, standing in a foot of water in total darkness, the pig remained silent until Ham and his father, seeing that the cover had been broken, walked over to the well and peered down, and only then did the pig begin to squeal for help.

Also, the pigs liked Ham. Or at least it seemed to him that they did. They let him scratch their dry, scaly backs and smooth foreheads and often came to the fence when they saw him there.

In calm silence the beasts would poke their snouts between the slats, and he would scratch them. One pig would even let Ham place two fingertips of one hand a short ways into its nostrils, dime-sized openings, as long as with his other hand the boy kept scratching the bony ridge of the snout.

They tried not to name the pigs. His father had pointed out that if they didn't give them names, it would help Ham avoid becoming too fond of them. "They're not pets. Remember that. No more reason to name a pig you're going to eat in a year or two than name a damn apple tree," he had explained.

Ham's mother had agreed, but later, when Ham accidentally revealed to her that on his own he had secretly continued naming the pigs year after year, she had merely smiled. Because he had referred to only one of the pigs by name, Anne, she asked him the name of the other.

"Tricksie. I named her that because she looks like the one we had two years ago, and her name was Tricksie too," he told her, pointing out the pig's unusually long snout and small ears.

"Tricksie and Anne. Why Anne?"

"I don't know. It just seemed to fit her," he said. Then he asked her not to tell his father that he had named the pigs, and she assured him that she wouldn't.

THE SEPTEMBER THAT Tricksie began her final season as a pig and Anne was more than half-grown, Ham and his mother harvested an unusually large crop of grapes. They were Concord grapes, large and purple and darkly sweet, that grew from several clusters of vines in front of the garden and along the south-facing side of the road.

For a week, every afternoon when school was out Ham would step down from the school bus and walk to the grapevines and work alongside his mother until suppertime. These were warm, pleasant afternoons for him, picking the dusky grapes in the golden September sunlight, talking quietly with his mother as they worked, chatting of school, his friends, his new teacher. He also liked asking her about what he was like when he was a baby, and she apparently enjoyed telling him. He asked her why she didn't have another baby, and she said, "Maybe I will," in such a way that he figured it was a decision. And that turned out to be the year before his sister Jody was born.

When he and his mother had finally picked all the grapes, having stored them each night in close-woven baskets in the cellar, his mother started making jelly with them. She'd never made grape jelly before, had never gathered a large enough crop, and she was excited at the prospect. She washed the grapes, and squashed them, and separated the skins and seeds from the pulp, the pulp from the juice. She saved the juice in Mason jars and used the cleaned pulp for the jelly. The skins and seeds, sloshing thickly in a five-gallon tub like a purple stew, she decided to feed to the pigs.

That afternoon when Ham got home from school, she asked him to carry the tub out to the pigpen and leave it for them. He dipped his fingers into the gooey mass and tasted it: sweet, and a little bit sour at the edges. But he was sure that the pigs, after a daily diet of grain mash and water, would consider it a treat.

Eagerly, he dragged the heavy tub across the back yard to the end of the barn where the pigpen was located, swung back the gate, and slid the tub inside. Closing the gate, he climbed up on the fence and watched Tricksie and Anne hungrily shove their snouts into the mushy substance.

After a few moments, the animals' rapid eating began to slow, and Ham, bored, left them alone and returned to the house. He wondered if, after such a huge afternoon meal, they'd be hungry again in the morning, and he decided yes, because, after all, they were pigs, weren't they?

The next morning, as he always did, Ham got up, dressed, came downstairs, and while his mother made breakfast, he went out to feed and water the hens, his father's fighting cocks, and the pigs. These were his daily chores. It was a sparkling clear morning, cloudless and dry, with a light frost that silvered the grass and made it crackle under his feet as he walked. He went to the henhouse first, completed his tasks there, and went on to the pigpen, lugging the bucket of watery grain mash he had made up in the barn.

As he rounded the corner of the barn and neared the pen, he started to call, "Soo-ee! Soo-ee! Here, pig-pig-pig!" Then he saw them. Tricksie, the larger of the two, was lying on her side near the fence, facing away from it. Anne was also lying down, a few feet beyond Tricksie. Ham thought they were sleeping, so he called again, expecting them to scramble awkwardly to their feet and rush to the trough. When they failed to respond to his second call, he thought, They must be full from yesterday's extra meal.

But then, coming closer to the fence, he realized that both pigs, though still the same size in relation to each other, in fact had nearly doubled in size. They both seemed as large and as round as hills, and as inert.

He put the bucket on the ground, reached around for a stick, and after a few seconds found the long, pointed maple branch he sometimes used to prod the pigs away from the trough while he filled it. Reaching through the slats of the fence with the stick, he poked Tricksie on the back, but got no result. She lay there as if she were a huge pile of sand.

Again he poked her. Nothing.

He then saw a purple trickle, like a string, from the pig's fig-shaped anus, and he knew that she was dead. He looked over at Anne and saw the same purple string dribbling down the inside of one of her hams, and he knew that both pigs were dead.

Grabbing the stick firmly, he started whacking it against Tricksie's hindquarters, her back, her swollen belly, swinging the stick in as long an arc as he could, whacking the pig's body all the way up to the head, which he couldn't quite reach, so he pitched the stick into the pen, climbed over the fence and jumped down into the muck, where he picked up the stick and resumed beating the carcass, swinging the stick from over his head, bringing it down hard against the pig's ears, eyes, and snout.

He moved to the other pig and began to thrash its belly and head, too, again and again, when at last the stick broke off in his hand. He threw the piece of wood away and stood there in the deep, dark mud, weeping, and through his clenched teeth brokenly cursing his mother, calling her stupid, stupid, stupid.

The Erotic Mouse

The winter that Ham's sister Jody was born, his mother asked him from then on when he was playing in the house to please play in the front room. He was nine that year, and because he liked building things, he took up a lot of room when he was playing and usually left a great clutter behind him. This was why his mother, still tired from having the baby and too busy with feeding and caring for her to cope with Ham's expansive play and the resulting mess, had insisted. "You never pick up after yourself, so from now on all your puzzles and model planes, *all* of it, gets done in the front room!"

The front room was an unfinished first-floor room to the right of the stairway as one entered the house, opposite the living room. In an earlier time it would have been a front parlor, a room set aside for special social events only. In size and window arrangements it matched the living room. It was almost exactly twenty-feet square, with two windows on the front wall and two on the side, a door that led from the front hallway and another that led directly into the back downstairs bedroom.

A standard Cape built late in the eighteenth century, the house, essentially foursquare, was filled to the eaves with symmetries. Downstairs, one could go from any one room to the fourth by walking in a circle centered on the chimney. Upstairs, the four small bedrooms, one of which Ham's father had converted into a bathroom, fanned out from the chimney like the arms of a Maltese cross, all four equal in size and placement. Ham's mother and father slept downstairs in the large bedroom, and Ham slept alone upstairs—at least until his sister Jody was no longer an infant, when one of the small bedrooms would be hers.

For years, ever since Ham could remember, the front parlor had remained empty, cold and unused—except when his cousins from Massachusetts came up to visit in the summer. Then, because of the mess and the noise of the three children, Ham's mother had insisted, as she would later for Ham alone, that they play there. Which they did, happily. It provided them with the privacy and freedom to make their noise and clutter uninhibitedly.

But now, for reasons Ham could not identify, he was reluctant to use the front room. For a long time he had avoided even entering the room. Unable to explain his reluctance to himself, he surely was unable to explain it to his mother, and all he could do was shrug off her questions and say, "I don't know, I just *hate* that room."

Eventually, however, he relented. One March afternoon he moved all his puzzles and games, his Erector set and tools, his model airplanes and his drawing pads and crayons and watercolors, into the front room, one thing at a time, slowly, as if he had been ordered to move out of the house altogether.

The following afternoon he returned home from school, and while he was sitting on the floor in the middle of the bare room, working on a balsa and tissue paper model of a P-47 Warhawk, he remembered the last time he had spent an afternoon there. It was when, the previous summer, almost a full year ago, his two cousins from Massachusetts had been "sent to the country" by their parents. Ham liked his cousins, especially the boy, Daniel, who was his age. But he also liked the girl, Virginia, even though she was older than the boys by four full years. Her parents had nicknamed her Ginger, and Ham had always assumed that it was because of her reddish hair, which somehow reminded him of what ginger looked like. She was a good-natured and attentive girl, and she never seemed to object to keeping company with two boys four years younger than she. She was able to lead them without necessarily dominating them, achieving a balance that pleased all three and, for Ham's mother, making the chore of suddenly having to care for three children less strenuous than it might have been.

But the last time they had come up to visit, Ginger had changed. Sullen, withdrawn and aloof from the boys, she had preferred staying in the kitchen with Ham's mother to playing in the front room or, on sunny days, out in the barn and yard with the boys. Ham saw immediately that she had changed. She spoke to him in a voice heavy with sarcasm and condescension, and she treated her brother Daniel with outright contempt.

"What's with her?" Ham asked Daniel after Ginger had sneered at the boys' request that she join them in a game of Monopoly. It was raining, and the boys were sitting by a window in the front room, slightly bored, watching the rain dribble down the glass.

"She's big stuff now," Daniel explained. "She thinks she's Miss America. All she does at home is look in the mirror. At night she locks herself in her bedroom and studies her titties in the mirror. No kidding, I seen her. I looked through the keyhole once an' saw her doing it."

"Doing what?"

"Looking at her titties."

"Her *titties*? Has she got *those*?" Ham didn't remember noticing any pointy things protruding from her chest when she arrived.

"Yeah, little bitty titties!" Daniel laughed. "I seen 'em, lots of times."

"How? Does she show them to you?"

"Naw. But I look at her through the keyhole in her bedroom door, and sometimes I walk in on her when she's taking a bath or getting dressed or something, like it was an accident. Boy, she hates that. And sometimes I sneak up on her from behind and yank up her shirt or sweater and take a look and run away before she can even hit me. She doesn't run as fast as she used to, so it's real easy."

"Yeah?" Ham was astonished by these turns in his cousins' lives, and he was equally astonished by Daniel's boldness.

"You want to see 'em?"

"See what?"

"Her boobs, the titties, stupid!"

"Sure," Ham quickly answered. "How?"

"Easy. You call her in here, tell her you want her to explain something to you, something like about the Monopoly rules, and I'll circle around through the living room and sneak up behind her and yank up her shirt. Okay? Got it?"

"Sure."

"But when I do, you better be ready to take off, because she really gets mad," Daniel warned.

Ham said he'd be ready, and Daniel went out of the front room into the living room. Then Ham started calling Ginger to come and explain something to him. "A Monopoly rule!" he yelled.

She sighed, got up from the kitchen table, and strolled through the downstairs bedroom to the front room. When she appeared at the door and asked, "Okay, what is it?" Ham momentarily lost his courage and was about to say "Never mind," when he saw Daniel tiptoeing out of the bedroom behind her, his blue eyes gleaming excitedly, his fingers and hands poised to grab her shirttail, which he did, snapping it up to her armpits and exposing to Ham's amazed eyes a tiny white brassiere strapped across her chest. Then, as she screamed, Ham started running, backward and out the door to the living room, through the living room to the kitchen and into the bedroom, where he ran into Ginger, who had remained standing in the doorway, her arms folded defiantly across her chest. Daniel, who had first fled into the kitchen and then had turned to follow Ham as he passed through, bumped into his cousin from behind and yelled, "Hurry up! Get going!" And then he saw her too.

They started to spin around and head back through the kitchen again, but she said, "Forget it, Daniel! I'm through chasing you. If you two want to be disgusting little sex fiends, go ahead. Here, take a good look," she said, and she lifted her blouse and showed them her brassiere. "Satisfied?"

Ham felt his ears redden at the sight, and he turned around and ran from the room, all the way upstairs to his bedroom, where he sat down on the bed and waited for Daniel to come looking for him. While he waited, he promised himself, over and over, that he'd never look at Ginger's titties again, no matter what her brother said, never.

EXCEPT WHEN HE happened to be in the front room, he hadn't thought about it since it had happened. It was like almost forgetting it, or like having only dreamed it, parts of it—the part where Daniel sneaks up behind her, his eyes gleaming, his fingers outstretched and hooked a little, like Dracula's, while Ginger stands in front of the door to the bedroom, talking peacefully to Ham about the Monopoly rules, when suddenly she bares her breasts to him, stands there leering, calling him a disgusting little sex fiend. That's what he remembered whenever he had to spend more than a minute or two alone in the front room.

And inevitably, if he remained there, he remembered two other things, both of which caused him discomfort that was extreme and similar in feeling to the discomfort caused by the first memory. Like the one, the other memories were of events that had taken place in the front room. In one of them, he is with Ginger. She is about ten, and he is only six, and they are looking at each other's genitals, touching them with fingertips, prodding, pulling tissue back, scrutinizing with excruciatingly gentle curiosity their respectively tiny organs.

They were not found out. No one burst in on them and pointed a huge finger and called them disgusting little sex fiends. Yet the memory gave Ham terrible discomfort, a deep sense of shame, and always, if at that moment he did not leave the front room, he would remember the other event that had taken place there. He would remember one spring morning, a Sunday before church, going into the front room from his parents' bedroom, taking a short cut to the stairs, and as he runs through the room, he glimpses a tiny mouse huddled on the fireplace hearthstone, a brown mouse the size of a man's thumb caught in a brick-walled corner. Ham stops and tiptoes over to the mouse, which cannot escape its corner and, as a final ruse, is stilled, trembling, waiting. The boy leans to his left and with his two hands removes a brick from the stack of a dozen or so that his father placed there, probably for some intended chimney repair, and the boy drops the brick onto the mouse, crushing its body but not killing it, so that it squeaks wetly, like an orange being squeezed for juice, and the boy must retrieve the brick, hold it up to his chin and drop it a second time, and then a third, and finally a fourth, when the mouse is dead.

HAM SLOWLY GOT to his feet and walked from the front room to the kitchen, on his way passing through his parents' bedroom, where the new baby slept in her white, gauze-shrouded basinette. His mother was resting. She was seated at the kitchen table looking at her fingernails. When he came into the room, she smiled and said hello to him and asked him to come stand next to her.

While she stroked his hair back with her hands, he asked her one more time if he had to play in the front room. She relented and said no, he didn't have to.

But she wanted to know why he hated that room, when he used to love it so.

He was going to tell her about the mouse, but when he opened his mouth to speak, he remembered that she already knew about it. It had never been a secret. He had run proudly from the front room to the kitchen and had brought both parents back to see the dead animal. They had been pleased and amazed. His father had patted him on the head and had said, "Good boy," and his mother had said, "I never would've been able to do that. I just would've run for the cat and let him do it!"

So he said nothing to his mother, nothing of the mouse and of course nothing about his cousins. He shrugged his shoulders and looked at his feet.

"You're a strange one, Ham," she told him, smiling. "But if you want to be here with me and the baby, I guess I'll just have to give in and let you."

After that he forgot about the mouse and did not remember it even when, now and then, because of some errand or helping his mother or father, he could not avoid going into the front room. And when he had forgotten about the mouse, he no longer remembered staring and poking at his cousin's body, or her hands on his. And eventually he forgot the day she pulled up her own blouse and exposed her breasts to him.

IF IT SEEMS strange that the daughter of a man like Hamilton Stark should treasure and retell in literary form these three tales of his childhood, the reader might remember that it's only in the light of these stories that she is able to justify her love for the man. Otherwise, she might be forced to regard her love for him as perverse, lost, tangled in ropes of ritualized grief and reenacted trauma, possibly for the rest of her life, and certainly his.

And if it seems strange that a hero's childhood should be described in this manner, please remember that my hero is both controversial and enormous, and therefore whoever would attempt to describe him objectively (excluding from his description the narrator's personal sympathies and antipathies for the subject) runs the risk of being dominated by the subject. That is the reason for the mask, the format of the tales, the realism, the lack of realism.

There will be other masks, other formats, other castings of reality. You may continue to call this one Rochelle, if you wish, and of course she will continue to play a major role in the events being described. She is, after all, Hamilton Stark's only child, and despite her having been deserted by him, she is crucial to our understanding of him. Actually, her absence from his life, because it was willed by him, is more revealing than her presence would be. I hope you like her. I do. She's twenty-six years old, a long-boned, precisely featured, red-haired young woman with green eyes and clear white skin that's almost translucent. She moves quickly but with grace and elegance. True elegance. If I were a younger man, I would court her. I would pursue her ceaselessly. For though she's the kind of young woman who tends to draw organized, purposeful, self-centered men into changing their lives suddenly, radically, and, very often, disastrously, she's also the kind of woman who's astonished when it actually happens—though, to one not so affected by her charms, it's never clear that she did not secretly desire the disaster.

But, to continue:

CHAPTER 4

Her Mother Speaks to Her of a Man She Calls "Your Father"

NO, REALLY, DEAR, I mean it. It's time everyone stopped all this dancing around the few trivial facts of the man and got right down to where you can stick your nose up against them, so to speak. Forgive me for saying it this way, but the man, your father, is a despicable man. Always was. Despicable, pure and simple, and everyone who's ever had the misfortune to know him knows at least that much about him, and especially everyone who's ever been married to him, among whom I count myself the first, as you know.

But you're his only child, dear, you've never been married to him, of course, so that's probably why you keep going through all this hero-worshiping nonsense with the man. But only child or not, don't forget the facts you have to ignore. Life's like that, it'll let you keep on ignoring the facts, practically forever, if you want to go that far, but eventually it'll make you pay for it—or your children, or your wife or husband, or maybe even your grandchildren. Anyhow, *somebody* ends up paying, and I don't plan on being that somebody for you. No, you're practically

grown now, old enough to know the truth about your father.
You think now that he's somebody to imitate, someone to admire
and recommend to all your friends, someone who'll defend you
against your enemies, a confidant, an advisor, a teacher, a chum.
When I get through, dear, you'll know better than to imitate
him. You'll know not to expect him to defend you against anything. Hah, you'll need someone to defend you against *him!* A
chum. Some chum.

YOU'RE PROBABLY WONDERING why I'm telling you all this now,
why I waited so long to turn you against him. Well, blood is
thicker than water, that's how I always reasoned about the matter, and besides, I never wanted him coming back at me that I
turned you against him, you his only child, the one he probably
claims to love so much, but of course, only later, when you're
practically all grown up and it's *easy* to love you, *easy* to be your
father now—not that you weren't a lovable child, no, of course
not, you were a wonderful, cuddly, curly-haired little thing,
everyone loved you, especially me, and I didn't want your father
claiming that I had turned you against him by only telling you
the bad things about him, or only telling you things in a light
that would make you think badly of the man your father. Let the
child find out for herself, that's what I always said, when people
asked me if you knew what kind of a man your father was, and
believe me, they asked, oh God, did they ever ask. They couldn't
believe it when you talked about him the way you did, when
you bragged about his being a pipefitter, when you told people
what a big shot he was, how he built the U.S. Air Force Academy
all by himself, that place in Colorado, as if that weren't one big
lie. Brother, the things that man could tell a child. I remember
my eyes filling with tears when I would hear you out on the
back steps telling your little friends how your father had been
a champion boxer. And when you told them he was a champion
runner. And when you described his cars. His ability to play the

saxophone. His enormous bicep. His black and thick hair. The curly mat of black hair on his chest. The broad shoulders, the hard-muscled back. The rocky thigh.

Well, you asked me for my thoughts and opinions and my memories of the man, and I'm going to give them to you, no matter what they do to your version of him. I know you'll be asking the same of his other wives—or, I should say, ex-wives—so I won't bother with what I know to be true of him after we got our divorce, because you'll get plenty of that from the women who knew him later and better than I did during those particular years of his life. And who knows, maybe he's changed. It sometimes happens. But even so, above all, I want to be fair to the man, because from what I've heard, he's been fair to me. From what I've heard, he's actually told people he still loves me, and that he loved me best of all, that I was his "true love." I can understand that. I mean, it doesn't surprise me. We were so young, and you know what they say about young lovers, first lovers. Oh, I've gotten over him, all right, I mean, I can admit now that he was my first love, my true love, all that sort of thing, but I'm over him now. Because after all, you must remember *he* was the one who left. Not me. *He* was the one who walked out. Not me. *He* was the one who wanted the divorce, the one who got himself a lover while he was still married to me. Not me. I never did any of that. It makes it easier to get over someone if you've never done anything wrong to him. You can understand that.

But I'm sure that when he says I was his first love he's telling the truth. I don't think he lied to me about that, and maybe even after all these years he still does think of me that way. It wouldn't be the strangest thing about him. You know what they say about first loves. We were young. I mean *young*. I was a fashion model then, for the Globe Department Store right here in Lakeland. A small-town girl, sure, but pretty. Some people said pretty enough to succeed as a fashion model in New York, even. You know all this, you've seen pictures, snapshots, and of course, you've talked to people who knew me then. Anyhow, that's not important, except that naturally it helped me land your father.

He came south to Florida that winter, it was the winter he thought he murdered his father, your grandfather. Someone'll probably go into all that in detail, so I won't bother here. It's a fascinating story, though. Whenever I tell people about it now, they simply refuse to believe that I believed it then, that he had killed his own father, I mean. But I always say, "Listen, if he believed it *himself*, why shouldn't I believe it too?" Not many people can come up with an answer for that one.

Anyhow, it was the winter he thought he murdered his father that I first met your father. He came south to Florida, hitchhiking, with nothing more than what he could put in a single battered suitcase. Why he chose Lakeland I'll never know for sure, but I think it had something to do with a construction job that was going on then. A lot of plumbing was involved, connecting up a couple of lakes in the area for a town water supply, something like that. I never paid much attention to the jobs he worked on, never really understood them very well, though of course I was a good listener and always made sure to praise him highly for his work, both to his face and behind his back.

He chose to stop running in Lakeland, after running all the way south from his family home in New Hampshire in the middle of the winter, hitchhiking on trucks, sleeping alongside the highway in places like Red Bank, New Jersey, and Raleigh, North Carolina. He had just turned twenty-two years old, big and strong and not afraid of anything or anyone, except the police, of course. I often think of him, now that you are doing the same thing at almost the same age, hitchhiking all over the country, sleeping by the side of the road and all, not afraid of anything or anyone, and you aren't even afraid of the police, naturally, because you don't think you have killed your father. Anyhow, I often think of your father during those years, and it gives me some slight comfort, because after all, he did the same thing, and no harm came to him for it.

I did say that he was big and strong then, didn't I? Well, indeed he was. Never in my life had I seen a man as big and strong as your father was then. It's where you get your height. He was wearing a T-shirt that showed all his muscles, and work pants, and he had come into the Globe to buy some underwear. He had just gotten off work at the pumping station. They were building a new pumping station that year and he had walked up to the foreman with his suitcase in his hand, and the way he told me later, he just said to the foreman, "You probably need pipefitters, and I'm the best damned pipefitter you're ever going to get the chance to hire, so you ought to hire me whether you need pipefitters right now or not." The foreman, who later tried to become your father's friend, Bucky Walker, you remember him, he said, "Anybody thinks that high of himself is either so damned good I can't afford to let him go, or so damned bad it'll be a pleasure to fire him. So you're hired, pal." That's how your father told it, and later, when Bucky told me the story, it was the same story, and Bucky had no reason to lie about it, because by that time your father had gone back up north and had left me with you as a baby here in Lakeland. Actually, Bucky was kind of interested in me then. He was hanging around the apartment a lot after work, drinking beer and talking about your father, wondering why he had gone and done what he had done. I often wonder what would have happened if I had gone along with Bucky the way he obviously wanted me to and had even married him after my divorce. And after he had divorced Sally, naturally. I mean, he was kind of a sweet man, and God knows, he was in love with me. I guess I never really told you much about all that, did I? Well, it doesn't matter, because I was still so in love with your father that I couldn't see the good side of any other man, even a man as sweet as Bucky Walker.

But I'm getting away from the thing I wanted to describe to you, how your father looked to me when we first met. I was modeling a pink one-piece Esther Williams bathing suit in a swim-wear fashion show on the mezzanine of the Globe, and I had just started down the ramp when I caught sight of him coming up the stairs from the first floor, where he had bought some underwear. He told me later that, noticing a sign about the swimwear show upstairs, he'd decided to come and take a look. There wasn't a beach at Lakeland, as you know, it's so far inland, and at that time he had been in Florida for over a month and hadn't seen a single woman in a bathing suit, and as he always said, that's what Florida was to him, "Women in bathing suits and Coney Island with palm trees." He'd seen the Coney-Island-with-palm-trees part, but so far he hadn't seen anything of the women in bathing suits. So he decided to walk up the stairs to the mezzanine and take in the fashion show. Your father was always like that, very direct and not at all self-conscious. It didn't matter to him that he was the only man in the place, or that he was dressed in a con-struction worker's clothes, all dirty and sweaty and everything.

I was walking down the platform, with mostly older women shoppers seated around the platform, my boss, Polly Prudhomme, describing the bathing suit I was wearing to the shoppers while I walked along, turning, strolling, kneeling, and then I saw your father's head as it came over the top of the stairs. Oh, I couldn't believe it. It was like a dream. A huge, smiling, suntanned face, a great toothy grin, tiny ears, dark eyes twinkling, a mass of black curly hair, a neck like a tree, and then his broad shoulders, thick chest, great brown arms swinging as he came up the stairs, and then that tiny waist of his, the long muscular legs, until finally he was at the top of the stairs, standing there with his legs apart, his hands in fists on his narrow hips, a big smile across his face, good-natured like a boy's, only somehow hungrier than a boy's could be. I was so taken by his appearance, especially the way it had gradu-ally come to me, piece by piece like that, like a mirage floating up from the floor—first the head, then the torso, then the legs—until at last standing there before me was a grinning giant, the handsomest man I had ever seen. Anyhow, I was so taken by his appearance that I stopped midway down the ramp, stood still, and stared straight at him, and I smiled. I smiled! All the women in the audience and all the girls waiting to come behind me and even Polly Prudhomme herself followed my gaze until they too were staring straight at him, most of them with their mouths open. Polly had stopped describing the bathing suit I was wearing and was gaping like the rest of us. It was a strange moment, silent, no one moving, your father standing at the top of the stairs, grinning, while maybe fifty women stared back at him, with me motionless up there on that ramp, smiling at him, as if I was a slave girl or something being auctioned off and he had suddenly appeared from the desert to save me from a fate worse than death. It was like the movies!

WELL, LIKE THE old song says, those may have been the best of times, but they were the worst of times too. At least for me they were. Your father, when he wanted to be, was the most charming, thoughtful, witty—oh, God, could he be funny—intelligent, tender, sexy, and all-around *interesting* man you'd ever want to meet. And when he was, those were the best of times. I was never a happier woman than I was then. I sang all day long until I got off work and could meet him at the door of the Globe, where he'd be waiting for me, standing there in the late afternoon sun, dirty from his job at the pumping station, chatting with the janitor, old Eddie Coy, who locked the door after the store employees had left. I'd come out the door, and your father would see me, and holding his lunch pail under one arm, he'd whip the other arm around me, and he'd lift me right off the ground and spin me in a half-circle and set me down again, and then he'd stare down into my eyes, and he'd say, in that deep, throaty voice of his, "Hi."

It was really something. I get a little weepy just remembering those days, the best of them. When it comes to the worst of them, though, all I have to do is remember a single one of them, just one of those days, and my eyes clear up pretty fast, let me tell you. There were Friday nights back then before we were married when I'd get off work and would come out the door, expecting your father to be there, as he'd promised, to take me out to dinner, and not finding him, would ask Eddie Coy if he'd seen your father, and Eddie would shake his head, No, not yet, so I'd wait and wait and wait, a half-hour, an hour, and hour and a half, until finally I'd know that he wasn't coming, and I'd walk on home to my apartment, fix myself some supper, take a long bath, and try to sleep—until along about one in the morning, when I'd still be awake, tossing and turning, and there'd come a loud banging on the door. Jumping out of bed, I'd rush to the door, and when I opened it, I'd see him, standing there, a vicious snarl across his face, bloodied lips and cut eyes, bruises and scrapes, torn clothing, with a half-emptied bottle of whiskey in his hand. "Ran into a little bit of trouble down at th' Tam," was how he'd explain all the cuts and bruises. Then, using nothing but the foulest language, he'd describe in gory detail how he'd single-handedly beaten up half a dozen sailors or brickmasons or electricians or "crackers," though I was never sure what he meant by the word, who he was referring to, exactly. Probably just anyone he couldn't identify any other way by uniform and such. Anyhow, he'd stagger into my apartment, brushing off my foolish attempts to clean him up and bandage his cuts, pushing me and any sympathy I might have away, physically shoving me into a corner of the room, where I waited, slowly growing frightened of him, as he talked to himself, only to himself, and drank the whiskey from the bottle, growling like a dog, literally growling and curling his lips back and showing his teeth, snapping and snarling, rambling on about his "enemies," turning everyone into an enemy—his parents, his sisters, his friends in New Hampshire and the people he'd met here in Florida, and of course, even me. Then, after a while, especially me. I was becoming his worst enemy. Every time he came in that drunk and torn up from fighting in the taverns, he would end the night by cursing at me, spitting out horrible names, a little more horrible each time it happened, a little more personally cutting, slicing into the parts of me that were the tenderest parts, taking the cruelest advantage of whatever fears and secrets I might have revealed to him some other night when we had been holding each other tenderly. Teasing and mocking me for my fears, threatening to expose my secrets, he'd call me "stupid" and "idiotic" and "sentimental" for a while, and then "selfish" and "insensitive" and "cruel," and finally, "whore" and "leech" and "nag"—those last three, it always came down to them, whore and leech and nag. That's what probably made them hurt so much, the fact that it always came down to the same three names. If he had just been lashing out at the world in general, he might've ended up calling me lots of awful things, sure, but all different. But because he always called me only those three, and all three, never one without the other two, he made me think that he really believed it about me, that even when he was sober and being kind to me, he still thought of me as a whore, a leech, and a nag. And of course, because I loved him and he was a man, I started seriously wondering if I was a whore or a leech or a nag, and there was just enough guilt for my own sexual interests in life, just enough dependency, and just enough nagging for me to slip slowly into believing that I *was* those things he was calling me, until I too thought of myself as a whore, a leech, and a nag. I even felt sorry for him for having to put up with me, for having fallen in love with me. So when he asked me to marry him I was so grateful, and so eager for the chance to prove by my loyalty that I wasn't a whore and by my wifely support and devotion that I wasn't a leech and by my trust and obedience that I wasn't a nag, that I said, "Yes," I said, "Oh, yes, yes, oh God, yes! Yes, yes," I said, "yes."

*   *   *

WELL, THAT'S WAY behind me now, and I've forgiven him, forgiven him for all of it. Really. I have. Part of it was my fault, I'm sure. I mean, I didn't understand him very well, so it was hard for me to give him what he really wanted and needed—though I'm not sure any woman would have been able to give him what he wanted and needed. He was lonely, terribly lonely, I could tell that much. I could understand that. A stranger in a strange land, like they say. No friends, except the few rough pals he made at work. No family, and unable to be in touch with his family in New Hampshire because of what he was sure he had done to his father. And Florida was just not the place for him—he said he was a man of cold winds and ice and snow. I remember him telling me that, very serious, as if he was telling me he was Catholic or Methodist or Episcopalian. He hated the heat, the sun, the white light of noon, said it made him shrivel up inside, said it made him feel closed off from the world. He was always complaining about the palm trees. "They're not trees. Why d'yer call them trees? They're giant weeds, that's what. *Weeds*," he called them. And he disliked the people who lived here, called them "crackers," even when they were from places like New York or Ohio. "Life in Florida," he would grumble, "is like living in a motel full of crackers." So actually, I wasn't surprised when he left Florida. I expected it. What did surprise me, though, was that he did it alone, that he didn't take the two of us along with him, his wife and his baby.

We hadn't been getting along for quite a few months when he left—not since I first told him I was pregnant, as a matter of fact, and you were three months old when he left, so that means we hadn't been getting along for about a year. But I had blamed that pretty much on myself, on the pregnancy and all and the way I was right after you were born, the way I was all wrapped up with being a mother. Like I said, he was lonely, and after I got pregnant it was hard for me to help him not be lonely.

•   •   •

OH, WHAT AM I doing this for? What's the matter with me? I sat down here to tell you the truth, and I'm not doing it, I'm lying, sliding over things, leaving important things out. I'm not telling the truth at all. It's just that I don't want you to be hurt by him any more than you already have been. But I can't keep on lying to you.

Life with your father was horrible for me right from the start. First there was that affair with Polly Prudhomme. Then there was the drinking. And after that there was all the violence, the fighting, the times he actually hit me. Then came the silence. He went silent on me. Shut everything down and just sat in his chair, reading sometimes, or looking out the window, or leaning back, his hands behind his head, and looking at the cracks in the ceiling. When you were born, he would come into the room where I was sleeping with you, and he would stand over your little bassinet and stare silently at you, no expression on his face at all. It was the strangest, scariest thing I had ever seen. It was as if he had died or something. I started going a little crazy from it. You can imagine the pressure it created, that silence, his expressionless face. I'd sob, "Do you love me?" and he'd say, "Sure," just that, as if he was answering a question about a new hat I'd bought. "How do you like this one, hon?" "Fine," he'd say. Except that I'd be sobbing, "What do you *feel* about me? What do you feel about the *baby*?" And he'd look up from the newspaper and say, "Fine." No expression at all on his face, no depth in his voice. Well, I know I went a little crazy from it. I'd sometimes find myself in the middle of the night lying on the bathroom floor, my face pressed against the cold tiles of the floor, sobbing hysterically, "Why don't you *leave* me! Get out! Get out!" And he'd be at the door, leaning casually against the frame of it, looking down at me with a strange curiosity in his eyes, and he'd say, "Fine." The next morning, silence.

It went on like that for many weeks until finally one morning

I got out of the bed I slept in, looked over at his bed and saw that it was already made, thought I'd overslept, and rushed out to the kitchen to make his breakfast. He was gone. He never left before seven-thirty. I looked at the clock on the wall. Seven o'clock.

He never came back. He didn't love me. He didn't love you. You were only a baby. He never even told you any nighttime stories or sang you any songs. You were only a baby. He should've loved you for that at least. But he didn't. I loved him. He might have loved me back a little for that. But he didn't. So he left us. Packed a suitcase, walked out, got on a bus, disappeared. He left me with some money in the bank, and once he wired me a hundred dollars from Colorado. Six months later, I got a typed post card from him. It said:

> Better get a divorce under way. I'll pay. My father is alive and well. Your lawyer can reach me c/o my parents, Barnstead, New Hampshire. Everything's going to be all right for you now. The hard part is over. For you, I do feel guilty, if you're wondering, but it won't do you any good. It doesn't even seem to do me any good either, so I won't be feeling it for long. As ever,
>
> *H. Stark*

That was all. Six months later we were legally divorced, and I never saw your father again, though, as you know, I did hear from him again, numerous times. But I was lucky enough never to have to see him again.

There were the post cards he sent you, but you also might as well know that your father called me for years afterward, usually late at night, often on a sentimental occasion, like our anniversary or my birthday or yours. He was always drunk when he called, and because I would be less than enthusiastic, he'd turn sour and angry almost immediately and would hang up on me. I never bothered at the time to tell you of these calls because you were too young to have understood, and he eventually stopped calling, probably when he was with his second wife, whom, I'm told, he loved intensely for a while, though frankly speaking, I don't believe it.

Your father beat me at least fifteen times in the year that we were married and living together. By "beat me" I mean hitting me more than once on any given occasion. I'm not counting all the times your father hit me only once.

YOUR FATHER SWORE and cursed at me constantly. He mocked my clumsiness when I was great with child.

YOUR FATHER LAY in my own bed with my best friend, Polly Prud-homme, who also happened to be my boss until I was too pregnant to model even the maternity dresses and had to quit my job at the store. He told me about it after everyone in the store and practically everyone in town already knew about it, and then when he told me about it, he gave me all the details of their times together. He praised her especially for her skill at giving him what he called "head," which meant sucking on his penis (you're old enough to know all this by now) and letting him ejaculate into her mouth and, he said, she swallowed the semen, though that's a little hard for me to believe. Yet he insisted that's what she liked to do and that she did it so well he almost became addicted to it. He told me they even had a code worked out so that he could make an appointment with her by teasing her in front of me, and I remember, when he came to the store to get me after work, his saying to Polly, as if he was teasing her about her name, "Polly want a cracker? Polly want a cracker?" And she'd laugh and say, "Naw, not tonight," or, "Later, maybe, after supper for dessert." I would scold him afterward for making fun of her name. "Besides, she doesn't know what you mean by 'cracker,' " I would say to him, and he'd just laugh, knowing that actually I was the one who didn't know what "cracker" meant.

Your father drank whiskey until he passed out on the floor, and he always did it on nights when he had promised to take me out to dinner and dancing.

YOUR FATHER HAD a fistfight with my only living relative, my Uncle Orlando—beating him senseless in his own front yard in front of his own wife and horrified children—all because Orlando had enough courage to stand up to your father and tell him what a selfish and cruel man he was to be treating me the way he was then (this was only a week before your father left me).

YOUR FATHER BRAGGED about his abilities as a pipefitter. He had no humility. He was convinced that, compared to him, all the men he worked with and for were stupid, lazy, and unskilled.

YOUR FATHER WAS frequently impotent, sexually inadequate. I won't go into it any further than that because there may well be reasons for it that we can never really know about, matters outside my experiences with him, childhood experiences and that sort of thing, but your father, I thought, was not quite right sexually. He talked too much about some of his friends' (men friends, mind you) muscles. Also, he seemd to enjoy a certain kind of intercourse which, I'm told, only homosexual men do regularly. You know what I'm talking about.

YOUR FATHER HATED cats. I won't tell you about how one time he killed a whole litter of kittens. It was horrible.

YOUR FATHER CHEATED at cards. Even bridge.

YOUR FATHER STOLE government property.

YOUR FATHER LIED about his taxes. He also told strangers that he made more money than he really did make. Sometimes he even told them he was making money on the side by playing the stock market, betting on the horses, betting on dogs, winning sports pools, bowling. He had me believing (until I had my lawyer check it out later) that he owned a lot of real estate in New Hampshire. "Half the side of a mountain," was how he put it, but my lawyer told me that your father's parents owned an old rundown farm, and your father owned nothing.

YOUR FATHER THOUGHT all flowers were ugly, though he once admitted he liked blue hydrangeas. "Mainly because they don't look like they're real," he explained to me.

YOUR FATHER DIDN'T know how to swim. He said it was on principle, but of course it was because he didn't want to be in a position of having to learn something that most people already knew about.

YOUR FATHER DIDN'T know how to ride a bicycle, either, and that too he said was on principle. I could never understand that.

YOUR FATHER HATED people of all races, creeds, and colors. He was an extremely prejudiced man, the worst I have ever known, even after living my whole life in the South. He would make fun of a person's background, no matter what it was. "Stupid Polacks." "Grabby Jews." "Dumb niggers." "Drunken Indians." "Thick-headed Irishers." He hated them all—even what he himself was, which he referred to as "common white trash" or sometimes "snot-nosed Yankees" and "backwoods New Hampshire shit-kickers." But whenever he used these terms, he somehow said them with a certain note of endearment. Somehow these slurs became affectionate nicknames. Not so for the others, though.

YOUR FATHER COULD play the saxophone well, but he only played it when he was alone or thought he was alone. He did not, as he claimed, play in the Guy Lombardo orchestra. He often referred to himself as "one of Guy's Royal Canadians" when people asked him about his saxophone, which he displayed ostentatiously on the coffee table in the living room of our apartment.

YOUR FATHER HAD a smile that people loved, and when, because of their love for his smile, they got close to him, he stopped smiling and never allowed it to be seen again. I cannot recall his smiling at me after we were married, and actually, I can't recall his smiling at me from the moment I told him that I was falling in love with him, which happened the fourth time I went out with him. Of course I know he must have smiled at me then, many times. It's just that I can't recall it.

YOUR FATHER TOLD wonderful jokes, but only to strangers. When he told jokes to people who were not strangers, the jokes were cruel and dark and only funny in a way that made you feel guilty if you laughed.

YOUR FATHER WOULD sneer at old people on park benches as if they disgusted him.

YOUR FATHER KICKED dogs and dared them to bite him for it.

YOUR FATHER WAS a jaywalker.

YOUR FATHER GROWLED. Like an animal. At night, if a car drove up, or if someone knocked on the door, your father would start to growl, low and deep from way back in his throat.

YOUR FATHER OFTEN ate the same thing for lunch that he knew I was fixing for supper.

YOUR FATHER LIED about having been a champion boxer. He was, however, a very good, that is, a successful, barroom brawler.

•   •   •

YOUR FATHER LIED about having been a champion runner, though he did have very muscular legs and seemed never to be physically tired, so he probably could have been a champion runner if he had tried. But he never even tried.

YOUR FATHER THOUGHT he had killed his father, but he never confessed to having any guilt for it. He blamed it on his father. Otherwise, he never talked about it with me. I'd ask him to tell me about it and he'd say, "It was all my old man's fault," and then he'd roll over and go to sleep.

YOUR FATHER TALKED incoherently to himself when he was drunk, and he was drunk at least one night a week, usually Friday night, after he had gotten paid.

YOUR FATHER HAD piles, which was unusual for a man as young as he was then.

YOUR FATHER WAS too big.

YOUR FATHER WAS afraid of going to the dentist. Also, he refused to see a doctor when he was sick or for his piles, and he refused to take medicines of any kind. Even aspirin. He was convinced that it would only make things worse. He always said, "If things can get worse, they will, but there's no reason to make it easy for them."

YOUR FATHER WAS afraid that his penis was too small, and in a way he was right, because, while his body was unusually large, his penis was normal-sized. Unfortunately, because he asked me, I told him that one night. He never made love to me afterward, but that came fairly late in the pregnancy anyhow.

•   •   •

YOUR FATHER SAID he loved his mother, but once when he was drunk he started to cry and roll around on the floor, yelling about how much he hated her.

YOUR FATHER WAS not a happy man. But he said it was on principle, and that it was for him a moral principle, what he called a "moral imperative," and that was why he tried so hard to make other people unhappy too. I could never tell for sure when he was joking, but I think he was joking then. But he may not have been. He certainly acted as though he thought everyone should be unhappy, that it was for him a moral thing and, therefore, by making people unhappy he was somehow making them better.

YOUR FATHER WAS the worst thing that ever happened to me.

YOUR FATHER REFUSED to admit that he was lonely, even though he had no friends he could confide in. But he said that was on principle, too, I mean the part about being lonely. I think he would've liked to have had a few friends, so long as he could've kept on being lonely at the same time. But he had too many principles.

YOUR FATHER HATED me.

OH, GOD, HOW he hated me.

CHAPTER 4

Addendum A

THROUGHOUT THE PRECEDING monologue, Rochelle listened atten-
tively to her mother, motionless and almost completely silent. Or
at least that is how she would later describe herself. She smoked
cigarettes one after the other. When she had smoked one down
to the filter, she would crush it out in the seashell ashtray on
her mother's Danish coffee table. Crossing and uncrossing her
long legs with that unself-conscious, almost inevitable grace of
hers, she never once took her alert eyes off her mother's expressive, changing face. The only sounds in the room were the con-
tinual drone of the air conditioner and the soft, southern voice
of Rochelle's mother and now and then the noise of a car in the
midday Florida heat slipping past the apartment building.

It's difficult to know how the content of her mother's jere-
miad affected Rochelle. We have only her self-description, offered
much later, when her attitude toward her father had been altered
considerably by the things she had heard from her father's four
other wives, from the testimony of numerous people, including
myself, who had known him over the years in one capacity or
another, from a lengthy interview with his dying mother and

another with his sisters and a brother-in-law, and when she herself had, as they say, "gotten in touch with her anger."

One could easily speculate about Rochelle's reaction to the news (and at that time it *was* news) that her father was in many ways a self-centered, immature, violent, cruel, eccentric, and possibly insane man. But I'm afraid that in my own case any speculation would be influenced by my personal relationship with her, and thus, however innocently, I would tend to work toward evoking in the reader deep feelings of pity and admiration for this amazing young woman. Also, I'm not at all familiar with the nature of Rochelle's relationship with her mother and therefore cannot confidently say that she did not have some secret use for refusing to believe her mother, i.e., that she did not, perhaps, need to think of her mother as a liar, as a bitter, middle-aged woman filled with self-pity, a mother in need of a villain to justify the absence of her husband throughout her daughter's childhood and adolescence.

Suffice it to say, then, that I'm not the best person to be in the position of presenting, with anything that approximates objectivity, Rochelle's emotional reaction to her mother's testimony concerning the character of her father. Frankly, I am too much in love with Rochelle to be of much good to anyone in this particular matter, except possibly to Rochelle herself, and probably not even that. I admire the woman, and I say it with practically no qualification whatsoever, and because I am aware of how deeply and sharply she has suffered and how she has endured with intelligence, dignity and selflessness throughout, I am filled almost to overflowing with compassion for her. Also, I confess that for several years I have desired her love in return, have sought her favor in every way I could imagine, taking advantage of every slight opportunity to court her that has come my way—and as a result, I have had to watch myself lie for her, to know that I was, on certain occasions, violating all principles, even those few principles

I had once thought inviolable. I say this without apology. I offer it merely as a warning.

My vulnerability to a woman like Rochelle is well known. Or at least it's well known to me. Many men have a weakness (I should say, a "weakness") for women with long, wildly flowing, deep red hair. And many men have a similar "weakness" for women who are tall, as tall or even taller than they themselves are, and who are thin without being gaunt, large without being big or heavy in any way. And, too, many men have a "weakness" for women who are well shaped, neatly and symmetrically proportioned. I am surely one of each of these types of men, and if that were all there was to my beloved Rochelle, I would be safe, as it were, and could report to you anything I might believe to be true of her without having to feel that I might be deceiving you to further my own rather special interests. But Rochelle is so much more than merely a tall, well-shaped woman with long red hair, that I am consequently that much less a reliable witness to her words and feelings.

I realize that so far I've not said a thing about Rochelle's character or her spiritual nature or intellect. Nevertheless, I would like to linger a little longer on what might be called her "body." She has skin on her body that is as smooth and white as a fine young onion, or as the flesh of an apple, or as an abalone shell worn smooth by a century's tides. Dark green (blue-spruce green, actually), her eyes are tear-shaped, slightly downturned, with long, dark lashes. Her nose is long, straight, slender, the vertical arc that insists on the perfect symmetry of her face. Her mouth is neither large nor small, but full and expressive nonetheless, with a sharp, slightly protruding upper lip, a pouting lower lip, and large, white, even teeth that seem as ready to nibble as quick to bite. Her forehead, cheeks and chin are smooth, symmetrical, but at the same time sharply defined by angles which are clearly visible in all but the severest light.

Ears—small, a happy maze of tender and delicate whorls, full-lobed. Throat—slender, long, white, and at the base, a mauve birthmark the size and approximate shape of a candle flame. And I have kissed that flame.

(PLEASE NOTE THAT I do not believe it would be appropriate for me to speculate on, or even to report what I know to be the case with regard to, Rochelle Stark's character, her spiritual nature, or her intellect. It seems to me that these attributes would be better portrayed, more interestingly and realistically portrayed, in action, *in medias res*, as it were, and therefore I will put off such portrayal until later in the narrative, when my beloved Rochelle's developed inner life can be made manifest more naturally and convincingly.)

CHAPTER 4

Addendum B

IN CHAPTER FOUR proper, Rochelle's mother—whose name, by the way, is Trudy Brewer Stark (she retained her married name after the divorce)—mentioned in passing that her daughter Rochelle was at present "hitchhiking all over the country, sleeping by the side of the road and all, not afraid of anything or anyone. . . ." From the text, it's also apparent, or should be, that at the time of the mother's speaking the daughter is approximately twenty-two years old. As it happens, this interview was made four years ago, which would make Rochelle twenty-six now, a figure that is consistent with the information she has personally made available to me on different occasions.

It is true, as her mother claimed, that when she was twenty-two Rochelle was traveling about the country in a somewhat casual manner. Or so it seemed. She carried all her worldly goods on her back in a large Kelty expedition pack, slept in a sleeping bag at the side of the road or wherever she happened to find herself at nightfall, and after a fashion "lived off the land" by shoplifting at supermarkets and fruit stands, stealing from gardens and orchards, and, whenever possible, picking wild berries, fruit and nuts.

She lived this way for about a year, most of which she spent retracing the footsteps of her father's fearful flight from New Hampshire, his wanderings that followed the desertion of his wife and infant daughter in Lakeland, Florida, and, when he discovered that in fact he had not killed his father and that his long hegira had been essentially in vain, his swift return home to New Hampshire.

Rochelle's journey, a fact-finding tour more than a hegira or pilgrimage, was not in vain. She returned home to her mother's apartment in Lakeland with the information she had gone out for. Essentially, the information was geographic and social, material that would help her realize her ambition to write a realistic novel about a man who was very much like her father, Hamilton Stark. She was young, and she had not traveled much, and naturally she had felt somewhat intimidated by the task she had set herself, especially when it came to writing about a character who had traveled rather widely in his youth and had spent most of his life locked inside the social confines of the working class. But her year-long note-taking journey reassured her that she would have little difficulty handling the geographic and social realism that her novel, as she had conceived it, would require. This was the point at which she began her series of interviews with her father's five ex-wives, several of his friends, and his mother, sisters and brother-in-law. As I have mentioned, the interview with her own mother was the first in this series.

CHAPTER 4

Addendum C

IN CHAPTER FOUR, which was narrated by Rochelle's mother, Trudy Brewer Stark, there were numerous references to Hamilton Stark's belief that he had murdered his father. Naturally, this belief was of considerable moment and consequence to Hamilton, a fact not lost on his daughter, Rochelle, when, some twenty-two or more years later, she began to write a novel about a man based closely on her father.

Therefore, since this episode has considerable bearing on the meaning of this, my own novel, and since Rochelle has evidenced herself to be an author far more naturally gifted than myself in portraying the circumstances, characters, emotions and actions that comprise the episode, I am including here her Chapter Eight, entitled "Return and Depart," which concerns itself most particularly with the events and circumstances that led up to Hamilton's "murder" of his father.

Note: There have been obvious name changes, as mentioned briefly in my Chapter Three, "Three Tales from His Childhood"—her Alvin Stock is actually my Hamilton Stark, who is, of course, my friend A. Rochelle's Feeney in "Return and

Depart" is Hamilton's friend, a man who in my novel remains nameless; he is not, as might be thought, the character C., nor is he myself; simply, I do not have a character in my novel who corresponds to Feeney, nor do I have such a person in my life. Nor does A. have one in his. In fact, Feeney may be a pure invention. The girl named Betsy Cooper is my Nancy Steele; in A.'s life, her name is B. Crawford is Rochelle's name for the place I have called Barnstead, which in A.'s life is the town of B. All three places happen to be located in New Hampshire. Rochelle's Loudon is the state capital, Concord, called that both in my novel and in A.'s life. As the chapter begins, Alvin (Hamilton, A.) has been discharged from the Air Force (the Army Engineers Corps, both for Hamilton and for A.), is twenty-one years old in 1963 (1948 for Hamilton and A.), and is returning home from Vietnam (Fort Devens, Massachusetts) to Crawford (Barnstead, B.).

A further note: The reader may wonder why I did not include with my earlier selections from Rochelle's novel (specifically in Chapter Three, with the three tales from his childhood) a schematic breakdown of the name and place correspondences between the two novels and "reality," such as I have included here in the note above. My decision was essentially founded on stylistic premises, but also I did not want to introduce too many characters into the novel too early for even the most organized and devoted reader to keep separate from one another. But the reader might well ask why, then, didn't I choose simply to continue here with my earlier practice of using the same names, the same as in my novel, for the excerpts from Rochelle's novel? Yes, I would answer, but then the reader might tend to believe that both Rochelle and I were writing about the same character, Hamilton Stark, when, of course, nothing could be further from the truth. Therefore, I reasoned, at some point I would be obliged to make the distinctions explicit, and this seemed to me the appropriate point for it.

Chapter 8
RETURN AND DEPART

Alvin came home to Crawford, a veteran, not a hero, for there was no war just then. He had spent all his discharge money traveling east and slowly north across the country, seeing his friends home, visiting a few days with each, eating large meals with the family, meeting the girlfriend, taking her friend to a movie or on a blind date, drinking afterward with his buddy until the local bars closed, and then catching the morning train, bus or plane as far as his next friend's home town, where he would repeat the ritual. It was a casual yet methodical itinerary, one the group of young veterans had worked out together with affectionate care during their last few weeks in Vietnam. Its logical and necessary conclusion, that Alvin would arrive home in Crawford, New Hampshire, last, alone, with no one left to pass through his home town on his way to someplace farther east or north, was a geographical accident. Consequently, when finally Alvin had been greeted at the Loudon bus station by his own family and in Crawford by his local friends, had put away his blue uniform, and had unpacked his duffel, his entire experience as an American soldier abroad as one of the military "advisers" in Southeast Asia was placed neatly into his past, as if into a trunk, and was stored away with his uniform in the attic.

This act, however, was not solely the result of an accident of geography (his having been discharged on the West Coast and returning home to a place farther north and east than that of any of his friends), though that was of course of some importance. But rather, it was also something he himself desired—to compartmentalize his past. He did not want any of his old Air Force buddies dropping by to spend several days drinking and talking about the past. He did not want any of his previous life overlapping his present and smearing onto his future. In a way, it was how he made himself available to himself: he now consciously thought of his past as a batch of differently shaped and variously colored boxes or blocks, all strung together in simple chronological order, like a chain of islands that happened to fall along a single meridian or degree of latitude. Among these blocks, Alvin numbered: Early Childhood; Early Adolescent Period of Self-Recrimination; The Religious Conversion Period; The Two Years He Wanted To Become a Minister; The Year He Wanted To Go to College; Giving Up; and In the Air Force.* To Alvin, no coherent relationship existed among these blocks of time except, of course, that of simple sequence. And by the time he was twenty-two, he was beginning to feel comfortable with that absence of relation. In fact, he was learning how to utilize and even to depend upon it—just to keep moving.

"Well, what d'you plan on doing now?" his father asked him across the table.

It was at breakfast, Alvin's first morning home. Having served him bacon, fried eggs, orange juice and coffee, his mother was now bustling silently, smilingly around the kitchen. "I don't know," Alvin said. "I just thought I'd call up a few people, maybe go see some old friends. You know . . ."

"I don't mean this morning."

"Oh."

"I mean, *do*. For a living. Or are you just up early because it's a nice fall day?"

Alvin wasn't sure he understood. "Where are the girls?" he asked his mother.

"Oh, they're still sleeping, Alvin. You forget, they're teenagers, and this is Saturday. No school." She smiled apologetically.

His father snorted.

"Yeah, well, I guess I'm just excited about being home and all."

"What're you planning to *do* now?" his father asked again.

---

* These comprise the sequences and subjects of the first seven chapters of *The Plumber's Apprentice*, the novel from which "Return and Depart" is drawn. It also marks one of the few places in the book where the narrator self-conciously becomes "the author."

Alvin put down his coffee cup and lit a cigarette. Inhaling deeply, he stared down at his half-emptied cup. "Pa," he said, "I don't think I know for sure what you're asking."

The older man looked straight ahead, across the table and out the window. "For *work*. A man has to *do* something. You're a *man* now, aren't you?"

"Yes."

"All right, then. What're you going to *do*?"

Alvin's mother had stopped her busy movement and now, looking down at her hands, stood motionless by the stove. None of the three people in the room was looking at any of the others. A gust of wind cracked against the house and whistled along its sides from north to south. Outside, the sky was stone dry and blue, a cool, windy, October morning. The ground was gone all to browns and yellows, and the trees had turned violently red, orange, yellow, purple. The dry leaves, about to fall from the branches to the parchmentlike ground, were clattering noisily in the wind and could be heard even from inside the house.

"Well," Alvin began, "I've thought about it. A lot. And I thought I'd drive over to Loudon on Monday and see if I could get a job working for the state. Department of Public Works, maybe. Then I'd take it from there—I mean, about where I'd be living and all, and when." Alvin spoke slowly, with care, obviously tense, as if he were lying.

"Okay. But before you do that," his father said, "I want you to consider this." The older man was still staring out the window. "Say you come to work for me again. But not part-time, not as a helper. As a pipefitter this time. Gradually, working together, we can take on a few bigger jobs. Schools. Maybe a hospital or something. Apartment houses. You know a few things about engineering now, and I know a lot about installation." He paused, as if waiting for Alvin to answer.

When his son remained silent, he went on. "We can get capital from the bank or the government. In a few years we can turn this one-man plumbing business into a regular contracting out-fit. Fifteen, twenty, thirty men laying pipe. Maybe doing some good-sized jobs all over the state."

Again, the older man paused, as if to gauge his son's response, and getting none, continued speaking, but more rapidly. "Here's the deal. You go to work for me on Monday, day after tomorrow, as an apprentice pipefitter. I can get you into the union. Easy. The Loudon local. I've already talked to the business agent over there. I'll pay you apprentice wages, what anybody else'd pay you. It'll take you five years before you can get your journeyman's license. If you're still at it then, and if you've given all you've got to make this into a solid, medium-sized plumbing and heating company, I'll make you an equal partner in the business. Where it goes from there depends on what we both decide. Together. In fifteen years or so I'll retire. Then the whole thing'll be yours. Assuming you're still at it and want it." He finally looked over at Alvin's face. "How does that sound to you?" he asked somberly.

Alvin sighed and rubbed his cigarette out in his saucer. He looked up and saw that both his parents were looking down at him, waiting for an answer. "Starting Monday, eh?"

"I already spoke to the union brass over in Loudon. They've got a couple of openings for new apprentices coming up this month. They'll hold one of them for you, if you want it."

"Five years?"

"Five years. On the job as a pipefitter early every morning. But doing a hell of a lot of estimating, too. And paperwork, engineering at nights and on weekends, too—making this operation into a regular contracting business. You can go on living here if you want to. Or you can get your own place. Up to you."

"Can I have till tomorrow, before I give an answer?"

"Sure. Take all the time you need. Between now and Monday morning." That was a joke, and Alvin's father smiled to indicate it.

Alvin laughed. "Ha!"

Then his father got up from the table, put on his old green cap and coat, and went out the door. After a few seconds, Alvin heard the pickup truck start and rattle past the house, down the dirt road toward town.

"Has he been planning this a long time?" Alvin asked his mother, who had gone back to work, this time at the sink, washing dishes.

"A *long* time," she answered over her shoulder.

HE ACCEPTED HIS father's offer. It didn't appear to him that he had much of a choice, so he accepted the offer with a certain reluctance and with the type of resentment that gets felt by everyone concerned but never expressed by anyone at all. He worked for his father—dutifully, methodically, punctually—but never more than was specifically required of him. His father told him, "Far as I'm concerned, you're just another apprentice pipefitter. A helper. And I'll treat you the same's I treat anyone else I hire out of the local. And if you don't do your job, pal, you can pick up your pay and head on down the road. Either you cut it, or you're down the road. Agreed?"

"Agreed." Alvin thought that was fair enough as long as he, for his part, was free to treat his father the same way he'd treat any boss he happened to be working for, any foreman whose crew he ended up on. He thought that, he decided it, but he never mentioned it to his father, his employer, his foreman.

The offer, then, almost as soon as it had been made and accepted, was corrupted. The bargain, sealed, was instantly broken open again—with the father treating his son like an employee but demanding in return filial loyalty and commitment, the son treating his father like an employer but resenting any demands placed on him which were not covered specifically in the union contract. Neither party, naturally, was satisfied. Each felt he was being cheated by the other.

Throughout the fall they worked together this way—father and son, boss and helper. Most of the work they did was small repair jobs, the kind of work Alvin's father had always done, jobs which Alvin hated because the work was often difficult, usually dirty, and frequently unacceptable to the customer. They replaced burst water pipes, cleaned out the drainage system in a supermarket, and installed several new oil burners in old furnaces. They repaired half a dozen water pumps, countless leaking faucets, clogged traps and toilets; installed washing machine drains, garbage disposals, drainage vents, lavatories, laundry tubs and bathtubs. They built furnace fireboxes, set toilets, installed radiators, piped up hot water heaters, and repaired sump pump systems. And in practically every case they were working on the plumbing or heating system of an old house, renovating or, worse, often merely repairing facilities, fixtures, equipment and pipes that had been used for several generations. Consequently, the work was filthy—in cobwebs, dust, soot, mucky water, shit and garbage. And it was always difficult, exacting work, trying to make an old piece of equipment work like a new one, trying to install pipes and fixtures where an architect had planned a closet or a stairwell, trying to run sharp-edged metal heating ducts where there was no basement, no light, and barely enough room between the floor joists and the cold ground for a man to crawl in. And because it was repair or renovation work, it inevitably took more time than the customer expected it to take, the equipment never functioned quite as well as it did when it was brand-new, and more parts and material were used than the customer had thought necessary. "Why can't you guys use more of the pipe that was already *there?*" was the typical complaint. And of course the bill always came to more than the customer thought the job was worth. Exhausted, filthy, Alvin would write out the bill and hand it to the customer, who would look at it, cluck his tongue, and say, "Jee-*suz!* I used to want my kid to grow up to be a doctor, but now I think I'll tell him to become a *plumber!*" In a way that Alvin couldn't quite name, conversations like that always left him feeling slightly humiliated.

Two or three nights a week Alvin and his father pored over blueprints, specifications, price books and long columns of figures, estimating and bidding on the kind of work they both wanted to do, each for his own reasons—shopping centers, filling stations, apartment houses, small schools, small-town office buildings. For Alvin, new construction meant work that was not dirty and was difficult only in a technical, interesting way. It was also somehow less demeaning than repair work. For his father, no such nice distinction seemed to exist. For him, the difference was strictly money. "All you can make on a repair job is your time and maybe a few pennies on the materials," he would grumble. "And for every job where you make a little more than what the job costs, you have two more that you lose money on, because either you took the job too cheap in the first place or the damn customer's a deadbeat."

On new work, however, there was a clear profit to be made. The two men would estimate all the costs, materials, time, overhead—and then they'd add up the figures and tack fifteen percent on top. That fall the Stock & Son Plumbing & Heating Company put out bids on six jobs—a school in Gilmanton, a filling station in Laconia, two garden apartment buildings in Loudon, and two ski lodges, one in Belknap and one in North Conway. But they were too high on all six. Not by much, but enough to be out of the running and in no position after the bids had been opened to bargain secretly with the general contractor against the other subcontractors, as was the practice. "Those fuckers all play footsie with each other," Alvin's father explained to him. "And the only way to get in on the game is to get in on the game fair and square. On your own. Prove you can do the job on time and for what you said you could. Next time, the big boys, the general contractors, will know to play footsie with you, too. But you still got to get that first job or two on your own. After that, you're golden." So they continued to estimate and bid for jobs two or three nights a week, Saturdays and Sundays, working the rest of the week "out of the pickup," as his father put it.

Alvin was a reasonably good plumber. He was extremely large and strong, close to tireless unless he got bored. And he was basically skilled—after all, he had worked for his father after school and summers since he was fourteen years old. On the other hand, he was more adept at estimating new work than his father was, because he was better able to read blueprints and to work rapidly with numbers. Nevertheless, he was paid only for the time he worked as a pipefitter, at a first-year apprentice's rate, and paid not at all for the time he spent estimating. To his father, that was part of the deal, the offer. To Alvin, it was not. But he said nothing.

He didn't gripe or grumble about it to anyone, not even to his friend Feeney, whom he saw frequently—whenever he wasn't working for his father. His social life then was actually not much different from what it had been during his last year of high school, four years before, except of course that he didn't attend any of the school functions and no longer could avail himself of the company of Betsy Cooper, his high school girl friend, who, then in her senior year at Mount Holyoke College, was engaged to marry a medical student at Columbia. Alvin drove around with Feeney, drinking at bars and in cars, picking up girls at roller-skating rinks, road-houses, country-and-western dances, and drive-in restaurants. He often successfully made love to these girls (in the car, or sometimes at Feeney's house, now that Feeney's father had left), and he usually got boisterously drunk, and he inevitably got into a fistfight with a stranger. These three activities he had rarely, if ever, indulged in as a high school student, and, therefore, people concluded that Alvin Stock had "changed" since coming back from the service. It was a reasonable conclusion.

His father told him, "I don't give a shit what you do on your own time. As long as you get to work on time in the morning and your hangover don't slow you down any. And as long as I don't have to bail you out of jail. Far as I'm concerned, you're free, white, and twenty-one. Except when you're working for me."

He smiled quickly, the movement almost unseen, like a lizard's tongue. It was a joke. Alvin was supposed to laugh.

His mother was not as sanguine, however. Every night when he went out, dark hair combed slickly back, clean T-shirt and khakis, loafers shined, Feeney outside in the car rapping impatiently on the horn, she would watch him leave and then would sit down and wait for him to return, no matter how late. In the kitchen, seated at the table, working a crossword puzzle and listening to the radio (turned low, so her husband, in the bedroom adjacent, could sleep), she would wait for her son to come home, and finally, at two or three in the morning, she would hear Feeney's car drive up, and she'd snap to attention in the chair, her eyes dry and red from sleeplessness and fatigue, and when he entered the house, usually by the front door, she'd call to him. "Alvin!"

"Whut."

"In the kitchen. Come in here, I want to talk to you."

He would tip and stumble through the living room and take a seat opposite her at the long table. "Whut." Sometimes he would be wearing a bruise across his face and lipstick across his shirtfront. Sometimes one or the other. Rarely neither.

Then she would begin: "Alvin. Son. You've got to get hold of yourself. Look at you. You can't *be* this way, you can't become the kind of person who . . . acts this way all the time. I'm worried about you, son."

"Well, don't. I am who I am. That's all," he'd answer, lighting a cigarette.

"You're unhappy, aren't you?"

"I wasn't . . . until I come in here and started gettin' nagged at." He looked her in the face, blew smoke at her. One mean bastard, he thought.

She coughed, got up abruptly, walked into her bedroom. "Good night. Shut off the lights before you go up." Angrily. It ended this way every time she waited up for him. She wasn't ever going to do it again.

"Yes, *ma'am*." Sneering. Rubbing out his cigarette in the saucer of her cup. Sliding away from the table and standing up. Going from the kitchen through the living room to the stairs and up to his bedroom, having left the lights on behind him. On purpose.

Whose purpose? He didn't know. He sat in darkness on his bed, kicking his shoes slowly off. Oh, what the hell, she was right, right about everything, for God's sake. The nights he turned into a bum, a nothing, a big slob screwing every whore in Belknap County, brawling in every bar and roadhouse, drinking himself sick all the nights he didn't have to work for his father . . . And she knew it, knew that these were the nights he turned into a bum, a slob, broke, drunk, fucked out, the taste of vomit on his teeth, his knuckles scraped, nose swollen, half the preceding six hours completely blacked out, erased from conscious memory, the rest remembered only in terms of sudden movement and roaring . . . And it was all her fault, his goddamned, sweet, nagging and high-falutin' mother's fault. She should've left him the hell alone, or else helped him get away to college, anywhere, just away . . . And it was all Betsy Cooper's fault too—that touchy, virgin, cock-teasing bitch, and all her ambitions, her promises to write letters to him, all her lies to him, how she didn't care what he did with his life, she would love and respect it . . . What a pile of crap that was! In a week she'd be home from college for the Christmas break. He'd go over to that big white barn of a house on the hill, and he'd tell her what the hell he thought of her, and then he'd fuck her, right in front of that big living room mirror, and she'd watch, and she'd love it, but she'd hate herself for loving it, and when he'd fucked her, he'd get off and stand up and laugh, laugh like a loon, laugh and laugh and laugh, Goddamn it. Goddamn it. Damn it. It was nobody's fault—but his own. He knew that. Impossible to deny. Impossible to blame anybody else, least of all his mother, least of all Betsy Cooper, both of whom were guilty merely of having thought him better, stronger, smarter, than he was, both of whom loved him—or had once loved him. He deserved himself. Everyone else deserved someone better. Only he was bad enough, weak enough, dumb enough, to deserve being who, in the final fact, he was . . .

IT WAS MID-DECEMBER, a blowy, snowy, Friday evening, cold enough that the wind crackled against the windshield of Feeney's Dodge, and the snowflakes, dry and hard as salt crystals, blew against the car and swiftly away from it, finally settling in long, wind-carved drifts along the sides of the road and edges of the woods and against the buildings they passed, as they drove back from Pittsfield to Crawford.

Feeney wanted a drink, had pulled a pint bottle of rye from the glove compartment as he drove, and poured a few ounces into his mouth, passing it across to Alvin when he had finished. Alvin silently recapped the bottle and replaced it in the glove compartment.

"Whassamatta, doncha wanta leetle drinkee?" Feeney teased him. Looking over at his dark friend, Feeney grinned, showing his small, brown teeth, and he wet his thick lips like a horse.

Alvin said no, explaining that he was tired tonight and just wanted to be out of the house, not out of his head, for chrissake.

Feeney chuckled salaciously and asked for the bottle again. Alvin passed it to him.

"You're just pissed we didn't scarf any quiffs at the fuckin' movies," Feeney said seriously, trying to be sympathetic. He noted the car's rapid slide toward the side of the road and whipped the wheel to the left, spinning the vehicle back into line, just missing a two-foot snowdrift.

"No," Alvin said. "Nothing like that. It's hard to get too down when you strike out with a batch of fuckin' sixteen-year-olds giggling in the back of a fuckin' small-town moviehouse. Besides, I really liked the movie," he added. *Picnic* it was, with Alvin played

by William Holden, Betsy Cooper by Kim Novak in a sexy lavender dress, the plot basically a brief, melancholy meeting between a
hungry, lonely, trapped woman and a profound man, the meeting
born in conflict between the characters, carried to tragic, compassionate fruition by sex and coincidence, resolved by the sad yet
spiritually necessary departure of the man. "That's my idea of a
good movie," Alvin said, half to himself.

Feeney handed the bottle back to him. "You sure you don't
want a slug?" he urged.

Alvin said no and continued staring out the windshield, the
snow firing out of the darkness into the path of the car. Without
looking, he put the bottle back into the glove compartment.

They drove a ways farther in silence, through Crawford
Parade, along the road to the Center, past the fairgrounds, with
the river on their right, iced over, the ice whitened by the snow,
following alongside the car as the vehicle wound a careful way
home. Driving into the Center, they approached Feeney's house,
dark and dilapidated, like an old railroad hobo, and Feeney asked
Alvin if he wanted to come in and have a drink and maybe watch
some television or play some cards awhile. "Christ, it ain't even
eleven yet," he said in a whining voice, pulling nervously at one
thick eyebrow with the thumb and forefinger of his right hand
while he steered the car with his other hand.

"No thanks. I might's well go on home. This snow's starting
to build up now and I'd probably have to walk if I stayed at your
place. Nights like this, I start to thinking about my grandpa,
y'know," he added half-jokingly. But half-seriously, too, because
it was true that he never remembered any of the stories of how
the old man, his father's father, had died, except on nights like
this, when there was a hard, cold snow falling in drifts, and he
remembered, pictured, a man he'd never actually seen stumbling
home in the dark, drunk, angry, snarling at the wind and snow,
and halfway home falling over a stone frozen into the dirt surface
of the road, and tumbling off the road into a high drift, forgetting

in that second of spinning collapse his anger, the hard, ancient center of his focus, coming softly to rest in the drift and letting go there, falling backward into sleep, at last—to be found there in the morning, rock-hard, with his hands and arms and legs extended, splayed, as if, when he had died, he'd been dreaming of swimming easily underwater, or as if he had been hurled to earth by a god. It was the reason Alvin's father did not drink, or so his mother had told him.

"Okay," Feeney said slowly. "I'll take you up the fuckin' road. But hand me that bottle one more time, will ya?"

Alvin once again retrieved the flat, brown bottle and passed it to his friend, who took a quick drink from it and blindly passed it back, bumping the bottle against Alvin's beefy shoulder in the darkness, spilling rye whiskey down the front of his wool loden coat and over his lap. Alvin grabbed the almost emptied bottle from his lap and cursed. Feeney apologized thickly, and they drove the rest of the way to Alvin's house in grumpy silence, passing no other car on the road, barely making it up the hill from the Center.

Alvin got out, said nothing, and walked through the snow to the house, stamped his feet noisily at the door, and walked in as Feeney drove off, the red taillights of his car swiftly disappearing behind high fantails of snow.

His mother heard him come in. "That you, Alvin?" she called from the kitchen. "I was worried, with the snow and all . . ."

"Yeah," he said sourly. He was standing near a table lamp in the living room, holding part of his coat out in front of him as he studied the whiskey stains on it. "Shit," he said in a low voice.

"Will you come and have a cup of tea with me, son? I'm glad you came home early," she called. Alvin could hear her get up from her chair and walk quickly, eagerly, to the cabinet over the sink for a cup and saucer.

Oh, well, why not? he thought. Maybe she'll know how to get the stain out of my coat. "Yeah, sure, I'll have a cup of tea with you." And he walked out to the kitchen, shedding his bulky coat as he entered the room.

She stood next to the counter by the sink, pouring him a cup of tea. Picking up the cup and saucer, carrying it across the room by pinching the saucer between thumb and forefinger, she walked past her son, tiny next to his enormous size, and suddenly, as she passed, she groaned, "Oh-h, Alvin!" With an expression on her face that joined disgust with self-pity, she placed the cup and saucer on the table in front of him, sat down opposite, and petulantly pushed the sugar and milk at him.

"What d'you mean, 'Oh-h, Alvin'?"

"You *know* what I mean!" she exploded at him. "*You!* You're what I mean! *You're* what's the matter. *Look* at you!"

"You think I'm drunk?"

"*Think!*" She kept stirring her spoon in the cup of tea, her hands shaking as she moved, her rage barely contained by the act. Her dark eyes glowered at him, her head twitching nervously from side to side, her feet tapping against the linoleum-covered floor. "You, you're nothing but a bum, a drunken bum! That's all! I don't know why I even bother to . . . to hope. You'll probably end up like your grandfather, the way you're going now."

"Not that one again. Jesus. My grandfather. As if ending up like my father is an improvement. Anyhow, I'm stone sober, Ma," he said quietly.

"You're a drunken bum! You smell like a brewery. You come in here smelling like a brewery, and then you have the gall to tell me how sober you are, and making cruel cracks about your father, too. You're a drunken bum, no good for anything. And now you're a liar, too."

"Ma, I am not!" he cried, and he stood up, facing her.

She wouldn't even look at him then, talked into her teacup instead and made him overhear her. "I work and I slave year after year, for what? For *this*? A drunk who can't even speak kindly to me? A thankless bum who can't say anything kind about his father?" She continued talking loudly at the teacup and about him, as if he were in an adjacent room, and he moved erratically away from the table, then back again, and finally grabbed her shoulder with one huge hand and shook her, which made her scream directly up at him, "Leave me alone! Don't you touch me! Get away from me! You're *drunk*!"

At that instant his father came crashing into the room from the bedroom. The man was dressed in a wildly billowing flannel nightgown, he was barefoot, and the gray hair on his narrow head stuck out like a spiky crown. His face was knotted in fury, and as he rushed for Alvin, he roared, "You son of a bitch, I'll *kill* you! Raising your hand against your mother! I'll *kill* you for that!"

Alvin turned, releasing his mother's shoulder, and caught the full force of his father's rush. Falling backward, he broke his fall with one hand and tried to ward off his father's punches with the other. The older man was swinging at him like a windmill gone berserk, hitting him on the head, face and shoulders, slamming him in the chest with his bony, naked knee, trying to keep him down on the floor while he beat him with his fists. Alvin reached behind him and knocked the cupboard door open, and with no conscious thought, or none that he would remember later, he reached into the cupboard, yanked out a large cast-iron skillet, and swung it at his father, hitting him squarely on the forehead. There was a thick, crunching sound, like that of an apple being broken in half by two strong hands, and the old man's body went limp and collapsed on the floor.

Alvin, dazed, dropped the skillet, stood up, heard as if from a great distance his mother screaming, "Alvin! You've killed your *father!* You've *killed* him!" and he ran from the house, grabbing up his coat as he ran.

Outside, it was dark and snowing hard. The wind had dropped, and the snow was falling straight down, like a gauze curtain. For a few moments he ran, then walked—down the road to the town, then through the darkened town to the highway, where the first vehicle heading south, a truck, stopped and picked him up.

"Where you goin'?" the driver asked from behind the red glow of his cigarette. He was a fat man a few years older than Alvin.

"Boston. Tonight."

"Okay by me. Your old lady kick you out or something?"

"Yeah," Alvin said, instantly constructing a scene that would justify his words. "Yeah, I came home too late and too drunk once too often, I guess. And she flipped her fuckin' lid. She'll probably cool off in a few days if I leave her alone. You know."

"Yeah, they always do," the driver said cheerfully as the truck picked up speed, plowing heavily, powerfully, through the falling, drifting snow.

(Here ends the excerpt from the novel.)

CHAPTER 5

*Back and Fill: In Which the Hero's Ditch, Having
Got Dug and the Pipe's Having Been Laid Therein,
Gets Filled; Including a Brief Digression Concerning
the Demon Asmodeus, Along with Certain Other
Digressions of Great and Small Interest*

AN ANONYMOUS CALL to the chief of the two-man Barnstead Police
Department, the large, barrel-chested, crew-cut man named Chub
Blount, who happened to be Hamilton Stark's brother-in-law,
brought the chief, as he preferred to be called, out to Hamilton's
house early one morning in February. The call had come in to the
chief's home around one A.M., waking the burly man from his
peaceful, nearly dreamless sleep. His wife Jody, Hamilton Stark's
sister, punched her husband's side with one of her sharp elbows
and woke him.

"Chub! Answer the phone!" she ordered crossly.

"Whut, whut, what?" His hand clumsily groped for the
telephone in the darkness above his face. Then he realized that
the instrument was beside him on the night table, and at last he
stopped its shrill ringing by picking up the receiver. "Yeah?"

"Barnstead Police?" It was a man's voice, hurried, thin, slightly overarticulated.

"Yeah. This's the chief."

"Good. There may have been a murder in your town. I thought you should know."

"Whut the hell . . . Is this Howie? Who the hell is this?" The chief sat up in bed and looked into the mouthpiece in the dark, as if trying to see who was talking into it at the other end of the line.

"Who is it, Chub?" Jody impatiently snapped.

"Never mind who this is. I just thought you might like to know that Hamilton Stark may have been killed this afternoon. You ought to look into it, that's all."

"What kinda crap you handin' me, pal? Hey, is this Howie? C'mon, Howie, is it you?"

"What on *earth* is going on, Chub? Is Howie drunk?"

"This is an anonymous phone call."

"Yeah, well, I don't believe you, pal. It's Howie Leeke, I know your voice, Howie, and I don't think it's funny, I gotta get up in the fuckin' morning and I don't like getting pulled outa bed in the middle of the fuckin' night to play games with a drunk."

"No, seriously, this is an anonymous phone call."

"Hang up, Chub."

"Howie, look, whaddaya doin', pullin' my chain like this in the middle of the fuckin' night?"

"You don't seem to understand. I'm anonymous. I'm not Howie Leeke or anybody else, either. I'm anonymous."

"Chub, hang up on him."

"Bullshit you're anonymous. It's Howie."

"No, really. I'm dead serious. I think Hamilton Stark has been murdered."

"Chub, will you hang that thing up!"

"Hey, Howie, ol' pal, where're you calling from? You calling me from a bar? You over the Bonnie Aire?"

"Why? Why do you want to know that? I'm anonymous."

"Jesus, Chub, it's one in the morning!"

"Shaddup, Jody. Howie . . ."

"Seriously, why do you want to know where I am? Are you going to try to trace the call? Go ahead, I'm calling from a public booth. It's only a waste of your time, though, because I'm calling to give you an important message about Howie, I mean Hamilton Stark . . ."

"Yeah, sure. Now listen up, Howie, whyn't you tell me where's that booth you're callin' from, you know, so's I can come on over an' have a drink with ya." Covering the mouthpiece with his hand, he said to his wife, "I'll get the bastard to tell me where he's calling from, see, and I'll send Calvin down there to pick him up for Drunk and Disorderly or Driving while Intoxicated. Teach that gabby bastard a lesson . . ."

"Listen here, now, this really is an important message. I think you ought to drive out to Hamilton Stark's place and look for him."

"Yeah, sure, that's all I got to do is drive around lookin' for that silly asshole. Now, c'mon, Howie, where ya callin' from? I'll come on down an' having a drink with ya. How's that?"

"I'm not Howie Leeke. I'm trying to remain anonymous, and you're not making it very easy for me, Mr. Blount."

"Okay, Howie, ol' pal, thanks for the tip about Ham," he drawled, reluctantly giving up the attempt to entrap his friend. "But one of these fine nights I'm goin' to catch you drivin' drunk or D and D, ol' buddy, and when I do, I'm goin' to hang your fuckin' ass from a fuckin' tree."

"No—"

The chief cut him off and hung up the phone. He flopped down into the warmth of his bed, bumping against his wife's bony knees and elbow as he squirmed back into the gully he had been sleeping in earlier, and quickly, with no further words, the two of them fell asleep.

But the next morning after breakfast the chief remembered the call, and saying to himself, What the hell, I haven't got anything better to do, he decided to drive out to his brother-in-law's house. He hadn't seen the man in several months, so they'd probably be able to think of things to say to each other, and what if the bastard *had* been murdered? It wouldn't be a shock to anyone—there were plenty of people in the world, hell, in the whole state of New Hampshire, who would be happy to see Hamilton Stark dead. Hung up on a tree with flies clotted around his mouth and eyes. Down a well, green in three feet of water, his body swollen like a jelly doughnut and held there with concrete blocks. Tied to a tree, with KILL THE PIG carved into his chest, his boots filled and overflowing with the blood from the carving job they'd done on him.

It wouldn't be any great loss, as they say, but even so, it would be murder, Murder One, right here in Barnstead, New Hampshire, where there hasn't been a genuine killing for several generations—not since the one over in Gilmanton, the one that woman wrote the filthy book about, *Peyton Place*. They should have burned that damned book. Maybe someone would write a book about this one, too. Killings up here are unusual. A few accidental shootings, hunting accidents, suicides, that sort of thing, sure, but no real live killings, he thought as he drove out of town, along the river, and turned left at the Congregational church, the only church in town, onto the dirt road that led to the narrow end of the Suncook Valley, where, in the shade of Blue Job Mountain, Hamilton Stark lived.

It was a cold, dark gray day, with the sour sky sagging down almost to the treetops. Along the sides of the narrow, winding road, the tin trailers and tarpaper-covered shacks seemed frozen into the several feet of old, leathery, late-winter snow that surrounded them, the vehicles outside and the leaning, dilapidated outbuildings scattered around them. Behind the dwellings and vehicles lay the woods, the dark, tangled third-growth pines and spruce—twisted, erratically spaced trees and groves laced together by the ruins of ancient stone walls and low, scrubby brush, a forest for squirrels and porcupines, creatures that run close to the ground or high above it.

As he drove, the chief squared his Stetson on his head, checked himself in the rear-view mirror, and hated his brother-in-law. He had not forgiven him. Although of course he told everyone that he had forgiven him long ago, which usually made the listener shake his head with surprise and admiration, for many of the things that Hamilton had done to the chief—not so much to the chief himself as to his wife Jody and her mother Alma Stark—were generally thought to be unforgivable. The chief usually explained the generosity of his spirit by saying, "Look, hey, the bastard's just not right in the head. I mean, what the hell, you don't think the bastard's *happy*, do you?" And no, no one thought for a minute that Hamilton Stark was happy, which proved the chief's assertion that the bastard wasn't right in the head. The chief liked being right, especially when he could prove it logically.

Two miles beyond the church there was a large cleared field on the right and, at the far end of the field, a driveway that led from the road along the edge of the field to a white-painted metal gate and, a little ways farther, the house. The chief turned off the road onto the driveway and in a few seconds pulled up at the gate. Easing his bulk out of the car, he walked around to the gate and unlatched it, stopping for a few seconds to study the piles of trash, most of them half-buried in snow that lay in the field in front of the house. Shaking his heavy head with disbelieving disgust, he squeezed back into his car and drove through the gate, following the driveway to the front of the house, where he came to a stop behind Hamilton's pale green Chrysler limousine.

Shutting off the engine of his own car, a Plymouth station wagon with the standard blue bubble on the roof, the chief slid out, zipped up his storm coat, slowly approached Hamilton's car from the driver's side, and immediately saw the three bul-letholes in the window, which caused him to unzip his storm coat and draw his revolver from the holster on his left hip. It was a smoothly executed series of moves. For a large man the chief was fast and balanced, and he practiced all his moves dili-gently in his free time. Poised on the balls of his feet, his head laid back and slightly to one side, and holding his revolver with his left hand, he switched off the safety and reached for the door handle with his right hand, slowly, as if he were trying to catch a butterfly without damaging its wings. He whipped open the door, shoving the snout of his gun down into the space where the driver's head ordinarily would have been situated.

Nothing. Empty. No blood on the seat. Slugs probably in the upholstery someplace—send the lab boys out to look for them later. Course, the slugs might be buried inside Ham's body. Hit the bastard clean and fast, got the body out of the car right away so they could wipe it down, dumped the body in the trunk of the hit car, then took off to where they could drop it into some open water. The nearest open water would be the Atlantic Ocean, the chief figured. Kittery, Maine. This was going to be a tough case to crack alone, he thought grimly. He was going to need some help.

Jamming his gun into the holster, he walked back to his own car and sat down in the driver's seat. He slammed the door behind him and started the motor and the heater, after which he slid a few inches to the right of the steering wheel to a posi-tion on the seat from which he could operate the radio comfort-ably. He stretched out his legs, plucked the microphone from the hook, and barked into its face. "Hawk! Come in, Hawk! This's Eagle! Come in, Hawk. This is Eagle, come in, Hawk!"

After a few seconds of answering static, a high-pitched voice cried, *"Hawk here, Eagle! Come in, Eagle!"*

"That you, Calvin?"

"Sure is, Eagle. What's up?"

The chief scratched at the nest of curly blond hairs where his throat met his chest. "I'm over to the Stark place, where Ham Stark lives? You know the place?"

"*Sure. The place up on Blue Job Road, used t' be his mother's place—*"

"Yeah, yeah. Well, listen," the chief interrupted. "I think there's been some kinda trouble up here. Looks to me like there's been a little shooting." Suddenly, as if the bank of clouds had parted and the sun had come out, the chief became frightened. Terrified. His head was located in his car precisely where he supposed Hamilton's head to have been when he had been shot. Whoever had shot Hamilton could as easily shoot his brother-in-law. The chief flopped down on the seat, his right cheek pressed flat against the cool upholstery, and went on talking into the microphone. "Look, Calvin, get over here right away, will you? Where the hell are you now, for God's sake?" he puffed. He was lying on his side, facing the glove compartment, and it was difficult for him to breathe.

"*I'm over on Route Twenty-eight, on my way to that guy Yanoff's, you know the guy, takin' his goddamned dog home to him. Herb Kernisch says he seen it runnin' deer last night and he'll shoot it next time it's out loose, you know Herb . . .*"

"Yeah, yeah, sure. How long will it take you to get here?" The chief was terrified. He'd walked into a trap. Shit, shit, shit. Those were rifle slugs for sure. Hit men from Boston. Probably Cosa Nostra. Mafia. Italian. They'd as soon kill him as pick a flower, and they could do it, too, the way he'd set himself up. They could pick him off from fifty yards, and all he had was his damned service revolver.

"*Oh . . . I dunno, twenty minutes, I guess, if I come straight over an' don't take this mutt back to Yanoff's. I ain't there yet.*"

"Well, for Christ's sake, hit your fuckin' siren an' get the hell over here!" he cried into the mike.

"*You okay, Chief?*"

"Yes. Yeah, sure. Just get the hell over here, will you, Calvin?" The chief was sweating, and his eyes were darting wildly back and forth across the narrow slab of leaden sky that he could see from his position on the seat. It was everything he could see—a rectangle of low, dark sky—but he expected that any second even that would go black on him, as three soft-nosed slugs penetrated his large, soft body.

"Ten-four, Eagle."

"Yeah, yeah. Ten-four." He looked for his hat, the white Stetson he'd bought last spring at the police chiefs' convention in Dallas. It was on the floor in front of him, getting dirty. He retrieved it and started brushing it clean with his hand. That goddamned Ham Stark, he fumed, as he brushed his hat with his thick fingertips. Getting me into this. Why does he always have to . . . whatever it is he does. I ought to just get the hell out of here, drive off and forget the whole thing. Not even mention it to anyone. Not even Jody. Except that Calvin's already on his way over here. *He* knows. Shit. Never should have called him. Jesus Christ, why don't things go right for me? Shit, shit, shit. Who the hell made that phone call last night, anyhow? *That's* who probably did it, got me into this in the first place. He studied his hat. It was white again, sparkling white, without even a bruise of dirt from the floor.

Taking a long-handled plastic windshield scraper from under the seat and sticking the wide end into his hat, the chief slowly raised his hat above him, hoping that, if they shot at it, they would miss. But no one shot. Silence. He held the hat in what he assumed was plain view for a minute, joggled it temptingly, and then slowly sat up beneath it, took the hat off the scraper, and squared it on his head, checking himself out in the rear-view mirror. He tried a little smile, the one that started with a sneer and ended there too, the smile he used to answer backtalking out-of-state speeders. He'd started practicing it when state troopers caught Ethel Kennedy, the murdered senator's wife, speeding on Route 93 on her way home from a ski weekend at Waterville Valley. The smile looked good. Tough, smart, mean. A smile that said he'd seen it all, seen it all twice last week.

How the hell had Hamilton got himself mixed up with Mafia hit men? the chief wondered as he settled back into his seat to wait for Calvin. Ham was a *plumber*, for Christ's sake, a pipefitter. Not a bookie or something. Maybe he was mixed up with a woman of some kind. Maybe this time the bastard went too far, got himself involved with a woman who belonged to someone who'd kill him for it. Serve the bastard right. Serve him right if some tough little wop in a three-piece suit kicked him in the nuts three or four times and then shot him in the face. Some women a man has to steer clear of. The chief thought of his own wife, Jody, her long, angular body, her grim mouth and flat voice. He studied the house in front of him, and as he hoped, forgot his wife. It was a nice place, he observed, a handsome white house, square, well kept, large but not too large, situated well off the road, with the mountain behind it and the valley in front. No wonder Ham was so attached to the place, he thought.

The house was a two-hundred-year-old, traditionally proportioned Cape, with an ell at one end that was connected to a small barn Hamilton had converted into a garage. Behind the house was another, larger barn, several outbuildings, and then the woods. Behind the woods was the mountain. The main house and the small barn had been built by Josiah Stark, and the place had remained in the hands of the Starks until now, which of course was a mightily significant fact about the place. But not to the chief. He could see only that it was a solid-looking, attractive and well-kept place, and that alone made it desirable. Oh, he knew that Hamilton had been born and raised in the house, and he imagined that that, too, probably made it desirable, at least to Hamilton. I can see why the bastard wanted the place so bad, he conceded. But I'll never know why he couldn't wait for his mother to die first. Never.

Though the chief had been a visitor to the house for decades, though he had courted and eventually married a woman who had been born and raised there, and though afterward for years he had visited his in-laws there, nevertheless, whenever he saw or thought of the house, he remembered only one event, a single night, the night Hamilton had taken possession of the house. Here is how it happened.

Or rather, here is the version of what happened that was generally accepted as the truth, accepted by all but one of the participants in the events of that monstrous evening, accepted as well by the townspeople of Barnstead, and accepted by hundreds of others who were told the story only because it could be said to have a certain universal "human interest," or because it was an example of horrid behavior, say, or of long suffering, or of a bizarre turnabout.

At any rate, almost any native of Barnstead, New Hampshire, the librarian, perhaps, or the town clerk, visiting a cousin named Mattie in Daytona Beach, Florida, might look up from her knitting and say, "Well, if you want to talk about your bizarre turnabouts, *here's* one for the books." Or, "If you think *that's* one of your long-suffering parents, let me tell you about Alma Stark . . ." Or, "Now, that's horrid, all right, but I can tell you something so horrid, Mattie, that it'll make you never want to have a son." And this is what she'd say:

"Up to Blue Job Road, oh, maybe a mile, mile and a half from town, you've got the Stark place, which has been in the family since it was built, probably some two hundred years, though of course it's lots different now, different from the way it was when it got built, because the Starks have always been hardworking and mostly in the building trades, the men, so they've fixed the place up quite a bit over the years—not so much the land, I mean, which is over five hundred acres, at least that's what they always got taxed for, 'in excess of five hundred acres'—no, they didn't so much fix up the land as the house and barns, putting on a dormer here, a new porch there, sort of constantly renovating was how the Starks have always taken care of their place, so by the time poor Alma and Horace Stark were up in their seventies and their children were all grown and married—there were three, the son Ham and the daughters Jody and Sarah—well, by that time the place was all modernized, you know, with electricity and aluminum storm windows and a new oil furnace, and the plumbing was just about the best you could imagine, because Horace was a pipefitter, like his father, who died pretty young in a sad way, but that's another story—anyhow, if there was one thing the Stark house was going to have, it was good plumbing. Oh, I guess Horace'd got to be about seventy or maybe seventy-one, and Alma was about the same age, when he got his first heart attack and had to retire from the pipefitting and stay in the house all the time, though of course he wouldn't do it, wouldn't stay in the house all the time, he was outside working on that place as soon's he could walk again, no matter he couldn't move half his face and couldn't even talk right anymore, though he never talked much anyhow. But now he couldn't even remember what you'd told him five minutes ago. Anyhow, all that man knew about life was work, work, work, and if he couldn't keep on working, he was dead, so he kept on working, putting in the garden, shingling the barn roof, building fences, cutting firewood—just about anything needed doing around the place, and lots that didn't need doing too. Poor Alma. She couldn't keep that man in and down the way the doctor had told her to, 'You keep that man in and down,' he told her, and Horace'd never been the easiest man in town to live with anyhow, kind of cross all the time, not very talkative and then grouchy when he did talk, but after he got the heart attack he got even crosser, scowled all the time, even when he didn't know you were looking at him. And because he couldn't talk right anymore, he stopped talking completely, left it up to Alma to do the talking for both of them, wouldn't even answer the telephone, would stand right there beside it and let it ring and ring and ring. He'd look at it like it was a design on the wallpaper or something. And the cost. Well, I know that heart attack of his cost them a pile of money, because Alma let me know with a few well-chosen words, she said, 'It's twice as expensive to be sick when you're old,' she told me one day, and I could have just cried for her, the poor thing. So proud, you know. But at least they owned the house clear and free, I told her, trying to comfort her, and at that time they did own the house clear and free, no mortgage, no debts of any kind, the way I heard it, so all they had to do was make do from month to month on Social Security, and I guess for a while that's what they did. Then Horace went and got his second heart attack, this time one of your real strokes, and he had to have surgery this time, so when he come out of it he couldn't even leave his chair without help from Alma, and all he could do now was sit in the living room in his rocker or his armchair, he liked to switch around, and watch the wrestling on television, a nice twenty-one-inch color set his son Ham, who was living over in Concord with his new wife, had bought him for Christmas. Ham was nice about that, the color TV, because he really didn't have to, they already had a black and white, but when it come to the question of how they were going to pay all the doctor and hospital bills, Ham told his mother, who was now the only one capable of making a decision, he told her to borrow the five thousand dollars from the bank and take out a mortgage on the house to guarantee it. Now naturally there was no way that poor old couple was going to be able to make the payments on a loan that size, so the son, a pipe-fitter like his father, but young, of course, and making good money working heavy construction over to Concord, he offered to make the payments for them, but so's he'd feel covered—that's how he put it, so's *he'd* feel covered—they should sign the deed of the house over to him, and he and his new wife would move into the house right off, 'to help take care of Pa,' he said. Now if you knew Ham's wife, you'd know how likely *that* was—she was his second wife, a fancy New York City tap dancer, used to be one of those June Taylor Dancers on the *Jackie Gleason Show?* You've probably seen her on TV, but it's hard to remember one from all the others. Anyhow, I can't blame her, not after what I know now, but that's how Ham put it: 'Annie and I want to be able to help take care of Pa, and we can do it a lot easier if we're living right there in the house with you,' he told his poor old mother, who naturally was terrified by all those bills and by the idea of having to take care of a man who'd become practically a vegetable—no disrespect, but that's truly what he'd turned into since the second heart attack, kind of leaning all the time off to one side there in his chair while he looked at the wrestling and the cowboy shows, which is what he liked the best, the wrestling and the cowboys, with the whole left side of him stiff as a door and the rest of him spastic as a cat with distemper. It was something horrible to see, so I used to go over there twice a week, to visit Alma and try to cheer her up some, and naturally I'd have to see Horace too, and even though he'd turned a lot sweeter, a whole lot, since the second attack and the operation, it was kind of sickening, if you know what I mean. I used to almost wish he was still all sour and grouchy, so he wouldn't try to talk to me, because now when I'd go over to spend the afternoon with Alma, he'd try to talk and smile, but all he could do was make these pathetic moans like a cow and toothy kind of crazy-looking smiles, which I know must have embarrassed Alma so much that probably even she was wishing the old man would get cross and silent again. I don't know, maybe Alma didn't have any other choice, because after all, Ham was her son and she *had* to pay those bills; so anyhow, she agreed to sign over the house and take out the mortgage and let Ham make the payments—he paid her a dollar, a single dollar bill, for the house, because when they signed it over there had to be some money change hands—and she also agreed to let him and his second wife Annie move into the house. They sold this little ranch over to Concord they'd owned and moved in that same week, going right to work fixing up the second floor entirely for themselves with a new bathroom and converting two of the little bedrooms up there into one 'master bedroom'—that's what he called it, a 'master bedroom'—and his mother and father went on using their old bedroom and bathroom downstairs. That was when the big dormer in back of the house got put in too, because Ham and Annie wanted a view of the mountain from their 'master bedroom.' It wasn't enough they already had a view of the mountain from the kitchen; no, they had to have one from their bedroom too. But of course all this time everyone, Alma too, thought that Ham was being kind to his mother and father. No one knew what he had in his head. No one knew that when the old man finally died, as he did that spring—very peacefully, thank heaven, just went to sleep and didn't wake up again, just like his own father died, only that was in a snowbank and he was dead drunk at the time—anyhow, when Ham's father finally died, no one knew six months later everything would blow up like it did. Ham went and put in a garden like his father had done every summer, and Annie got herself involved a little bit with the town, joined the Ladies' Aid Society and so forth, and Alma seemed happier than I'd ever remembered seeing her, because everyone knew that Horace had been a difficult man to live with. He was so cross all the time, even as a young man. Anyhow, as fall comes on, Annie stopped going to Ladies' Aid, and Ham was seen drunk a lot in town, and ever since he was a boy in high school, practically, he's been nasty when he's drunk, and he was being nasty all right, scrapping and fighting in the Bonnie Aire over to Pittsfield, wrecking his car one night by driving it dead drunk into the Civil War Memorial down to the Parade. So people started getting the idea that things weren't going all that smooth at the Stark place. And they sure weren't, as we later found out. What was happening was that Annie had decided she didn't like living way out in the country with no one but her mother-in-law for company all day, and so she'd started nagging Ham about moving to Connecticut or someplace where she could have the kind of life she preferred, and like I said, I can't really blame her. After all, being married to that man must have been no picnic, like they say, and since she was a big-city girl, a famous dancer and all, living way out at the end of a dirt road in an old house with an old woman must have been pretty boring for her. She was sort of a pretty woman then, and she was actually a nice woman when you got to know her, and she couldn't help it if fate and Ham had put her in a place that could only be boring to a woman like that. So they did a lot of fighting, she and Ham, and one of the ways she got around being so bored and doing so much fighting was to take week-long trips down to New York City, where she stayed with her aunt in an apartment in the Bronx, she once told me. That made it easier for everyone, I suppose, probably even for Ham, though who can say what makes things easier for that man? Anyhow one night in October when Annie was down to New York, Ham came home drunk and late, around nine o'clock or so. Alma'd made supper for him, and so she was ticked off that he'd come in so late and drunk, and I guess she must have let it out a little, because he got to fighting back at her, yelling that this was his house and he'd come home when and how he damned well pleased to come home, and so forth, until finally she said, out of anger, you under-stand, not really meaning it, 'All right, then, I'll leave,' and he said, 'Fine.' He went and phoned up his sister Jody, who thank God lives in town with her husband Chub, the chief of police, and Ham told Jody to come pick her mother up, she was moving out. Jody was shocked, naturally, but what could she do, so she drove up to the house and picked up her mother, who had refused to show that man any emotion over the thing and had gone right ahead and packed her bags, and Jody drove the old woman back down to the Center where she and Chub and their twin boys have a trailer, and lucky for everyone, it's one of those two-bedroom trailers, so they had room for Alma. Then Chub went and called Ham and asked him what was going on, sort of man to man, and when Ham told him to mind his own GD business, Chub got mad—and he's not the kind of man you want to get mad—so he hopped into his car and drove up to the house and stormed in, but when he got into the house he found Ham standing in the middle of the living room with a rifle pointed at him. I mean it. A rifle. Pointed right at Chub's heart. That's the kind of man Ham Stark is. Or was. I really wouldn't know now, because I haven't seen the man to talk to, even assuming I would talk to him, which of course I wouldn't, for what, twelve years now, ever since that night . . ."

THERE ARE TWO versions of what happened following the moment when Hamilton confronted his brother-in-law with a 30.06 rifle. Both are widely believed. Here is Chub's version:

"I come in there and the bastard's got his thirty-ought-six aimed and cocked. I can see he's drunker'n a fiddler's fart, so I start trying to humor him, you know, because your drunk man can pull the trigger when your sober man won't. So I start saying things like, 'Hey, Ham, ol' buddy, you don't want to shoot your ol' buddy, get yourself in all kindsa trouble.' You know, stuff like that, just talking to him, while all the time I'm circling around the room and closing in on him, trying to look real casual, like I'm just checking out the furniture or something, but with each step getting closer to the guy, not being obvious about it or anything, of course, until finally I'm maybe only two feet from the tip of the barrel. That's when I make my move. I look quick off to my left, like there's someone at the window, and he follows my look, and I grab the barrel of his gun and yank the thing out of his hands, and then I throw it on the couch behind me with one hand and reach around his neck with the other arm, yank his head back, and throw a hammer lock on him until he blacks out and goes limp. He's a pretty big guy, bigger'n me, but he doesn't have my training, of course, so there's not much he can do against me, especially since he's drunk and all. Anyhow, after a few seconds he comes to, and realizing what he's done, the guy starts bawling like a baby, pounding his fists on the floor and everything, just like he's a little kid. I can see he really isn't right in the head, so I says to him that he ought to get himself to one of those psychologists or something, a head doctor, only he tells me to go to hell, starts laying me out like that, so I says the hell with him and I walk out, and I haven't seen the bastard, not socially, since that night."

THE SECOND VERSION of that confrontation was, naturally, Hamilton's own, which he conveyed by means of a typed post card to his daughter Rochelle, when in a letter she asked him specifically what had happened at that particular point in the evening, "the night you and your family quarreled," was how she delicately put it. Here is his post card:

> Big Chief broke into private domicile. H. S. ordered him off property with aid of 30.06 Winchester. B. C. eagerly complied. Nothing else. Later phone call from B. C. threatened H. S. with bodily harm. Promises never kept. Boring story. Tell about how your great-great-great-great-grandfather stole 700 acres from Abenookis. You need some humor in your book.

Her father's literary advice, offered gratuitously, was not followed, which is perhaps unfortunate, because possibly the only significant flaw in Rochelle's novel is its lack of humor.

At the time she received the above card from her father, she was especially unlikely to heed the kind of advice he was offering, for at that particular moment in the writing she was exploring and expounding her theory that her hero, Alvin Stock (Hamilton Stark), was actually possessed by a little-known demon named Asmodeus. Although, to be sure, Rochelle later on gave up this somewhat bizarre notion, so that in the completed manuscript there is not a single reference either to demons or possession (with one possible exception, in her Chapter Two, "Conversion," where she describes a vision of the archangel Raphael that was experienced by the hero, Alvin, at the age of sixteen one night after a high school dance in the Pittsfield High School parking lot), nevertheless, the terms of her theory are significantly revealing, not only of how Rochelle perceived the extremity of her father's behavior, but also of the man's behavior itself.

While in many ways a courageous and rigorously rational young woman, Rochelle, especially during the period when she was writing her so-called novel, was nonetheless capable of profound superstition, and further, was capable of structuring her superstitions to help her evade uncomfortable truths. Of course, she was very young at the time (still is), and besides, one can hardly blame her. Even if she had been drawing on nothing more than her own direct experiences of her father, she would at some point have been forced to confront the facts that he had mistreated her mother, that he had deserted her in her infancy, that later, as she grew into young womanhood, he had mocked her attempts to express her love for him, and that he had rejected outright her final attempts as an adult to create a friendship with him. Additionally, he had done all this as if he had intended to do it from the beginning! As if nothing could have pleased him more! His villainy was all of a piece. Thus, no matter how much one would have liked to, one could not have forgiven Hamilton Stark for his weakness, nor understood him for his stupidity, nor sympathized with him for his pathology—because he so consistently had insisted that everything he did was intentional, was deliberate, and in the long run was happiness-producing. And if all this, which was no more than her own direct experience of the man, were not sufficient to send her flying to the warm solace of superstition, at the time of her novel-writing Rochelle was interviewing and corresponding with many other people who had been involved with her father, either as wife, sister, brother-in-law, or even friend, and thus she was being literally overwhelmed with tales of selfishness, of rage, drunkenness, lust, greed, of eccentric violence and destructive manipulation, of betrayal, disloyalty and deceit. She could find people, men as well as women, who said they had loved him, who even seemed to be obsessed with him, but she could find no one who could tell her tales of sweetness, of gentleness, kindness and generosity, of affectionate big-heartedness, humility and steadfastness. And yet, oddly, the more of the man's nature she uncovered to herself, the more she loved him and the more her obsession with her father dominated her thoughts and actions.

How else, then, to explain to herself (or to others) such a compelling attraction to a man she knew in all ways to be morally obnoxious—unless she could believe that he was possessed? An otherwise sweet, gentle, kind and generous man, she decided, an affectionately big-hearted man, a humble and steadfast man, was tragically possessed by a demon, she believed, and he had thus been transformed into a wholly selfish man, a raging, drunken, lustful man, a greedy man, a man of eccentric, unpredictable violence and pointless manipulation, a master of betrayal, disloyalty and deceit.

And it was not unnatural, once she had determined that her father was possessed in the first place, that Rochelle would happen on the demon Asmodeus. She had what might be called a lively religious curiosity, possibly the guilt-motivated residue of an adolescent conversion experience and the falling away that had followed. She had been raised rather casually as a Presbyterian, southern (and therefore highly emotional regardless of how casual one might be in keeping the rituals), and when she underwent what in those sects is referred to as the "conversion experience," whereby Jesus Christ, heretofore a mere abstraction, becomes one's "personal savior," she brought with her the intellectual apparatus and energy that were her genetic birthright, and as a result she succeeded in making herself into something of a biblical scholar before, at the age of eighteen, she commenced to fall away from the organized forms of religion. Thus, later on, when the young woman began looking around for the proper demon, she had little difficulty remembering Asmodeus. (It might be worth noting also that in the meantime, between her falling away from her religious faith and her "discovery" that her father had been possessed by the demon Asmodeus, she had undergone almost a year of Jungian psychoanalysis, and consequently it was not especially difficult for her to credit non-Christian deities and other mythical figures with immense power in determining the behavior of individuals who in all ways were unconscious even of the mere existence of such deities.)

Rochelle knew that Asmodeus, or Ashmedai, though imported from Persian mythology into Palestine, showed up rather frequently in Jewish literature, where his original func-tion was to cause frustration in marriage, usually by provoking rage and violence. There was a crucial link with lust, however, a particularly non-Jewish and non-Christian (although perhaps not non-Protestant) link between rage and lust. Rochelle's adolescent studies had shown her that the Jewish Asmodeus had probably originally been the Persian "fiend of the wounding spear," some-times Aeshma Daeva, from the root *aesh*, meaning "to rush for-ward" or "to be violently self-impelled." He was a storm spirit, a personification of rage, one who took deep pleasure from filling men's hearts with anger and desire for revenge. In contrast to the modern world, where anger is regarded as a thing of great value, as something not to be suppressed but rather as a "feeling" to be experienced as a type of ecstasy, in the ancient world anger was regarded as something pre-eminently evil and nonhuman and, therefore, dependent upon interference from outside forces for its visible expression.

According to Jewish stories, Asmodeus was the son of a mor-tal woman, Naamah, either by one of the fallen angels or possibly by Adam himself before the creation of Eve. In the testament of Solomon, written between A.D. 100 and 400, he is reported to have remarked, "I was born of angel's seed by a daughter of man." Described there as "furious and shouting," he not only prevents intercourse between husband and wife, but also encourages adultery. "My business is to plot against the newly married," he boasts, "so that they may not know one another . . . I transport men into fits of madness and desire when they have wives of their own, so that they leave them and go off by night and day to others that belong to other men with the result that they commit sin. . . ." A peculiar function: to frustrate desire so that he may arouse it elsewhere. In another account, the book of Tobit, written around 250 B.C., Tobias marries Sarah, who has had seven husbands before, all of whom were strangled by Asmodeus to prevent them from lying with her. On the advice of the archangel Raphael, Tobias cooks the heart and liver of a fish, and the smoke repels the demon and drives him off.*

For Rochelle, the peculiar sequence of the demon's evolution—from a demon of rage to one who infected men with uncontrollable lust to one who meddled with the mainsprings of marriage—was sufficient to qualify him as the one responsible for her father's equally peculiar combination of what she had no choice but to regard as social and moral inadequacies. Of course, to connect Asmodeus to the life of her father, Rochelle was also forced to ignore or to explain away as "corrupted sources" and "mistranslations" long chains of bizarre imagery and anachronistic, minor attributes of the demon. All she cared about was the fact that he was the only figure who combined rage with lust and loosed these emotions onto the

---

* The Latin version of Tobit adds that Tobias and Sarah defeated the demon by successfully remaining chaste for the first three nights of their marriage, which was the beginning of the later custom "Tobias's Nights." In fact, right down to the nineteenth century in parts of France, Germany, and the Balkans, it was customary to follow the example of Tobias and Sarah, and in medieval France, husbands were often permitted to pay a fee to the Church for a license to disregard the rule.

institution of marriage. To do this, she had to overlook, for instance, the efficacy of the smoky fish liver. She also had to sidestep all ancient attempts to describe the demon physically, because his attributes, if she visualized them, would have made her suspect herself of having drifted into "imaginative zeal," which she abhorred in others as much as in herself. How, for instance, could she have pictured her father as being possessed by a figure who was said to have the enormous feet of a cock (a bird, one might note, well known for its indiscriminate sexual vigor)? How could she have accommodated herself to those several Jewish tales that have Asmodeus as the king of the demons and residing on top of a mountain from which he regularly journeys to heaven where he takes part in the learned discussions that supposedly go on there? How to make peace with the tale that has the master magician, King Solomon, force Asmodeus and the other devils to construct the Temple at Jerusalem,* after which Asmodeus takes his nasty revenge by seizing the ring in which all Solomon's magic power resides and, tossing the ring to the bottom of the sea, sends Solomon into exile and reigns in his place until, miraculously, Solomon recovers the ring from a fish's belly and proceeds to imprison Asmodeus and all the other devils in a large jar? And how to honor the source called the *Lemegeton,* a highly respected magic textbook, which, providing a long list of demons, asserts that when Asmodeus shows himself to human eyes he rides a dragon, carries a long spear, and has three heads, that of a ram, a bull and a handsome youth, asserting further that only a bare-headed magician may summon the demon, whereupon the demon will respond by making the magician invisible and will lead him to great treasure? How indeed? And what is meant by "bare-headed"?

---

* Oddly, when asked which of his many construction jobs had given him the most personal satisfaction, Hamilton replied, "The Temple of Jerusalem," which remark, at the time, was interpreted by the interrogator as meaning that none of his many jobs had given him personal satisfaction.

Nevertheless, despite such pathetic imaginings, Rochelle successfully managed to incorporate the demon into her vision of her father and, for a single, early version of her novel, her vision of Alvin Stock as well. Happily, she saw the irrationality and the personal psychological use such a vision implied, and because she is as brave a woman as she is intelligent, she purged the novel of all references to demons and possession, and though she did not in that way simplify the character of her father, she did succeed in seeing him more clearly, more *realistically*, one might say.

On the other hand, perhaps by coming to regard her father in such a critically analytical light, she lost something, too—a depth, the shuddering, vibratory quality that a proper description of his character required, especially if the reader were to understand the intensity with which Hamilton Stark (Alvin Stock) could simultaneously attract and repel people who, for whatever reason, came close to him. One is left, with regard to Hamilton Stark, with the two-dimensional vision of the chief of the Barnstead Police Department, Chub Blount, who, unable to imagine (or if he imagined them, to care about) the qualities of life associated with the Stark house simply because it had been owned and lived in by the Stark family for over two hundred years, and not mentioning those qualities to himself, thus saw the house in what may be called a "realistic" light. To continue the analogy, one would be forced to deny oneself any vision of the house that explained how a man could commit irrational acts of loyalty to a mere wooden structure. One would not be capable of understanding why a man, who from adolescence had resolutely refused to pray for anything, suddenly had found himself on his knees one night next to his bed in his modest ranch house in Concord, steadfastly praying for ownership of the same house his ancestors had owned. No, if the reader relied on the chief's view of the relationship between Hamilton and the house his ancestors had owned, he would see a merely selfish, aggressive man using the occasion of a deed and his old and sick parents' desperation to work out his hostilities and gratify his greedy whim to own the house outright and exclusively.

Knowing about the patina of time and family that in Hamilton's mind had surely been laid over the image of the house—an inescapable aura, when it's available, for any imaginative American of our time—knowing that, however, the sensitive reader may add to the chief's opaque view of the dispossession the vision of a man obsessed and terrified, a man determined to attach himself to the one thing in his life that seemed capable of connecting him to the thread of time that potentially runs through the fabric of every family. In most cases, especially in this country and among the members of all classes but the most privileged, this thread is broken at every turn. Given geographic relocation, eager divorce, homes for the aged, distant, private schools for the young, housing developments for the middle-aged and insistence by all generations that the adult life of one generation will not be repeated as a life again, it should be no wonder when, having endured all that discontinuity, a man who sees a possibility to attach himself to his familial past by means of a two-hundred-year-old farm and house will grow desperate and impatient beyond reason. He will conceive plans and schemes, will see potential heirs (such as his two younger sisters) as threats to his very life, will even see his own mother as a likely breaker of the thread, and will see his father's death as a piece of great good luck. Who then is to say this is mere selfishness and aggression? For a man such as Hamilton Stark, emotionally severed from his parents and sisters since childhood (and perhaps, because of the conventions, since birth), a man unable to attach himself to the life and history of a wife or even, at the deepest level, of a friend or of his only child, a daughter he can barely remember and for whom he is unable to create any loyalty except in terms of conventional guilt, which he rejects as both inappropriate and insufficiently personal—for a man such as this, it seems natural that an old frame house and seven hundred acres of rocky, overgrown hillside would become, for all practical purposes, mystical emblems, badges which, if his, would connect him to the rest of the universe.

Obviously, while the chief sat in his patrol car in front of this very farmhouse and let his mind drift across the unpleasant details of his near-violent (or possibly violent, in fact) encounter with his brother-in-law, even though the encounter had taken place some eleven years ago, nothing like sympathy or understanding organized his thoughts. They merely drifted across the surface of the remembered event, and if a question were raised about any possible deeper motivation lying behind Hamilton's outrageous behavior, he answered it immediately, saying to the questioner with complete confidence that what happened is what happened, and what happened is the kind of man Hamilton Stark is, a guy who's mad at the world and wants as much of it for himself as he can get, no matter who gets in the way, no matter if it's his mother or his sisters or anybody else. That's how the chief would probably put it. In fact, that is pretty much how he did put it when, one afternoon, he was asked about that particular evening by Rochelle.

Poor Rochelle. Even though she loved her father, she still did not understand the potentially mystical aspect of real estate in New England (the reader may recall that Rochelle was raised in central Florida), and thus she was unable to understand what storms of emotion Hamilton had been responding to when he had dispossessed his own mother. Naturally, this created a sharp conflict for her. No matter how diligently she analyzed the details of that evening, no matter how many interviews she conducted, visits to the house, careful reconstructions of the minutes of the evening and the months that preceded it, she was unable to get around the conclusion that her father had behaved in a wholly reprehensible way. And as a result of her examination, she (unlike the chief, who had no need of, nor interest in, neutralizing all emotions but love for the man) experienced considerable pain. If the chief were to read the final version of her novel, which describes in agonizingly honest detail her pain in this regard, he probably would agree fully with her description of the events that prompted her painful judgment of her father, but he would not understand why that judgment, once she had made it, gave her any trouble. As far as he was concerned, when you love somebody who turns out to be a bastard, you stop loving him. And not without a certain relief, probably.

Some of this was going through the chief's mind that gray February morning while he sat in his car outside the Stark house and waited for his assistant to arrive. I.e., When you love somebody who turns out to be a bastard . . . Yes, even for the chief, it was difficult to look at the house and not drop into examinations and speculations concerning the kinds of love and hate these Starks bore for each other and for themselves. They were no noisier than any other family in town, nor were they unconventional by way of education, travel or economics, and except for Hamilton, they were as careful to avoid eccentricity or drawing attention to themselves as practically everyone else in town. All this made it difficult to explain the intensity of their feelings— not so much the fact of the intensity as the fact that people were allowed to see that those feelings existed at all. It was unusual to know that much about a person or a family, especially when the family was as reticent and close-mouthed, as *ordinary*, as the Starks.

Suddenly the chief's ruminations were intruded upon by the whining voice of his assistant, Calvin Clark. "Hey, Chief!" the man cried through the closed window of the chief's car. "What's up?"

The chief squeezed his large belly past the steering wheel and got out. "I got an anonymous tip last night that Ham Stark might've been shot," he said, "so I came up here this morning to check it out. I figured it was just Howie Leeke calling me drunk from the Bonnie Aire or someplace—you know Howie, how he does—or I would've come out here last night."

"Sure, sure, Chief." Calvin was gulping air, a habit that made it almost impossible for him to lie successfully. Whenever he became even slightly insincere, he found himself unable to keep from gulping while he talked, as if he were about to be beaten for his insincerity. Luckily for him, or perhaps merely as a result of his habit, he rarely lied outright. Politeness, however, often made it necessary for him not actually to lie but rather to speak with little or no sincerity, and since he was a polite man, he frequently found himself gasping like a fish out of water.

"Yeah. So anyhow, I come out here this morning. Just to check it out, you know?"

"Sure, Chief, sure." Gulping.

"And I found *these*," the chief said dramatically, pointing with a thick finger at the trio of bulletholes in the window of Hamilton's Chrysler.

"Holy shit!" Calvin gasped appropriately. "What are they?"

"Bulletholes. Thirty-thirty, I'd say. Maybe bigger."

"Yeah, sure, sure. Where's Ham? He seen these yet? Boy will he be pissed. You know Ham."

"No, you . . . *Jesus!*" The chief stomped back to his car and got into it.

"Where you going, Chief?" Calvin called.

"Nowhere," he answered, almost whispering it. Then, with authority, "Listen, take a look in the house for Ham. I'll poke around out here and in the garage."

"Right, Chief," Calvin said, promptly jogging toward the front door of the house. It was locked, and in a second he had disappeared around the corner of the house, checking the side door at the porch. The chief, sweating, restarted the engine of his car. After a few moments, Calvin appeared at the front of the house again, spreading his empty hands to show that he'd been unable to find Hamilton.

"Not out here either!" the chief hollered out the car window. "It's probably just some kind of crazy . . . Let's head back to town, you can check by here late this afternoon!"

Calvin walked slowly up to the chief's open window. "You don't think somebody *shot* him, do you? I mean, *somebody* hadda shoot them holes in his car," Calvin reasoned.

"The bastard probably did it himself. You know Ham."

"Yeah. Then who was it called you last night?"

"I dunno. Probably Ham. It still could've been Howie, but I kinda doubt it now. Probably Ham made the call, just to get me pissed."

"Yeah," Calvin gulped. He was shivering from the cold. The gray sky had seemed to tighten and lift a bit, and flecks of snow were drifting slowly down.

"I'll see you later, back at the office," the chief announced. He cranked up the window, dropped his car into reverse, and backing around Calvin's car, entered the turnaround behind it, spun the wheel hard to the left, and fled down the long driveway to the road.

By the time he reached the center of town it was snowing hard, as if blankets of the soft flakes were being tossed against the ground. Boy, snow in February is depressing, the chief thought, and then he decided to go home for the rest of the day. He figured, with the snow and all, he'd be out on emergency calls most of the night, so he'd better catch some sleep while he could.

CHAPTER 6

Chapter Beginning as "His Second Wife Speaks of a Man She Calls 'Your Father' (from a Tape Recording)"

HIS SECOND WIFE speaks of a man she calls "Your Father" (from a tape recording):

"Yeah, my mother, she used to sit back in her chair and she'd clap her hands together, like this, and she'd say to me, 'Annie, oh, Annie, you're so pretty with that smile and those legs. With those legs, honey, you, you're going to the *top!*' She said, she said it often enough, boy, once a day at least, and she wasn't the only one saying it, either. My God, Uncle Zack, my Aunt Harriet. I mean, even old Grover said it, old Grover the janitor in our building on East Eighty-sixth, even he said it, so by the time I was, say, oh, I dunno, twelve, thirteen, by that time I really believed it myself. I really, I believed it was gonna be *true*. I was going to the top. And you know what that meant to us, 'getting to the top,' it meant Show Business. SHOW BIZ. I guess because we were New Yorkers. You know. But also because we were all jokers, all of us, the whole family—comics, singers, mimics, like that. This was before television, of course, back in the forties and all, so to us Show Business didn't mean TV, it meant the stage. The Musical Stage, honey, right up there in front of a live audience, people who really love ya, and you can feel 'em loving ya, nobody cares if you feel it, so you just take it in like the sun's rays, and the more you get the better you get, no kidding, that's how it works, Show Business. With the stage, I mean, not TV or movies. It's different there, TV, the movies, because the audience there hates you if you look like you can feel 'em loving ya. They want to see you as if you're all alone in the world or something, you know, as if they're look-ing at you through one of those one-way mirrors that depart-ment stores have for detectives. Anyhow, to be good, *really* good, on the stage, you have to get special training, of course. No matter if you're talented—talent's as cheap as daisies and'll do you about as much good as a dozen of 'em—unless you get the training, because you might, you maybe wouldn't think so, but it's not so easy to stand up there and let 'em love ya and let 'em know you can feel it, let 'em know you love it. Which of course is what keeps them doing it, loving ya. It really is not easy. I don't care what you might think. It's work. Hard work, honey. You wouldn't believe—you've never been in show busi-ness, have you? I can tell. Never mind, I mean, I can tell from the way you walk and how you're sitting, stuff like that, though of course you've got the looks, you could do it, I mean if you had the training and all, though you might be too old for it now. I was only a kid when I got started. I had the looks too, but like I said, talent's cheap. Nothing. Nuth-ing. So I had to get started early, before I was ten, even, I got started. At first all I could do was sing, you know, like a little kid, but cute, I mean cute enough to get me on 'Uncle Bob's Rainbow House' eight times in one year, and then when I started taking lessons it didn't take long before I was good enough to sing with Ma-jor Bowes, and after that I did the 'Rinso White' commercial on radio. Did you ever hear that one? 'Rinso *White!* Rinso *White!* Happy little washday *song!*" You're too young for radio. Another radio show I was on was 'Our Gal Sunday,' where I had a singing part for thirty-six weeks running. And all this time I'm taking voice lessons, training to be *heard*, honey, not seen, not yet, anyhow. First things first, you know what I mean? But around the time I was eleven my mother says I ought to start getting ready to be seen, people are really starting to talk about how good-looking I am anyhow, so she starts me taking tap and modern ballet, and three afternoons a week the accordion. Things you can do out in front of people. Not like the piano or the cello or something like that, that hides you. My mama really had it figured, she really knew what she wanted for me and how she could get it for me. She wanted me to be seen, and naturally, to be loved for it, for being seen. Oh yeah, my mama just knew it, people were going to love me for letting them see me—and I was going to let them see everything I had, too. I was going to turn myself into a beautiful girl gracefully dancing up there on the stage, long white legs shining in the lights, feet in silver shoes tapping miraculously fast in complicated rhythms while the whole upper body and the accordion would swing back and forth in a slick kind of counterpoint! *That* girl was going to be *me!* That girl up there tap-dancing and playing the accordion, her fingers and arms moving as fast and as graceful as her feet and legs, with the music of the accordion and the crackle of the taps joined by the sweet sound of her own singing—*that* girl was going to be *me!* 'Lady of Spain I Adore You.' Sure. I was going to become an entire musical production, with the movement, the rhythm and the melody all together in a single body placed in the exact center of an enormous stage! I mean it, she meant it. That was my mama's dream, God rest her soul, and naturally, before I was very old, it was *my* dream too. I guess when, I guess you're more likely to do that, make your parent's dream into your own. You know, when your parent dies young. Maybe, I don't know, to work off the guilt or something. You know. Hell, I don't know. It doesn't matter. Why, I mean. Anyhow, it sure became my dream awful fast, and especially after mama died, which was the summer I turned sixteen and was starting to take voice with Estelle Liebling—you probably know who that is, Beverly Sills studied with her, though I didn't know her then, even though we were about the same age. I guess we had our lessons on different days or something. I could hit a high G above high C then, would you believe, and that's as good as Beverly Sills, though like I said, talent's cheap, you have to have a lot more than talent to be a Beverly Sills. Anyhow, when my mama died I was sixteen. Cancer. My father died when I was two. Car crash. I went to live in the next block, over on Eighty-seventh, with Uncle Zack and Aunt Harriet and just threw myself into my lessons, tap-dancing and singing and playing the accordion, all of them, practicing eight and ten hours a day, probably driving everybody in the building nuts, but no one ever complained, because just like my mother, they were all sure I was going to the top. They all knew that someday I would make it big. Big. And then they could remember when. You know how people are. They like to be able to remember you when. And if you yourself are a true believer, I mean really believe, even to the point where it's never actually occurred to you that you might not make it big, never even once occurred to you, pretty soon everyone who knows you starts thinking the same way. It never even occurs to them either that you won't become a star. So long as you're not a complete idiot, of course, so long as you've got *some* kind of recognizable talent. That's the one thing you really need talent for, to convince people you're not crazy because you happen to believe you're going to become a star. It's what makes them *believe*. In you. People, strangers practically, would start telling me on the elevator, 'Annie, I just *know* you're going to make it big! I can already see your name up in lights on Broadway!' they'd say to me. Stuff like that. Only, the trouble was, pretty soon I was, I not only had to live up to my poor dead mother's expectations for me, but the expectations of everyone who lived in the building too, and all my teachers, even my friends. So if the thought ever did occur to me that I might not make it, get to the top and become a world-famous tap dancer and accordionist—or the even more horrible thought that I might not really *want* to become it—well, you better believe those were thoughts I put out of my head in a hurry. I can remember lying in my bed in my room on Eighty-seventh, my legs and ankles stiff and aching from ten hours of practice, and suddenly I'd be thinking, I might not make it. I might not be good enough. I might not be lucky enough. Stuff like that. And pretty soon I'd start to think that those were thoughts that were being put into my head by my poor dead mother's restless spirit, just to sort of test me. To discipline me. No kidding, that's how I got around any doubts I felt in those days. I just figured it was Mama, doomed to wander through purgatory or someplace until I made it to the top. Mama somewhere out there helping to guarantee my becoming a star by toughening me up with bad thoughts. So I'd give the right response, I'd say, I'd tell myself, 'Not a chance I won't make it, not this kid, not me, not Annie Laurie!' And then I'd roll over and fall asleep, probably with a smile on my face . . .''

If I may, I'd like to state now that the above is a partial transcript of a tape recording made by Rochelle Stark during a series of lengthy interviews with her father's second wife, Annie Laurie Stark, who now resides alone in a shabby tenement in Manchester, New Hampshire, middle-aged, depressed (I'm sure) and angry in ways she herself can never know, or she would probably try to kill someone—her ex-husband, a randomly selected stranger, or even herself.

I will try to explain. I have not offered the transcript in its entirety here because the whole tape is too long, too painfully depressing and, finally, because of the several secrets she must keep from herself, a little confusing to the listener. Also, unless you happen to know the woman personally, boring.

For one thing, if you do not actually *hear* the tapes, if you must read them, you cannot hear her tough, New York accent, its glitter, and thus cannot hear it cut against the enervated, listless quality of her language, the words she uses. It makes an interesting conflict, creating an effect of stoic bravery, that accent and those words. And then, of course, there are the secrets, what she cannot mention, cannot bring herself to talk about to anyone, not even to patient, kind Rochelle, who, sitting across from her in the dusty, cluttered living room, knows what those secrets are. For while, naturally, you who read this account cannot see Annie, Rochelle, in interviewing the woman, could see her, and among the several things she could observe was that Annie Laurie is obese, is almost grotesquely fat. And because she will not speak of it under any circumstances (and no interviewer would be so callous as to force her), Annie's obesity remains a secret. Well, not anymore.

But there is a second secret which I cannot bring myself to reveal. Not yet, at least. At least not with this character. Perhaps never. (This is a *novel*, for God's sake, not a court case.)

Anyhow, the tapes of her interview with Annie Laurie Stark are among the documentary materials that Rochelle chose to use in the making of *her* novel. How they happened to come into my possession is not worth going into here, but it is enough to say that she made them available to me, with full knowledge of the use I would make of them. I have tried to give credit to Rochelle and her materials wherever in my novel I have consciously drawn from them or from her novel itself. And because her novel will never be published (for reasons that I will go into later), I do not feel any particular misgivings over certain of my appropriations—even though I am sure there are people, literal-minded readers with a facility for legalistic short division, who would construe my truly creative operations as plagiaristic or, at best, as derivative. To such readers, I offer neither apology nor explanation. To the rest, the above ought to be sufficient as both apology and explanation.

BUT THE TAPES. When I first sat down in my chair and listened to them, a process that consumed an entire evening, long into the winter's night, I was astounded. Appalled. Aghast. Amazed. (I can see now that I'll be unable to keep Annie Laurie's second secret to myself. It's fast becoming part of the novel. Oh, Annie, Annie, I'm sorry.)

Immediately, I called my friend and neighbor C., the thinker, a man whose sense and sensitivity I trust explicitly because both sense and sensitivity happen to be driven by a deep curiosity about the nature of the universe rather than by any purely personal considerations. "I have something here that I want you to listen to," I explained to him, after first apologizing for calling so late.

"*Now?*" he petulantly asked me, understandably, for it was three A.M.

I assured him that it could wait until the following morning, that I had just got carried away by a rush of perceptions that had led me to a state of extreme agitation and, as a result, moral confusion. An orderly progression of perceptions makes the moral life easier to accomplish. When a flood of perceptions washes over one, however, one's moral certainty gets swept violently away. This is possibly why it's so rare and difficult for the aware man to be much of a moral example to others. One is always safer if one can save that role, the role of moral example, for the dull and the stolid, the insensitive, the practically insensible.

But to return, I explained to C. that I needed an objective response to some tape-recorded interviews I had recently obtained, materials that I wished to use, in a much modified form, of course, in my novel about Hamilton Stark, which C. well knew to be in fact about A. I told C. that the reason for my excitement and my need for him as an objective listener derived from my bewilderment, which in turn was a consequence of my inability to trust any longer certain conclusions I had drawn prior to my having heard these tapes, conclusions which, of course, had to do with Hamilton Stark's character.

"I thought I *knew* this man!" I exclaimed to C. "I thought I had a clear idea of the quality of his attractiveness, its limits and uses. I thought I knew how he had been perceived by the people who loved him as well as by those who hated him, and thus I thought I knew how to perceive him myself and to make him available, visible, known, to people who knew nothing of him except by what they got through me. But now . . . now I'm just not sure anymore. I've heard some things in these tapes that simply don't belong there. Or rather, they don't belong in the same moral universe as the one I have cast my novel into. I'm finding myself tempted to break into that universe, like some kind of sneaky rapist climbing through a bedroom window, with secrets, information, data, stuff, I had wanted to keep out. I need someone to confirm or deny what I think I'm hearing on these tapes before I can go on. Am I making myself clear?" I asked him.

"*Not at all,*" C. answered.

"Please bear with me. I know it's late. But this may be the most important chapter in the book. It'll be either the final chapter or the sixth of eleven," I explained.

"*Well, what are you hearing?*" He yawned noisily onto the mouthpiece, letting me know that he wished to go back to bed.

"I'd rather not tell you until after you've told me what *you* hear." I didn't want to prejudice him any more than necessary. I told him only that the tapes were an interview made with D., who was A.'s second wife, the one he now and then refers to as "the hussy" and sometimes as "the actress." He once told me, concerning D., that the trouble with a woman who has been an actress is not that she will lie but that you will never be able to believe her.

"Ah, that *one*," C. said.

I decided to tell him nothing more until he had heard the tapes himself. I promised him that I'd have two bottles of a fine California wine, a pinot noir from a small vineyard outside Sonoma that we are both especially fond of, and he gladly promised that he would come over to my house and listen to the tapes tomorrow evening after dinner.

HE ARRIVED AT about nine, still sucking his teeth, as was his habit following an enjoyable meal. It was a blustery cold night, clear and starry, the kind of night that sometimes occurs in mid-February when a spring wind stirs the midwinter cold. I helped him out of his overcoat and escorted him into the library, where I had a large, cheering fire crackling well along and the wine and glasses set out next to the armchair.

He descended into the hug of the chair, taking possession of it as if with great physical need, lit one of his thin cigars, capped a light belch with his gopherlike front teeth, and indicated that I should pour the wine. Our visits are characteristically embellished by a certain ritual, a ceremony. This was a typical one. The purpose of our little ritualistic parading around, our wheezing, sighing, genuflecting, our litanies, and so on, which either would go undetected by a stranger or, if detected, would be thought curious yet boring, is that we both are trying to create as much as possible of the atmosphere that we assume prevails at meetings in, say, London or Brussels, or Belgrade even, between two wholly civilized intellectuals. The underlying assumption, of course, whether held consciously or not, is that by creating such a particularized atmosphere (no matter that we must imagine the model for it), we will therefore find it easier to behave as wholly civilized intellectuals ought to behave—not a simple feat for two middle-aged, middle-class, American men living in a village one hundred miles from even a minor seaport or a major university. But this kind of imitation has always been characteristic of American intellectuals, I suppose. We are, in our own odd way, neoclassicists, regardless of our low opinion of other neoclassical people or ages and in spite of the fact that we have never enjoyed a specifically classical period in our cultural development. Perhaps it's too late to have one. We have lost our innocence. We must imitate, and we also must imagine what we imitate. Thus we always seem to be at least twice removed from true sincerity, true, innocent authenticity. It's hard to tell if that's a problem or a solution to one.

I poured the wine, standing next to C.'s chair while I poured, as if I were the wine steward and my library our club library.

C. tasted the wine, just a sip, almond-sized, and made a slightly dissatisfied face. "Cheese. A small slice of Gouda to neutralize the taste buds."

I strode to the kitchen and returned with a wedge of Gouda on a small wooden plate, which I placed on the table next to C.'s chair. Then I filled both our glasses.

C. sliced a sliver off the wedge, popped it into his mouth, quickly chewed and swallowed. He cleared his mouth, as if to make a speech, and tasted the wine again.

Still standing, I waited through the sniff, the flip of tongue, the hold, and the drop.

"Excellent," he pronounced.

As if relieved, I crossed the room to the fireplace, where, my glass held casually in one hand, my free arm draped like a sweater across the mantel, I assumed a posture that in the dim half-light of the carpeted, book-lined room would make a disinterested viewer think of Oliver Goldsmith. I watched C., legs crossed at the ankles, one hand flopping across the thick arm of the chair, the other posing his wineglass beneath his nostrils as if he were holding a long-stemmed rose, his cigar building a white tubular ash in the ashtray beside him, assume a posture in his chair that would make that same disinterested viewer think of my friend as Ford Madox Ford. Sometimes it was Paul Valéry, but usually, especially in winter, for some reason, it was Ford Madox Ford.

"You said something about listening to some tapes?" C. wheezed at me. Ordinarily he affected the wheeze when he was unsure of the direction of the conversation. It seemed to settle him down, make him the center of the room regardless of where the conversation might wander.

The recorder was inside a cupboard next to the fireplace. Leaning down and switching the first reel on, I quickly told C. that what he was about to hear was an unedited interview made by Rochelle Stark (whose real name C. of course was familiar with) with Hamilton Stark's (A.'s) second wife, to whom I am referring here as Annie Laurie. "You've never met this woman, and I don't believe we've ever discussed her before, have we?" I suddenly realized that I was speaking with the voice of an attorney addressing a jury. I couldn't tell, however, if I was the prosecuting attorney or the attorney for the defense. I wasn't even sure who the defendant was.

"No, although you *have* alluded to the fact of her continued existence. Somewhere in New Hampshire, I believe."

"Yes. Manchester."

"Ah. The Queen City."

And here the tape began:

"What, what's that thing you got there, a tape recorder? Is it on, is it turned on, honey? You aren't going to *record* this, are you? Listen, honey, if you're going to put this on tape I'll have to be a lot more careful of what I say, especially with you being his kid and all. I mean, you know what they say about how blood and water don't mix, don't you? I'm not interested in a feud, starting some kinda family feud, not anymore, not now.

On the other hand, I mean, what the hell, maybe it doesn't matter anymore, I mean to him. Or anyone else either. There's a lot of water gone under the dam, you know. What can it matter now, after all these years? I mean, so what if he happens to hear what I've got to say about him now, there's plenty others who could say lots worse by now, I'll bet. Besides, he can't hurt me any, not anymore, not anymore. And it's not like I was interested in making a good impression on him, if you know what I mean. Pretty hard to do now, ha, ha, ha. It's been what, ten years now I've been sitting around thinking about what happened between your father and me, and you know what? Most of what I thought was true back then, ten years ago, when I divorced him, I really don't think is true anymore, not that I'd do it all over again if I had the chance, believe me. I wouldn't marry that man again in a million years, and I wouldn't divorce him either. What's done is done, and marrying and divorcing a man like your father is something you only want to do once. Jesus, isn't it amazing how you never know what's happening to you when it's actually going on? You have to wait until it's all over and done with before you can find out, and then it's too late, you've forgotten too many things, you can't remember what people said, or what they even looked like, or even the order, you can't remember the order of things anymore, if you ever knew the order of things in the first place, for God's sake. Makes you feel kind of helpless. I guess you can never know what really happens to you, not even afterward. Right? It's kind of crazy. Think of all the trouble you'd save, though. I mean, if you knew what was happening at the same time as it was actually happening. Hah, it's probably a good thing you don't. You'd probably just kill yourself and save yourself the trouble of your whole life. Here I am, look at me, running on about nothing, old motormouth, that's what your father used to call me. Old Motormouth. I'm sorry, honey, I know I talk too much, I'm really a great talker, or at least I used to be a great talker. I don't get too many chances anymore, so I don't know now, I mean, maybe I'm just a lady running off at the mouth . . ."

"How old was she when this was recorded?" C. asked in a flat voice.
"Thirty-one."
"Not old."
"No."

" . . . twenty when I first met him, about your age, a few years younger, even. Jesus, we were a beautiful couple, I was really thin then, no kidding, I had to be, I was dancing with the June Taylor Dancers on the *Jackie Gleason Show* every week, national TV, and they did a weight check every Thursday night, like they do with boxers, because after all, our bodies were our meal tickets, honey, our livelihoods, and if we put on a pound more than we were allowed, there was a dozen girls standing right behind each one of us ready and able to take our places on a moment's notice. It was a grind, lots of pressure. Once you stepped out of that line-up, honey, you stayed out. We worked harder than anyone who hasn't done it can know, new routines that the choreographers more or less made up on the spot and as we went along, practicing seven and eight hours a day right up to the dress rehearsal, which really wasn't your actual dress rehearsal at all as much as it was just the first time we could do the entire number all together from start to finish, and usually there were half a dozen last-minute changes that we'd have to fit in before Saturday's show, and then we'd have Sunday off, and then on Monday the whole thing would start over again. The life of a chorus girl isn't all it's cracked up to be, honey. We really were a lot like your professional athletes, like boxers or something. Except that we had the summers off, but not many of us could afford to loaf, or wanted to anyhow, so most of us took summer stock and chorus line jobs in musicals or nightclubs, which is how I met your father. I was in the chorus line, with a singing part, too, at the Lakeside Theater up in Laconia. You know the place probably, it's pretty famous, over there by the lake, at that place they call the Weirs. Anyhow, your father went to see the show one night, alone, and he picked me out of the chorus line, so he says, and sent me a dozen yellow roses and a note backstage after the show. Believe it or not, it was the first time that had ever happened to me. A stage-door Johnny! Imagine! Me, little Annie Laurie, singled out of the chorus line by a man in the audience! Remember, honey, I was only twenty years old at the time, and sure, I was a big-city girl and he was supposed to be a country rube, but I'd been raised like a flower in a hothouse and he'd been brought up like a piece of moss on a rock, a chunk of lichen or something, so when he tried the old dozen-roses-and-a-note routine, I fell for it. Hook, line and sinker. Also, I was pretty lonely, spending the summer like that in the sticks, away from home for the first time, really, because back in New York I was still living with my Uncle Zack and Aunt Harriet, who had raised me after my mama died. So here I am, backstage in this dingy little barn theater beside the lake, taking off my make-up, and one of the stagehands comes knocking on the dressing room door with a dozen yellow roses and a note for 'The Tall Blond Singer in the Chorus Line.' That's how he'd addressed the card, and since I was the only one in the line with a singing part, one short number, which I had because it was a six-girl line and I was the only one who wasn't completely tone-deaf, I knew the note was for me. I can still remember pretty well what it said. It was in that style of his, the way he wrote all his notes or letters or anything. Even the way he talked, most of the time. *Flowers a token of esteem from member of audience. Would you have drink with sender. H. Stark.* The note was typed, you know, with a typewriter, but it's strange, I didn't even notice that, or if I did, I certainly, I didn't think anything about it, you know, like, What's a member of the audience doing with a typewriter in his lap? I should have, of course. Thought about it, I mean. I guess he must've typed the note out at home before he came to the theater and brought it with him, and that's strange, don't you think? I mean, it was opening night. He couldn't have known who he was going to send the flowers and note to until after he'd already got to the theater. The note on the flowers was in handwriting, somebody's, probably the stagehand's. I should've thought about stuff like that, at the time, I mean. I sure have since then, but a lotta good it's done me. If I'd thought about it then I would've been able to know quite a lot about your father before I even set my eyes on him, but I guess I was too flattered and lonely to notice even. All I cared about was whether or not he was going to be young and handsome, so I asked the stagehand, and he told me sure the guy was young, you know how stagehands talk, and yeah, the guy was handsome. 'Okay-looking,' was probably how he said it. 'But the guy's pretty big,' he told me. I remember that clear as a bell. I remember picturing to myself this tall, handsome stranger, as big as John Wayne and handsome as Robert Taylor, so when, when I walked out the stage door and saw your father, I had to pinch myself on the arm to be sure I wasn't dreaming. He was very gallant, like they say, I mean at first he was. Real old-fashioned, kind of making these little bows when he'd open a door for me, attentive to every detail of the evening, like making sure that when he brought me a corsage, which he did every time we went out, at least at first, but making sure too that he had on a lapel flower that was the same as was in the corsage. Jesus, what a Romeo he was, that guy! But not one of your Latin lover types. Different. All the time serious as a preacher or something, talking like some kind of weird professor in that flat metallic voice of his about things that usually were pretty interesting, if you listened close, like about the history of Lake Winnepesaukee, which is the lake the theater was located on, or maybe discussing the fine points of the show, pretty well informed on theater, he was too, almost like one of those critics for the *Times*. I was really, I was surprised, up here in the woods like that, and all of a sudden here comes one of the local yokels, and it turns out he has this interest in theater and travel and history, all kinds of stuff, stuff I thought only New Yorkers were interested in. Jesus, honey, what a sucker I was. Twenty years old, getting sweet-talked by some big hunk of country meat. And by the time I let him sweet-talk me into bed with him, I was pretty much in love with him. He wasn't my 'first,' but he *was* the first man I fell in love with, really deep, you know? That was also the first time I saw him drunk, too, but it was too late for me to get out by then, the bastard. He had me hooked, so when he started getting mean and wild and drunk all the time, instead of running away from him, which is of course what I should've done toot sweet, I tried to comfort him. You know, to soothe his fevered brow, like they say. Wrong thing to do, honey. Dead wrong. You know, to soothe his fevered brow. All my hand on his brow did was jack up the temperature about ten degrees. Jesus. I'll never forget his face, the way I saw it then, that first night in the motel with him, like the face of some kind of beast, all the time roaring and shouting stuff that didn't make any sense at all to me, stuff that didn't have anything to do with me, although he'd stare right into my face when he shouted, so naturally I thought at first he was shouting at me, that's what anyone would've thought. It was the most frightening, scary thing I'd ever seen, I thought he was . . ."

C. was refilling his glass. "Old A. doesn't seem to've been able to hold his liquor, eh?" He smiled tolerantly. "Not really a man's man."

"So it would seem," I said. "But listen, this is interesting here."

" . . . until finally he flopped onto the bed and passed out, and afterward, after I was sure he was out cold, I crawled into the bed next to him, but under the covers, he was lying on top of everything, and I tried to sleep, which I guess I eventually did, for a while, anyhow. I woke up, I woke up before he did, and in the early morning light looked at his face. Oh, Jesus, it was like a baby's face. Peaceful, innocent, curious, good-natured. You know what I mean? Like a baby it was. The exact opposite of what it had been six or seven hours before. I'd never seen such an incredible switch. I wondered if maybe I'd imagined the whole thing, you know? But anyhow, even though I was wondering this, I still expected him to act all hangdog and guilty as hell when he woke up. Naturally. I mean, I was all set to forgive him. I'd even rehearsed a couple of speeches where I forgive him for getting drunk the first night we spend together and we talk awhile about his childhood and he promises never to drink like that again. That's the sort of thing I figured would happen. No kidding. I never expected him to do like he did. To wake up and just act like nothing had happened. It was something weird, honey. One for the books. He acted like I was an old pal or something, just somebody who happened to be there in the morning after a night out with the boys shooting pool or bowling or something. He brushed his teeth and shaved and got his clothes back on—one of the last things he'd done before passing out was take off all his clothes and pound on his chest like Tarzan, no, more like a scowling gorilla, the real thing—and then, all the time humming and cleaning up the room, he waited for me while I dressed too. Finally I got up the nerve and I put it to him, I asked him straight out, 'What about last night, Ham?' And you know what he did? Get this. He winked at me! Real slow and sexy. Just crunkled up his cheek, smiled a little, and *winked!* Then he pats me on the ass and pushes me gently toward the door, saying as we go out that he's hungry as a bear. That was the first time your father made me feel I was crazy . . ."

I reached down and snapped off the recorder. In the sudden silence that followed, I placed another log on the fire and refilled both my and C.'s glasses.

"I don't . . . I don't quite understand," C. said slowly.

"No?"

"No. There's something . . . *peculiar* about her tale." He held his glass by the stem and twirled it slowly. "There's a gap between the story she's telling, all that business about a man she was married to long ago, a man she met over a dozen years ago, for God's sake, a gap between that story, as data, and the way she's telling it. She's in no way still in love with the man, that's obvious. Not like A.'s first wife. This woman is brighter, more conscious of herself, than the other. Tell me," he said, peering over the rim of his glass, "is this, this *gap*, what you were so eager for me to hear and speculate on?"

"Well, yes, but there's more." I was alarmed that he'd picked up the distance between the content of her story and its formal elements. It meant that for him to be able to respond intelligently to the tape he would have to know the secrets about Annie Laurie that I had hoped to keep out of this book. Her obesity, already revealed, at least to the reader, was but one of several pieces of information concerning her that I was loath to expose—for several reasons. First, it would make it easier for some readers to identify Annie Laurie's model, D., if they happened to see her on the streets of Manchester or in one of the local department stores, say, or coming out onto the stoop of her building to get her welfare check from the mailman. And if one of my readers happened to be her mailman—oh, almost too cruel to imagine!

When I began this project I was under the impression that I would be able to keep certain secrets, an impression that increasingly looks false. I wanted my story to seem true-to-life, as it were, which meant to me that a great deal of it had to be redundant. Also, I was aware from the start that Hamilton Stark in many ways could be seen as a grotesque, an exaggeration of a merely neurotic human being, and to ground him sufficiently in everyday life (as well as to justify my view of him as something quite superior to a merely neurotic human being formed and contained by his social circumstances), I felt it necessary to surround him with plain fare, pea soup and porridge people. Not exotics. Not three-hundred-pound ex-tap dancers whose sadly diminished lives are spent reminiscing over a few tattered clippings and an unpleasant night spent years ago in a lakeside motel. I had to go this far, however, to reveal this much: there was no way I could keep it out of Rochelle's novel, after all, and certainly there was no way I could legitimize my altering the transcripts of her tapes. And as for revealing Annie's great weight, I could not withhold that fact without misrepresenting Annie's narrative altogether. What if the reader were to infer, as he naturally would, that Annie was still beautiful, still slender and long-legged, that her memories and childhood ambitions were not mocked outright by her present physical condition? That reader would have heard something quite different from what I and C. and the rest of us have heard. But . . . was it sufficient that I reveal only her enormous belly, arms like the legs of a hippo, throat like a tire tube, cheeks and forehead smooth and round as basketballs, hands swollen like sausages? Was that alone sufficient? Well, I hoped my friend C. would tell me. If C. heard nothing odd, nothing that was not mildly moving and interesting, then I would probably not even bother to tell him as much as that the woman he had been listening to was an almost impossibly fat woman. If C. found himself slightly bewildered by the tapes, however, if he detected, as he did, a "gap" between form and content that was not quite comprehensible, then I had decided I would reveal the fact of her obesity. If still he was not relieved and was not permitted comprehension of her testimony, if he was neither moved nor interested by it, however mildly, then . . . well, then I would probably have to reveal more.

"Would it clear things up for you," I said to C., "if you knew that the woman is unusually obese? A frighteningly fat woman?"

C. thought for a moment. "You mean like the fat lady at the circus? Freakish?"

"Yes."

"Well, no. No, not unless *this* makes no sense to you . . . or to me, of course," he said, indicating with his diction and furrowed brow, pursed lips, index fingertips pressed to chin, that he was about to launch a speculation, a ship of theoretical thought. "We are, all of us, so unsure of what is real and not real, that whenever we encounter a person, especially one of the opposite sex, for some reason, who behaves as if the question of what is real and not real were a simple one to answer, and further, when that person then proceeds to proffer an answer that completely denies the simple evidence of our senses, we are, all of us, likely to forsake our sense and cleave to the other. Essentially, that's the role our parents play for us when we are infants and small children. They define what is real and what is not real, and quite often, *usually,* in fact—because as children we don't understand even the basic physical laws of the universe yet, not even the laws of perspective or of Newtonian physics—quite often what our parents tell us is real denies completely what our senses have indicated is in fact the case. We say, for example, 'The moon is bigger than the sun.' It's obvious to us. But our parents contradict us: 'The sun is thousands of times bigger than the moon.' Often they even laugh at us, and they always explain away the contradiction with some piece of nonsense, like, 'It only appears to be smaller because it is so much farther from us than the moon is.' So even though we're presented with a contradiction that is then justified only in terms of nonsense, we nevertheless accept it wholly. At that time, the power of the contradiction seems to depend on two things: the physical size of our parents compared to our own tiny displacement and their self-assurance. 'Ho, ho,' they say, 'the sun is thousands of times bigger than the moon!' We as children have neither size nor self-assurance.

"Now, my friend, here's the point. Evidently certain women, and possibly a number of men as well, when encountering a man of A.'s enormous physical size and self-assurance —which to my mind borders on the psychotic—find themselves reduced back to the level of children when it comes to their ability to separate what's real from what is not real. Your man was apparently able to induce in Annie Laurie the emotional equivalent of a child's relation to its parent, in particular as regards the parent's having been thrust into the position of arbiter of reality, a kind of metaphysical supreme court of no appeal. That's evidently what made our Annie Laurie, I mean D., think she was crazy. Unfortunately for her, she was made dependent upon him, and her dependence increased in geometrically multiplying degrees every time such an encounter as at the motel occurred. I'm curious. Did his denial of her reality in so absolute a fashion take place only after one of his episodes of drunkenness and rage?"

"The fact of her obesity doesn't really alter your comprehension of her words?" I queried hopefully.

"No. Of course not. Don't be silly. But tell me, did A. deny D.'s perceptions of the world only after one of his episodes of drunkenness and rage?"

Somewhat relieved, I answered him. "Apparently what he could not remember simply did not happen, as far as he himself was concerned. According to the tapes, portions you haven't heard, he could not remember *anything* he said or did while drinking, and he could never remember what he had said when he was enraged, which was often, and he could not recall what he

experienced during sex. I'm summarizing, of course, but there's
no point in your listening to seven hours of tape. Most of what's
there is self-centered trivia and small talk between two women
who don't know each other very well. The important facts about
Hamilton Stark, A., though, are, one, he believed passionately
that if he had no memory of a particular act, speech, or emotion,
he did not commit it, speak it, or experience it. It wasn't his. It
was someone else's. And two, he never remembered what he did
when he was drunk, said when he was angry, or experienced
when he was copulating. A third fact of consequence might be
that he was often drunk, frequently enraged, and regularly had
sexual relations with women."

"You speak of him in the past tense," C. said with a smile, "as
if he were dead."

"It's a narrative convenience. Ignore it."

"Fine. But it is odd," C. opined, and again my heart fluttered
with dread, "that the man would seem so deliberate about his
offenses. Do *you* think it was deliberate on his part? Is that why
you want to immortalize this cad? Do you think his awful personality was the expression of a consciously held idea, a philosophical idea, about the world and how to be in it? That is, after all,
what's fascinating about religious leaders, isn't it?" (That's one of
the things I love about C.—he refuses to deal with personalities;
he goes straight and deeply into the abstract, historical heart of
the matter. It's why I referred to him earlier as a thinker.)

"Oh, I don't know, I'm no longer sure," I said sadly. "I feel
like Saint Peter making one of his denials." For the first time
in my celebratory examination of my hero, I was aware of the
strong possibility that he was not only a churl, but a noncon-
scious churl. A true churl. I was suddenly afraid that my man's
life was out of his control, when my original perception of him,
the very reason I had decided to celebrate him in the first place,
for heaven's sake, was that he, of all people, had gained control
of his life without suppressing his life. For an instant I thought

of telling C. about the cataclysmic end to Hamilton's marriage to Annie, and also the final secret. But then, like Peter after the cock crowed and the prophecy had been fulfilled, I felt a sudden surge of belief—possibly welling from my knowledge of how C. would interpret the information and the secret, possibly for an even less defensive reason—but regardless, like Peter, I was once again rocklike in my steadfastness, and I was no longer ready to give up on my man, my Roarer, my Crank, my Colossal and Cosmic Grouch and Bully Boy, my Man Who Hated Everything so as to Love Anything, my Man Obsessed with a Demon so as to Avoid Being Possessed by One—my one last possibility for a self-transcendent ego in a secular age!

OUR CONVERSATION DAWDLED on into the late evening, but we, neither of us, could add anything substantial to what has already been described here, especially since I had by then decided to withhold a quantity of specifically cruel qualities demonstrated by my man, and by eleven o'clock, C. and I decided to have a nightcap and end the evening's conversations with a . . .

CHAPTER 7

Ausable Chasm

THIS IS THE story of how Hamilton Stark almost went to college. Unavoidably, it will be the story of numerous other events as well—other people, other missions, other conflicts resolved and unresolved—but mainly, it will be the story of how Hamilton Stark almost went to college.

Not many people know it, know that he even wanted to go to college in the first place or that he actually came close to doing so in the second. Naturally, you'd never have heard it from the man himself—he carried a number of odd, perhaps even (now that we know what we know) defensive prejudices against people who had gone to college.

"You take your college-educated man," he frequently proposed, "and I'll show you a capitalist dupe. Not that I mind your capitalists. Shit, no. I *admire* capitalists," he said. "It's your *dupes* I can't stand. I'll stomp a capitalist dupe before I'll stomp a communist true believer, and you know what I think of your communist true believers," he reminded me.

Needlessly, it turned out, for I did indeed know what he thought of people he chose to designate "communist true believers." I knew that he despised them. Possibly despised them to the point of violently attacking them, for, though I personally have never actually *seen* him physically assault a so-called communist, nevertheless I have heard stories that, frankly, I'd rather not relate here. Let it suffice to say that Hamilton Stark, in the barrooms of central New Hampshire, was a well-known, militantly forceful anticommunist. Every morning he read the Manchester *Union-Leader*, a newspaper widely regarded as the nation's most rabidly right wing, a newspaper with red-ink headlines such as MUSKIE WEEPS WHEN SHOWN HIS OWN WORDS and HALDEMAN AND EHRLICHMAN QUIT UNDER LEFT-WING PRESSURE. That sort of garbage, which Hamilton, oh, my Hamilton, seemed to choose to believe.

There was a brief period when he and I were still willing to argue politics. I am a moderate Christian Socialist and at the time of this writing have cast my presidential ballot for the following individuals: Adlai Stevenson, John F. Kennedy, Rogers Morton (write-in), and Morris Udall (write-in). Hamilton, though he has voted in every presidential election since 1948, has voted for only one man—Ezra Taft Benson. At least that is what he tells me. And I have no reason to doubt that if Hamilton votes in 1976, he will vote yet again for Mr. Benson, even though by then Benson may well be dead and out of the running altogether. And who knows, Hamilton may write in Benson's name anyway. He used to quote Benson to me until, my ears burning, I begged him to stop. "You want to hear what a *wise* man said? 'It's just too bad, it's really sad, but there has to be a loser.' Now that's *my* idea of presidential wisdom!" Hamilton would exclaim. "I *love* that . . . 'it's really sad,' heh heh heh. You talk about your Kennedy wit. What about the *Benson* wit?"

I suppose in a certain perverse light Benson's remarks could have been seen as witty, but to me they seemed cruel and shallow. The difficulty in arguing politics with Hamilton was that I could never tell for sure whether or not he was being serious. It was never clear that, by taking such an extreme position and then defending it with quotes from someone like Ezra Taft Benson, he wasn't mocking me. Here are some other sentences Hamilton quoted and claimed were uttered by the man: "There's no way a man can live a useful life without stepping on a few people's toes." "It's in the nature of freedom not to know what a man will do with it." And, "The best defense is the one you never have to use." Actually, this last sentence I heard myself as it came from the crinkled lips of the ancient parchment-skinned Ezra Taft Benson. He gave the graduation speech at Ausable Chasm College of Arts and Science, Ausable Chasm, New York, in 1969. I was in the audience because Hamilton Stark was in the audience; he was there, first, because his hero Ezra Taft Benson was giving the graduation speech, and second, because his daughter Rochelle was giving the valedictory speech. Frankly, I think Benson's speech meant more to Hamilton than his daughter's did—Hamilton either fell asleep or pretended to fall asleep during the latter—but for me, that day was momentous. It was the day I first met Rochelle, Hamilton's daughter. Benson could have collapsed from a heart attack during his speech and I wouldn't have noticed or cared. And the only reason that today I can recall the merest scrap of his speech—"The best defense is the one you never have to use"— is because Hamilton quoted it to me a dozen or more times during the drive back to Barnstead.

I had never met Rochelle, though of course I knew of her existence, had listened to Hamilton talk about her for years, and had seen pictures of her, first her grade school photographs, then junior high school, and most recently, four years ago, her high school yearbook photograph. So, in a manner of speaking, I knew what to expect. I had seen her image change, gradually, year by year: from that of a bright-faced, wide-eyed, mischievous three-year-old (taken at nursery school), in which she wore a kelly green daysuit that contrasted beautifully with her then

flame red hair; to the image of a gap-toothed seven-year-old grinning proudly into the camera, her now deeper red hair in braids
tied around her head, her green eyes flashing with innocent
affection; to the image of a sober-faced, sexually serious adolescent, an intense face already full of intellectual grace and sensual
force, with a touch of the bewilderment that such rare presences
in such inordinate quantities must have caused her; and on to the
most recent image, the tall, almost statuesque, even though delicate and slender, young woman, her deep red hair now tumbling
roughly, densely, over her shoulders, her eyes warm, intelligent,
disciplined, her mouth in a slight smile as if about to speak, full
and promising, her neck long, proud, elegant. And of course,
because these photographs were all inscribed to her absent,
never seen nor even directly remembered daddy, I was able to
trace the development of her character over the years by studying the changes in her handwriting and the language she used to
inscribe her photographs. From her nursery school photograph
(precociously, I thought):

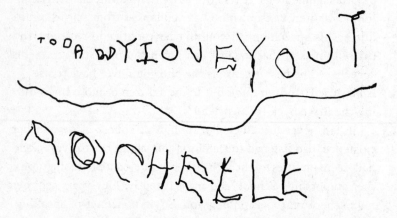

And then, sadly asserting her relation to him, a six-year-old
who could no longer even recall the presence of the man, who
knew him only as a name and burning need:

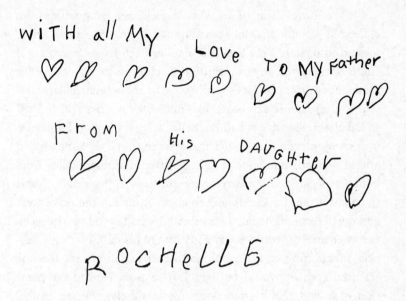

WITH all MY LoVe To MY Father

FRoM HiS DAUGHTer

ROCHeLLE

Here she is at ten, obviously after having read a bit of Shakespeare (one wonders what her mother made of the little girl's reading habits: a fifth-grade child poring over Lear?):

From Cordelia to her Lear, with love and loyalty forever

And here, in her own, mature, self-aware hand, at the age of seventeen, describing the true nature of her relationship with the man while at the same time offering him its positive denial, which was, of course, the nature of her daily experience of the man:

... love, even from such an inhuman distance, for my father. Rochelle

It was never clear to me why Rochelle was graduating from college in Ausable Chasm, a small tourist town, once a mill town, located in upstate New York a few miles from Lake Champlain. I could not imagine anyone sending his child to such a college for academic reasons (unless the child were unable to matriculate anywhere else), and so far as I knew, Rochelle's mother still resided in Lakeland, Florida, as had Rochelle, at least through her senior year of high school. It didn't make sense to me that she should attend a small, nondescript college fifteen hundred miles from home, especially when there were so many right around home to choose from. I asked Hamilton about it during the drive west and north from his home in Barnstead. He had called me the week before to ask if I would accompany him to his daughter's graduation, mentioning, as if it would help me decide to come, that the featured speaker would be Ezra Taft Benson. He did not mention, of course, that his own daughter would give the valedictory speech, or that it would be in Latin (of her own choosing—the first time in the history of Ausable Chasm College of Arts and Science that the graduation speech had been given in Latin!). He told me about that, offhandedly, in Burlington, Vermont.

"Why," I asked him as he drove his car onto the ferry at Burlington and we began the crossing of Lake Champlain, "why does your daughter happen to be graduating from a small, obscure college in upstate New York, when all along I thought she was living in central Florida with her mother and presumably would have gone to either a well-known, prestigious college in the New England states or else one near her home? Did they move north while she was in high school?" I prodded. I suspected there was a story here to be told me by someone.

It was a beautiful, sunshiny, mid-June day stuffed with bright yellows and jade greens. The mountains, the broad valleys, the almost giddy blue of the lake—it made me want to be either a farmer in this valley or a tourist. I could not decide which role would give me more of the place. It's an ancient dilemma: We can never choose between the experience itself and our memory of it.

Hamilton's answer didn't make much sense to me. Not then, anyhow, except to let me know that he didn't wish to discuss it. He simply told me that the girl was obviously trying to get closer to her father now that she was no longer wholly dependent on her mother, but that Ausable Chasm was as close as she dared come to where he happened to be. So I let the subject drop and tried to enjoy the day, the smooth lake, the immense sky above it.

At the campus, a complex of half a dozen small, square, brick buildings that from the outside resembled a munitions plant, we met Hamilton's daughter, Rochelle, he for the first time since she was an infant, me for the first time ever. As we got out of his car—he was driving an air-conditioned, dark brown Cadillac Coupe de Ville at that time, quite luxurious—I asked him if Rochelle knew he was coming. He grunted that in response to her invitation he had sent her a post card so indicating.

"Is this the first time you will have seen her since she was an infant?" I asked him.

Again he grunted his answer, which was yes. I could tell from his grunts that he was somewhat tense and possibly even a bit frightened of the occasion. One could hardly blame him. I'm sure that, although he never mentioned it, her acceptance of him was fully as important to him as his acceptance of her was to Rochelle. What if she saw him and, flooded with memories of her mother's angry descriptions of the man, said to him, "No, I have changed my mind, I don't want you here, I don't want you to come to my graduation!" Would he try to comfort her, try to convince her that he truly wanted to be there, reassuring her with his kind, soft and urgent words? Or would he simply spin on his heels and walk away, back to his car, and go home?

Luckily, when Rochelle came up to him and introduced herself, saying that she recognized him from snapshots her mother had shown her, he smiled graciously—one of the few times, perhaps the only time, I've seen Hamilton Stark smile graciously—

and he took her hand in his and thanked her for inviting him. Rochelle was already six feet tall, a young woman with electrifying beauty, and as she stood there in the parking lot outside the auditorium in her royal blue gown and mortarboard, her hand in her father's hand, her green eyes staring directly, searchingly, into his brown eyes, which were squinting from the bright sunlight, I felt tears running over and down my cheeks.

Though she and I barely spoke, except for the moment when Hamilton introduced us to one another, it seemed to me then, and was later confirmed by her own testimony, that we both felt a deep bond between us. Years later, six, to be exact, I was able to ask her about that first meeting at Ausable Chasm, to ask her how she had perceived me then. We were lying in bed together, drifting languidly from passionate peaks through hazy valleys all the way to the gray light of dawn, the time of night and first intimacy when lovers ask one another how they were seen before, when they were not lovers. It's an ancient form of talk, one of the few reliable ways of finding out how one actually is in the world.

I lit a cigarette for her and, naked except for my socks and garters, walked across the room to the dresser—we were at my home, in my own bedroom, this the conclusion to an evening that had begun as a literary discussion on the subject of the modern novel—and fixed her a drink, cognac and soda. "Tell me," I said to her, returning to the bed with her drink, "on that day we first met, your college graduation day, the day you told me about your father's wanting to go to college and how he had failed to satisfy that desire and how that was all tied up with your desire to attend Ausable Chasm—on that first day, how did you see *me*? How did I seem to you? Can you remember?" I asked, handing her the glass. "You don't mind telling me this, do you?" I asked, suddenly worried that I might have embarrassed her with my question. I still did not know how to anticipate her reactions to anything I might say or do, nor do I even today. She is more intelligent than I, but her thought sequences are linked in patterns and systems that are not as logical as mine, and consequently she is unpredictable to me. Excitingly so, however! I find myself enlarged, enriched, and challenged by her unpredictability. She accomplishes it, expresses it, in our relationship in such a way that it never makes me feel arrogant or humiliated (the two most conventional responses in a male to a female's unpredictability).

"No," she said in her low, early morning voice, "I don't mind." She was tired, I knew, as was I, but we were both nonetheless stimulated by the occasion. It produced in her a kind of languid animation that, whenever it appeared, made me want to make love to her again. But I resisted the impulse and attended her words.

"I saw you immediately as an ally," she told me. "I looked into your face and watched how you watched my father. I knew then that you were probably the only other person on earth who was obsessed with him in a way that corresponded to my own obsession with him." Then she stopped a second. "But you don't want to hear about my *use* for you, do you? I mean, after all, as an ally you were useful to me. You were going to become a way for me both to justify and satisfy my obsession with my father. I did have other perceptions of you, perceptions that had nothing to do with any possible *use* I might make of you. Wouldn't you rather hear those?" she gently asked me.

Indeed. I had an erection to cope with now. The milky light of dawn was entering the room like a thief, stealing the nighttime and our disembodied, anonymous voices, thrusting us back into our particular, constraining bodies, those vessels, those jugs, those ridiculous, pajama-shaped symbols of our true identities. (I believe this, I have always believed it. I have never regarded myself as anything more than my disembodied voice and have never thought of myself as more clearly seen, known, than when I am heard. This, of course, lies behind my need to pursue and understand Hamilton Stark—at least it's what presents me with a rationale for my pursuit—for he is the only human being I have known who did not seem to exist solely through his disembodied voice.)

That day at Ausable Chasm College of Arts and Science, though, I almost gave up on Hamilton. I came closest then to believing that the entire view I held of him was nothing more than an objectification of my own psychological and philosophical needs. For the first time, and, I hope, the last, I seriously entertained the notion that I had, in essence, made up Hamilton Stark, had invented him, had taken an ordinary man with an unusual personality disorder and had structured his numerous symptoms into an image that satisfied a set of secret, shameful needs in me.

My true weaknesses always seem to derive from my sympathies. Hamilton has told me this, and it's true. You will recall my sympathy for his second wife, the one he called "the actress," and how my sympathy for her made me question his very authenticity. Well, the same thing happened, only in a more extreme fashion, that day when I first met Rochelle, discovered that she was giving the valedictory speech, saw her reaching out for her father's love and part of his life, and saw him yank both back. I was horrified. This was going too far, I thought. Surely, cruelty has its metaphysical use and meaning, but there must be a point where it is simply and purely cruelty and has no use or meaning except for the perpetrator.

"I'm glad you came," she said to him in a voice that, to me, seemed remarkably calm.

He squinted into the sun and, expressionless, said that he had come to hear Ezra Taft Benson speak, a privilege that heretofore he had been denied.

Rochelle asked him if he understood Latin.

He shook his head no and asked, surprised, if Benson were going to speak in Latin.

"No, not that I know of," she said, smiling easily. "But *I* am. Would you like a translation of my speech?" she asked him coyly. "I've copied it out for you."

Again he shook his head no.

The half-hour that followed was extremely strained. The three of us strolled around the parking lot, Hamilton in the middle, Rochelle on one side, and me on the other. We looked at the automobiles, commented on the makes and the number plates, and asked one another questions that could not be answered. At least not by any of us.

ROCHELLE: "Are you happy to know that your daughter is graduating from college?"

HAMILTON: "Seems like a good idea."

ME: "What are your plans, now that you're graduating from college?"

ROCHELLE: "Everything depends on one thing."

ME: "And what is that?"

ROCHELLE: "I'm not sure yet, and I can't tell what I *think* it is."

HAMILTON: "What kind of a car is that, the little convertible sports job with the raggedy roof?"

ROCHELLE AND ME: "I don't know. Custom made, maybe?"

HAMILTON: "Don't you hate custom-made cars?"

ROCHELLE: "I don't know. I never thought about it."

ME: "Why?"

HAMILTON: "Who knows? Maybe I'm just trying to make conversation."

ME: "Oh."

ROCHELLE: "Have you been friends with my father for a long time?"

ME: "Relative to what?"

HAMILTON: "Yeah, relative to what?"

ROCHELLE: "I don't know. Forget it. I was just trying to make conversation."

ME: "Oh."

HAMILTON: "Where are we supposed to sit?"

ROCHELLE: "I don't know. Anywhere in the auditorium, I guess. Wherever you want to sit."

HAMILTON: "All right if we go and sit now?"

ROCHELLE: "If that's what you want."

HAMILTON: "That's what we want. Right?"

ME: "I guess so, you're the host today. Or are *you* the host, Rochelle? I mean the hostess."

ROCHELLE: "I'll show you where the auditorium is. Then I'll have to leave you and join my classmates for the march. I'll be sitting on the platform."

HAMILTON: "With Benson?"

ROCHELLE: "I don't know. I presume so."

ME: "Well, should we wish you luck, Rochelle? Or are you the overconfident type?"

ROCHELLE: "Who knows? Relative to what, eh?"

ME (LAUGHING): "Right."

HAMILTON: "Let's go find a seat."

ME: "Okay."

ROCHELLE: "The auditorium's right through those doors, straight ahead and to the right. Think you can find it all right?"

HAMILTON: "Sound simple enough."

ME: "No problem. Right, Hamilton?"

HAMILTON: "No problem. Right, Rochelle?"

ROCHELLE: "No problem. Right?"

ME (LAUGHING AGAIN): "Are you making fun of me?"

ROCHELLE: "I don't know. See you after the speeches."

I REALIZE THAT I'm not explaining many things that the reader doubtless would like explained. Please believe me, I'm not leaving these questions unanswered merely because I have a perverse love of mystery. Quite the opposite; in fact, I despise mystery. Mystery is the last resort of the hysteric. It's a frantic, final attempt to organize chaos, or rather, to give the *appearance* of having organized chaos. None of that for me. It's too easy and too cheap a way out for a man who feels, as I do, morally compelled to abide with chaos all the way to the end, until either he has succeeded in answering all the questions at hand, unraveling all the tangles, explaining all the puzzles, solving all the riddles, or else he has succumbed to the snarl of chaos altogether. For such a man, for me, the middle, where "mystery" lies, is definitely excluded. I am an *emotional* man, yes, but I am *not* a romantic man. And though I may never ascend quite to those airy levels of pure reason where, for example, my friend C. strolls about so comfortably, at least I am clear about the nature of my goal and can measure with accuracy the distance I remain from it. This particular clarity and the measuring that results therefrom comprise, for me, the only possibilities for a moral life. All else is either fantasy or determinism.

For this reason, that day at Ausable Chasm I persisted in try-ing to find out why Rochelle was graduating from college here in the North. Ordinarily, if Hamilton indicated that he didn't wish to discuss a subject, I deferred to him and changed the subject, never bringing it up again unless and until he indicated readiness. But my fascination with Rochelle, then, at the actual sight of her, drove me to push in ways I would have otherwise found rude, if not downright boorish, in myself as well as in anyone else.

"What's the story?" I asked him. "What's the explanation? How come?"

All of which he answered with a shrug, a downturned mouth with pouting lower lip, like a carp's, a helpless flop of open hands at his sides. And after a while it occurred to me that he didn't know the answer either, that it was likely, when he had learned that his daughter was graduating from Ausable Chasm College of Arts and Science, that he had been as surprised and puzzled as I.

I therefore ceased asking the man about it and promised myself to ask Rochelle instead. Unfortunately, whenever I was with her, I became so addled by her physical and spiritual presence that I forgot my promise altogether, and now, six years after making that promise, I still have not kept it, and thus I do not know why Rochelle graduated from an obscure college in upstate New York rather than one in central Florida. This distresses me. For now it is too late to keep that promise. Rochelle is gone from me except in memory and imagination. I will never know the answer to my question, and the reader will never know either.

To RETURN: I handed Rochelle her drink and joined her in the bed. (This happens to be the imaginary point from which I can most easily recall the events of the day I spent in Ausable Chasm.) We were talking about the day we first met each other and how we had perceived each other then. She said that she had thought of me as a small man, short and slight, but later, after having seen me numerous times alone, realized that it was because I had been in the company of her father that first time and thus, when compared to his great height and overall bulk, had appeared much smaller than, in fact, I actually was. She was pleased, she told me, when she discovered that I was the same height as she and that, while my musculature was not exactly overdeveloped, 1 was nevertheless wiry and in quite good shape for a man my age.

Waving her compliments away, I gently asked her if she had seen her father and me from the speakers' platform while she had been giving her speech. I wanted to know if she had seen my attentiveness. I confess it. Hurt somewhat by the comparison between her father's and my physical size, I wished to have her compare my rapt attention with her father's cruel inattention. So I risked causing pain. I risked the chance that, by invoking the image of her father sitting in the audience and apparently sleeping through her speech, with me perched on my chair, rapt and admiring next to him, she would feel again the pain that moment must have caused her.

"You were an angel," she said, smiling into my face. She had cut through my ruse in one stroke, had comforted me without mocking me and at the same time had spared herself the pain of the memory. What a woman! Then, with laughter, she began to talk about Ezra Taft Benson's speech. "Remember it?" she asked me. "That funny little old man with all that crazy fervor?"

Actually, I recalled nothing of Benson's speech, except for the one line that Hamilton had continually quoted to me all the way back home in the car. I promptly related it to her: "The best defense is the one you never have to use," I said.

She giggled, then reminded me that when Benson had uttered those words Hamilton had broken into applause, mortifying me, perhaps astonishing Benson, and inducing a few scattered, sheeplike souls in the audience to join him. I had completely forgotten that awful moment and for a few seconds relived my embarrassment, which had been quite painful. I wasn't so much embarrassed because I was sitting next to a person who seemed to be reacting to a banality with inappropriate enthusiasm, as I was embarrassed because that man happened to be my hero. I did not point this out to Rochelle. I didn't have to. After all, he was her hero too.

I may not have listed it among my earlier encomiums, but Rochelle's memory is prodigious, photographic. Mine, of course, is ordinary. But she could recall details, entire conversations, books, films, any text at all, things and events in their entirety that I could but barely invent. Catalogues of things passed by on an afternoon's drive in the country, newspaper articles and editorials verbatim, entire chapters from the Bible, the first paragraphs from novels she had read years ago, news accounts from radio and television that she'd listened to but moments before—it was unnerving, slightly otherworldly, and at all times not quite believable. I could never rid myself of my initial response to one of her recitations, which was that there must be a trick to it, a crib, a way of faking it somehow. At any rate, on this morning, when she noticed that I had preferred being amused by the Benson speech itself to being embarrassed by the associated image of

Hamilton's suddenly applauding a remark of, well, questionable morality, she quickly and kindly proceeded to recall for me the introduction given Benson by the president of the college, a Mr. Carlisle Bargeron.

"Remember," she said, "in President Bargeron's introduction, this bit of deathless prose: '*Ezra Taft Benson was conditioned early in life for the political buffeting that was to come. In fact, he experienced mob abuse early in his life.*' " Rochelle giggled and put on a pompous expression that mocked President Bargeron and continued. " '*Secretary Benson is not a ministerial man in appearance.*' " She was recalling his words effortlessly; they came back to me as she spoke them. Surely she was making them up; but if she were, how could I recognize them as she spoke? " '*He could be taken for a well-groomed businessman, over six feet tall and weighing two hundred pounds. He greets you with a pleasant smile and has an easy laugh.*' " She smiled at me. "He must have written that speech from old publicity handouts from the Eisenhower administration. Because there was old Benson, sitting right next to Mr. Bargeron in a folding chair, tiny, shriveled, scowling like a Puritan minister!" She laughed. "Do you remember the crescendo of the introduction?"

I shook my head no. Good God, until she had started quoting it, I had forgotten that there had even been an introduction in the first place.

" '*Secretary Benson stands at the crossroads, seeking in turn the tide!*' " Then, wrapping her long arms across the front of her body, she broke into goodhearted laughter. Utterly without malice, her laughter seemed to enfold the very object of her mockery, President Bargeron, and even Benson himself in a hug of compassionate understanding. For a second I felt that her laughter included as its object Hamilton too, and even me. Swinging her long, tanned legs over the edge of the bed, she got up and, naked, unself-consciously crossed the room to the dresser and made herself another drink.

I must tell you that I was happier at that moment than I could remember ever having been before.

When she returned to the bed, she went on quoting, this time in a wheezy, high-pitched voice designed to affect the quality and tone of Ezra Taft Benson's aged voice. " *'We need,'* " she said sternly, " *'as we need no other thing, a nationwide repentance of our sins! In our rush for the material things, we have, indeed, forgotten to serve the God of this land. We must look beyond the dollar sign! Our greatness has been built on spiritual values, and if we are to survive we must find again what we once had and now have lost. I am speaking of the inner strength that comes from obedience to divine law!'* "

Taking a sip from her drink. Offering me a sip. Then, amazingly, going on. " *'At least twenty great civilizations have disappeared! The pattern is shockingly similar. All, before their collapse, showed a decline in spiritual values, in moral stamina, and in the freedom and responsibility of their citizens. They showed such symptoms as excessive taxation, as bloated bureaucracy, as governmental paternalism, and in general a rather elaborate set of controls and regulations affecting prices, wages, production, and consumption.'* ' "

She paused again, and then she began a recitation that to me was indeed beyond belief (I could not believe that she had merely heard the speech once; she had to have read a copy at some point), for she was now quoting Benson as he quoted yet another speaker, and she was quoting both exactly (as far as I knew): " *'After reviewing the decline and fall of these great empires and appraising the lessons taught, the historian Glover of Oxford University makes this cryptic comment: "It is better for the development of character and contentment to do certain things badly yourself than to have them done better for you by someone else."'* ' "

Her voice, ordinarily low for a woman and tender, had tightened in her mimicry and had risen and, to be sure, had harshened somewhat. I was struck dumb by her ability not only to remember the man's exact words but also to mimic his voice and mannerisms. What a woman! I said to myself.

"And remember how he ended his speech?" she reminded me.

I had not remembered at all, of course, until she began to quote it, and then as she spoke there returned to me in a rush a second embarrassing image, the image of Hamilton's second outburst, which, fortunately, had not been perceived by Rochelle. It came as Benson was reaching the rhetorical peak of his message. The little man, visibly trembling with the emotion of his message to these young graduates, had cried out to them, "*I love this nation! It is my firm belief that the God of Heaven raised up the founding fathers and inspired them to establish the Constitution of this land! This was ingrained in me as a youngster by my father and mother and by my church! It is part of my religious faith! To me, this is not just another nation! It is a great and glorious society with a divine mission to perform for liberty-loving people everywhere!*" Here he hesitated a moment to wipe the spittle from his lips with his handkerchief. Then, continuing with fervor, he shouted, "*Freedom is a God-given, eternal principle vouchsafed to us under the Constitution! It must be continually guarded as something as precious as life itself! It is doubtful if any man can be politically free who depends upon the state for sustenance! A completely planned and subsidized economy weakens initiative, discourages industry, destroys character and demoralizes the people!*" At precisely this moment as Benson stepped away from the microphone, Hamilton had leaped to his feet and, brandishing one huge fist like a club, had bellowed, "Live free or die!" It was the New Hampshire state motto!

The rest of the audience had begun to applaud and a few individuals had risen to their feet, to prove their patriotism, perhaps, but possibly because of their genuine enthusiasm for the secretary's words, and thus, luckily, Hamilton's cry was lost on most of the people in the auditorium. Not on me, however, nor on the dozen or so people seated near us. And not on Ezra

Taft Benson, either. The old man, by a quirk, happened to have been looking straight at Hamilton as he finished his speech, so when Hamilton leaped to his feet and bellowed the New Hampshire motto, Benson must have thought an enormous fanatic, an outsized Puerto Rican or some kind of Balkan anarchist madman, was about to attempt a suicidal assassination. The old fellow went white and staggered backward, clutching at his chest, clawed at it, and fell to the floor, where he began kicking his feet like a child having a tantrum.

In a second Mr. Bargeron, Rochelle and the minister who had offered the prayer at the beginning of the ceremonies had reached Benson and had pulled him back to his feet. Apparently they had not seen the cause of his fall and assumed he had tripped over a microphone wire because they were, all three, apologetic and concerned mostly that he might have hurt himself. The secretary, who by this time had realized he was not to be assassinated, smiled painfully and limped from the stage, disappearing quickly behind the curtain, ashen-faced, shaken, mumbling to himself.

Rochelle and I must have been remembering the same image—old Benson staggering backward, grabbing at his chest, falling over and kicking his feet on the floor, then being helped off the stage—for suddenly she looked at me in the gray, melancholy light and in a soft voice asked, "What *really* happened? What made that old man act like that . . . so *terrified* . . . as if someone were going to kill him? Did something happen that I, that I didn't see? Did my *father* do anything?"

I knew that she wanted me to say no, to keep it a puzzle, but I couldn't lie to her any more than I could lie to myself. So I told her, told her how her father had stood up fiercely with his enormous fist raised and had cried out the New Hampshire state motto, which, as she could tell immediately, was indeed threatening. To a timid listener it could sound like, "Live free or I'll kill you!"

"Did he do that because he was carried away with enthusiasm for Benson's speech?" Her voice was shaky, frightened, pleading.

"Oh, God, I don't know. I just don't know anymore. But he has a way," I explained, "as you probably know all too well, of praising a thing by condemning it and of condemning a thing by praising it. He has a way of making a positive statement from a double negative, and a negative statement from a double positive. The first skill is not rare, but the second is. You aren't a native New Englander, as I am and as your father is, so you're probably not as aware as I of the degree to which the skill operates in the culture as a means for self-expression. Practically any old Yankee farmer will let you know how cruel and relentless his winter has been, not by condemning it, but by smiling and perversely praising the facts that his thermometer has frozen, that his cattle and pigs all froze to death in January, that there was still ice on the lakes in mid-June. It's almost an ironic point of view, an extremely highly developed form of sarcasm that they're not even aware they possess. The late Latin poets possessed it, consciously, of course, and certain eighteenth-century English authors owned it also, again quite consciously. But rarely, if ever, has it been characteristic of an entire people. Hamilton, your father, seems to have developed it to an extremely high degree, mainly because at some early age he must have become conscious of it and realized that, if he pushed it to a still more extreme point, he could gain a much wider range of reference for it, could use it to criticize matters more complex than last winter's awful weather. At least that's my theory, Rochelle. And because I love the man, I choose to believe it. So I guess it's more than a theory, it's also a rationalization. I wish it were more than a rationalization, though. I wish it were a description."

"I know," she said softly, in almost a whisper. "If it *were* a description, you could believe that he despised Ezra Taft Benson, had utterly rejected him, and yet had managed at the same time to avoid subscribing to your and my liberal notions. Wouldn't that be a profound and mature politics?" she said in a voice filled with wonder. "To be free to criticize and even to despise the old man's reactionary position without, as a result, having to endorse any other. To offer yourself essentially as a *critique*, to be able to trust yourself that much! Why, you'd have to be a political genius to accomplish it!" she exclaimed. "Or some kind of Kierkegaardian ironist," she added thoughtfully.

"That's precisely what keeps me from deserting your father's side at moments like that, like the time he shouted the state motto at Benson or when he fell asleep during your valedictory speech or mocked me for voting for people like Morris Udall . . . or all the other things he's done that, on the surface, seemed mindless, cruel or intolerant." Our enthusiasm for the man was growing again. Our fear and mistrust were on the wane. With bright eyes and rapid words we cheered each other on, and before long we were both loving and admiring him without qualification again.

It was more than merely possible that he had intended all this, had even foreseen it, and that it was his method of teaching us to see and understand the world more independently and with steadily increasing clarity. He was in many ways like a Sufi master or a wizened old peyote-chewing Indian shaman or a Zen Buddhist teacher who by indirection points direction out. But we are so naïve and ill-formed that, in our search for wisdom, we run around expecting to find it only in stereotypical figures— like desert-browned Sufis or raucous old Indian grandfathers or crisp Buddhist monks—never realizing that it is more in the nature of true wisdom that, for us, wisdom reside in the familiar form of a New Hampshire pipefitter who can't seem to get along with people.

Reaching over, I took her by her smooth shoulders, pulled her to me, and felt her cool breasts press against my chest. "Oh, Rochelle!" I cried. "We must be strong! And I do believe that we're stronger together than we are alone! Your father is probably the greatest man either of us will ever have the good luck to meet in our lifetimes. Alone we weaken, we forget how difficult and tangled is the path to true wisdom. But together we are strengthened, toughened, encouraged to push through the intellectual and emotional tangles and our own most private fears and insecurities and conditionings to the end, where we, too, can offer ourselves as critiques, as double positives, and finally, in the largest sense, as human beings!"

Needless to say, I was hovering somewhere between ecstasy and hysteria when suddenly, and thankfully, Rochelle taught me the utter ridiculousness of my feelings, showed me how far I still had to go before I could claim to possess a shred of the cloth Hamilton wore. She showed me also how much further along that path she had gone than I, showed me that while I might have glimpsed the master's garment, she had actually touched it.

"I don't think you understand the nature of religious experience," she said evenly. "I'm sorry, but when a person reaches the point where he or she can claim to know what you are now claiming to know, he or she should be free to enact it. If he or she can't, if he or she still needs help, then he or she really cannot say that he or she has the requisite knowledge. I'm sorry, but you're much closer to the path when you're greedily interrogating me about my father, when you're splicing together your own personal and acquired knowledge of him, making of the man's life a text, if you will, that will guide you straightway into the invention of your own life." Gently, she pulled away from me and took a last sip from her glass. Then she smiled. "If you'll fix me another drink, I'll tell you how my father almost went to college."

"What?" I was stupefied by the sequence—first a collusion, then a collision, and now a collusion again.

"Sure," she said brightly. "I'll tell you everything I know about him. And it's quite a lot. I've done four years of research on his life so far, for that 'novel' of mine. You know, *The Plumber's Apprentice*. I don't feel possessive about that material anymore. I'm

no more a professional novelist than *you* are, for heaven's sake!"
she laughed, and I had to laugh with her. "Go ahead, honey, fix
me another drink and I'll tell you all about how my daddy almost
went to college." She smiled and spoke with a southern accent
that, as I rushed across the bedroom to the dresser where I had
placed the cognac, soda and ice, nearly made me swoon.

"After all, honey," she drawled from the bed, "you told me
something this mo'ning I didn't know about before, that stuff
about how Daddy stood up and shouted the state motto and all?
I oughta do the same thing for you now, shouldn't I?" And she
winked at me. *Winked!* What a woman!

I was certainly very confused. How, *how* had I lost control of
the situation like this?

Then I remembered: it was the ecstasy and the hysteria—or
rather, it was my having reached the point halfway between the
two. After that, everything had gone haywire for me. Rochelle had
taken complete control of the conversation, and of me, until there
I was fetching her a drink in exchange for a tale I hadn't even
particularly wanted to hear anymore, and to make matters worse,
I was doing it in a swoon. How would I ever be able to remember
the tale, let alone determine its importance to my own tale? Oh,
reader, dear reader, remember this, and let it be an example to you.
In the book of your life, never permit yourself to invent a woman
or a man who is capable of bewildering you while he or she seduces
you. You will lose the thread of your argument, you will find your
story line impossibly tangled, your plot utterly overthrown, and
your faith in your powers of observation and analysis sliced to
limp ribbons of insecurity. Call it love, call it whatever you will,
but know the risk. If you must, as I must, think of your life as a
novel and of the creatures therein as "characters," then unless you
keep yourself from falling in love with one of those creatures, you
will have to give up the idea of control. You will have to become
not an inspired author, but one who is simply not in control of his
own novel. It happens, it happens frequently.

"I'm sorry," I said, my voice hushed with contrition. "You're right, you're quite right, of course." I handed her drink to her, and holding on to my own as if it were a kitten, I sat down next to her on the bed. "Please. Please tell me how Hamilton, how your father almost went to college. It's a chapter in his life I know nothing about. I'd even forgotten it existed, that you had mentioned its existence that day after your graduation ceremonies, until you mentioned it again tonight, I mean this morning."

"Yes, this morning. It's late," she yawned, stretching her long white arms in the milky light, and once again I found myself having to deal with my own tumescence.

"Tired?" I asked.

"Yes," she answered. "But still, I want you to hear this. It might help you to know important things about him. It's a short story, I can tell it to you in a few minutes, and tomorrow, later today, I mean, I'll let you have the chapter from my novel that describes the adventure. As a matter of fact," she went on, "I've been thinking of turning the entire manuscript, even my notes and tapes, over to you, to let you use in any way that pleases you." She yawned again, as if with disinterest in my response.

I was shocked. "*What?* What do you *mean?*" Her novel, the obsession-driven activity of her last four years? Give it up, just like that?

"Yes. I've made a decision. I think it's a waste of my time to be writing a novel about the man—I mean that kind of self-consciousness, that kind of objectification. It all seems to run counter to what I'm to learn from the man. From what I am learning. It's hard to describe. *You* write the novel. If you can. I can't. And even if I could, I'd never bring myself to *publish* it," she added with a wry smile.

I was twice shocked. She sat there, looking straight ahead into space, apparently close to emotionless, as if she had once witnessed a glory or a horror that I hadn't, announcing as she was to me in a passionless voice that she was canceling out the work of four years of her young life, hard, diligent work, boring research, arduous travel, careful visioning and revisioning, until she had nearly perfected a style and had mastered the content. I, her most confirmed admirer, could not believe that she would cancel this enterprise, that she, simply and practically without feelings, would turn the manuscript over to me for my grimy use. (Relatively speaking, of course. I can't pretend to be *that* self-deprecating.)

"Listen," I said to her, "I *love* your novel!"

"*Do* you?"

"Yes!" I exclaimed. "It's so . . . so . . . *realistic!*"

She said, "Well, you've still got a lot to learn, I'm afraid. But *I* can't teach you. I'm still an initiate myself, you know. Here, here's the story," she began, and leaning back against the pillows, as the new day's sunlight spilled into the room for the first time, she took a sip from her drink and told me the story of how Hamilton Stark almost went to college.

SHE WAS RIGHT. It wasn't much more than a short story (she told it at one sitting), and, to fully understand the event, its subtler aspects, I did need the manuscript, which she delivered to me late that same afternoon. It was entitled "Fighting It, Giving Up," Chapter Four, from *The Plumber's Apprentice*. I've included it here, rather than try to summarize it or provide my own version, for the usual reasons: her handling of the material seems so much superior to what I could accomplish that only an insensitive egoist would proffer his own version instead. The name changes are the same as indicated earlier, when other portions of Rochelle's novel were quoted. There is, however, one additional character here, the youth called Feeney, and though he appeared briefly in a chapter quoted in my Chapter Four, Addendum C, Rochelle's Chapter Eight, "Return and Depart," at that time I said that no one corresponded to Feeney in Hamilton's, A's, life. It now appears that I was wrong. Rochelle, through diligent, wily research, has uncovered the prototype for Feeney, a man named F., who now works as a machine operator in a tannery in Penacook. He and A. rarely see each other these days, and then only by accident.

Chapter 4
FIGHTING IT, GIVING UP

It positively amazed Alvin that he could get in his car and drive it over the hills for four hours roughly north and west, stop the car, get out, walk into a bar, order a drink, and be served legally. Well, not quite legally, even here in New York State, because he was only seventeen, but even so, it was still enough to astound him when he and Feeney strode through the door of the Valley Café in Ausable Chasm, New York, and each ordered a Seven-and-Seven, that the bartender merely served them and took their money.

It was a Friday in November, Alvin's senior year in high school. He was a football star and a good student, "especially in math." Everyone said so. He had driven to Ausable Chasm this day for an interview with the dean of admissions of the little-known engineering institute located at the edge of the small town. Feeney had gone along to keep him company and "for laughs," he'd said, and while Alvin was being interviewed, he'd taken the car and had driven around the town looking for a bar that he thought, from its appearance, would serve them without asking for IDs. "I got a sixth sense for these things," he had explained as he drove off in Alvin's Ford.

It was a raw, rainy day, blustery and dark, and Alvin wore only a lightweight cloth raincoat over his charcoal gray flannel suit, and he carried no umbrella, so by the time he had located and entered the brick, armorylike administration building, his clothes, hair and shoes were soaked through. Miserably uncomfortable and smelling like a wet, long-haired animal, he sat through a painful fifteen-minute interview with a blond crew-cut young man who never once smiled as he asked Alvin questions about the size of Pittsfield High School, the percentage of the graduating seniors who went on to college, and the range of courses offered there. "We've never had an applicant from your school before," the somber young man explained.

"Oh, I see," Alvin said.

A few minutes later, when, in answer to the dean's inquiry as to the possibility of Pittsfield's football team winning the state championship, Alvin had laughed and said, "Never!" it was the dean who said, "Oh, I see."

It had gone on like that, the two of them saying soberly, "Oh, I see," perhaps half a dozen times each, ending with Alvin's pointing out that he would need a scholarship, a full scholarship, to go to college, because his parents were unable to help him financially. "My father's a plumber," he added helpfully.

The dean had said, "Oh, I see," one more time and then, "Yes," and then, "Well, yes," and had ushered him back to the outer office, where they shook hands and grimly parted.

By the time Alvin reached the coffee shop near the campus where he'd arranged to meet Feeney, he was again soaking wet and he was growling. He was still growling when he sat down across from Feeney in the plastic-seated booth, and Feeney laughed.

"Let's get the hell outa here," Alvin said. "I gotta get *plowed!*"

Feeney went on laughing. He always laughed when Alvin started growling. That Alvin Stock, what a crazy guy! He gets pissed at something, he starts growling like some kinda mad dog or something. Really growling, and loud. Anybody can hear it. Like he was gonna tear somebody up with his teeth. What a crazy guy!

The growl was new—or rather, it had only recently been noticed by others. Alvin himself was still not quite aware of it,

not even when it was timidly pointed out to him. He wasn't sure
what people heard when they laughed and said, "Hey, man,
calm down! You're *growling,* for chrissake!" But he knew what
he felt—a knot, at first tightening in his chest, high up, and
then slowly loosening as it rose in his throat and finally, between
clenched teeth, squirted from his mouth. For him, the sound was
merely that of his breath exhaling under pressure from below,
scraping against resistance from above, the physiological opposite of a sigh.

But what others heard was a frighteningly literal growl.
For them it began with a deep rumbling from Alvin's chest that
thinned, tightened, and rose in pitch as it moved up his throat.
Then, finally, after resonating in his mouth, the noise would flow
like a metal ribbon between his teeth, usually driving anyone
near him back a step or two in surprise and, for a second, fear.
Then, when it was apparent that Alvin was not conscious of his
noise, came the nervous laughter, the light mockery. In turn,
his response was usually one of irritation and slight embarrassment—irritation that he was being distracted from expressing
his anger, embarrassment that he was not fully aware of how he
was being perceived. And too, from some corner of his mind,
embarrassment that he was angry at all and had been found out,
betrayed, almost, by a noise his body seemed to make involun-
tarily.

THE VALLEY CAFÉ was a neighborhood tavern located in a row of
wood tenements south of the center of Ausable Chasm at the edge
of the Ausable Chasm River, which, a few miles downstream,
emptied into Lake Champlain. It was a small place, a storefront,
actually, with a dark bar along one side of the room and a dozen
or so red plastic-seated booths along the other. At the back
were three doors, one leading from behind the bar to the small
kitchen, the second leading to a pair of filthy, unventilated rest-
rooms, the third, marked by an Exit sign, leading to an alley. At

the front there were two large plate glass windows painted dark green from the low sills to eye level, with a small red neon sign in each pane that rapidly blinked VALLEY CAFÉ.

The place was quiet, dimly lit, almost empty. In its own toughly cynical way, the bar was friendly. It worked hard at seeming to be no more than what it was, a neighborhood bar. Anything that was deliberately atmospheric, as if to attract strangers, would not have made sense, no more to the patrons than to the owners. A juke box was allowed, was not thought pretentious or, worse, naïve, but only if the songs were the type of melancholy love songs that celebrated stoical loss, songs ten years out of date sung by middle-aged crooners who'd broken in with the big bands in the thirties and forties.

Alvin and Feeney walked up to the bar and ordered Seven-and-Sevens from the beefy, T-shirted bartender. He was a chin-less, balding man in his fifties, his thick arms covered with faded red and blue tattoos. His T-shirt was stretched tightly across a belly that clung to the front of him like a tortoise shell, below which he had tied a white apron like a bib. He served the boys quickly and went back to his post at the front of the bar, where he had spread his newspaper. Planting both elbows on the counter, his chin resting against his knuckles, he resumed reading, slowly moving his lips as he read.

In a few seconds, having grown accustomed to the semidarkness of the room, the boys took a look around them to see where, in fact, they were and who was there with them. At the far end of the bar, in a bank of shadows, hunched a man in his late sixties, a serious afternoon drinker with a shot of blond whiskey and a glass of flat draft beer arranged precisely in front of him. In one of the booths, with his back to the bar, a young man in khaki work clothes was arguing in a hissing voice with a tubby, bleached-blond, middle-aged woman who was barely listening, but now and then making a low-voiced comment that would set the young man off and hissing again. He chain-smoked from a pack of Camels in front of him, and she affectionately studied her pink-painted fingernails. For a minute Alvin wondered why the young man was haranguing her. Were they married to each other? Lovers? Brother and sister? He gulped down the last of his drink and called for another.

Maybe she was a prostitute and he was her pimp. Naw, impossible. The guy's wearing work clothes. Besides, she's too old and fat to be a prostitute. What's it like, he wondered, to fuck a woman that old and that fat?

She was looking across at him then, not quite staring, but openly, undeniably, looking at him. Alvin returned her gaze. Feeney, staring down into his glass, went on chattering, something about California, L.A., swimming year-round, beautiful cars, a '49 Olds 88 . . . Alvin noticed that the woman's face was not unattractive. She had bright, dark, heavily made-up eyes that were wide apart and low on her face, and a full mouth that she had painted pink, to match her fingernails. Her hair was short and curly, fluffy almost. The color of vanilla ice cream, Alvin thought. She was wearing a maroon short-sleeved sweater and a navy blue wool skirt, both of which clung tightly to her bulky, round torso. Her arms and breasts, though exceptionally large, looked firm to Alvin. Maybe she's not really that old, he thought. In her late thirties, maybe. And the guy is her brother-in-law and he's complaining about something that his wife, her sister, did to him, and she really doesn't give much of a shit because she doesn't like the guy much in the first place and he's constantly whining in the second place. And anyhow, what she's really interested in is *me*. Finishing off his drink, he ordered another.

Feeney ordered another too. "Gimme a coupla Slim Jims, will ya?" he said to the bartender.

Other people, mostly men, came into the bar, drank awhile, and left. It grew dark outside, and the bartender turned on a set of rose-shaded lights. Alvin played the juke box, half a dozen

Frank Sinatra songs, and while the records played, Alvin, back at the bar, snapped his fingers to the beat. He drank, ordered again, and drank again.

Feeney started talking about the drive home, four hours, and Alvin said, "Yeah, yeah, sure. Later, later," and because it was Alvin's car, Feeney forgot about it. What the hell, he could always sleep in the back and let Alvin worry about the driving. He was only along for the laughs, he explained—but Alvin didn't seem to hear him.

A pair of sailors, quite cheerfully drunk, wandered into the place and took stools next to Alvin and continued their drinking. The young man with the woman in the booth started to get up to leave, but as he rose from his seat, he saw that the woman was looking intently at Alvin, who was leaning off his stool in her direction, like a tower about to fall, and the young man quickly sat down again.

One of the sailors, a thin, red-headed boy with freckles swarming across his face, elbowed Alvin in the side and, grinning good-naturedly, said to him, "You got somethin' goin' with Blondie over there, ain't you?"

Slowly Alvin turned and looked at the sailor. All he could see was the red-headed boy's huge grin, a tooth-filled half-moon, and to Alvin at that moment the sailor's great, good-hearted grin was the silliest, weakest thing he'd ever seen, so he said, "Whyn't you mind your own fuckin' business?" and watched with pleasure the collapse of the grin.

"Fuck you," the sailor quietly offered, and he turned away.

Satisfied, Alvin resumed watching the woman in the booth, who had now placed herself so that Alvin could see her legs, crossed, halfway up her thighs.

By this time Feeney, too, had realized that Alvin's attention was focused solely on one person, and also that the person's attention seemed to be focused on Alvin as well. "Go easy, Al," he warned. "We're a long ways from home, y'know."

Alvin brushed his friend's warning aside with a crooked smile, and the next thing he knew he was standing beside the booth, staring down at the blond woman. "Buy you a drink?" he asked, flashing the same crooked smile he had given Feeney a moment before.

The woman looked up at him, her face wide open and pleased, but before she could answer, the man seated opposite her snarled, "Screw, kid. Get fuckin' *lost,* will ya?"

In a dead voice Alvin said, "I didn't offer to buy *you* a drink." And for the first time he saw that the man was actually quite a bit older than he'd thought, was in fact the same age as the woman, probably in his late thirties. Up close, Alvin could see that the man was large, and muscular too, red-faced from working out-side, with large tanned hands crossed with pencil-thick veins.

The man jammed an unlit cigarette between his thin lips, and with one motion he snapped open his lighter and lit the ciga-rette while with his free hand he pointed first his index finger at Alvin's chest and then a hooked thumb at the barstool Alvin had just left. Inhaling deeply, blowing the smoke from flared nostrils, the man repeated his instructions: "Screw, kid. The lady's with me. Now get fuckin' *lost,* will ya!"

The woman smiled helplessly up at Alvin and remained silent.

Alvin looked coldly into the man's pale blue eyes. "Shut up," he said evenly. "I'm talkin' to her, not you."

"Lissen, honey, maybe some other time, okay?" the woman said to him in a husky voice. She was still smiling up at him.

"I'm from outa town, I'm leavin' tonight, so whyn't you let someone who's just passin' through buy you a drink? Whaddaya drinkin', anyhow?" Alvin peered down into her glass, as if peer-ing down a well.

"Gin and tonic."

"Gin and tonic!" Alvin called to the bartender. "An' another Seven-an'-Seven!" He started to sit down next to the woman, who quickly slid over to make room, when suddenly the man reached across and clamped onto Alvin's wrist, stopping him.

"Kid," he hissed, "if you don't turn around an' get the hell outa here I'm gonna take you apart."

Swinging his other hand around in front of him, Alvin wrenched the man's hand free of his wrist and threw it against the table. "You ain't takin' anybody apart tonight, pal."

Alvin felt wonderful. Like a tractor or bull or tree. And fast, like a cobra or lariat or chain saw. And fearless, like a block of ice or a surgeon or the wind. Here was a big man who was older than he, a tough, wiry man facing him with threats and anger, yet to Alvin the man was like a curtain that could easily be brushed aside. So he turned all his attention to the woman, asking her name and did she live around here.

The man stood up and grabbed Alvin's right shoulder. "Let's go. Out." His voice was hurried but low and smooth, almost pleasant, as if he were putting his cat out for the night.

At the bar, Feeney, the sailors, the bartender, and three or four other customers, all older men, were watching intently. Only Feeney looked frightened. He got off his stool and took a step toward the booth, then a sideways step toward the door that led out to the street and Alvin's car. From the juke box at the back Frank Sinatra was singing "On the Road to Mandalay," but otherwise the place was silent, still, and waiting.

Alvin looked down at the man's hand clamped to his shoulder. He said, "You wanta step outside *with* me, pal? 'Cause that's the only way I'm goin'."

"Some other time, kid. I ain't got time to play games with punks like you. Now get outa here."

"Screw you. Either you step outside with me, mister, and get the shit pounded outa you, or you just pick up your little lunchbox there and trot home alone. I plan to sit here awhile an' have a drink an' a talk with Mary. Is that your name, honey? What's your name?" he asked the woman with the vanilla ice cream hair.

"Helen."

"Terrific. Terrific. What's you say you were drinkin'? Gin an' tonic?"

"Yeah."

"Okay, honey. Bartender, let's have a gin an' tonic an' a Seven-an'-Seven over here!"

"Okay," the man in khakis said. "You want your head beat in, you're gonna get it. Let's go, sonny. Outside," he said, and he let go of Alvin's shoulder and strode angrily for the door in back that led to the alley.

Alvin grinned and slid out of the booth without looking back at the woman.

Feeney grabbed him by the arm. "C'mon, Al, let's get the fuck outa here. Whaddaya doin', for chrissakes? That guy'll kill ya!"

Pulling silently away, Alvin started for the exit to the alley, and Feeney shrugged his shoulders and followed his friend, averting his eyes as he passed the woman in the booth.

Jumping from their stools, the pair of sailors followed. "I hope the bastard gets *creamed,*" the red-headed one said.

The bartender, wiping up the bar with a dirty gray cloth, shook his head as if disgusted and slightly bored by the whole thing. "Fuckin' kid drinkers," he mumbled to one of the men at the bar. "Who needs 'em?" Then he called over to the woman, who was lighting a cigarette from a lit butt in the ashtray in front of her. "Hey, Helen, you still want that drink?"

"Yeah."

"Who's payin' for it?" the bartender asked, winking to the men along the bar.

"Whichever one comes back, Freddie. Whichever one comes back." She laughed and started studying her pink fingernails again.

The man in the khaki work clothes was at least six feet tall and broad-shouldered, but still he wasn't as tall as Alvin or anywhere near as wide. He was thick and compact, though, one of those men whose muscles are flat and short, an efficiently built, heavy-boned man with thick wrists and large hands.

When Alvin stepped out of the bar into the alley, he saw the man standing, facing him, a half-dozen paces away at the edge of a circle of light thrown by the single bulb burning over the door. In back of the man was a cinderblock wall about nine feet high, and beyond that was a belt of the dark gray, almost black sky that rose straight up from the river below. Next to the back door of the bar on either side were overflowing garbage cans and collapsing, rain-soaked, card-board boxes. The ground was puddled and muddy, and a nasty, erratic wind was blowing.

Alvin shed his suit jacket and handed it to Feeney, who tried to lean himself casually against the side of the building. The sailors came out and stood next to him, grinning, their arms folded over their chests. With one hand Alvin unknotted his necktie and passed that to Feeney.

Feeney said, "Thanks."

Alvin said, "Yeah."

The man said, "C'mon, kid," and crouched slightly, his fists in front of him, his head pulled down into his bulky shoulders, his feet planted firmly on the ground. A puncher.

Taking two quick steps forward, Alvin drew his fists up in front of his face, quite high up, leaned slightly off the balls of his feet and then, for the first time in his life, he started to fistfight. As if he were in a trance, thinking consciously of the mechanics of what he was doing no more than he would if he were eating a meal, he slid to his left, feinted once, and jammed his right fist, twice, as if firing it, under the man's left arm, crashing his fist against the rib cage, driving the man off-balance to his side, where Alvin caught him with a knee slammed into the crotch as the man fell away. The man grunted and swung a couple of slow punches at Alvin's head, both missing weakly, and Alvin started moving swiftly in and out, his fisted hands attacking the man's neck, chest and belly, like a pack of dogs tearing at the sides of a wounded deer, moving too fast, too relentlessly, too automatically, for the man to avoid them. As he started to collapse backward toward the cinderblock wall, with Alvin driving on like a crowd, the man, spitting blood, groaned, "Enough!" Alvin grabbed him by the shirtfront, held him at arm's length, and whacked him, hard, across the temple with one enormous paw, flipping the man out of his grasp into a heap in the mud. Walking over to him, he picked him up again and threw him back down again. He kicked him once on the shoulder. Then he left him alone.

"Jesus Christ!" Feeney yelled. "You did it! You really took the guy!" He was clapping Alvin on the shoulder and staring down at the man on the ground.

Alvin pulled his jacket and tie out of Feeney's other hand and shoved his arms into the jacket and slung the necktie around his neck without knotting it. He turned and started straight down the alley toward the street.

"Hey! Where ya goin'? What about the broad? Where ya goin'?"

"Home," Alvin grunted and kept on moving, head down, for the street.

"Okay, I'll get your raincoat. You left it inside," Feeney called to him.

"Yeah." Then he was gone from sight.

Feeney turned around, a puzzled but still exhilarated expression on his face. "Jesus." The sailors had gone back inside. The man on the ground was slowly, awkwardly getting to his feet. "You okay?" Feeney asked him quietly.

The man was bleeding from the mouth and nose. He stood, bent over, clutching his left side, breathing laboriously. His clothes were smeared with mud and fresh blood. "I gotta . . . busted . . . rib. I think. . . . Tell Freddie . . . C'mere. Th' bartend-er . . ."

"Sure." Feeney walked somberly inside, told the bartender he'd better check the guy out and maybe get him a doctor or something, the guy seemed pretty busted up. Plucking Alvin's tan raincoat from the coatrack, he pointedly avoided even a glance at the woman in the booth next to it and started walking out the door at the front.

"Where's the other one?" the bartender asked. He had come out from behind the bar and was on his way toward the back door. "I don't wanta see him in here again. You tell him that."

"No sweat," Feeney said, grinning. "No sweat at all." Then he looked down at the woman. Serious-faced, she was sipping from her gin and tonic. She caught him staring, and without removing her pink lips from the rim of the glass, gave him the finger.

Feeney laughed and strolled happily out. When he reached the car and got in, he looked over at Alvin behind the steering wheel. He was smiling and the car motor was running.

"Feelin' pretty tough, ain't ya?" Feeney observed.

"Yeah. Like a bucket full of nails." Then he jammed the car into gear, and they headed back to New Hampshire.

I WAS GRATEFUL for the story, grateful to Rochelle for having delivered it to me, for having written it in the first place. But the story complicated things for me far more than it simplified them. I asked Rochelle if it complicated things for her, too, and she said no, not really, which surprised me.

"But he sounds so *ordinary*," I pointed out to her, "like almost any young man already determined at adolescence by social and familial past, one of those angry American youths locked into patterns of violence, drunkenness and sexual exploitation. Even if he eventually raised his consciousness to the point where he could direct his anger politically, rather than mutely against himself," I observed to her, "he'd still be little more than another feeble example of the type called 'working-class hero.' " And both Rochelle and I were claiming much more for him than that.

It was not exactly what I had been looking for in a story about Hamilton's brush with a college education. I had wanted him to be offered a full scholarship, say, by Harvard or Princeton or Yale, and after visiting one of those campuses and encountering there for the first time an example or two of the academic mind, to reject the offered scholarship with some sort of truth-telling gesture of defiance. It would have made a marvelously effective vehicle for social satire.

"My father is *not* Holden Caulfield all grown up," Rochelle said, sounding a little hurt.

I couldn't tell if it was her author's pride that had been bruised or the pride of a daughter who believes that she understands her parent better than any stranger can. In either case, though, she was justified in feeling hurt, so I apologized, first for my persistently soft-headed expectations that Hamilton's past could be anticipated any more than could his future, and second, for not having immediately expressed my enthusiasm for the skill and restraint with which she had told her story.

"As always," I explained to her, "your literary gifts amaze and delight me. Especially when placed next to my own awkward attempts."

She smiled politely.

"Look," I brightly said, "the sun has risen above the trees! Shall we go downstairs for breakfast? Or would you like to let me make love to you?"

"Oh, you devil. Don't you ever get tired?"

"Eventually," I confessed.

"You some kind of billy goat, honey," she purred in that southern accent of hers, the one that stiffens me with lust.

CHAPTER 8

100 Selected, Uninteresting Things Done and Said by Hamilton Stark

1. He drove past a hitchhiker without picking him up. The hitchhiker was a long-haired youth in an army field jacket whose stance and bulky physical proportions reminded him for a second, as he later said, of the author's younger brother, now dead, whom Hamilton had met only once, several years before.

2. He bought a new saxophone (tenor) but still preferred the old one.

3. After placing a classified ad in the Concord *Daily Monitor,* he sold his new saxaphone for $25 less than he had paid for it. He considered the loss not bad at all. "Self-knowledge always has a price."

4. Between his second and third wives, he perfected a technique for getting out of bed in the morning in such a way that he had to make the bed only once every ten days or so. The technique involved spreading his legs under the covers to the far corners of the bed and then dragging his long body toward the top of the bed, where, springing his weight with his arms against the brass rail headboard, he lifted himself to the floor.

When he married for the third time he ceased this activity, but when the woman left he resumed it until he married again. He also employed the technique between his fourth and fifth wives and after his fifth wife had left.

5. He changed his brand of cigarettes twice in his life—from Chesterfields to Camels to Lucky Strikes, which he now smokes at the rate of one pack a day.

6. He never learned to fly an airplane, though he often expressed a desire to do so.

7. When he was twenty-six years old he learned to drive a bulldozer, an activity he still enjoys. So much so that when he was thirty he purchased his own bulldozer, a small Caterpillar that he painted black and keeps waxed and shiny, even the blade, which he retouches with black enamel after each use.

8. In winter he usually wears a navy blue woolen watchcap. He rarely covers his ears with it. They are small and turn red from the cold, but he doesn't seem to notice or care.

9. He cut down a dying maple tree behind his barn and that winter used the wood for his fireplace. He remembered having looked at the tree from his earliest childhood, and he thought of this while he was cutting it into fireplace-length pieces. He used his chain saw for the cutting, used it expertly, especially for a man who was not a bona fide woodcutter.

10. He never in his entire life wore a pair of sandals. Never even tried them on in a shoestore.

11. He never defaulted on a debt, and his checking account was never overdrawn. Once, however, he was tempted to default on a television set he had bought on time from Sears, Roebuck & Co. He made his payments punctually for fourteen months, and when the set broke down for the fifth time, he threw it away in anger, tossed it over the fence into the field in front of the house. With ten months remaining, and no television set to be repossessed or repaired, he threatened in a letter not to make any more payments, but instead sent his checks in nine days late

each month until the balance was paid. After that he was reluctant to purchase any more appliances on time; he said it made it more difficult for him to get rid of them when he wanted to.

12. At the end of each year he threw away the old calendar and posted a new one, making a careful point of using a different calendar altogether, different size, picture, advertiser, etc. He preferred calendars from plumbing and heating wholesale supply houses. The pictures were usually of New Hampshire winter scenes, though sometimes they were of bathrooms or furnaces.

13. One winter morning, as he prepared to leave for work, he observed that he always put his left glove on before his right. He reasoned that this was because he was right-handed. For the same reason, he reasoned, he always shaved the right side of his face before the left.

14. One summer afternoon, a Sunday, he tried to draw a picture of his house from the field in front of it. He made three careful attempts but wasn't satisfied with any of them, so he threw them away.

15. "If I was governor of this state, I'd let them all go to hell. That's the only way to govern." (He was speaking to Democratic and liberal Republican critics of the present governor's policies.)

16. The most horned-pout* he ever caught in one night was twenty-two, on June 17, 1964, on Bow Lake, alone.

17. Because of his size, he often had difficulty buying clothes until he was about thirty, when he came across an L.L. Bean catalogue in a privy. After that he always bought his clothes by mail order from L.L. Bean.

18. This is the sequence in which he read the several sections of the Sunday newspaper: comics; sports; obituaries; headlines and front page; editorial page; letters to the editor; classified ads. He followed this pattern with the weekday editions too. On Sundays, however, he was more conscious of there being a pattern and of his being free not to follow it if he so desired.

---

* A local, smaller, coldwater version of the well-known catfish.

19. He talked to dogs in a gruff voice that seemed to send them cowering away. Once, however, he was almost bitten by a friend's unusually courageous dog, which ended the friendship, such as it was.

20. Drawn into a leather-goods shop in Concord by the attractive window display, he was about to purchase an eighty-dollar briefcase, but at the last minute he changed his mind and bought a new wallet instead. "I like the smell of new leather," he later explained.

21. To an insurance salesman as the man stepped from his car: "Get the hell outa here! If I'd wanted to buy anything, I'd have sent for you!" The frightened salesman drove off quickly enough to satisfy him.

22–39. Once a week, at various, though unvarying, times, he performed the following chores:

a. dumped his rubbish in the field in front of his house;

b. buried his garbage in a pit in the field in front of his house (except in winter, when the ground was frozen solid, in which case he simply permitted the garbage to freeze solid, until spring, when he could cover the moldering heap with earth);

c. swept out the barn and cleaned off his workbenches;

d. added a quart of STP additive to the crankcase of his car;

e. checked the tire pressure of all four tires, plus the spare, of his car;

f. in summer, mowed the lawns; in winter, chipped off any ice or snow that had accumulated on the gutters and scraped away any ice or snow on the walks and driveway that he had missed during the week (he shoveled and plowed out his walks and driveway immediately after every snowstorm, but often,

because of the lateness of the hour or other responsibilities, had to leave the finish-work for the weekend);
in the fall, raked any leaves that had fallen that week
into a pile, which he burned (the ashes he piled next
to the garden in back of the house until spring, when,
before turning the soil, he spread them); in the spring,
worked at least three hours cutting and pruning in the
wooded areas surrounding the house and along the
path up the mountain.

g. drove to Pittsfield, where he bought groceries at the
IGA for the coming week, filled his car with Shell gas,
stopped at Maxfield's Hardware Store for any tools,
nails, screws or other items he might need or had
run out of during the previous week, stopped at the
state liquor store for a half-gallon of Canadian Club
and at Danis's Superette for a case of Molson ale, and
returned home;

h. except in winter and late fall, tended his flower beds and
vegetable garden, usually between 4:00 and 6:30 P.M. on
Saturday; in the late fall and winter, during these same
hours, he cut and stacked firewood for the fireplace and
the two wood stoves in the kitchen and barn;

i. read the New Hampshire *Times* (the Sunday edition of
the Manchester *Union-Leader*);

j. repaired any furniture, appliances, tools, machinery,
lamps, cupboard doors, faucets, shutters, shingles,
gates or fence posts that, during the previous week,
had broken or had begun to malfunction, leak, buzz,
flap, or lean;

k. drank half a gallon of Canadian Club and a case of
Molson ale, one shot and one bottle at a time;

l. watched one, and no more than one, sporting event
on television;

m. sharpened, on the wheel in his workshop, all his butcher knives, axes, hatchets, and handsaws; sharpened his Swiss Army pocketknife while he was at it;

n. fired at least twenty rounds from his Winchester 30.06 rifle—at bottles and tin cans in the field in front of the house; sometimes he shot idly at crows in the field in front of the house; sometimes rats and woodchucks, and when his garden was up, rabbits;

o. as a spiritual exercise (though he never called it precisely that), once a week went twenty-four hours without uttering a word to another person; because of the requirements of his job, this usually took place at home on Sundays, where it was easier to accomplish without complications;

p. walked to the top of Blue Job Mountain behind the house and looked out over the land below, wished it were his as far as he could see, all the way to the limits of the horizon;

q. checked all the above items off his list, one by one, as he performed them, and when necessary, revised the list to accommodate the upcoming week and any changes in routine that might be necessitated.

40. As a matter of course he tossed all mail addressed to Occupant into the trash can in the kitchen or in winter directly into the wood stove. Once, though, as if on a whim, he opened and read a plea for contributions to Boys' Town. After that he resumed tossing all such mail into the trash can or wood stove, as before.

41. He liked to open the glove compartment of his car and find it neat and orderly. Flashlight, registration, New Hampshire road map, sharpened pencil, matches, extra fuses lightly rolled in a strip of electrician's tape.

42. To his third wife (Jenny): "I'd as soon wipe my ass with a corncob as this damned stuff. Can't you buy better toilet paper than *this*? It's like sandpaper, for Christ's sake!" To his fourth wife (Maureen): "You trying to give me piles or something? How much d'you save, buying this cheap shit? It feels like emery cloth!" To his fifth wife (Dora): "This stuff feels like pie crust, for Christ's sake! What *gives*?" He figured that, because of his size, he was more sensitive to the texture of toilet paper than normal-sized people were. He also knew that made no sense, but he didn't care. Whether a thing made sense or not had nothing to do with whether it was true or not.

43. He didn't like dogs. "All tongue, lips and flapping tails. No sense of their own worth. Which makes them worth*less*."

44. He didn't like cats. "Sneaky bastards. They love dying even more than death. Which in *my* book makes 'em unreliable."

45. He didn't like horses. "Should've gone extinct forty or fifty years ago, when they couldn't compete with tractors or trucks anymore for work or with cars and bicycles for transportation. Besides, they're ridiculous-looking. Bodies're too big for their legs. I'd like 'em if they were the way they used to be, before the Arabs started screwing 'em up—dog-sized things, like white-tailed deer, only smarter. Probably made good eating."

46. He hated domestic fowl of all kinds. "I don't even like to eat one of the bastards, unless it's cut up so I can't recognize what kind of animal it was when it was still alive."

47. He liked pigs. "Now you take your typical pig. That's an animal with a developed understanding of its life. No delusions. Not like cows. Cows are under the impression that people keep them around because they *like* them. Pigs never make that mistake."

48. What he hated about sheep was the way most people regarded them: "Most people think sheep are sweet and gentle. The truth is, sheep sleep twenty-four hours a day. As far as being

alive goes, they're located only one step this side of lawn furniture. Three stomachs covered with a woolly mitten. Personally, if it wasn't for the mutton, I'd rather see a flock of cotton bales."

49. "I'd make a lousy farmer," he confessed. "Plants are okay, though. I don't mind being around plants, long as they don't get too cute, if you know what I mean."

50. He claimed not to know his birth date. "I was barely there, for Christ's sake." When asked how old he was, he would answer, "About thirty-seven," or, "About forty-two," or whatever, always, of course, giving his correct age. He claimed his sense of time was different from most people's in that it was more precise. Doubtless he knew his birth date and, when required by law, provided it, for he possessed a driver's license, union card, Social Security card, and so on, like the rest of us.

51. Whenever in conversation the word "Florida" came up, he would interject, "Coney Island with palm trees."

52. He did not believe in God. He said that when God believed in *him*, then he'd believe in them *both*. He made his statement somberly, with care, apparently with full awareness of its theological, philosophical and psychological implications.

53. He had lifetime subscriptions to *The Farmer's Almanac, Reader's Digest,* and *National Geographic.* Frequently, however, he sneeringly referred to an individual as, "The type of man who has a lifetime subscription to *The Farmer's Almanac,*" or, " . . . to *Reader's Digest,*" or, " . . . to *National Geographic.*" Once, when someone had the temerity to point out that he himself owned lifetime subscriptions to these very periodicals, he answered, "Of course. How else do you think I'd know the types?"

54. He woke at six o'clock every morning of his adult life, even when he did not have to go to work. He did not own an alarm clock and could when necessary wake himself earlier than six and at exactly the time he wished to waken. He seemed to require no more than five hours' sleep a night. In providing this information, he explained that this was because when he went to

bed he went to sleep immediately and when he slept he concentrated on it. "Like a machine," he explained. "No, like a rock," he added.

55. Exposés and public scandals seemed to make him sad, as if he were suddenly reminded of some great loss from his childhood.

56. "I hate a melee. If you want a fight, you ought to make it personal. Insult somebody. Insult his mother, his girl friend, his manhood, whatever it is he thinks needs protection."

57. He never permitted any of his wives to make breakfast for him. Once Jenny, attempting to curry his favor, got up an hour earlier than he and prepared a breakfast of fried eggs, pancakes, sausages, fresh biscuits, coffee, and melon, and when he came downstairs and discovered this lovely meal, he was enraged and stormed out of the house. Later, when describing the event, he explained his rage by pointing out the control a woman can obtain over a man if he lets her imitate his mother. "Good intentions can't dull a sharp knife," he aphorized. In fairness, he also pointed out the control a man can have over a woman if she lets him imitate her father. "It's how I kept all my women in line. While I kept them."

58. He despised throw pillows, bric-a-brac, knickknacks, and souvenirs, scatter rugs, doilies, and imitation chandeliers, flower decals, pink appliances, the color off-white, and whitewall tires, decorated mailboxes, and lawn sculpture, and David Susskind, and game shows, and television weathermen. He believed that you are what you love, and therefore he despised people who loved any or all of these things. He also believed that you are not what you despise, and since you cannot very easily control what you love and thus cannot very easily control what you are, you therefore ought at least to make a concerted attempt to avoid being what would disgrace you. For him, then, the most interesting person was the one who hated more things than anyone else, and the least interesting was the one who loved more things than

anyone else. Errol Flynn, he thought, was an example of an interesting man. Lee Harvey Oswald and Arthur Bremer were interesting. Gerald Ford, Marilyn Monroe and the Beatles were not.

59. He loved compression when, as a quality, it was joined to symmetry—as in algebra or symbolic logic, a portable tape recorder, a double-bitted ax, or a Maltese cross. In fact, his favorite design was a Maltese cross, and he frequently left it doodled behind him, on restaurant tablecloths, condensation on windows, sand, snow, and dust.

60. He wore no jewelry and carried no watch. "On principle," he claimed. As with so much else.

61. He did not wear glasses.

62. The men were unloading a truckload of twenty-foot lengths of six-inch galvanized pipe. He was the foreman on the job site, and because it was only eight-fifteen in the morning and the four men unloading the truck were moving very slowly, two men to each length of pipe, he grew annoyed and left the shanty, where he had been laying out the day's work on the blueprints, and told the crew they were unloading the pipe as if their intent were not to get the truck unloaded but were instead to avoid hurting themselves or tiring themselves out too early in the day, at which point he himself began unloading the pipe, yanking a length by himself from the pile, hefting it to his shoulder and carrying it to the stack twenty feet away, and there laying it gently, so as not to damage the threaded ends, down. The men looked at the sky and the ground. He came back to the truck and did it again. Then again. The men stood aside and watched him work, confused as to the point he was making. After he had unloaded ten lengths of pipe, he stopped before the men and calmly said to them, "You have to lift until everything turns black. Lift till you black out. You have to do it every day. The job will always be more than you can handle, anyhow, so the only point is to lift until everything turns black." Then he walked back into the shanty and resumed

laying out the day's work. The men turned to each other for a second, grinned good-naturedly, and went to work unloading the pipe, as before, two men to each length, and moving slowly, with care, pacing themselves.

63. He suddenly remembered his father's walk, his stride, efficient and regular, like a dog's involving his body only from the hips down. He tried to imitate it and discovered that to do so he didn't have to alter his own stride in the slightest. The discovery gave him a moment's extreme pleasure, not because it meant that he resembled his father even more closely than he had thought (which would not have pleased him at all), but rather because he believed that his discovery of the similarity between his imitation and the remembered image had led him directly to a momentary awareness of the nature of *all* human beings. And who, indeed, would not experience such awareness, however momentary, with pleasure?

64. He visited his father's grave only once after the funeral, the following summer, when the grass had returned. He walked about the plot for a few moments, admired the view of the river from the hilltop cemetery, and got back into his car and drove home. From the top of Blue Job Mountain behind his house, he could see the cemetery, three miles distant. His ancestors for two hundred years were buried there, and once, when this was pointed out to him, he seemed surprised and confessed that it had never occurred to him, even though he made it a habit to climb to the top of Blue Job once every week.

65. To Trudy, his first wife: "I can't tell you I love you because I don't know what the word means. I mean the word 'I,' not 'love' or 'you.' "

66. To Annie, his second wife: "I can't tell you I love you because I know what 'you' and 'love' mean and I don't know what 'I' means."

67. To Jenny, his third wife: "I can't tell you I love you because I know what 'you' and 'love' mean."

68. To Maureen, his fourth wife: "I can't tell you I love you because I know what 'you' means."

69. To Dora, his fifth wife: "I can't tell you I love you."

70. With regard to all five wives, he observed one evening that it would have been possible for him only to have told them he did *not* love them, because he would then be lying and thus he would know what he meant. He meant to lie. By this it seemed that he believed that the only statements a person could make, and also could attribute meaning to, were statements known by the speaker to be falsehoods.

71. Asked by a friend why he continued to marry, feeling as he did toward women in particular and things in general, his response was to shrug helplessly and say, "When you don't despise a thing, you let yourself be powerless to resist its advances, when and if it advances."

72. He disliked most curtains and drapes, all venetian blinds, overhead lamps, tools that were not kept in immaculate condition, and collections of any kind. "I believe in sets of things, not collections."

73. " 'Everything implies its opposite.' I read that. The writer didn't understand what he was writing. He thought it was about logic instead of the world."

74. He refused to return the greetings of his immediate neighbors, the people who lived along the road to his house, and after a while they ceased greeting him or waving to him when he drove past their homes on his way to and from town and work.

75. He seemed to attract the adulation of adolescent boys, and as long as they remained in awe in silence, he did not discourage it. But as soon as anything more was asked of him, a declaration of loyalty or affection, say, a simple explanation, he in turn asked more of them, and this inevitably drove the boys away, usually hurt, often angry, and always confused as to who had failed whom.

76. On a number of occasions, with something like glee, he quoted a well-known Jamaican proverb: "Me no send, you no

come." He claimed that it meant, "If I didn't send for you, then you're not here."

77. He combed his hair the same way all his life—straight back without a part, cut fairly long, trimmed by a barber every three weeks. Even in his forties, he had no gray hair, and as a result it was difficult to guess his age. People took him for anywhere between twenty-five and fifty-five, depending on their opinion of how old they themselves looked.

78. He kept himself physically very clean, and every morning he shaved himself meticulously, using no cologne or aftershave lotion on his face other than coarse rubbing alcohol. He used a straight razor, which he honed daily on a two-inch-wide leather strop, and a mug and brush. The razor, strop, mug and brush had all belonged to his father, and every morning while he shaved he thought of his father every morning shaving who must have had some other way of calling forth his father, for the grandfather, the one who had died drunk in a snowbank, had been a bearded man. In that way, every morning while he shaved he was able to think of his grandfather, a man he had never met and who had never shaved. This process satisfied him doubly because it demonstrated for him the way he believed everything worked.

79. He participated in no sports, had not played a game of any kind since his adolescence. The only kind of fishing he did was what is called "bottom-fishing," and though he owned numerous firearms, both rifles and handguns, he hunted only what he called "pests," crows, woodchucks, rats that scavenged his rubbish and other used-up household articles dumped in the field in front of his house.

80. Where other people saw only white, he claimed to have recognized twenty-one different shades of the color of snow. What he said he saw were eight shades of gray, seven of yellow, and six of blue. His favorite snow color was "blue number four." Black and white, as colors of anything, were unknown to him, he insisted.

81. Drunk, regardless of whether he was speaking to a stranger or to an acquaintance, he usually spoke in accents— Irish, Southern, Italian, and so on. Then after a few more shots of Canadian Club and bottles of ale, he would begin to speak in foreign languages, or what the people around him took for foreign languages. If a French-Canadian were present, he would speak a bit of French. Occasionally, if it came out that the person he was talking to was fluent in some other foreign language than French, in Spanish, say, or German, he would start dropping sentences, phrases, words, as well as entire paragraphs, that seemed to be in Spanish or German. No one ever challenged him on his proficiency, and surely no one dared to challenge his veracity. The people usually just smiled and nodded, the way they would if someone had merely introduced a pleasant non sequitur into the conversation, which by then would have been drunken, loud, and digressive anyway, full of fits and stops, starts and interruptions. What matter, then, if some of the fits and stops came in foreign languages that no one in the group, except the speaker, seemed to understand? In this way, he had spoken in recent years with dozens of French-Canadian lumbermen, millhands, and fellow construction workers, an Italian-American formalist painter from New York City with a summer house on Bow Lake, four Creole-speaking Jamaican transient farmworkers, a Portuguese fisherman visiting relatives in Fall River, a pair of Russian chemists at a convention in Breton Woods, a Venezuelan student at the University of New Hampshire, many Greek cooks, restaurant managers and waitresses, a Chinese Bible salesman, and six Japanese tourists. Additionally, in what he claimed were the original languages, he had made references to and quotations from numerous works of literature written in ancient Greek, Latin, Sanskrit, and Hebrew. As he rarely bothered to translate these into English, it was not known how accurately he was quoting the original, if at all. And of course, always at these times he was extremely drunk,

and the personality he was exhibiting was so vivid that, while it could not be ignored, neither could it be taken seriously—that is, as literally a personality.

82. He wore size 13 EEE shoes, over-the-ankle, moccasin-toed workshoes with a steel-reinforced toe and heel. At all times he owned three pairs of these shoes, one brand-new, one two years old, and one four years old, all of them purchased by mail from L. L. Bean in Freeport, Maine. These were the only shoes he owned, and every two years, when he bought a new pair, he threw away the oldest pair, just tossed them over the fence into the field in front.

83. He sent the apprentice pipefitter, his very first day on the job, to the toolshed for a glass-stapler. After a while the boy returned, saying he couldn't find it, and then, timidly, asked him what a glass-stapler looked like. He stared at the boy with apparent disgust and after a moment told him it looked just like it ought to look. "Keep in mind the function, and you'll figure out the form," he said grumpily and walked off. The boy asked the other men, who smiled and sent him on several wild goose chases before the boy finally figured out what was happening, and then everyone had a good laugh together. "You can't find what doesn't exist," he advised the boy. "But remember, you can't lose it, either." The boy nodded somberly, as if understanding, and the men looked from one to the other and grinned knowingly. Later in the day, one of them said to the boy, "He's a little crazy, y'know. But don't let it worry you none, because he never lets it interfere with his job."

84. He picked up the phone and dialed the first three digits of his sister Jody's telephone number. He had prepared one sentence; it was: "Hello, let me speak to my mother." From there on he planned to improvise. He had, however, forbidden himself to explain or apologize for *anything*. All else was permissible, depending on what she or his mother said. Then he stopped dialing and put the phone down. "If I'm not going to explain or

apologize for anything, then I have no reason to be calling her. She should be calling me," he later reasoned.

85. Inside his house, he walked around in his stocking feet. His shoes were always neatly set on a wicker mat next to the door.

86. He could find the cube and square roots of extremely high numbers in his head with nearly the rapidity of an electric calculator. He dismissed the feat as a trick of concentration that any fool could teach himself if he weren't so happy being a fool.

87. He owned no photographs of himself. Whenever one came to him, he threw it away, just tossed it into the trash can under the sink without even examining it to see whether it was a good likeness or not.

88. Nor did he own a single photograph of anyone else, not a snapshot. If one were presented to him (as by his daughter Rochelle, numerous times), unless it was personally inscribed (as were all his daughter's), he pitched it into the trash can under the sink. His explanation (no apology) was that he already knew what the subject of the photograph looked like; he didn't need any machine to tell him what he already knew. If he were going to save any photograph, it would have to be of a person he'd never seen before, but he'd never found any reason to do that yet, as evidenced by the fact that he even threw out pictures of himself.

89. Suddenly everyone noticed that he was growling, his lips curled back, his eyes gone cold, his scalp drawn back from his face. A moment before, everyone had thought he was speaking in what he said was an Ashanti dialect of Twi, still spoken, he had told them, in parts of Ghana. He had seemed to be directing his utterances to a black woman reporter for the Detroit *Free Press* who was in the state to cover the presidential primary election. In fact, he had been directing all his attention toward the young woman in the gray-tinted aviator glasses, as had she to him, and here he was now, growling like some kind of trapped beast. The

others at the table all started talking at once, each of them trying separately to change the subject, whatever it was. Soon he had ceased growling and his face had returned to normal. By then someone in the group was telling the others how little he thought of this guy McCarthy's chances of beating LBJ in the primary. The black woman avoided looking at him, and when she spoke to anyone at the table, it was only to answer a quiet yes or no to a direct question. He in turn seemed to withdraw into himself, and after a half-hour, he got up silently and left the bar for another.

90. In his lifetime (thus far), he had made love, as it were, to nineteen different women. The first was when he was seventeen years old. The woman, five years older than he, a French-Canadian down from Quebec for the summer, working as a waitress in a resort hotel on Lake Winnepesaukee, was "experienced." He was drunk at the time. The most recent was a forty-seven-year-old divorcée who works as a compositor in a Concord printing plant. He met her at the leather-upholstered bar of a cocktail lounge and took her back to her dingy apartment where they made love, as it were, on a Murphy bed. He was drunk at the time.

91. He saved all personal correspondence—all letters, post cards, telegrams, inscriptions, memos and notes—everything directed to him that was in the slightest way personal. Then he filed everything alphabetically by sender (he called it "author").

92. Though he was married five times, he never wore a wedding ring. His reason was that in his work he might catch the ring on something that would rip his finger off. He'd seen it happen, lots of times.

93. He worried about diseases of the rectum, though he had never suffered from any such disease or affliction. He used his size as rationalization: anyone his height and weight made things hard on the rectum.

94. Whenever in conversation the words "New York City" came up, he would snort, "Babylon!"

95. After an act of violence, however minor (or major), he was extremely calm, clear-eyed and physically relaxed. Indeed, much more so than anyone else in the area. It didn't give the effect of release as much as it seemed he had regained something precious that had been lost, something he had luckily plucked from the flux.

96. Every year he received four Christmas cards: one from each of his sisters, one from the union business agent for the Concord local, and one from the chairman of the New Hampshire Republican party. The first two were always signed in ball-point with just the first name of the sender; the other two were always unsigned, with the name of the sender printed by machine. The first two he filed alphabetically by author; the other two he promptly threw away. He himself sent out no Christmas cards, although his wives had all participated in the rite, secretly, however.

97. When other men told stories from their experiences in the military, he never contributed any stories from his experiences in the Army Engineers Corps, although, if questioned directly, he would not deny that he had had such experiences. In that way he usually gave the impression that he had been involved with "security matters" that simply could not be discussed without clearance from above. He did nothing to correct that impression, naturally. The same was true when the men he worked with told stories from their childhood or adolescence; he merely would not deny that he, like other people, had gone through a childhood and adolescence. The impression given was that either his childhood and adolescence had been totally uneventful and bored him to think or talk about now, or else he had suffered so profoundly that it was extremely painful to him to think or talk about now. Again, he did nothing to correct either of these impressions.

98. One rarely spent an evening or afternoon with him without his at some point asking this riddle: "If you can hold six eggs in your right hand, how many can you hold in your left?"

Most people, whether they knew the "right" answer or no, said, "Six," whereupon he placed six eggs one by one into the person's right hand. Then he placed six more eggs in a group on a tabletop and instructed the person to go ahead and hold them in his left hand—without, of course, first emptying the right. His riddle answered (i.e., three or four, depending on how many eggs the person could pluck and hold with the fingertips of his left hand), there followed a demonstration of the denial of that very answer. He deposited the dozen eggs onto the tabletop, and then, as if plunging both his hands into a vat, he placed them simultaneously over all the eggs, covering them completely, and when he lifted his hands and turned them over, he was holding six eggs in his right hand and six in his left. On his face was a broad smile of triumph, as if he had proved, not to his audience but to himself, something that couldn't be believed.

99. He knew that if he had been a small man, people would have behaved differently toward him. But he also knew that if he had been a small man, he would have behaved differently toward them. "Different solutions create different problems," he concluded.

100. One night, shortly after his mother had moved out, he discovered a photograph album that she had accidentally left in an upstairs closet in a dark corner of the overhead shelf. Most of the pictures in the album were snapshots of him as a child taken in the summertime at the river, by the sea, in the sun-dappled meadow. He studied each picture for a long time, and when he had finished, he took the album downstairs and walked outside, coatless in the cold night air, and heaved the album over the fence, sending it in a long, fluttering arc into the darkness.

CHAPTER 9

The Uroboros: Being a Further Declension of the Central Image

Sometimes there is such a thing as too much integrity.

—ERROL FLYNN, My Wicked, Wicked Ways

IT HAD OCCURRED to me, on my own, that in my apparent need to justify, to myself if not to anyone else who cared to listen, the peculiar nature of my relation to Hamilton Stark, I may very well have been guilty of misrepresenting Hamilton's peculiar relations to others, in particular to his mother. This would not be an unusual error or failing on the part of an author in my position. In fact it's almost normal for those who come after a great man to distort that man's relations to others, his parents, friends, other disciples, and so on, in order to cast one's own role in the great man's life in as interesting and favorable a light as possible. One wishes not only to spread the word, as it were, but to establish one's version of that word as the authoritative one as well.

Thus, one evening when my friend and neighbor C. told me flatly that I had so far slighted Hamilton (A.) by my failure to address the question of his treatment of his mother, I had to agree.

On this particular evening C. had come over carrying a paper bag containing his bath soap, shampoo and towel. Every late August and September he visits me once every three days to bathe and later to drink a little wine and chat. His well, a dug well, goes dry every year at this time, whereas mine, a drilled well several hundred feet deep, continues to provide water, and naturally, it pleases us both to turn this neighborly service into a social occasion. While C. splashes about in the tub like a walrus, I often pull a kitchen chair up to the closed bathroom door and converse with him. I think at times like this, if someone could see us, he would believe that we were lonely men, and he could be right, except that we are not lonely at all. One way in which Hamilton has helped me in my well-known solitude, incidentally, is his insistence on maintaining the distinction between solitude and loneliness. And I believe that I, in my turn, have taught it to C. A solitary man is not necessarily a lonely man, unless he permits himself to fuzzy the distinction between his particular solitude and loneliness in general. That fuzziness inevitably results in self-pity, and self-pity necessarily drags along loneliness for its escort. It insists on its oppressive company, because self-pity, as if compulsively, always slaps at the presence of anyone who might offer pity and understanding instead. We are always alone, but we need not ever be lonely. What Hamilton demonstrated is that our recognition of the former, which is true whether we believe it or not, makes possible the reality of the latter, which is true if and only if we believe it so. Far be it for me to presume, but it made sense of some of his otherwise inexplicable enthusiasms, homeopathy, for instance, whose main maxim is, "Like cures like." If you are lonely, he would say to me, don't run out and fill your life with friends and acquaintances. Instead, direct all your attention to the inescapability of your solitude, your absolute oneness. The only way to cure a glutton of gluttony is to force-feed him. Starving him will only increase his appetite.

Most of us can understand and respect the logic of such a position, but few of us are strong enough to enact it. Hamilton, of course, by his example, shows us simultaneously both the price of exacting it and also the rewards. What more can one ask of his teacher? I ask you. And what less?

These thoughts, however, were not part of my conversation with C. He was sloshing about in the tub and shouting through the closed door about Hamilton's (and A.'s) mother, Alma Stark (M.), and how, by my having neglected to present in any detail or believable complexity the nature of her relationship with her son, I had not merely been remiss as an author of a novel, but I had also invited the reader to deal superficially with my characters. "An otherwise excellent and amusing novel," he warned me through the door, "can be robbed of its *significance* if you make it easy for your readers to deal superficially with your characters."

I'm afraid that at first I found his theory specious, but I knew he was right about my having slighted poor, long-suffering Alma Stark. It kept her two-dimensional, robbed her of the true human complexity that I had granted, say, to Hamilton's wives (so far). And I also knew C. was right in that by my slighting Alma, describing her as merely victim, I had also slighted my hero, Hamilton. I had made him appear as merely victimizer, insofar as I had described his relationship with his mother at all.

No, C. had me all right. I was going to have to stop in my accelerating rush toward the climax of this novel and go back, not to the beginning, but at least to Chapter Five, "Back and Fill," and bring to bear a more scrupulously observant point of view than the one offered there, the town's librarian's, as I recall.

•   •   •

LET ME TRY my own point of view. I don't really know the woman very well, have not met the woman she's modeled after, A.'s mother M., more than twice, and casually at that, and of course I was not there the night Hamilton threw his mother out of what everyone thought was her own home. But I do know Hamilton (or rather, A., the man *he's* modeled after) quite well, as well as anyone, with the possible exception of his daughter, knows him. And I've had numerous opportunities to discuss that evening with him, to draw out of him as much of his own point of view as he's willing to share with anyone else. I think, therefore, I can give a fairly reliable account of what led up to and what followed from that evening, thus creating a somewhat different account of what actually transpired *during* that evening, the particulars of which, because they've been included in an earlier account, the librarian's, and referred to several times, by Police Chief Blount, for instance, the reader is already doubtless quite familiar with.

Hamilton's mother Alma had a habit of wringing her hands and, when they seemed to have been wrung out, of tweaking with her thumb and forefinger the loose skin under her chin. Wring and tweak, wring and tweak. I don't know when she developed this habit, but Hamilton told me that he never recalled her to his mind's eye without seeing her first wringing her hands and then pulling at her throat. He never recalled her with her hands in the air, palms out, in glee or happy surprise, or down at her sides, empty and disappointed. He could not remember her clapping her hands in excitement. Always they were wringing and tweaking, wringing and tweaking.

This image did not make him feel particularly happy. As a youth, he had responded to the gesture with shuddering, deep waves of guilt for nameless offenses, sins of omission as much as commission. In general, other people than Hamilton, strangers even, tended to respond to Alma Stark in much the same way.

One had to ask oneself, even when meeting her for the first time, if one had not somehow, inadvertently, injured this woman, disappointed or deprived her, imposed on her, if one had not added, somehow, to her already unfairly heavy load of woe. For most people, the answer to the question of culpability was a simple denial. After which one tended to regard her through a skeptical lens tinted with pity. For, to most people, she proved immediately to be potentially manipulative, which was why most people felt justified in objectifying her somewhat by pitying her.

In a patriarchy, or any male-oriented society or household, husbands and sons are especially vulnerable to the trap that results from real or imagined injuries to women. It's one of the very few routes to power for their wives and mothers, which, naturally, invites them to specialize in it, and, through disuse, all the alternative routes gradually get broken up and overgrown, until soon they are impassable altogether. Thus, Hamilton and his father were especially vulnerable to Alma's particular specialization. They were both willing and conscious participants in a patriarchy, they were both raised, as conventional New En-gland Protestants, to prove their moral and spiritual worth by the nature and extent of their works, that is, by their worldly success, and they were both reared, in the Victorian manner, to be ashamed of human bodies. Since neither the father nor the son, for various and different reasons, had experienced much of what is conventionally called worldly success, and since both father and son had human bodies, they were forced into employing extreme and often cruel-seeming means of resisting the trap Alma's generalized woe had created for precisely them.

To neutralize the effect of her wringing and tweaking, her sighs, her constantly wet eyes, her self-denying anticipation of needs he himself never even knew he had, Hamilton's father applied the old male strategy of grim condescension. He disregarded her point of view, treated it as he would a simple child's.

She thinks *she's* suffered, he would snort. Hah, she doesn't even know what suffering is. She doesn't know how lucky she is!

But this strategy couldn't work as well for her son, because for Hamilton she was someone whom he first knew and continued for several years to know from the point of view of utter dependence. Condescension comes hard to sons, no matter how easily it comes to them later as husbands or fathers. For him to neutralize his mother's wringing and tweaking, her long-suffering wet eyes, her whole series of practically irresistible invitations for him to draw on his guilt quotient, Hamilton had to devise a different and even crueler-seeming strategy. It was to affirm, as much as possible, his mother's point of view. Let his father deny it, condescend to it, reject it any way he could. Hamilton would honor it, would validate it, would meet all its most stringent demands on him. If she felt injured or disappointed or deprived somehow, if she felt that her unfair burden of woe had been unfairly added to, he would do what he could to justify her feelings—to provide an objective correlative, as it were—by injuring her, by disappointing and depriving her, by adding, even if only slightly, to her burden of woe.

His description of the process by which he validated and honored her point of view went something like this: "When a lady makes a request, a gentleman has no choice but to meet that request. Sure, he can ignore it, but he wouldn't be much of a gentleman, would he?" He was smiling, but the smile was characterized more by resignation than good cheer.

I had asked him pointblank why he had behaved toward his mother in a way that the rest of the community had regarded as a heinous way to behave toward one's mother. He had first obtained the power, legal and financial, to evict his mother from the home she had lived in all her adult life, the house she had raised three children in and where she had lived in wedlock with a man, his own father, for over forty years, the house that had become the source and final resting place for a lifetime's most personal memories and associations. He had obtained the power to evict her from this house, had obtained it under the guise of helping to care for her in her dependent old age, and, *horror,* he had *used* that power. He had gone ahead and evicted her. He had forced her to accept the extra room in her daughter Jody's small and crowded trailer and to have the costs of her room and board paid by her other daughter, Sarah. Hamilton had forced Alma into becoming her daughters' burdens of woe, he had forced her into deepening their sense of having been injured. He had given them, thereby, control over her. For he had forced her into the role, for the first time in her life, of victimizer, of depriver, of oppressor.

This was not, of course, what the community saw in it, but it is what eventually I came to see in it. Gradually, as I pondered Hamilton's cryptic, seemingly irrelevant answers to my questions, I came to believe that his eviction of his mother that night was an almost inevitable consequence of the years in which he had honored her need to be injured. Doubtless, in time she had gradually come to realize that he did not feel guilt for his role as injurer, at which point she played her last card, so to speak. She would force him to reject her altogether. She would up the ante. Which, from Hamilton's point of view, gave him no alternative but to raise her bet and force the next round of the game into play. Did she want him to be *that* ungrateful a son? All right, if that's what she wanted, it's what she got. After all, she was his mother and he could do no less for her than try to provide for her what she really wanted.

"I learned something about women from that experience," he told me one evening at the Bonnie Aire, where we had gone for a few drinks. It was a hot, overcast, Friday night, the July following his eviction of his mother.

What had he learned about women? I asked him (having at the time intimations of some future troubles with women, whom I then understood almost not at all).

He learned, he told me, a woman's greatest power over a man is her ability to turn her suffering into a virtue. She converts the one into the other, completely. She makes a condition of being female—and a wife and mother—into an ethical feat, which feat we as men have no choice but to reinforce. Most men don't understand this conversion, he explained, and that's why most men, rather than reinforce the conversion, deny that it's even taken place. They treat their women as if they were still suffering. But what we're *supposed* to do, what they *want* us to do, is to reinforce the conversion by acknowledging it and making it possible for the process to continue. So, naturally, what they want is for us to increase their suffering, to build their supply of it back up at least to where it was before they managed the difficult task of converting it into something that gave them power, the power of possessing virtue.

He paused and chugged down his glass of ale as chaser to the shot of Canadian Club he had tossed down right before speaking. I remained silent. Hamilton seldom spoke at this length (not to me, not about a subject that he knew was important to my understanding of him), and I didn't want to distract him with my presence.

"And I'll tell you something, something that I've not told anyone else," he said, looking down at the empty glass, turning it in his huge hands. "It ain't easy, giving them what you know they want. Especially when it's your mother. Because the spring the whole thing, the conversion thing, works off is guilt. Male guilt." He explained that it's only to a man that a woman's suffering looks like an ethical feat. Other women look at it with envy, or, if they're a little protective of their own brand of pain, they see it as pathetic, or maybe they look at it with fear, because they know a woman who suffers more than they do cannot honor their own conversions. But a man sees it differently. Only a man can admire the pain, can acknowledge the bearer of it as virtuous. And the reason a man sees it this way is because he bears with him a quantity of guilt, nameless because he's born with it, having been born male in this world where one-half of the species dominates the other half. Hamilton wasn't saying it was right or wrong, that domination. He was just saying that it exists. The dominant one in any pairing off feels guilty for that fact, whether he knows it or not. And because most men don't know they feel guilty, guilt in general, rather than in the particular case, most men don't see what's being asked of them by the particular cases before them.

He was sweating across his forehead and upper lip. Two large fans, one in each of the back corners of the tavern, were not cooling the place much. The temperature outside was the same as the temperature inside, and all the fans accomplished was to create movement in the heated air, which was sufficiently close to body temperature so as to be incapable of cooling anybody. The bartender leaned morosely on his elbows and stared at the front door. There were no customers aside from Hamilton and me. The waitress, a tubby woman with frizzy orange-dyed hair, sat on one of the barstools, her tray plopped on her lap. Hamilton and I were in a booth close to the door.

A man's guilt, he told me then, wants him to eliminate the suffering of the particular case in front of him, so gradually he tries, and sometimes he thinks he succeeded, only to see it reappear a moment later, in her face, her hands, her voice. Some men, after a while, realize that the particular case has nothing to do with their generalized guilt, and what they do is to dismiss the particular case, to deny its hold on them. As Hamilton's father had done. He had ended up ignoring Alma's virtue and had treated her suffering "as a plain pain in the ass," to use Hamilton's words. It's easier on the man that way, he explained. But harder on the particular case, the woman. The only honorable thing a man can do is, first, realize that this particular case's pain has nothing to do with his guilt. That lets him deal realistically with the particular case, but it also means that he can't kid himself about there being any easy removal of his generalized guilt. "No," he declared, "you've got to learn to live with it. You're not going to change society, so you just have to learn to live with it. Right?"

"Right. Right."

"But that doesn't mean it's easy, any of it. You've still got to face down that guilt every time some woman comes up to you wringing her hands in despair," he went on. It's hardest, he explained, when the woman is your mother, because if she practiced "smotherhood" on you while you were young and helpless and completely dependent on her for information about the world, then she's going to have a strong hold on your guilt. She won't be able to help it. "Smotherhood," he said, glossing the term for me, is a self-defeating, usually unconscious way of deluding a son into thinking that all his guilt is directly related, as effect, to his mother's pain and apparent powerlessness. And this delusion gets set into the son's mind long before he can think for himself. So that later on, when he tries to respond rationally to the demands some woman's pain is putting on him, if that woman happens to be his mother, he's still got to deal with the old, deep-seated delusion that his only honorable response is the guilt-ridden one. In the particular case of Hamilton's own mother, he felt that he had been put to the ultimate test. She had made it clear to him that the only way he could honor her conversion of generalized suffering into particularized forbearance was to kick her out of her own house. Which, after a lot of tugs in the opposite direction, he did. "It wasn't easy," he sighed. Then he waved to the waitress for another round.

"I bet it wasn't," I said admiringly. Perspiration was running off our faces. I unbuttoned my cuffs and rolled up my sleeves to the elbows, then loosened my collar and took off my necktie. I had long since removed my sport coat. Hamilton was wearing a clean white T-shirt and work pants—not that it matters, except peripherally with regard to what happened next.

The waitress, whose name was Linda, a cheerful type who seemed resigned to spending the rest of her life doing just what she was doing then, brought us another round, our third or fourth, I can't recall, and slowly, her tray slapped her thigh, walked back to the bar and hitched herself up onto a stool and resumed staring at the front door. The bartender, whose name was Lee, a town "character" who played Rudoph the Red-nosed Reindeer every year in the Kiwanis Club's Christmas Pageant, went on peering morosely into the hot empty space a few feet in front of him. He was obviously lost in thought, puzzling his way around a bit of supper caught behind a tooth, his mind a single, low-frequency hum of passive attention that, having fallen upon his tooth, seemed glued there. In the corners of the room, the two standing fans whirred uselessly away at the heated air as the screen door swung open and a woman walked in from the street, alone. The door banged behind her, and she looked around the room, smiled at Hamilton and me slightly, and walked directly to the bar, where she ordered a gin and tonic.

She was around forty, a good-looking woman, more hand-some than pretty, wearing a sleeveless blouse that exposed her muscular arms and drew attention to the amplitude of her bosom. Her corn-blond hair, long and healthy-looking, was wound into a Teutonic bun behind her head. Her white Bermuda shorts were tight and made of such heavy cloth that they seemed to armor her lower body rather than merely to cover it. Though she had been in town, living in an apartment over Paige Realty, for no more than two weeks, certain things about here were already known by just about everyone else in town: She was the new school nurse, she was from Concord, the capital, where she had previously worked in an old-age home, she was unmarried, prob-ably had never been married, she had a loud, commanding voice and a hearty laugh and she liked, on these hot evenings in July, to come out of her sweltering apartment around nine for a couple of gin and tonics and a little conversation with "the boys." Her name was Jenny, and within two weeks she was Hamilton Stark's third wife.

"WELL," I SAID to C., "that ought to make things more 'significant.'" We were in my library on the ground floor. C. had finished his bath and dressed, and we had adjourned to the library where he could drink a little wine, an excellent California burgundy that C. had not yet tried, and warm ourselves by the fireplace. It was a chilly evening, not yet cold enough, of course, to turn the furnace on, but quite cold enough to welcome a room's being heated by an open fire. C. was seated in his favorite armchair, resting from the exhilaration of his bath, as was his wont, and I had taken my accustomed place by the fireplace, standing with one elbow resting on the mantel.

C. was wheezing slightly. "Ah, yes. Yes, that's fine, fine." He uncrossed and recrossed his feet at the ankles on the ottoman. "Tell me, if you don't mind giving things away, tell me," he wheezed, "do you *personally* agree with Hamilton's rationalization for his . . . behavior toward his mother in particular . . . and women in general? After all, it implies an attitude toward women that's not exactly fashionable, you know." He almost chuckled. "You may get yourself into deep trouble with your female readers, heh-heh."

Letting himself sink back into the chair, he went on. "Two questions. Did you indeed have 'trouble with women' later on? And did the understanding of women that you gained, apparently through Hamilton Stark, help you out of your trouble? Obviously the two questions become one, and obviously, again, that single question is an attempt to determine if your novel can be used as a pragmatic guide. For we all, if we are men, have 'trouble with women' from time to time and wish, especially at such times, that we understood them better." C. smiled benevolently and nipped off the end of his cigar with his front teeth. I don't think the burgundy suited him.

"Yes, yes, of course. But that was just a personal aside there, that business about my intimations. It really refers to nothing that should concern my readers.* Probably, because it does intrude on the narrator's locus of attention, and therefore the reader's locus of attention as well, I'll revise it out of the final version of my manuscript. I will say this much, however: If you want to use this novel as a guidebook, then you'll have to accept Hamilton Stark as your guide. That's the only rule for reading it, the only condition I'll attach—except of course that you know the language well enough to recognize a persona when you hear one."

"Ho, ho!" C. laughed.

I refilled his glass. That should quiet him, I thought. I had expected him to respond, not to my slip of a reference to my own, later, personal difficulties (which are well outside the scope of this book), but rather to the peculiar juxtaposition of Hamil-

---

* It might be worth noting, however, that the intimated troubles did occur later, very recently, in fact, and naturally enough concerned the only woman in the author's life (at the time of this writing). That woman was Rochelle Stark, and the author's "troubles" with her arose from her gift, and his literary use, of the voluminous materials and several texts of her novel, *The Plumber's Apprentice*, which, the reader will recall, were formally presented to the author in his Chapter Seven, "Ausable Chasm." For, when it became apparent to Rochelle that the author intended to incorporate extended pieces of her more or less completed narrative directly into the body of his own narrative, her reaction was surprising to the author. He had taken her at her word, that her research materials and other texts were his to use, however he wished to use them, in the writing of his own novel. Thus he had hoped that she would be pleased by what he regarded as his imaginative use of those texts, especially since he had credited her for them and had so elaborately praised their qualities (even when, naturally, with this fastidious an author, there were sections that displeased him somewhat). And if his hopes of her gratitude and delight could not be met, then he fully expected her, at the least, to provide him with an objective appraisal of his use of those materials, as one craftsman to another. In other words, the author hoped she would be flattered by his deployment of her help, and if he

ton's confession regarding his mother in particular and women in general, and the sudden appearance in the narrative of his third wife, Jenny, the nurse. After all, if it's specifically the custodial compulsion of some women that you find most disturbing, one would expect you to be especially wary of women who are custodial by profession—nurses, housekeepers, babysitters, prison guards, and so on, professions that have no product as issue. It certainly surprised me—Hamilton's speedy courtship and marriage to Jenny, I mean, and, that night at the Bonnie Aire, his quick switch from the painful (to him) description of his relationship with his mother to his moves on Jenny. For, no sooner had she sat down at the bar and ordered a gin and tonic than Hamilton arose from our booth and joined her at the bar. He opened his conversation with a discussion of the weather, the evening's dominant fact, and moved quickly to questions about her—where she was from, her job, her impressions of the town and its people, what she did with her earnings—to a suggestion that they dance (Hamilton is well known as a dancer, an excellent dancer), whereupon he played "On the Road to Mandalay" by Frank Sinatra on the juke box in the corner, and the two of

couldn't get that much from her, then he expected *more* help, this time in the form of critical analysis. Instead, as the reader may have guessed, Rochelle's reactions were more complex. She would not criticize. No, indeed, quite the opposite; she lavished him with praise for his imagination and wit. And she would not let him believe that she was sincerely flattered. "Oh, my goodness! I'm so happy that you were able to take so *much!*" she exclaimed. "And that you had to change so *little!*" This was the beginning of the author's "troubles" with Rochelle. A sensitive person, he was able immediately to break her code and perceive that her exclamations were actually whimpers of pain, a woman's pain, the kind of pain no self-conscious man can perceive without recognizing its cause—man himself, or rather, that aspect of himself which is characterized by gender (as opposed to sex or any other personal manifestation of manhood). At first the author permitted himself the standard, expected reaction of personal guilt. After all, her suffering certainly seemed personalized enough, a particular kind and dose of pain caused by a particular person's offense. He therefore apologized. She told him not to apologize. He sounded ridiculous. She was honored. Why should he apologize for having honored her? He apologized again. She rejected his apology again. He tried to minimize his actual use of her materials. She agreed, ashamed of their irrelevance. He came back and defended his need

them danced, slowly at first, in the oppressive heat, then in large, graceful circles around the small room, between tables, from the door in front to the bar at the back. They played "Moonlight in Vermont" by Andy Williams, and danced again, serious-faced, athletic, the two of them, a pleasure to watch, certainly, but somehow embarrassing, for, in this heat in the all-but-deserted tavern, with their somber yet intent expressions, it was a rather intimate dance they were doing. Then they played the theme from the movie *Picnic,* and I think we all, the bartender, the idle waitress, and I, became extremely self-conscious and turned away from the dancers, the bartender to a chore in the kitchen in back, the waitress to painting her fingernails pink, and I to a copy of Peterson's *Field Guide to North American Birds* that I happened to have in the pocket of my sports jacket, which I had removed some time earlier.

It was several minutes later, when, as I was committing to memory the call of the brown creeper (*Certhia familiaris*), whispering to myself "see-ti-wee-tu-wee," that Hamilton interrupted and informed me that he and Jenny were going for a walk to the top of Blue Job, where it would be cooler, and if I wanted a lift

---

for them, their utter relevance. She didn't believe him. He insisted. She believed him, and again, honored, she rejected his apology, this time in advance of its being offered. He grew suspicious of her expectation that he apologize. She must think he had something to apologize *for*. He denied having done anything wrong. She agreed, nothing wrong. He said lots of novelists had done it. She was happy to know there was a tradition for this sort of thing. He demanded to know what she meant by that. She said nothing. He said he knew irony when he heard it, and sarcasm too. She doubted that. He laughed sarcastically. She apologized—for misleading him, for having been unclear. She had been perfectly clear, he said ironically. She wrung her hands. He stalked about. She apologized. He told her not to be ridiculous, he felt honored by her gift. Why should she apologize for having honored him? She apologized again. He rejected her apology again. She began to deprecate the materials, pointing out his good judgment in deciding to use so little of them. He agreed, depressed by what he feared was their irrelevance. She came back and defended their relevance to his novel, especially the way he had integrated them. He didn't believe her. She insisted. He believed her, and again, feeling honored by her gift, he rejected her apologies for the meagerness of the gift. What, she asked him, made him think she wanted to apologize for her gift? He must think her ashamed of her work, espe-

back to his house, where I had parked my own car, he would provide it. I smiled hello politely to Jenny, who was sweating profusely, and said no, that I'd stay here awhile and would catch a ride out for my car later in the evening.

Hamilton seemed relieved, or at least he did not scowl as he usually did when I abridged or altered one of his suggestions with a plan of my own, and the two of them left together, as silently and intently as they had been dancing.

The next time I saw Hamilton, not three weeks later, he had married her. "Well, I married her," he said.

"Who?"

"Jenny, the school nurse," he said, as if I should have expected it. I did not, of course. Quite the opposite.

C., HOWEVER, WAS not surprised.

"Well, let me tell you, it surprised *me!*" I fairly shouted, startling him back into his chair.

"Goodness!"

Certainly it surprised me. Hamilton had but barely shed his second wife Annie, and he had only just met this new one. Also,

---

cially in relation to his work. She told him hers was just as beautifully done as his. There was nothing wrong with it. He agreed, nothing wrong. At least, she informed him, she was working in a tradition. He was happy for her, as for so many other writers, that there was a well-established tradition for them to work in. She demanded to know what he meant by that. He said nothing. She said she knew irony when she heard it, and sarcasm too. He doubted that, judging from her work. She laughed sarcastically. He apologized. He said he was guilty of having been unclear. After all, he depended on a tradition as much as she did. Oh, no, he had been *perfectly* clear, she told him, wringing her hands. He stalked about. She wept. He apologized. And so it went, around and around again, like a uroboros. They had been transformed, and two separate people, hitherto linked solely by their love for one another and their shared obsession with a third person, had suddenly found themselves capable of connecting only viciously, auto-cannibalistically, wearing a single body, yes, but a body with its tail in its mouth. And since neither the author nor Rochelle could distinguish the head of the beast from its tail, they could not break this self-devouring connection, and rapidly their love for one another turned to fear for their own survival, then desperation, then hatred of the other. Their old shared obsession broke apart also, and they began to attack each other's viewpoint and interpre-

because of her profession, as I have mentioned, and because of her rather ordinary life so far, which, I assumed, gave her a rather ordinary mind, and because of her appearance, this new one did not, to me, seem to be Hamilton's "type." She was a handsome woman, in an athletic way, but her overall appearance was Prussian, almost manly. Both of Hamilton's previous wives had been physically delicate by comparison, even Annie, who did not start to gain weight until after she had married him. This woman seemed invulnerable, which surely only reinforced what I assumed (from her profession) was a custodial temperament. How could Hamilton have thought he would be happy with such a woman, especially so soon after the dissolution of his second marriage and that final encounter with his mother and the insights into what he called "smotherhood" gained there?

It wasn't difficult to understand or to predict, my large friend assured me. According to him, though my even larger friend, Hamilton, might well be conscious of a particular image dominating his relationship with his mother, he might even be conscious that the same image had dominated his rela-

---

tation. Where one found meaning, the other saw projection and egoism. Where one found sublimity, the other saw wishful thinking. Each began to think the other soft-headed, sentimental and self-indulgent on the subject of Hamilton Stark. Yet they could not separate. The uroboros is a mesmerizing image. It is, in spite of the entrapment it signifies, a securing, containing, utterly stable image, and if the author had not recalled his earlier conversations with Hamilton and had not decided to enact certain of the aphorisms learned there (and set down earlier in this chapter), it's possible that their lives, the author's and Rochelle's, would be locked together even today by the image of the self-swallowing serpent. For the author, as the reader doubtless knows by now, bore a typically heavy burden of typical male guilt, despite his years of study with the master of neutralizing precisely that guilt. And Rochelle, in turn, bore a typically heavy burden of typical female pain, despite her relative freedom from any oppressive relationships with particular men (heaven knows, her father had never participated in any such relationship, and her love affair with the author had been essentially the connection between two acolytes, with nothing in their role as acolytes to permit an inequality between them). Thus, by the time the author finally remembered Hamilton's advice and example and their applicability to his own situation, he had grown feeble and confused, and it took an

tionships with his other wives, and possibly his relationships
with all women (an awareness, C. pointed out, that so far I had
not granted Hamilton); in spite of this awareness, this self-
consciousness, the man might still be compelled to go on living
in its dominion.

At first I didn't understand, but then C. explained that it
depended on the image, its qualities. A uroboros, for example,
is an image of closure, a frightening image of compulsive, ritualistic repetition. To have one's life organized under the dictates
of a uroboros would be painful, indeed, and if one were unfortunate enough to be conscious of that image, one might find it
even more painful, for all one could do would be to raise the
repetition to a higher level, hoping to avoid it there, only to find
oneself once again repeating oneself. What one would have in
that case would be a spiraling uroboros, as it were. In Hamilton's case, by becoming conscious of his compulsive attraction to
women who wanted to "smother" him and his resultant revulsion at the indebtedness incurred, that is, his "guilt," his only
recourse seems to have been to introduce "wrath," so as to speed
up the process, to spin the wheel a little faster, hoping thereby

---

enormous effort of will for him to face down the forces that conspired to keep him from
applying that advice and example, the forces of his own conventions, the threat of public
disapprobation, his fear of loneliness, and naturally, his love of Rochelle. There was a
further consequence that threatened him: he doubtless would end up unable to use the
materials of her novel in his own novel, either because she would forbid it or because he
would be too ashamed, purely and simply, of a cruelty that, at such a point, would be
merely gratuitous. And possibly illegal. But even so, he was at last capable of meeting this
coercive array of forces head-on. One afternoon following a particularly vicious turn of
the wheel they were locked into, he went to his desk and drew out of a drawer all the
notes, tapes, genealogical charts, maps, photos, and all the carefully typed manuscript
pages of *The Plumber's Apprentice*, wrapped the materials fastidiously in brown paper,
and drove to the post office, where he mailed the package to Rochelle, who at that time
was still living in a boarding house in Concord. To the top sheet of her manuscript, he
had clipped a typewritten note, which read: *I have read your manuscript and related materials with care, and, as you know, with a predisposition to enjoy them because of the person
your character Alvin Stock is based on. I have found, however, that, whether taken as a work
of imaginative fiction or as a* roman à clef, *the manuscript fails to interest or amuse, and I*

(one must assume) that the pain for the woman and confusion for himself would be lessened.

Rochelle's demon Asmodeus was not a wholly imprecise way of perceiving her father's behavior, C. reminded me. It explained a great deal—his fervent seductions, his cold withdrawals, and, finally, his wrathful rejections. If you concede sincerity to such a man, then his behavior does indeed seem possessed. The difficulty with the image of Asmodeus, however, is that it holds out the possibility of exorcism. Magic. The right combination of aspects of the moon, chants, artifacts and fetishes, and *voilà*! he's free. A daughter's love, a *spurned* daughter's love, explains her attraction to it.

But, I, as C. quite rightly pointed out, I was no man's daughter, spurned or otherwise. Which was doubtless why I had chosen to describe the same man with the image of the holy man, the man outside all social prescriptions for meaningful behavior, the man who uses his life as allegory, who, to demonstrate human ordinariness, heaps ashes on himself, who, to demonstrate the vanity of human wishes, forgoes all normal access to praise and achievement, the man who, to demonstrate

---

am therefore returning it to you with my thanks. You are obviously quite intelligent and at times show evidence of talent, and I would not wish to discourage someone who is at the very beginning of her career as a writer, but it occurs to me that you might consider trying some other aspect of writing than fiction. Have you ever thought seriously of writing articles for women's magazines? This can be extremely lucrative, and you would be free to travel. In any case, I am flattered that you cared to solicit my opinion of your work, and if you wish to have me read any of your future writings, I would be delighted to do so. Good luck to you in your career. She never knew, of course, that as he typed this letter the author wept. Nor would he have told her or even hinted at his pain if they ever happened by chance to meet again. It was the end of Rochelle's lovely presence in his life, he knew that. He also knew how she would remember and imagine him from that day on—as a senselessly cruel man, possibly psychotic, a man unable to give love because he was unable to accept love, a *dangerous* man. And he knew that, in so describing him, she would bring him closer to the way most people described her own father, and that possibly her experience with him, the author, would lead her finally to view her father as others did. Her inescapable image of him, the author, as villain would, by its similarity to the other, lead her to accept an image of her father that she had resisted so bravely these many years. He knew that this

the possibility of self-transcendence, denies the claims the rest of us honor.

We are the only creature that does not know what it is to be itself, C. went on. We are the only creature that must perceive itself through the use of images. The limits and the possibilities implied by those images, then, are the limits and possibilities for our perceptions of ourselves. And because we can hardly be expected to exceed the morphology of our perceptions, then it's clear that our images of ourselves determine the morphology of our very lives. Rochelle saw her father through the image of a particular kind of demon-possession, one that combined and thus explained his peculiar juxtaposition of drunkenness, lust and rage. I had tried to convert her to my point of view, which depended on her coming to see him as a holy man. C., in his turn, was recommending that I see Hamilton as a spiraling uroboros. We were all three trying to perceive him, to imagine him into a reality in our own lives, by means of a coherent image. Yet he persisted in resisting our imaginations. The demon had fallen away in the face of Hamilton's obvious intentionality. No man possessed could be that willful. And the holy man was rapidly being secularized by what appeared to be compulsive behavior rather than self-conscious, exemplary behavior designed to be taken as allegorical. And now this somewhat pathetic and depressing image of the self-devouring serpent had come to control my perceptions of the man. The time had come to try to discover how Hamilton perceived himself, if at all. And if this could

---

conversion, or lapse, would deprive no one of any particular truth—not Rochelle, not Hamilton, and not the author. And finally, he knew now that he himself was going to have to research and write all those sections of his hero's life that he had originally counted on being researched and written by Rochelle. That meant work. Hard work. He did not enjoy reading realistic fiction; still less did he enjoy writing it. But he had no choice. Rochelle was gone, used up and thrown out with the rubbish of his imaginative life. And her novel was gone with her. He was alone in his book now, a solitary. (Except, of course, for the company of his friend C. and Hamilton Stark himself.)

not be determined, to ask oneself if, indeed, one had invented him altogether.

Thank heaven for C.! If it hadn't been for his presence in my life, his very presence that evening in my library, I would at that moment have felt wholly alone.

CHAPTER 10

Graveside

THIS IS A painful chapter for me to write. Before I'm through with it, I will have lost my best friend, will have sent him from my house into the snowy cold, leaving me behind, remorseful and, to counter remorse, desperate for justification. A dangerous state for a rationalist: it's when he is most tempted to depart from reality and fly off into the soothing heavens of reason.

It began with the death of Alma Stark—not the actual fact of her dying, but later, in my describing it. It's possible that it began earlier, of course, in Chapter Nine, where I told of Hamilton's meeting and consequent marriage to Jenny, but I was not aware then of any irreconcilable differences between my and C.'s points of view. At that time, despite the differences between us, I was still able to use C.'s point of view to inform my own, as I had been doing all along. So that at the end of Chapter Nine, while I may have seemed disconsolate at having to lose Rochelle, I could still console myself with the continued presence of C. But all that was before I had told of the death of Alma Stark.

The death itself was not especially poignant or wrenching. It was expected. She had been ill for most of the previous winter and had fended off an attack of flu and then pneumonia, but clearly she was weakening and, in fact, had not been expected to survive the winter at all. She was eighty, still mentally alert, but no longer able to resist ordinary onslaughts against her body. The following November, she came down with a strep throat, and despite massive doses of antibiotics, she developed double pneumonia and had to be hospitalized in Concord, where, after struggling on for two more weeks, she died, quite peacefully in her sleep, of heart disease.

Though her last years obviously had been scarred by the wound Hamilton had inflicted on her when he had evicted her—a wound she could close only by refusing after that night ever to see her son again, refusing and regularly renewing that refusal, for the cut was deep and could be staunched only with diffi-culty—those last years, nevertheless, had been relatively com-forting to her. She was able to convert her dependence on her daughters, Jody and Sarah, into something which caused *her* to suffer, and thus the integrity of her personality was sustained. Her daily round of activities included helping Jody with house-work, cooking and cleaning up after the children (twin boys entering adolescence, people who, to her tongue-clucking satis-faction, seemed to regard her presence as they would a maid's—or at least that's how, sighing, wringing her hands and tweaking her throat, she would put it to her friends at the Ladies' Aid Society, always adding, of course, "It must be hard for them, hav-ing an old lady suddenly come to live in a crowded little house with them"). After the first year, Chub had added a small bed-room to the trailer, off the back at the middle, like an awkwardly placed appendage, and she spent most of her evenings there, and while her daughter, son-in-law and their two children watched TV in the living room, she crocheted, wrote letters to the Barn-stead boys in Vietnam, and read the Bible. It was a nice room, pine-paneled, with a single window that faced Chub's gravel pit (a supplementary source of income for the family). She had her own bed, a dresser, a small desk under the window, and even a closet of her own, which she had filled with the rest of her possessions—her clothes, photograph albums, Christmas tree decorations, and the quilted spread that she had made the spring she married Hamilton's father and that she had used on their bed for over forty years. But now she slept alone on a narrow, cotlike bed. It would look foolish, she remarked, if she used the quilt to cover this little bed. But she couldn't bring herself to give it over to Chub and Jody, to lay it across their wide Hollywood bed in the master bedroom. She thought maybe she'd just leave it to them in her will. She'd leave the photograph albums to Sarah, who seemed more interested in them anyhow, perhaps because she was childless. At least that's what she told the ladies at the Ladies' Aid Society while they knitted, sewed, crocheted, and wove handy, warm articles for the Barnstead boys in Vietnam. As it turned out, however, she wrote no will; Sarah ended up with the quilt and Jody took the photographs and Christmas tree ornaments.

During these years, between Alma's loss of her home and her death, no one in the family spoke to Hamilton or saw him socially. If one or several of them accidentally came up against the fact of his presence, at a bean supper or the Fourth of July Band Concert or in McAllister's General Store, for instance, they ignored that fact and would not acknowledge its existence even to one another. One time Chub had backed his cruiser—his own station wagon, actually, outfitted at the town's expense with a siren, blue glass bubble on top and two-way radio—into one of Hamilton's cars, a year-old Cadillac, the car he'd driven to Rochelle's graduation in Ausable Chasm, New York. Chub had driven up to Danis's Superette without noticing Hamilton's car and had parked next to it, both cars facing the store, and then, recognizing the dark brown Cadillac, he had realized that the owner doubtless was inside the grocery store and that they would unavoidably pass in the aisle, so he had immediately dropped his cruiser into reverse and had backed out quickly, clipping with his right front fender Hamilton's finny taillight. While the glass was still tinkling to the ground, Hamilton had emerged from the store and had stared, expressionless, as Chub spun the wheel of the cruiser, tromped on the accelerator, and roared away.

No one spoke to Hamilton of the event that for all intents and purposes had severed him from his family, and naturally, he never brought up the subject himself—not necessarily because he was ashamed, however. It just was not his way to discuss his personal life, not even with people who happened to participate in his personal life, his wives, for instance. In fact, none of his wives learned of the split in the family from Hamilton himself, and there were three of them (wives) who came to live with him in the very house that had been as much the symbol of that split as cause. They found out from their friends and other associates in town, usually when someone, eager to obtain and circulate Hamilton's point of view, would ask Jenny, the school nurse, or, later, Maureen or, still later, Dora, why on earth her new husband had kicked his mother out of her own house. Jenny, or Maureen or Dora, would demand to know what on earth the person was talking about, whereupon she would hear the generally accepted version of the story, so that the interviewee became interviewer, first of the friend or associate who happened to have made the query in the first place, then of Hamilton himself.

"Why on earth did you kick your mother out of her own house?" she would ask him finally.

His answer always went something like this: "A, it wasn't her house. B, it was my house. And C, I didn't kick her out against her will." And that's all he would offer as explanation or description of what had happened that night. If his wife of the moment persisted with questions, he would simply announce that his mother was the only person to whom he would explain or describe what had happened, but only if she first indicated to him that she neither understood nor remembered what had

happened. "And so far," he would say, "she's given no such indication of stupidity or lapse of memory." At which point it was
clear that the interview had ended. Hamilton would go back to
reading the paper or weeding the garden or repairing the toaster,
and his wife would promise herself that she would inquire further into the matter, to be sure, but she would ask other people
than her husband.

His first wife, of course, never heard as much as a rumor about
the event, but his second wife, Annie, "the actress," who had
been visiting her aunt in the Bronx at the time, had been forced
to rely on the town's version of the story as much as any of the
wives who came later. When she came back from the Bronx and
her mother-in-law was no longer living with them in what Annie
had regarded as her mother-in-law's home, Hamilton had refused
to tell her any more than he later told Jenny or Maureen or Dora:
"A, it's not her house. B, it's my house. And C, I didn't kick her
out against her will." This, to Annie's bewildered, "Where's your
mother? Where are her clothes? Her *things?*" Though she never
actually judged him for what had happened (she always said,
"Whatever it was that actually *did* happen that night"), it nevertheless was one of the things that she cited later when she chose
to list her reasons for eventually becoming so frightened of him
that she left and divorced him.

His third wife, Jenny, however, left and divorced him for no
other reason than his supposed treatment, his mistreatment, of
his mother and his refusal to confirm or deny the local description of that mistreatment (there was no local *explanation* for it, of
course). It was assumed by the townspeople that because Jenny
was middle-aged, childless, and, it was discovered, an orphan,
she had married Hamilton with the hope of obtaining thereby a
ready-made family. When it appeared that he was as orphaned
and childless as she, and thus could not deliver what she desired
from him, she had swiftly returned to her previous way of life
as the school nurse and, later on, as athletic director of the girls'

sports program. Some people thought that Jenny may have been a lesbian and that her marriage to Hamilton had been a last, vain attempt to kindle and warm herself with a "normal" sexual relationship, but to believe that, they would have been compelled to attribute "normal" sexual proclivities and needs to Hamilton, which by then no one was willing to grant him. Not that anyone suspected he was homosexual. Rather, no one could imagine his being tender. People could easily understand why women were initially attracted to him—"After all," they said, spreading their hands and lifting their eyebrows, "he *is* good-looking, in a largish way, and he makes a decent living, and he has a nice house, now. And he *is* a beautiful dancer. He's a smooth talker, too, when he wants to be. So if you'd just met him, and if he wasn't drinking too much, not drunk, I mean, well, who knows, there's lots of women who might think he'd be a good catch. At least at first." And indeed, five women in Hamilton's lifetime so far had thought so and, as a result, had pitched themselves into his lap. And he had married them for it. As he put it when, after each divorce, he was asked why he had married the woman in the first place, especially as with each consecutive wife the courtship and marriage became more and more abbreviated: "Hey, what's a man to do? When a woman tells you she loves you, you can't tell her not to. And if you don't particularly dislike the woman, there's no point in telling her you dislike her. No woman wants to hear a lie like that, even when it's true. And frankly, I never met a woman I disliked." In recent years, however, he would add, "Course, I never met one I liked, either. Maybe if I had, I wouldn't have gotten married so many times, heh, heh, heh."

His fourth wife, Maureen Blade, only eighteen when she married him, probably was too young to be able to evaluate her new and much older husband's past behavior, or even his present behavior, for that matter. That's both the advantage and disadvantage, for the elder, of choosing a mate who is still not much more than a child: she has not yet been exposed to enough adult behavior to recognize when it is abnormal. The whole idea of "normality" depends on the availability of a fairly large sampling, which would necessarily be unavailable to an eighteen-year-old girl, no matter how precocious. And Maureen was not thought to be especially precocious. By the time she had been Mrs. Hamilton Stark for six months, however, she had aged considerably, if not matured as well, and the whole question of precocity was no longer relevant. After her divorce from Hamilton, she resumed the use of her maiden name, Blade, but to no avail. No one could think of her as a maiden anymore. She was a young divorcée, a woman with a complicated past.

But Maureen was the only one of Hamilton's five wives who already knew the story of his break with his mother when she married him. A psychiatrist might suggest that, in marrying him, she was working out, through identification with his well-known acts against *his* parent, her own desires to behave similarly toward *her* parent, a drunken lout, Arthur Blade, a chronically unemployed lout who had mistreated his eldest daughter for years, beating her and, it was rumored, even making sexual advances against her. One might, if one were that same psychiatrist, also suggest that in marrying Hamilton she was seeking a replacement for her father, for, not more than a month before the marriage, Arthur Blade had been committed to the New Hampshire State Hospital in Concord, where his extreme alcoholism could be treated, at least temporarily.

In any case, Hamilton refused to act the father for her, no more the kind father than the cruel; he treated her the way he treated any other adolescent, tolerating her enthralled presence, exchanging goods for services and vice versa, and whenever she asked for something more, some direct expression of his personal affection, say, he responded by demanding more of her first, such as more room in which to move without having to explain or justify his moves. "If you think you can make a man report back to you who he is, where he goes and where he cannot go, and that by doing so he will be acting out of love for you, you're dead wrong. A man will do these things for you only if he is afraid of losing you. And fear of losing a woman and loving her are not the same thing. Actually, they may be opposites," he told her, and immediately Maureen fell into confusion and despair, a state he encouraged and she endured for six months, until she at last realized that she would be rid of her confusion and despair only when she had got rid of her husband. She knew that she would then, as a direct result, have many other unpleasant thoughts and feelings to live with—such as what it meant to be an eighteen-year-old ex-wife in a small New Hampshire town—but she no longer cared. Besides, she could always say that he had treated her no better than he had treated his own mother. Then everyone would understand her leaving him, especially those people who had not been able to understand why she had married him in the first place.

So she told him that she wanted a divorce. He said, "Fine with me, if that's what you want." He would not contest it, as he had not contested any of his divorces ("I never contested the marriage, did I? Why should I contest the divorce?"), as long as there were no demands for alimony and no demanding property settlement. She could take whatever she wanted of what she had brought with her. Anything else she wanted he would sell to her at one-half the market value. So she packed her clothes in her battered suitcase and went back to live in her father's house, to care for her five younger brothers and sisters until her father was released from the state hospital, at which time she hoped to move down to Manchester or some other city, maybe Boston, where she could find a job in a factory and get an apartment of her own and maybe buy a red car.

His fifth wife, Dora, on the other hand, until Alma's actual funeral, knew nothing of her husband's break with his family. Naturally, she knew about his other wives and his daughter Rochelle, for he made no secret of their existence. (Oddly, for such a talked-about man, he made no secret of anything; there was no question he would not answer; it's just that very few people knew what to make of his answers or how to avoid having their next question manipulated by the answer to the preceding one.) She had asked, as did all but his first wife, if he had ever been married before, and he had answered, "Of course." She asked him how many times. "Four." So many! Were there any children? she wondered. "Yes." And how many children? "One." Hamilton never offered information gratuitously, so if you didn't know ahead of time precisely what your question was, and then asked it, it was likely that he would never provide the answer. For instance, in the above interrogation, what Dora really wanted to know was, "Who, if anyone, do you love more than you love me?" To that question, he probably would have simply said, "No one." Whether or not she felt comforted by his answer would depend on whether or not she had been able to assume that he loved her in the first place. Dora, however, believed that when a person told her he loved no one more than he loved her, he had already answered the question of whether or not he loved her in the first place. Thus it was not till later, after Alma's funeral, that it even occurred to Dora to ask her husband if he loved her at all. "I can't tell you I love you," was his answer. Her next question, even though they had been married for no longer than a few months was, "Would you give me a divorce if I asked for it?" And, once again, he said, "Fine with me, if that's what you want." And by then, indeed, it was what she wanted. She had seen enough, heard enough, by then. The form of the interrogation, more than its content, and Hamilton's strict and what seemed to some his almost fanatically pure adherence to the form had trapped her. As she would later say, "He didn't exactly tell me to leave, but it was obvious to me that I had no choice."

When she first met Hamilton, Dora knew nothing of the stories about him that had circulated for years in and around Barnstead, mainly because, until she married him, she had never been to Barnstead. She had been living in Concord at the time, in a small and rather drab apartment. And since her divorce six months earlier from her first husband, Harry Franklin, a man she had loved deeply and loyally for twenty-three years, she had lived there alone, extremely depressed, quietly trying to heal the deep, suddenly inflicted wounds that had precipitated the divorce. What had inflicted the wounds was her accidental discovery that her husband Harry Franklin had been a lifelong philanderer, and she alone, of all the people who had known him these many years, she alone had been unaware of this aspect of his character. In fact, to her embarrassment, she had thought of him as sexually cold, almost unresponsive, not just to her but to all women. She had even developed a kind of condescending, maternal affection for his nature, often referring to him as a cold fish, a stodgy haberdasher on whom, she felt, all sexual innuendoes and provocations were lost. And when finally his true nature came out (broadcast hysterically by one of his girl friends, who, not as trusting as Dora, had trailed him and had discovered that he was betraying her, too), she had felt as if he had yanked her legs out from under her. And when, through some perverse determination to "clear his conscience once and for all," Harry had revealed to his poor wife the names of all the many women he had slept with over the years, continuing for weeks to remember and then to confess yet another old and all-but-forgotten liaison, when his confessions were finally over, Dora felt as if her life had been cut to pieces, the pieces cast into the sea, like so much garbage, to float there, swelling in the sun, picked at by gulls above and nibbled by passing fish below. It was in such a state, then, deeply depressed, beaten—a woman so deceived that any further deception would be meaningless, for there was now nothing left to "protect" her from—in such a state, one night after work, she had stopped for a drink alone in a cocktail lounge next to the typesetting shop where she was a compositor, and she had met Hamilton Stark.

They were seated at the leather-covered bar in the artificial gloom; he was a little drunk, and soon so was she. Perhaps she was attempting to put a little cynicism into her life, to see if it could lift her spirits a bit, even if only briefly, and when he had idly mentioned his displeasure with the place, what he called its "ad-man décor," she had just as idly suggested that they adjourn to her apartment for the evening, where, she said, the décor was "early Woolworth's." He had asked her if she had a television set; she had said yes, a color set, and he had been delighted. There was a Frank Sinatra special on that night that he wanted to see. "Ol' blue eyes," he had called him. "You know that song he sings, 'I Did It My Way'?" he asked her. She thought she knew the song. "Well, that's me," he said.

She married him within a week. The reasons were obvious to everyone who knew her. "She's marrying the pipefitter because of what it'll do to Harry," they said. It was presumed that she did it so Harry Franklin would regard her new marriage as the act of a broken, possibly deranged woman, and therefore, people reasoned, he would feel guilty. "As well he should," they clucked. It was, of course, no less possible that her marrying Hamilton after knowing him over drinks and color TV for only a week was the act of a broken, possibly deranged woman, in fact, and that how Harry the haberdasher might feel about it had never once occurred to her. But no one thought of that possibility. People tend to see ulterior motives everywhere these days, even in grief and woeful distraction.

They were married by a justice of the peace, a man who ran a large dairy farm and ice cream stand in Northwood, and a few days later, Hamilton's mother died. Dora had barely unpacked her clothes and color TV. The kitchen set and bedroom suite they had purchased together, as a cynical nod to the forms of sentiment, had been delivered that afternoon, and she had just finished tucking in the linen, placing her combs, brushes, make-up and jewelry neatly on the dresser, moving first one article, then removing them all and starting over again, trying to make these dozen articles look as if they had been on top of that dresser for twenty-three years, when the phone rang. It was the first time it had rung in the three days since she had moved in, and she rushed out to the kitchen to answer it.

It was Sarah, Hamilton's sister, she knew, even though they had never met, calling to inform her that her new mother-in-law, after a lengthy illness, had died in her sleep the night before. Funeral services would be held at the First Congregational Church in Barnstead at 1:00 P.M. on Saturday, December 1, two days later. Dora started to respond to this news and the, to her, peculiar way in which her new sister-in-law had conveyed it, but before she could utter a word, even a stammer of sympathy, Sarah had hung up.

That evening, when Hamilton came home from work (he was then the foreman for the plumbing, heating and air-conditioning systems on the new Tampax factory being built in the southwestern part of the state and was driving forty miles each way to work every day), she told him, word for word and in the same tone of voice, what Sarah had told her. She prefaced her bulletin, naturally, by telling him that his sister had called him that afternoon with some "shocking" news.

"Oh? Which sister?"

"Sarah."

"What was the news?"

She told him.

"Anything else?"

"No, nothing else. Just 'click,' " Dora said, miming the act of hanging up a telephone receiver.

" 'Click,' eh?"

"Yes. 'Click.' "

Hamilton sat down slowly at the kitchen table in the chair that faced the window. It was where his father had always sat. At breakfast he could see Blue Job as it caught the day's first light, and in the late afternoon he could watch it lose light and slowly turn gray until finally it loomed darker than the sky that surrounded it.

He asked her to tell him when the funeral was to be held, and she repeated Sarah's message. It *was* a message, she assumed, even though it had come in the form of an obituary notice. She wanted to ask him about Sarah, about his other sister, Jody, and about his mother, too, but she did not dare, not now. Until this moment, she had not once wondered about these people; she had been too preoccupied with how her marriage to Hamilton fit or did not fit into her own private, truncated past. And now that she wanted to know about his past, if for no other reason than to be better able to comfort him at such a bad time, she was afraid to—for he had begun to growl, low in his chest and throat, like a large and vicious animal. He sat there, looking dead-eyed out the window at the gathered darkness, his hands fisted heavily on the tabletop, and growled.

Very slowly, one silent step at a time, she backed away from him, and then left the room altogether. In seconds she had left the house and was outside in the front yard, standing next to the car, a green Chrysler airport limousine he had recently purchased, wondering if she should flee down the road in his car, which so far he had not allowed her to drive, or return to the house and try to comfort him. She had never heard anyone growl aloud like that, and she had never seen a person's eyes go dead before, and she was terrified. Harry Franklin, when *his* mother had died, had cried like a baby, she remembered with sudden affection. And she had held him in her arms and crooned soothingly to him while for hours he had catalogued his childhood memories of the woman. What could this woman have done to Hamilton to have evoked such an enraged response? Clearly, it was rage— those eyes, that growl, the enormous fists on the smooth Formica-topped table—but rage at whom? Somehow it did not seem directed at his mother. No, the rage belonged elsewhere, and that was why Dora was so frightened that, rather than try to comfort him, she had fled from him, had tiptoed out to stand coatless by the car in the cold November twilight and wonder if she should flee still farther from him.

Suddenly he was there, standing at the door, his bulk filling the doorframe, his face burning darkly across the yard at her. He slowly reached one hand out and pointed a finger at her, as if it were the barrel of a gun. "Where the hell are *you* going?" he demanded in a low voice.

"I . . . well, I don't know. I thought . . . I thought you wanted to be alone." She started to wring her hands. The ground that lay between them, freshly frozen but already as bleak as tundra, seemed to undulate in slow waves, and she knew she was weeping. From across the field a wind chipped at her back, and she began to shiver from the cold.

"Get in here," he ordered. "One woman already left me today. Don't make it two." He turned slowly around and disappeared into the darkness of the living room, leaving the door wide open for her.

She hesitated a second, then, still wringing her hands and shivering from the cold, quickly walked across the dead yard and followed him into the house.

He did not speak to her again that evening, nor did she attempt to engage him in conversation of any kind. As swiftly and unobtrusively as possible, she prepared their meal, a frozen sirloin that she broiled, frozen french fries and peas (his favorite meal, he had told her one evening the week before at her apartment in Concord when, quite by accident, she had presented him with the very same fare). And after they had eaten in silence, she had quickly cleared the table, washed the dishes, and had gone into their bedroom, which had once been his parents' bedroom, adjacent to the kitchen. Off that room was the cold, unused front parlor, empty of furniture, curtainless, with a fireplace that he had blocked up years before. A few days earlier she had looked on this house as having what she called "marvelous potential," and she had imagined redecorating it, starting with that old, tomblike parlor, which, because of fair days it filled to brimming with morning sunlight, she had thought would make an attractive master bedroom, then converting his parents' old bedroom into a large and luxurious bath and dressing room. The upstairs, where there were two bedrooms and a connecting bath, she planned to use for guests. Her mother could come from Chicago and visit them, and her sister in Pittsburgh could come, and her father and his second wife, and her friend Gladys from Massachusetts could drive up during her vacation next summer. She had imagined new curtains, new carpeting, fresh paint. The house was squarely built, meticulously maintained and spacious, and it coaxed out all her most hospitable fantasies and plans, even though for the last six months she had been a woman who had felt that all her life's plans had been for another, a previous life.

But that night, as she sat on the edge of the double bed that she and her new husband had purchased a few days before, she looked around her, and all she saw was hopelessness and dark retreat. It was not the kind of hopelessness that was characterized by disorder or sloth, but the kind that makes itself known first by the ruthless paring down of the elements of a life to its essential, molecular units, then by a compulsive ordering of those units, a deliberate placement of remnants in self-referring relations that were abstract, geometric, intellectually pure, controlled. The house and its contents seemed suddenly, hopelessly, cold to her, like an arctic wind, and she began to think with fond nostalgia of her small, crowded apartment in Concord, its warm disarray and thoughtless clutter. (She did not dare to think of the house she had lived in before that, the house she had shared for twenty-three years with Harry Franklin.) She snapped off the light next to the bed, got slowly undressed in the dark, and slipped into the bed. She began to think that she had made a terrible mistake. It might not be too late. Harry was a good man, though flawed, cruelly flawed . . . and he had cried when she left him, cried like a baby. . . .

Hamilton did not come to bed that night. Or at least not to their bed. Possibly he had slept in one of the upstairs rooms and had made the bed when he got up, but when she came into the kitchen at six-thirty, the ceiling light above the table was burning and his coffee cup and breakfast dishes, as usual, were soaking in the sink, and his car, as usual, was gone.

She heard the furnace kick over and start its low hum, and she checked the thermometer posted outside the kitchen window. Fourteen above zero. She hoped it wouldn't snow for the funeral. Oh, God—the funeral. What should she do about the funeral? As the gray cold day wore on, she worried more and more fixedly about it. How was she supposed to act? What was expected of her? She could not understand how such a thing could have become problematic, but it had. She was surprised that she actually did not know what was the proper and appropriate thing to do. Funerals and weddings and birthdays—these were events in a life that were such integrated parts of its overall texture that one almost never questioned what was expected of one as a participant in those events. One simply knew. They were rituals of the culture, and she was one of the people who lived inside and sustained that culture. Why, then, was she so unsure of herself, so incapable of deciding what was expected of her by her husband, her sisters-in-law, the townspeople they lived among? She felt as if she had accidentally wandered into an alien land, where the rituals were obscure and exotic, where a wrong guess could be disastrous for her because outrageous to everyone else.

Around four in that afternoon, as it grew dark and the temperature began to fall again, she called the only florist in Barnstead, Herb Cotton, and ordered a large arrangement of white chrysanthemums to be sent to the church the next day in time for the funeral. She knew that she should have sent the flowers to the funeral home, but Sarah hadn't said anything about which funeral home her mother's body was lying in or whether there was to be a service there, and she didn't dare call Sarah now and ask her.

"*What should the card say?*" the florist, presumably Herb Cotton, asked in a high, thin voice.

"What?"

"*The card. What should we put on the card?*"

"Oh . . . Well, I suppose . . . the usual, I guess."

"*The usual?*"

"Yes . . . you know, 'From Mr. and Mrs. Hamilton Stark,' " she said with hope in her voice.

"*This Mrs. Stark speaking?*"

"Yes."

"*I see.*" He paused. "*Ham's wife, eh?*"

"Yes."

"*Yep. Wal, don't you an' ol' Ham worry yourself. We'll get these over to the Heywoods' Funeral Home tonight. They'll still look good at the church tomorrow.*"

"Oh . . . Well, thank you."

"*Good woman, y'know. That Alma Stark. That's Ham's mother, y'know.*"

"Yes, I know. I . . . I never knew her."

"*Yep. Bye, now,*" he said sharply.

"Good-bye," she said, and she hung up the phone.

That evening, Hamilton arrived home three hours later than usual, only slightly drunk, but dark and glowering and filled with smoldering silence. She bobbed around him, gave him food, and stayed in the bedroom for the remainder of the evening, listening to him as he tramped heavily in and out of the house from the barn. Every now and then she could hear sounds that told her he was sorting out the tools, equipment, materials—"a place for everything and a thing for every place." One minute she imagined him doing something that was wholly intentional, deliberate, no matter how bizarre-seeming. She imagined him, for instance, building a coffin for his mother, a hearse from his car, a graveside marker. But a minute later she could only imagine him doing something that was determined wholly by forces outside his conscious will, compulsive acts, no matter how ordinary or normal-seeming—and she imagined him sorting out jars of nuts and bolts, inventorying pipe and fittings, stacking kindling endlessly.

That night she slept alone again, and again she didn't know where her new husband slept if he had slept at all, for when at seven-thirty she went out to the kitchen, even though it was Saturday and not a workday, once again the light was burning and his breakfast dishes were in the sink and his car was gone. Around nine he returned, with the newspaper and the week's groceries, ale, and Canadian Club. He had begun his regular weekend routine. Dora, of course, did not know this yet, but by eleven, when she had watched him several times perform some menial or trivial task in the yard or house and then pull a pen and small black notebook from his shirt pocket and make a mark in the book, she realized that he was indeed performing a weekly ritual. That's when it occurred to her that the man had no intention of attending his mother's funeral. She could not say with confidence, however, that it was his intention, actually, not to go, for she also believed that he was *unable* to go, that forces beyond and stronger than any of his intentions were keeping him at home on this day, notebook and pen in hand, checking off his chores, one by one, as he did them.

She decided it was safe to tell him, simply and straightforwardly, that she would be going to the funeral. Whatever ritual he was going through, she knew that it did not include her, at present, in any way, and that she was free to attend the funeral or not. So, as he strolled whistling through the door with an armload of split wood for the kitchen woodbox, his face red and dry from the cold, she told him that she wanted to go to the funeral but had no way to get there.

"I'll get you there," he said cheerfully, clattering the wood into the box next to the large black stove. "What time's the service?"

"One."

"Well, you'd better hurry. I'll drop you off on my way to Pittsfield," he said, as if he were agreeing to drop her off at the library. "I forgot to stop at Maxfield's this morning for some eightpenny nails and friction tape. By the time I get back from Maxfield's, you ought to be ready for a ride home, so wait outside the church and I'll pick you up as I come by," he instructed her, and then he made another mark in his notebook and walked out to the barn.

Grateful, though somewhat perplexed, she quickly put on a dark gray, simply cut wool dress, hat and coat. By then it was a quarter to one, so she went out to the barn and presented herself. "I'm ready," she announced.

When she came in, he had been filing the points on a circular saw blade, and when he saw her, he quickly put down his file and the blade, strode from the barn, got into his Chrysler, and started the motor. She slipped in next to him and tried to draw herself back and down into the seat. Somehow she felt he was doing a great favor for her, and in spite of his apparent cheerfulness and easy manner, she believed that the less space she took up the better.

They rode in silence for the mile and a half along the road to town, past the bleak, leafless maples and elms and clustering pines and spruce at the edge of the fields. The day was clouded over again, and everything was cast in shades of gray and tan— the dead grasses, the brush and weeds, the bony branches of the trees, even the houses and barns, trailers and cabins, that huddled in shabby groups alongside the road.

The First Congregational Church, located at the center of the village and facing the Parade, a square patch of open ground, was shaped like a long barn with a bell tower at one end. Though it was painted white, in the chill light it looked cement-gray and somber, more like a mausoleum than a barn or church. A dozen or so cars and pickup trucks, and a single black hearse, were parked on the road outside the church, and Hamilton had to pull out into the middle of the road to get past. But as he started to slow and stop at the end of the line of cars, a short, stout woman, then a tall, gaunt woman, followed by a thick man and two brittle-looking teen-aged boys, got out of a station wagon with a blue light on top. Hamilton drew in just beyond the car and came to a stop.

"That group getting out of the cruiser?" he asked her. "That's Sarah, the short one. Jody and Chub Blount are the others, and their boys, Alfred and Alvin. Twins. If you want to go to the graveyard for the burial, ride out with Sarah and her husband, Mooney. Sam Mooney. He's probably inside the church, getting set to ring the bell. He's a deacon."

"Is it all right?" She had opened her door and had one foot on the ground.

"All right? Well, I guess you'll have to ask *them*. Sarah and Mooney. *They're* the ones to tell you if it's all right. Not me."

She decided to risk it. She had got out of the car completely and was peering in at him through the open door. "Hamilton, I'm sorry, but *please*, tell me why you aren't going to the funeral."

He gripped the steering wheel with both hands. "Go," he said stiffly, not looking at her. "Go on. You haven't imagined being dead, so you go on. It'll help you keep from imagining it a while longer." He paused a second and pursed his lips as if he were about to whistle, then went on. "To me, not imagining being dead is like believing in Santa Claus, you ought to do it as long as you can. So go ahead, you deserve it," he said, suddenly smiling into her puzzled face. "We all do."

So she did go, as he instructed, first to the funeral service, which was appropriately somber and brief, and, after the ceremony, she left her seat at the back and paraded with the others past the coffin and looked down, once, at the embalmed, parchmentlike face of the old woman, and then filed out of the church, where she joined the rest of the people at the roadside and where she introduced herself to the stout woman Hamilton had pointed out and who had by then been joined by her husband, also stout and as short as his wife.

When Dora asked if she could ride with them to the cemetery, it was the man, Mooney, who smiled and said, "Of course," and when they had driven the three miles out of town to the cemetery on the hillside overlooking the frozen, lead-gray Suncook River, it was the husband, Mooney, who briefly told her what she by then suspected, that Hamilton and the rest of the family had been engaged in a "feud" for over ten years, "maybe even longer, maybe since he was born," Mooney added. But he hadn't enough time to tell her much more than that, so in many ways, and in a few new ways, as she got out of Mooney's car and crossed the narrow cemetery lane to where half a dozen people she recognized from the church and the pallbearers and the minister were gathered around the casket and open grave, she was as confused as she had been back in front of the church when she had first stepped out of Hamilton's car.

There was a sharp, steady wind blowing off the river. The mourners had positioned themselves at the head of the grave, behind the waist-high granite gravestone, with their backs to the wind. Dora walked quickly around the grave and the four or five floral arrangements at the foot, noticing as she passed the large fan of white chrysanthemums among them, and took a place at the end of the line, next to Mooney, who, like most of the others in the group, had jammed his hands into his coat pockets and was staring at the ground. One or two of the men had folded their arms over their chests and were staring into the sour sky, but all of them were standing in postures that to Dora seemed more defiant than mournful, more angry than grieving. Mooney's face was set, his soft chin and cheeks held tightly back, almost as if he were wincing. Next to him Sarah, far from indulging in the expected filial weeping, was scowling darkly down at the bleached-out ground, and beyond her, Jody, too, scowled and worked her lips against her teeth. Chub was one of the men whose thick arms were crossed over their beefy chests and who looked up at the sky and flexed the muscles in their jaws. Even the twin boys, Alfred and Alvin, in their awkward way, stood angrily at the head of their grandmother's grave and looked as if they were about to have a tantrum.

Dora didn't know what to make of this show of apparent anger. She felt as if she had walked into the middle of a play, one of those modern plays where the characters never speak and act in the ways you expect them to speak and act. Even the minister looked angry, standing there at the foot of the grave, his Bible in his hand, glaring down at the gravestone and then scowling into the book as he read the half-dozen sentences that committed Alma Stark's mortal remains to the earth. Was this how the people of this town expressed their grief? Who were they angry at? It almost seemed they were angry with God Himself for having taken the old woman from them. But she knew that couldn't be true—surely, Alma had not been that passionately loved a mother and grandmother, that steadfast and selfless a friend and neighbor. Surely, she could not have been so desperately mourned that her survivors would blaspheme the God who had taken her from them.

The minister, having completed the requisite benediction, gave the signal to the two men from Heywoods' Funeral Home to lower the casket, and then he spun around and stalked across the roadway to the car, with the others immediately following. As the casket hissed hydraulically into the cold, dark earth, Dora suddenly found herself alone, and she started to rush after Mooney and his wife Sarah, who were already grimly getting into their car. Glancing back at the gravestone as she passed alongside the grave, she saw with mild surprise that the single large stone had been put there to mark two graves, not one. On the left of the polished face of the stone it read HORACE MOORE STARK, with the dates 1892–1963, and on the right half of the face it read ALMA BRAITHWAITE STARK, with the year of her birth, 1893– and a blank space left for the year of her death, 1973.

Was there something about this stone, Dora wondered, that had angered them? Why? What was wrong with the stone? It seemed perfectly appropriate to her—the husband, Horace, had died first, in 1963, she could see that, and naturally the wife, knowing she would someday be buried next to him, had placed a single stone to mark both graves, leaving blank the place where the year of her own death would eventually be carved. Dora was sure that many surviving wives and husbands handled the matter precisely in this manner. The alternative, she thought, as she got into the back seat of Mooney's car, was to employ two separate stones and to leave the selection of each stone and its placement entirely in the hands of the survivors of each partner, which, she reasoned, would probably be a slightly more expensive and com-plicated way of doing it, but at least it would have the advantage of not trying to anticipate the order in which the various mem-bers of a family would die, who would be the survivors and who would not. And one would not, year after year, every time one came out to the cemetery, to pay one's respects to the memory of one's dead husband, have to look on one's own gravestone, with that blank space for the date of one's death beckoning to one, impatiently reminding one who was next, suggesting by its very incompleteness that one was late, was overdue, urging one to rush, to come down sooner to the earth.

They were almost back to the church, and none of the three in the car had said a word. Then, in a low, frightened voice, Dora asked, "Did Hamilton have that gravestone installed on his own?"

knowing that the answer would be yes, and knowing that he had done it without ever having mentioned it to any of them, not to his mother and not to either of his sisters, and knowing, too, that they had discovered its presence one afternoon, doubtless one Memorial Day, when they all had gone out to the cemetery with Alma to place flowers on the old man's grave, which up to then had probably been marked by a modest brass plaque laid flat in the ground, the conventional way for survivors to put off the expense and the usually painful negotiations with one another that accompany the selection and purchase of a large, permanent, granite marker.

Mooney stopped in front of the church. Hamilton's green Chrysler was slightly ahead of him and on the other side of the road. Dora had reached for the handle to open the door when suddenly Sarah spun in her seat and faced her. Her wide face was torn unexpectedly with furious weeping and she bellowed into Dora's shocked face, "You *fool!* You *fool!* I don't even feel *sorry* for you!" Then she began to sob and turned away, burying her face in her hands. Her husband said nothing. He reached one hand across and patted his wife's knee; it was a practiced gesture, a fruitless one, but one he could not let himself forgo.

Slowly, silently, Dora got out of the car, crossed the road, and started to walk to Hamilton's car. She knew the woman was right, Sarah, her husband's own sister. For she *was* a fool, a pathetic, middle-aged, solitary fool, and she deserved no pity for it, none at all. Opening the heavy door of the car and holding it open for a second, she looked in at her husband, the man whose name a week ago in a dark haze she had attached to her own, and she decided, as she got into the warm interior of the car and closed the door behind her, that she would leave him, she would flee this man as soon as she dared, as soon as she no longer feared he would kill her for it.

THE RINGING OF the telephone next to my bed clanged into my dream and woke me. I groped for a second, half-blind in the semidarkness, and found the receiver and finally stopped the ringing. As I drew the receiver to my ear I checked my watch—Was it morning or evening? What day? What night? As if by answering these questions one might know who would be calling and breaking so unexpectedly into one's sleep. And while my eyes, fixed on the luminous face of my watch, told me that it was 6:25 A.M. and that the day was Monday, February 5, and that the year was 1975, my ear, pressed to the cool, smooth, plastic face of the receiver, told me that it was my friend C. who was calling me at this early hour, still a half-hour before sunrise.

He spoke sharply, before I myself had said a word. *"Did I wake you?"*

My mouth felt sourly dry—too much cognac and too many cigars the night before. "Well, yes, but it was time to get up anyhow. I was up late last night," I said, as explanation for my still being in bed a half-hour before sunrise. (C. sleeps almost not at all, or rather, never for longer than two or three hours at a time; over a period of twenty-four hours, however, he probably averages eight full hours of deep sleep—but as a result, he has lost touch with normal, if not exactly "natural," sleeping habits, and thus I never know when he will call me and I never know when not to call him.) "Working," I added guiltily.

"Ah, yes. On your novel."

There was no point in my denying it, so I said nothing. The room was filled with soft, dark shadows, as if it were under water, and I sensed a snowstorm coming.

"Well, I wanted to know if she's all right."

"Who?"

"Oh, sorry! Dora. Or the one you call Dora. I've been reading your Chapter Ten and sitting here pondering her fate, and I must confess it, you've given me cause for concern, even alarm."

"Alarm?" This surprised me. "For whom?"

"Why, for Dora. Or whoever she is—A.'s fifth ex-wife. Is she all right?"

"All right? Well, yes, yes . . . I mean, I suppose so. She left him over a year ago, you know. Why, what's wrong?"

"*Is she back with her husband, the haberdasher?*" he asked nervously.

"Oh, yes, certainly. They were married again, the day her divorce from Hamilton, A., came through. Sometime early this winter, as I recall. No. C., Dora's fine now, fine. She's even gone back to her old job at the typesetting company. I imagine her time with Hamilton, I mean A., seems like a bad dream to her now. Which, of course, is a shame."

"*How's that again?*"

"Eh? A shame. I said it's a shame that she considers her few months with A. as she would a bad dream."

"*Well, if you asked me, and I'm beginning to think that you wouldn't, but if you asked me, I'd tell you that I think she's damned fortunate to be able to think of it as a bad dream. She's lucky to be able to think at all!*"

"Wha . . . ?"

"*The man's dangerous. And surely you see that,*" he said, his voice suddenly lowered.

"Ha, ha, ha, ha, ha!" I laughed. "Dangerous? Perplexing, yes. Frustrating, certainly. But dangerous? No, my dear friend, I think not."

"*You sound irrational, man,*" he informed me quietly. Was there a tainting touch of condescension in his voice? I couldn't tell. Perhaps he actually believed what he was saying, perhaps to him I did sound irrational. But to me, his assertion that Hamilton was dangerous, and was dangerous specifically to Dora, his ex-wife, was, well, hysterical. No, if anyone sounded irrational this gray predawn, it was my old friend C., the man I was accustomed to regard as an almost pure thinker.

"C.," I said calmly, "what's got you off on this 'dangerous' tangent? If you're afraid for Dora's welfare, for heaven's sake, or her physical safety, you might as well be afraid for mine as well," I said.

"Indeed." His voice was still low, and then very carefully he began to try to "reason" with me, as he put it, though I must say right here and now that what he had to say did not sound particularly reasonable at all. I will concede that he was sincere, however, and that he was not condescending to me. And I do believe that the man was genuinely afraid that Dora, and possibly I myself, were in danger of being killed by Hamilton Stark. Yes, that's right, *killed*. By Hamilton, *my* Hamilton, good old Ham Stark. My *hero*, for God's sake!

The way C. saw it, he told me, the very inability of practically every intelligent or sensitive person who came into close contact with Hamilton to determine with confidence whether the man's behavior was deliberate and intentional or out of control and compulsive—that very inability made the question of whether Hamilton was dangerous or not a very real question, one that any responsible person, as well as any other kind of person who chose to associate with Hamilton, had to try to answer. Then C. went down a quick list of people who, close to Hamilton in various ways, had been unable to determine whether his behavior was intentional or compulsive— Rochelle, who tried so hard for so long, and for all I know may still be trying as she reads this, and Rochelle's mother, and Annie, Hamilton's second wife, and probably Alma, his mother, although, from the evidence, one couldn't be sure, and Dora, and then, of course, me. On the other hand, people like Jody and Chub Blount, probably Sarah and her husband, Sam Mooney, too, and Hamilton's third and fourth wives, Jenny the nurse and Maureen the waif, and most of the townspeople who knew Hamilton considerably less than intimately—these people all were convinced that the man was stark raving mad, out of control, dangerous. They had no doubts. Whether they could come up with a sure diagnosis or not didn't matter; they believed he was ill and that the nature of his illness put them in various kinds of danger.

The rest of us, according to C., couldn't decide whether the man was ill or transcendently healthy. We were attracted to him quite as much as we were repelled. And that, according to C., made the question of his potential danger a real one. He went on briefly to cite a few famous cases that he thought were historical parallels—Juan Perón, Howard Hughes, Mary Baker Eddy, and several others I've forgotten. In all these cases, C. insisted, the very thing one person used as evidence of the hero's madness, his illness, another person cited as evidence of his genius, his transcendent good health. Usually, this produces a stand-off, a static situation, which no responsible person should abide. (I thought C. did sound a bit self-righteous there, but basically I agreed with him.) At which point, according to C., the person recognizes that he or she is faced with the choice of either becoming one who follows the hero or one who flees from him, and because of the nature of genius on the one hand and this particular type of illness on the other, one is forced to forgo one's reason, one's reliance on objectively considered evidence, and rely instead soley on one's intuition, which, C. said, was precisely what all of us—Rochelle, her mother, Annie, Dora, and I—had attempted to do.

Apparently it was easier for people like Rochelle's mother and Annie and, eventually, Dora to trust their intuition. Though they never actually were able to conclude, in a syllogistically sound way, that the man they had married was insane, they nevertheless had ended up acting as if they had so concluded. Though they had all three decided, after the fact, to regard certain bits of his behavior and certain physiological manifestations as evidence of his madness, it was wholly on an intuitive basis that they had reached their conclusion. After all, C. pointed out, the very same bits of behavior and physiological manifestations these three people used to prove their ex-husband's madness, Rochelle and I had cited as evidence of his genius—the cryptic, self-denying, aphoristic utterances (which, C. reminded me,

I had once regarded as "double positives" and a higher form of wisdom); the absurd ritualization of petty tasks and minor events (to me, the absurdity was admirable and was in fact the whole point); his inability to demonstrate "normal" feelings toward others (a willed characteristic, which, I had claimed, functioned mainly to make us more conscious of our "normal" feelings); his growling out loud, the "dead eyes" cited by Dora (to me, evidence of a yogic state of meditation employed by Hamilton to help him cope with deep frustration without having to resort to simple repression); and numerous other minor acts and behavior patterns. The point C. wanted to make, apparently, was that none of this was evidence that could justify our feeling one way or the other about the man. For on that level Hamilton resisted penetration or analysis. One could not confidently project oneself onto him, which, said C., is indeed as much characteristic of genius as it is of madness, for we are, none of us, one or the other. Rochelle and I, C. believed, had taken longer than the others to decide one way or the other, had continued to entertain the question, letting one ambiguous, open-ended image of him fold into another just as the first image seemed about to close, because we were probably slightly more intelligent than they, or at least were more worldly-wise in the way of paradoxes.

Up to this point I had not found it especially difficult to agree with my old friend, and actually, as the conversation progressed (it was more a monologue than a conversation), I had felt grateful to him for taking the time and thought to put the matter in this particular perspective. In my quest for an understanding of Hamilton Stark, C.'s point of view was still of value to me. The bedroom had gradually filled with a milky light, and because of the peculiar stillness, I knew that it would soon be snowing. I lay back down and propped the receiver against the pillow next to my ear and continued to listen.

But, unfortunately, this was where C. started to assert a point of view that, to my mind, not only revealed an intolerable intellectual arrogance but actually undermined his carefully stated previous position as well. Essentially, what he started to do was cite what, to him, was clear-cut evidence for the madness of Hamilton Stark, what he, C., called *"a particularly virulent form of madness."* I listened with dismay as he described Hamilton's absurd overritualization of petty tasks and acts as a compensatory device for his failure to participate any longer in his society's "normal" social rites. Then C. went on to recall for me Hamilton's youthful belief, *"on rather suspiciously flimsy evidence,"* that he had killed his own father in a quarrel. That, plus his unseemly rush to supplant his father later, after the old man's first stroke, by taking over legal title to the property, indicated to C. the presence of a *"deep and unresolved oedipal conflict."* As further evidence of this unresolved oedipal conflict, he also pointed to what he described as Hamilton's strong need to keep his mother at a safe distance, even going so far as to *"toss the old woman out into the cold"* and to withhold all expressions of feeling for her, even at her death.

By now, quite frankly, I was too appalled to stop him. And thus C. went on uninterruptedly, dragging out one bit of so-called evidence after another, each time reasserting his diagnosis of *"unresolved oedipal conflict,"* sounding more and more like a college psych major. I could barely believe what I was hearing! There was the pattern of Hamilton's passively aggressive stance toward the women who became his wives—why there were so many of them, C. insisted. There was his inability to declare his love for any one of them, which, conjoined with his inability to say that he did *not* love any one of them and his apparent belief that the only alternative to loving someone, in particular a woman, was to hate him, or, in particular, her. And then there was *"that gravestone business,"* as C. called it, which indicated to him that the man was by now dealing with only barely repressed desires to remove the object of his obsession, the object of his *"unresolved oedipal conflict,"* by wishing her dead. And so *"natu-*

rally," C. had felt a rush of concern for Dora's welfare, for with Hamilton's mother finally dead and buried, his dark obsession would turn to the next closest substitute, his wife, and even if she were his most recent ex-wife, she would still be the next closest substitute for his dead mother. *"Murder, my friend, is always the madman's way out of an overpowering love-hate relationship."* Hamilton was giving evidence, to C., at least, of an increasing inability to sustain any relationship at all with a woman, as shown by the increased pace of his marriages and divorces. *"How can I not be deeply concerned with the welfare, even for the very life, of any woman who falls prey to the charm of his enigmatic ways and his manipulative passivity, especially now, when he seems so close to losing what little ability he has had in the past of repressing his murderous impulses?"*

How, indeed? I thought sarcastically. Yes, how? Oh bitter disappointment! Oh solitude! Oh inevitable betrayal! Oh silence, exile and cunning!

"You there?"

Oh lost and by the wind grieved point of view!

"Are you still there?"

Oh deep-wounding reason! Oh overreaching Apollonian perspective!

"Hello? Operator? Anyone there? I think I've been cut off. Operator? I think I've been cut off. I think the connection's broken. Operator? Is anyone there?"

CHAPTER 11

An End

"A fine setting for a fit of despair," it occurred to him, "if I were only standing here by accident instead of design."
— KAFKA, The Castle

Let me lie here in the snowfield and die warm.
—"Stone-People-Long-Song, Stave 12" (ABENOOKI
CREATION EPIC, LaFAMME AND BRÔLET, TRANS.)

THERE WAS NOTHING left for me to do but return to A.'s home in the town of B., locate the man, seek him out and face him there, and gather from that confrontation the evidence and information, the data, that would let me rest easily with my having at last rejected C.'s point of view. I was extremely distressed, perhaps even desperate. Everything was either falling apart or else was about to come together. I felt that if I stayed at home this bleak morning and continued to write my novel, for instance, or cooked a ham or read a bit of Livy, by nightfall everything indeed would have fallen apart. If, on the other hand, I drove

myself across the center of the state to the town of B. and scrupulously searched A.'s house and adjacent grounds, I just might
be able to discover a clue to where he was, and then I could follow the clue to where he was and meet with him there, my mind
racked by dread and paradox, and the meeting would somehow
set me at ease again.

Surely, I thought as I lay there in my bed and slowly put the
receiver back on the telephone base next to me, surely, this is the
final test of my faith. Never again will I ask myself to question
the very sanity of my hero, and thus my own sanity as well. Never
again, I swore, would I permit myself to be so torn, so divided, so
alone. By the end of this day, I would have committed myself to
following and, to the best of my abilities, emulating the man, or
else I would have purged myself of him forever, would have freed
myself at last from the glittering beauty of his image.

Thus my desperation and dread and fatigue were mixed
with a certain gladness, for I knew that after today, one way or
the other, my agony of self-division would be ended. For a second I wondered if the whole thing had been engineered by A.
himself, as a final test of my loyalty and spiritual insight. But I
quickly shoved that thought away. After today I would no longer be asked to plague myself with such fearful speculation, and
knowing that, I also knew that any speculation today was pointless, was but the idle habit of my deeply troubled mind. Once a
divided mind foresees resolution as inevitable, it no longer has
sufficient cause to be divided.

I bounded from my bed and got dressed quickly in a woolen
shirt and heavy flannel trousers—after having first glanced out
the window at the cold, overcast day. It hadn't yet started to
snow, but clearly it was about to. Neglecting to shave or even to
brush my teeth, I hurried downstairs to the kitchen, where I sat
down and laced on my boots, pulled on my overcoat, cap, and
driving gloves, and walked quickly, briskly, to the garage.

By eight-fifteen I was in Concord, headed west toward

the town of B. As I skirted the downtown area and began the gradual climb away from the Merrimack Valley to the Suncook just beyond, the snow started falling, scattered flakes, hard and wind-blown. They came like bits of ash at first, tiny, dry flakes, isolate, drifting slowly to the ground as if settling to the bottom of a motionless sea. Soon, though, the snow was falling in swirls and waves that blew from the roadside in powdery sprays and fantails as the car, winding downhill from the ridge west of Concord, reached the Suncook River and brushed along the road that followed the river north and west toward the narrow uplifted head of the valley, where, near the horizon, I could make out the dark gray hump of Blue Job Mountain. Here the river, where it meandered, broadened, and then slowed, was frozen from bank to bank. The ice was invisible beneath the thick blanket of old snow. Sledges, sleds, snowmobiles and people afoot had left trails, paths and tracks across the smooth white skin of the river, scribbles and doodles that, from the road, looked random and pointless. Doubtless, when they were first laid down, the tracks and trails had followed a deliberate pattern, had logically sought a goal—just as had the black, curling ribbon on the road itself, which, seen from a map, would also look random, pointless, dropped from the sky to lie however it fell, as if only accidentally tying together two distant, named points on that grid. But, in fact the road had not been randomly drawn. It had been laid down atop the still narrower, unpaved, wagon route that nineteenth-century Yankee traders had built to carry granite and lumber from the mountains to the sea, and that road in turn had been laid down atop the old market road built by eighteenth-century farmers in the valley, who, in their turn, had been following the still older footpaths that the earliest settlers had worn smooth, their paths laid atop the Indian paths, which had followed the migratory movements of the animals, the deer and moose, the bear, and even, before these, the bison. And the animals had been following the river, this very river before me now, its smooth white surface crisscrossed and scribbled over, like a used sheet of paper, with the tracks, trails and footpaths following the invisible rivers, valleys and ridges of the makers' whims and impulses.

Far out at the center of the river, where beneath the ice the water ran deepest and coldest, there were several clusters of tiny windowless huts. Inside each hut, a fisherman sat hunkered over a head-size hole cut in the ice, drinking whiskey and warming his red hands over an oil heater, each man closed into his own kerosene-lit world, as shut off from the others by the cold and the wind as planets in separate solar systems. And though their huts were clustered together in the same galaxy, the fishermen were together for no reason of comfort or sociability, but only because here, in this region, the river ran deepest and coldest and the fish would take the bait.

A little farther on there is a place, where the river is at its broadest and makes a long, slow sweep around a gently rounded plain, that has been marked by a plaque placed by the state historical society beside the road as it curves along the arm of the river. The plaque tells the traveler that there, in the spring of 1703, the first party of settlers in the town of B. spent their first night in the valley. There, on this slight swell of land, they made camp, and the next morning, as dawn broke and the mist lifted from the river and the trees turned gold in the hazy sunlight, the settlers were surprised by a war party of Abenooki Indians and in the ensuing battle lost one of the original incorporators, a man named Lemuel Stark.

By the time I reached the outskirts of the village, where the river narrows to rapids and the mills were built, the gristmill, the sawmill, and later, in the nineteenth century, the shoe factory, now a storehouse for a local well-drilling company, the snow had started to fall densely, in semitransparent curtains down and across my field of vision like veils dropping away first to reveal a face and then to cover it.

At the Parade, the large common square of ground at the center of the town, as I approached the Congregational church and the turnoff to Blue Job Road, I saw the police chief's car, Chub Blount's Plymouth station wagon with its blue glass bubble on top, come out of Blue Job Road, turn onto the main road, and pass swiftly by me, heading in the direction I had just come from. The snow was falling too heavily now for me to have seen his face as he passed, but I recognized his white Stetson hat and saw that he was alone. A few seconds later, I was passed by another car with a blue glass bubble on the roof, this one driven by the chief's assistant, Calvin Clark. I assumed that the two had come directly from A.'s house, and I responded to the fact that they both were alone with a peculiar mixture of relief and disappointment—relief that they apparently had not found A., or if they had, that they had not arrested him; and disappointment because, if *they* had failed to locate him at his house, then how could I expect to succeed? Of course, it was also possible that they *had* found him after all, had found his body, that is, and thus had no reason not to be alone as they drove back to town. But then, I reasoned, I would have seen only one of the two police officers, for surely Chub would have left Calvin back at the house to watch over A.'s body and to make sure no one tampered with or accidentally disturbed the evidence.

But evidence of what? I asked myself. How do I know a crime's been committed? Maybe nothing unusual or disastrous had happened to *anyone*—not to Dora, not to A., not to Chub Blount, not even to *me*—and maybe the chief and his assistant had not even been at A.'s house in the first place but had been out on Blue Job Road this snowy morning on some other and wholly unrelated police business. Quickly, I ran down the bits of evidence—the three bulletholes in the car window, the strange circumstances of the car's presence and A.'s absence, with all the doors of the house locked, the gate closed, and even though yesterday had been a Sunday, week's end, the absence of any freshly tossed out trash at the edge of the field in front. Yes, it's true, I thought. It's true. The evidence points with equal force to numerous conclusions, and many of the conclusions do not constitute crimes or disaster or even anything especially unusual whether in A.'s life or Dora's or Chub's, or my own. As I slowed the car to make the turn at the church onto Blue Job Road, I finally admitted to myself that, yes, I may have made the whole thing up. I may have imagined everything.

But then, as soon as I was on Blue Job Road, I started to laugh at myself, not out loud, but with a low, ironic giggle. An hour before I had been wondering seriously if the whole thing, this very thing I was now afraid I had imagined, had been engineered by A. I felt light-headed, almost giddy. This was self-mockery taken to the edge of hysteria.

By then the snow had covered the road sufficiently to obliterate any trace of its surface, and I was only able to keep to it by following the high banks of old, ice-hard snow on either side. The windshield wipers clacked back and forth, cutting a pair of half-moons for me to peer through. In a few seconds I entered the short stretch of the road where the conifers grow to the very edge of the road, their branches interlacing between them and across the road above me, making a rough, dark tunnel and it seemed suddenly that it was no longer snowing and a great arching space had opened around me. The woods here, most Scotch pine and dark spruce, grew scruffily into the shaggy wall of an outdoor cathedral, and I remembered then that it was there, just yesterday afternoon, that I had looked hopefully for the figure of Rochelle, as if she were a sister or daughter whose recent death I still mourned and had not yet accepted as real, whose familiar form and hair and green, hooded loden coat my eyes still habitually searched for.

Then, as quickly, I was out of the wood and into the snowstorm again, peering anxiously through half-moons, aiming the car rather than driving it, for the road was slightly slippery under my tires. I passed several battered house trailers and tarpaper-covered shacks, the homes of A.'s neighbors, barely glimpsing them through the falling snow, noticing only that, covered with the layer of fresh snow, the buildings and the cluttered yards looked cleaner, more orderly, as if the snow could tend to them more capably, more energetically, than could the inhabitants.

A few seconds more, and I slowed the car and turned onto the lane that led to A.'s house. I glanced over at the large, hummocky field in front of the house and saw that it, too, had been transformed by the fastidious care of the falling snow, had been made over to look more like a natural, cleared meadow in winter than an open dump, a private trash receptacle.

When I drew up to the gate and prepared to stop so that I could get out and open it, I saw, with surprise, that the gate was wide open already. Hadn't I remembered to close it the day before? It was enough of a habit that I didn't have to think consciously of it in order to close it after passing through, therefore I couldn't be sure. Was this "evidence" of anything—that the gate, normally closed, was now invitingly wide open? I looked up the long driveway to the house and garage. Everything was as I had seen it yesterday afternoon—A.'s Chrysler parked facing the closed garage door, the house darkened and apparently empty, the large expanse of smooth, freshly whitened yard encircling the house from the fence down in front to the woods in back, and beyond those woods, the rising shape of the mountain. No, except for the new pelt of snow and the open gate, everything was the same. Everything.

Very slowly, the snow creaking under my tires, I drove up to A.'s car and parked directly behind it. Then I got out of my car and walked around to the window at the driver's side of the Chrysler. There they were, the three bulletholes connected by a network of tiny cracks, like spider webs. I touched each of the holes with my finger. One of them unexpectedly crumbled at the edges from the pressure, and my finger poked into the cold interior space of the car, startling me. Frightened by something nameless, I quickly withdrew my finger and nervously yanked on my gloves.

It was totally silent, windless, the snow falling straight down, as if being drawn to the ground by the ground itself in some guilty need to hide itself. I left the car and checked the garage door, which was locked. Then I crossed the yard to the front door, determined that it was locked, went up to the side porch and yanked on that door too. Leaning close to the glass to block out my reflection with my shadow, I peered into the kitchen. It was dark inside, but when my eyes had grown used to the darkness, I could see the outlines of the stove, sink, refrigerator, and the small, wooden table and single stool A. had built to replace the Formica-topped table and chairs he had once owned with Dora and that now lay beneath a foot or more of old snow in the field in front, the chromium legs rusting, padding from the seats spilling from rips torn one afternoon last April by high-powered rifle slugs. I could see the calendar on the wall near the telephone. Below the four-color photograph of an oil burner was the sheet for the month of February, for the year 1975—just as it should be. Yet somehow I was surprised. Somehow I had expected to see some other year, some other month. The house seemed to have been deserted long, long ago.

Slowly, I stepped down from the porch and took a few steps into the yard. The only sound was the constant rattle of my own voice inside my own head. The snow was still softly falling, and I couldn't see clearly more than a few feet in front of me. There was nothing left for me to check, I thought, except the footprints, and that was quite impossible now. Everything was buried under several inches of soft, fresh snow, so that the only footprints I could see were my own. They dribbled along behind me, tiny, crumbling craters slowly filling with new snow. I knew that in a few minutes even these, my own tracks, would disappear. And that would be the end of the "evidence." Any further pursuit of A. would have to be based solely on abstract reasoning, speculation, empty theory. Or else I simply would have to *guess* at his whereabouts, randomly placing him here and there, then rushing to seek him here and there, and if he was not to be found at either place, to guess again. I did not want that. No man wants to believe that his life has finally gotten so out of his control that he either must theorize about it or else be forced to *guess* at its nature. He'd rather believe in magic, fetish objects, totems, dreams. This is how a real life becomes a fiction, I thought, dismayed.

Suddenly, as if remembering a scene from a dream, I remembered driving through the cathedral-like woods on my way over this morning and how, for a few hundred yards, where the branches of the trees wove themselves together overhead, the snow had seemed almost not to be falling. If there had been old tracks on that ground, I thought, footprints laid down beside the road yesterday or the day before, anytime back to the last heavy snowfall, then they would still be visible. Like the faces of type in a printer's matrix, they could be returned to after the type itself had been destroyed and read again. With a matrix, yesterday's or last week's newspaper could as well be today's or tomorrow's.

Stepping quickly, almost bounding, around the side of the house to the back, where the second barn and an old chicken house and tool shed were located, I reasoned that if A. or anyone else had decided in the last few days to walk into the woods, for whatever reason, his tracks would probably still be visible near the trees and would remain so until the wind came up and blew the new snow into obliterating drifts. I knew that A.'s habits and routines seldom led him into the woods, so I knew that any trail. I saw would be a sign that something out of the ordinary had occurred—and I desperately needed just such a sign at that moment to break the impasse, the painful balance that hung between all the signs of normalcy and all the signs of variance.

Of course, I also knew that his habits and routines led him at least once a week to walk up the path to the top of the mountain, so any variation from the tracks that the habitual walk up and back ought to have left would be meaningful, too.

With a hunter's eye, I scrutinized the exposed, old, packed snow that lay in corrugated sheets beneath the tall pines, cedars and spruce growing along the cleared ground behind the barn and outbuildings. Nothing. Several times I walked back and forth along the edge of the clearing, looking into the woods. Nothing. An occasional rabbit's trail, the scattered scratches from birds, the small spirals left by squirrels—that was all. Then, as my spirits sank, I came to the path, the narrow defile between the trees and bushes that slowly switch backed up the gradually rising incline all the way to the top. And there they were—A.'s tracks, his easily recognizable 13 EEEs, each one a yard from the next, leading swiftly from under the smoldering blanket of new snow on the yard directly into the woods and on. This I had, of course, fully expected to see, especially after a weekend, when I knew that A. had made his weekly trek to the top of his mountain, Blue Job, two thousand feet or so above sea level, a huge lump of granite and glacial till that had been his family's property since the days of the earliest white settlement in the valley. It comprised almost the whole of seven hundred acres for which they had been taxed these two hundred years, that mountain and the three- or four-acre apron at the base of its south face, where the house and fields were located. Except for its lower half, where every fifteen years or so timber could be harvested, the land was not arable. The upper thousand feet of its height, at this latitude, was so close to the tree line and so free of loose soil that it was almost completely clear of vegetation—a gray gnarl of rock and bony plate and crevice.

I took a short step onto the path, and the snow suddenly seemed to cease falling. My vision cleared as if a screen had been removed from before my eyes. I straightened and peered around for the second set of tracks, A.'s return set. But there was none! How could that be? If he'd gone up, then he must have left tracks coming down. There was no other route for him, up or down, especially at this time of year. The northern slope was precipitous and notched with crevices and sheer drops of hundreds of feet onto ledges and broken shards of stone. The east and west slopes, once you got off the knob, no easy descent, and entered the trees, were practically impenetrably dense with low scrub brush and face-whipping birches left from the last timbering. Besides, they eventually flattened into fields that were owned by other people, people A. had refused to permit to trespass on his property. He was not very likely to trespass on theirs, not unless he was in the direst of circumstances, and probably not even then.

But how to explain the presence before me of tracks leading up the mountain, and no tracks leading down?

I could not answer my own question. Emphatically I decided again that there would be no more speculation. I would follow the tracks through the woods to the rock, and I would follow what I knew was A.'s usual path across the rocks the rest of the way to the top. I knew that my answer lay there, at the wind-blown top of the mountain, not here below, in the shelter of the forest.

I pulled my cap over my ears, gave my gloves a tug, and started trudging uphill along the path, first easterly, then westerly, switchbacking through the trees. As I ascended, the trees became shorter and more twisted, and soon I could see patches of gray sky over me and fresh snow falling on the path. In a short while, the trees were not much higher than my head, briary Scotch pine and dwarfed and gnarled spruce, and when I looked down to check on A.'s tracks, I could no longer see them, for the snow was by then falling heavily on me and on the path, erasing my own tracks behind me as quickly as, a few minutes before, it had erased A.'s. But I was familiar with the path, had walked it many times before, and I knew that A. had come this far and that he must have gone on, so I continued to climb. It became more difficult, for I was out of the trees altogether, and the path was rougher and more circuitous as it wound around huge boulders and skirted short but dangerous drops. The new snow on the old, hardened snow below made my footing less sure. Several times I slipped and almost fell, and once I kept myself from tumbling back down a steep stretch of the path only by pulling myself forward with my hands on a long, jagged outcropping adjacent to the path. The wind was high now, and it whipped the snow against me in wet, adhesive sheets, plastering my hat and coat and face. I could not see more than a dozen feet in front of me and then only when the wind momentarily hitched or shifted and blew the snow from behind me. My progress was slow, I knew, but I didn't have much farther to go. I had reached the crown, where the path abruptly steepened for a final hundred and fifty feet and then leveled off at the top. Increasing my effort, even though I was panting like a racer and, despite the cold and the wind, sweating heavily, I made the final scramble to the top, where I finally came to rest on the table-sized ring of flat stone there. I could see nothing that I could not reach out and touch. The snow had covered my entire body and had turned all but the red sun of my face as white as the whirling white space that surrounded me. If there had been another human face on that high flat tabletop, that altar, I would have seen it, I would have fallen to my knees before it, for I would have seen nothing else but that face. But there was no other human face there to match mine. I was alone, completely alone. I knew that if I took another step, I would walk off the altar into empty space, a swirl of white, and then nothing. Nothing. *Unimaginable nothing.* I turned slowly around and began the descent.

THE RELATION
OF MY
IMPRISONMENT

Remember death.

UPON THE DAWN this drear and soppy month just past, in a year now some twelve years past, it happened that as I began my daily work at the building of coffins, which is my calling, I was prevailed upon by certain superior officers of the town to cease and desist from this work. I had left my young wife's kitchen and had arrived at my workshop at the side of the house and before the road, where, as had been my procedure since completing the apprenticeship of my youth and embarking singly upon the practice of this my calling, I had commenced to lay out the day's labor and to organize that labor into precise allotments of time. Thus I was bent over my various plans and figures at my bench, when there appeared at the doorway a friend and neighbor, a man who must be nameless here but who was one of my chief supports in the early days of my tribulation. This man, all breathless and screw-faced with haste and concern, related to me that this very morning, while passing through the marketplace across the common from the courthouse, as he was on his way to cultivate his fields, which lay on the far side of the town from his dwelling place, he had learned that the chief of civil prosecution in the parish had sent an order to the chief of civil prosecution in the town, to the effect that from this date forward all those men and women residents of this town who engage in the manufacture and/or sale of coffins, or of gravestones or of other such markers of graves, or of vestments for the dead, or of floral or other memorializings of the dead, or who in any way embalm, decorate or otherwise handle and prepare the dead for burial, must henceforth cease and desist from their activities. If this order is not immediately obeyed by those residents of this town who heretofore have participated in such activities, they will be arrested and charged with the crime of heresy and prosecuted to the fullest extent of the various laws.

Because my friend loved me, he wished, however, to do more than merely to warn me of my impending arrest and trial and imprisonment. He attempted as well to persuade me to close the doors of my shop immediately and, upon the eventual arrival at my shop by the officers of the chief of civil prosecution in the town, to deny that I was engaged now in any such activity as had become so recently a heretical activity, for, as my friend pointed out to me, I was an esteemed member of the community, welcomed among them for my comportment and orderliness and the consistent charity of my mind, and therefore the officers of the community would be reluctant to scourge me from them. My skills as a maker of coffins, my friend showed me, could easily be applied to the manufacture of items which the community felt it needed, rather than items which it had deemed not only unnecessary but dangerous to the public weal. He then told me of a growing desire among the better-off families for high wooden cabinets with glass doors for the purpose of exhibiting fragile and expensive possessions.

Having delivered himself both of his warning, which I received with gratitude, and his suggestion regarding my future activities, which I received with the thought that my friend was perhaps putting his timorous self in my place (out of his love and fear for me, however, not of love or fear for himself), he began to gather up my drawings and figures and contracts for the several coffins I then had underway, wrinkling and folding them as if to toss them into the fire.

No, I said to him. This seems not to be our only recourse. Let us think a moment and look into our hearts before we decide what is the proper action. How would it seem to others of our persuasion, with regard to the matter of the dead, if their coffin-maker were to run and hide and, if found, lie outright? Come, I said to him, be of good cheer, let us not be so easily daunted, our case, to care for the dead, is good, so good that we will be well rewarded, finally, if we suffer for that cause. If, however, we deny our cause, and others like us, seeing our example, also deny the cause, then we will suffer ten hundred and infinitely more times over for the denial. For if we will not remember the dead, who among the living will remember us when we join the dead ourselves, as all men must? (*I Craig.,* xiv, 12.)

My friend persisted and pleaded with me none the less, until I begged leave finally to closet myself briefly for prayer and guidance in this question and proceeded to close myself into the coffin that my father had employed his brother, the revered master to my apprenticeship many years ago, to build for me. And as so often has occurred in times of woe or quandary, the face of a beloved ancestor, in this case the wise face of my mother's great aunt, passed before me and gave me these words: Your guide in life can proceed from no other source than the mercy you tender the dead. To suffer for such tenderness is to receive mercy back from the dead when no others will show it to you.

Whereupon I arose from my coffin and confronted my good friend with these words: Leave me, if you wish, and tend your fields, and turn your coffin into a sideboard, if fear is what determines your actions. But as your fellow man who loves you, I am compelled to go on as before. I further stated that since coming to know myself, I had showed myself hearty and courageous in my coffin-making and had made it my business to encourage and teach others the skills and the meanings of the skills I now possessed, and therefore, thought I, if I should now run and make an escape, it would be of a very ill savour in the land. For what would my weak and newly converted brethren think of it? Nothing but that I was not so strong in deed as I had been privately in word. Also I feared that if I should run now when there may well be a warrant out for my arrest, I might by so doing make them afraid to stand forth some time after when but great words only should be spoken to them. And still further, I thought the world thereby would take occasion at my cowardliness, to have thus blasphemed the dead, to have then some ground amongst themselves to suspect the worst of me and my profession.

Sadly, but with freshened understanding, my friend clasped me to his bosom and departed for his fields, and I retrieved my wrinkled and folded drawings and figures and continued as before to lay out the day's work. And at a quarter past ten in the morning, while I was planing a mahogany headboard for the coffin of a young woman living in a village seven miles from ours, three officers of the chief of civil prosecution in our town entered my shop and read to me the orders issued by the chief of civil prosecution in the parish and by that perogative ordered me to cease and desist my activities as a maker of coffins. I carefully restated all the arguments above, and I continued with my planing as before. The officer in charge, a decent man I have known since we were schoolmates together, then placed me under arrest, and after having released me into my own custody on my own recognizance, wrote out a summons, that I was to appear the following morning at the court of the chief of civil prosecution in the town, there to be heard for indictment and if indicted to be remanded to the parish jail to stand trial at some future date for the crime of heresy. He escorted me outside my shop to where my wife anxiously awaited me and closed and sealed the door to my shop and posted the summons thereon. He was a peaceable and methodical man, as were the junior officers with him, and I believe that they persecuted me only with grave reluctance. May they be remembered, therefore, at least for their inclinations to mercy, even if it happened that they were too weak to enact said mercy. (*II Vis.*, xxx, 4.)

Upon the following day, at a quarter of nine in the morning, I presented myself, in the company of my good wife, who had fearfully dispatched our five children to the home of her cousin in an adjacent parish, at the court of the chief of civil prosecution in our town. Here follows the sum of my examination by His Honor Mister Dome.

Dome: What is the work that you practice in the wooden structure attached to your dwelling place and facing the roadway? And how long have you been at that work?

Self: I am a builder of coffins for the express purpose of tendering mercy to the dead. And I have been such since boyhood, when it became imperfectly known to me that any skills I might obtain while among the living would be without meaning unless bent wholly to that purpose.

Dome: You admit, thereby, that you have all your adult life participated in an activity that the larger community has now declared illegal. Do you also admit that you have consistently and diligently enjoined others to do likewise?

Self: Only those others who give evidence of possessing such gifts as I possess and who, with long instruction and example, can acquire the necessary skills for coffin-building. To those who give no evidence of possessing these gifts, and who therefore ought not to be encouraged to acquire these skills, I merely encourage in a general way to know themselves, so that they may pursue a more truly characteristic way of tendering mercy to the dead. For while there are many paths homeward, there is but a single calling. (*Trib.*, vii, 38.)

Dome: Do you admit that you meet together privately for the purposes of giving and receiving instruction?

Self: It has always been customary to do so in this land, and more efficient also.

Dome: You have before me this day confessed to acts which, though in the past have merely been heinous in the eyes of the community, are henceforth regarded as illegal and, therefore, punishable by law. As is my sworn duty, then, unless you first swear before me at this table that all such activities will no longer be tolerated by you or by those under your care, I will be compelled to indict you for persisting in heresy and to remand you to stand trial in the court of the chief of civil prosecution in the parish. Do you so swear?

Self: I cannot of my own will free the dead from the care of the living, any more than I can of my own will free the living from the care of the dead. It is in the nature of things.

At which words His Honor Mister Dome was in a chafe, as it appeared, for he declared that he would snap the neck of these heresies.

Self: It may be so. But I am not able to aid you, for I am already bound over.

Dome: I find against you, Sir. But if you can locate sureties to be now set for you and thus guarantee that you will appear as ordered for trial at the next quarter-sessions, and also that you will cease and desist, pending the findings of said trial, all coffin-making and other such activities as have been declared illegal, I will set you over to return to your home and family until you are called to court.

Self: I understand that any sureties I obtain will be bound against my further coffin-making, and that if I do build a coffin, their bounds will be forfeited. But since I will not leave off the building of coffins, for I believe this is a work that has no hurt in it but is rather more worthy of commendation than blame, then any who will provide sureties for me will soon hate me. I do not believe that I will be able to uncover any friends willing to provide sureties for me who would also be willing to hate me.

Whereat he told me that if my friends would not be so bound, my mittimus must be made and I sent to the jail and there to lie to the quarter-sessions, some nine weeks off.

Thus have I in short declared the manner and occasion of my first being in prison, where I lie even now, calm in the knowledge that to suffer as a result of the errors and weakness of the living is to be all the more prepared for the demands made by the dead. Let the rage and malice of the living be never so great, they can go no further than the dead will permit them. Even when they have done their worst, I will yet love only that greater power over them, the everlasting dead.

AT THE VERY commencement of my imprisonment it was one of the chiefest pleasures of my days to converse at intermittent times in his rounds with my jailor, whose father had been a higgler from my own town and who often had spoken fondly of my own father to this said man when he was himself a child. It was his recognition of my surname, therefore, that brought him to present himself to me early on my first morning in confinement there. Thus my jailor seemed from the outset to rest in a certain sympathy toward me, for he could not understand how I was a dangerous man that had to be locked away from the company of my fellows, like some beast whose uncontrollable lust it was to tear at living flesh. Nor could it be shown to him that I had destroyed or stolen private or public property or that I had made any claims or abridgements against the lawful liberties of other men.

Yet despite this wondering of why it was that I had been imprisoned, my jailor all the same could not understand why I did not leave off my activities as a maker of coffins and apply my skills instead to some task that the majority of my fellow men wished to see promoted, such as the building of glass-fronted cabinets (he cited the same fashion among the newly wealthy as had my friend earlier, prior to my arrest).

But I have met my calling and the meaning it lends to my formlessness more sweetly here in this cell than in the world outside, I told him. To show it my back and numbly acquiesce to the demands of the majority of the living would sour the very air that fills my body.

Could you not do more good if you were set at liberty than you can while locked here in a cage? my jailor inquired. He was a decent fellow, and I did believe and believe especially now, many years after his passing away from me, that he was concerned that the most good be done. And what in particular offended him about my confinement was that it seemed to do no one any good. He was thus a man whose compassion was essentially an act of logic, and his view of mean and cruel men was that they were merely illogical. We could not agree on this, for my own view has been that such men are mean and cruel because they will not perform the rites and other acts of worship which would purge them of their meanness and cruelty, which purgation would thereby permit them to enact goodness in the world. Mercy, I explained to my jailor, is a quality of feeling toward others that must be obtained at some source outside the human heart. My brethren and I believe that it can only be obtained by devoting oneself fully to the worship and further contemplation of the power of the dead. For a man cannot see or hear or touch the world born and dying daily around him until he has first seen, heard and touched the infinite. (*Wal.,* v, 41.)

When I had lain in prison for along about twelve weeks, and not during that time knowing what they intended to do with me, upon the fifteenth of May there came to me a Mister Jones, clerk of the court, having been sent by the several justices of the parish to admonish me and demand of me submission to their regulation of my activities and the curtailment of any future making of coffins or of teaching others to do likewise or of recommending such activities and the wisdom and sweetness thereof to any others, especially to the youth. But since I knew that my case had

not yet been publicly tried and that I was merely under indictment and had not yet confessed to any act of heresy but had
merely argued as to the legitimacy and rightness of my calling, I
knew the admonitions and demands put to me by Mister Jones
were but part of a strategem designed to control me without having as well to defend in public the court's interest in breaking the
neck of the people's growing love for the dead and their gradual
awakening to acts of worship and contemplation of the dead. For,
as all men knew, there was in those years a new spirit moving
over the land which was compelling the people toward a deeper
delight in life that was by necessity and grace derived from their
growing knowledge and experience of the dead. The finite is but
the flesh of the infinite, and the living the breath of the dead.
(*Flor.,* ii, 14.) Here is how Mister Jones, clerk of the court, made
his conversation with me:

When he was come into my chamber, which I had in various
ways and through the aid of my young wife made as comfortable and cheerful as such a stony place could be made, he called
heartily out to me, Neighbor! How do you do, neighbor?

I thank you, Sir, said I. Very well, blessed be the dead.

Said he, scratching at his nose, Well, Sir, I have come to tell
you that it is desired that you would submit yourself unto the
laws of the land, or else at the next quarter-sessions it will go far
worse with you, even to be banished and sent away from out of
the nation or else even worse than that.

I said with all seriousness, looking briefly onto the face
of my jailor for confirmation, that I did desire only to demean
myself in the world, as becometh a man and a worshipper of the
dead. Whatever denied me that benefit could not be pursued, I
explained.

Still he scratched his nose, as if there were situated there
some devious growth or some question that by a steady scratching would get answered. You must leave off these unholy and
illegal practices which you have long been wont to participate in

and endorse among others, for the statute is now set up against them, and here am I now, sent by the justices to tell you that they do intend to prosecute the law against you if you will not submit.

Sir, I said modestly but with natural authority and a reasonable man's knowledge of procedure and law, Sir, I conceive that the laws by which I am imprisoned at this time, the laws of indictment, do not reach or condemn either me or the practices of tendering mercy in various accepted, codified manners to the dead. I have come forward and made myself known unto the world, and now you and your justices must do the same. The dead will decide who is in the right.

I believe that the clerk of the court was a weak and easily frightened man, for at this he turned and stalked furiously from my presence. My jailor was at first moved to laughter, but after a moment, when he saw that mirth had not been my intent, he sombered and declared his affection for my methods, though he said he was repelled by my cause. This did not dismay or discourage me, for I had long ago undergone the type of self-scrutiny that weds method to cause; and therefore I knew my jailor's lack of affection for my cause was only due to his ignorance of it, whereas his appreciation of what he called my methods could only be due to a clear readiness for conversion.

And indeed, before the next quarter-sessions came to term, my jailor, whose name was John Bethel, had begun to open his heart and understanding to the mystery of the dead and had commenced joining me in my cell for evening prayer and contemplation. He had not yet his own coffin and therefore was compelled to close himself in his arms where two walls meet, as is the custom for those among the brethren who, for reasons, have not their own coffins at ready access. But when he had frequently observed my emergence from prayer and had glimpsed indirectly thereby the grace and relief obtained, he thereupon had each time attempted to elicit from me the name of one by whom he himself might have a coffin built.

I greeted his repeated request with deeply troubled feelings. On the one hand, I took delight from what appeared to be a case of genuine conversion to the understanding that supercedes all understanding, and I knew that without his own coffin in which to closet himself for prayer and contemplation, my brother John Bethel would eventually see his questing fall back upon itself, like a vine with nothing to attach itself to, there to wither and die. This possibility, nay, this likelihood! grieved me, and I would determine at once to provide him with the name of one of those among us who would build him a coffin, when, as I paced my cell waiting for my jailor to make his evening round and appear to me, it would seem to me that his request for information, such as the name of one who would build him a coffin, was but a subtle ruse designed to induce me to expose and incriminate and thereby condemn one of my beloved brethren to the fate I now endured. And thus I would close my mind as if it were a fist, and I would swear never to reveal the names of my fellow worshippers of the dead, even if tortured and brought to the very gateway of death itself. I had no fear of torture in those years, any more than I do today, for I was filled with the knowledge that if one among the living were to bring me to the very gateway of death and there threaten to hurl me through, it would be as if he were threatening to hurl me into the arms of my dead parents and long-departed ancestors, and I would at such a moment urge him onward, not to confound him, as I am sure it would do, but so as to end this agony of separation.

While I was yet enduring this quandary with regard to the question of the conversion of my jailor John Bethel, as it was now some weeks beyond the second quarter-sessions of the meeting of the justices of the parish for the purposes of trying all those previously indicted and not yet tried in public court and still I had not yet been called forth so to be tried, though I continued to languish in jail fully as if I had indeed been tried and convicted of those crimes for which I had merely been indicted and had not confessed (except as to argue against the legitimacy of the laws which prohibit acts of worship of the dead such as my brethren are known to participate in), came the time of the solstice. Now at the solstice there is usually a general releasement of divers prisoners, by virtue since ancient days of the high feelings surrounding the event, in which privilege I also should have had my share. But they would not take me for a convicted person, unless I were willing to sue out a pardon (as they called it), by means of which I would recant all my previous statements and activities as had got me indicted in the first place. Therefore, since I was no more willing under these new circumstances to recant and deny than I had been when under more durable and oppressing circumstances twenty weeks before, I could have no benefit of the solstice. Whereupon, while I continued in prison, my good wife went unto the several justices, that I might be heard and that they would impartially take my case into public consideration.

There were three, and the first that my wife did plead unto was Judge Hale, who was celebrated for his learning and deep probity and who was known for his leniency towards dissenters of various sorts. He very mildly received her, telling her that he would do her and me the best good he could, but he feared, said he, that he could do none.

The following day, lest the judges should, by the multitude of their business, forget me, she did throw another petition onto the table of Judge Twisdom, who, when he saw it and had read it through, snapped her up and angrily informed her that I was a convicted person already and could not be released unless I would promise to make no more coffins and not to teach others, &c.

After this disappointment, she went unto Judge Bester, who, in the mild presence of Judge Hale, stood and declared loudly and angrily that I was convicted by the court and that I was a hot spirited fellow, whereat he waved the petition in the air above his head and shouted that he would not meddle therewith.

But yet my wife, being encouraged by the seeming kindly face and manner of Judge Hale, did persist, saying that I had been indicted merely and had confessed to no crime and had not been tried, yet I was both confined to prison and at the same time was not to receive the indulgences prompted by the solstice that all other prisoners were to be granted. The place where this interview took place was called the Lion's Chamber, where there were then situated the two judges and also many gentry and officers of the several towns in the parish. My wife, coming into them with a bashed face and a trembling heart and voice, began her errand to them in this manner:

Woman: My Lord (directing herself to Judge Hale), I make bold to come once again to your Lordship to know what may be done with my husband.

Hale: Woman, I have told you that I can do you and your husband no good, because they have taken that for a conviction which your husband has already spoken at the indictment. And unless there be something done to un-do that, I can do you no good.

Woman: My Lord, he was clapped into prison. . .

One of the gentry in the room, interrupting her: My Lord, the man was lawfully convicted! Why waste your precious time?

Woman: False! False!

Whereupon Judge Bester answered very angrily, saying that my wife must think that judges could do whatever they wished, whereas it seemed instead that her husband, meaning me, was the one who at this very moment was standing at prison for attempting to do whatever he wished. Did she desire that they too, meaning the judges and various gentry in the room, should end standing in prison alongside her husband? He laughed loudly at this.

Woman: But my Lord, he was not lawfully convicted.

Bester: He was.

Woman: No, he was not.

Bester: Indeed he was!

Hale: He was.

One of the gentry: Get this woman from out the room! She is a disrupter!

Bester: He was convicted! It is recorded! It is recorded! he continued crying, as if it must be of necessity true because it was so recorded. With which words, he and the others in the chamber, for they had taken up the cry, attempted to stop up her mouth, having no other argument to convince her but, It is recorded! It is recorded!

Here Judge Hale, trying to restore order, but not so greatly interested in restoring justice, interrupted and declared that none should talk about this matter any further, for he (meaning me) cannot do whatever he wishes, and he (meaning me again) has proved himself a breaker of the peace if not a heretic.

Woman: He only desired to live peaceably and that he follow his calling, both that his life and his family's be properly maintained, and moreover, my Lord, I have five small children that cannot help themselves, of which one is born blind, and they and I now have nothing to live upon but the charity of good people.

Hale: You have five children? You are but a young woman to have five children. And a slender woman to have five children. (He seemed to wish her proven a liar of some sort.)

Woman: I am, my Lord, but stepmother to them, having not been married to him yet two full years when he was first arrested. Indeed, I was with child when my husband was first apprehended, but being young and unaccustomed to such things then, I was smayed at the news and fell into labor and so continued for eight days, then was delivered, but my child died.

Whereat Judge Hale, looking very soberly on the matter, said, Alas, poor woman!

But Judge Bester declared that she made poverty and pain her cloak and its lining.

Here the woman fell to weeping, albeit in silence, for while she had up to now endured great woe and tribulation, this attack upon her very integrity, coming as it did from such a height and, as it seemed to her then and to me now, with no other cause than that of idle malice, came with a heaviness all out of proportion to its mass, as if it were a chain cast from lead and placed around her narrow shoulders solely to bear her down.

When she had left this place called the Lion's Chamber and had brought herself directly to my cell and had recounted to me the details of her several interviews with these mighty persons, I saw that it would be this way with me now for my life time, unless I could contrive to get my name placed upon the calendar for the quarter-sessions of the meeting of the court and thus could come to trial and either be found innocent, and freed in that way, or else be convicted, and thence freed by the power of the general amnesty associated with the solstice. While my wife wept in despair, for she had at last given up the fight for my freedom, I negotiated with my jailor, who, at my direction, had determined to obtain the calendar for the quarter-sessions of the meeting of the court and place my name thereon, thus compelling the justices to hear my case, for, with my name upon that calendar, they would have no choice but to call me to come forward. I allowed myself the pleasure of admiring the symmetry between their claim that my confession and judgement were already recorded and my own new claim that my name was recorded upon the calendar. Their foolish worship of the record would compel them to proceed in a manner that they had earlier deemed undesirable if not wholly repellent.

My jailor, John Bethel, here proved his devotion to my cause, as well as to my method, for he went out from me and under the cover of darkness stole into the courthouse where the records were kept and added my name to the calendar, so that the following day, when he was instructed by an officer of the court to deliver the various named prisoners who were to be tried that day, he was able to come to my cell and bring me forth. As I passed him in the hallway, I whispered unto him that he would soon have the coffin he required, and together, I and seven other prisoners, under the careful guard of my brother John Bethel and his two assistants, came to the courthouse, there to present ourselves for trial.

I was not at first noticed standing among the others in the docket, but before long one of the justices, Judge Bester, saw me there and signalled in whispers to the other two judges that I was present, whereupon all three began to glare heatedly at me while they listened to the various cases being put before them. This glaring of theirs distracted them somewhat, for on several occasions they compelled the prisoner before them to repeat his testimony of defense, and in all seven cases they were able to agree unanimously on the guilt of the prisoner before them, even without the usual discussion amongst themselves, so as to hurry toward the calling out of my name. This calling duly came, whereupon Judge Bester reddened with fury and with a roar charged that I had somehow contrived to alter the calendar and that he would see me punished horribly for such a crime. Judge Hale, more calmly than his brother judge but in a rage none the less, called my jailor forth and put to him these questions:

Hale: John Bethel, you were posted throughout the night in your office at the prison, were you not?

Jailor: It is my duty, Sir.

Hale: Did this man pass you or was he in any way absent from his cell during the night?

Jailor: No, Sir, he did not and he was not.

Hale: How, then, do you think he altered the calendar?

Jailor: I am but a jailor, Sir, and thus I have no thoughts on the matter. Since, however, it was recorded that he was to be brought to trial here today, I did not know what else to do with him but to bring him straightway here so that you might try him. To delay or otherwise obstruct his being tried, Sir, would be to foul the law and the numerous statutes of procedure.

Bester (interrupting): The calendar has been secretly altered! Hang him for it! We shall try him, oh, we shall try him indeed, but we shall try him for altering the calendar! (He was at this point too vexed to continue speaking and began to sound as if he were chewing upon a piece of cloth, and he left off trying to speak and instead turned away and faced the back of the court-room in a fume.)

Hale: Have you (meaning me) anything to say for your defense?

Self: With what, Sir, am I charged?

Hale: With having altered the calendar.

Self: I have not been properly indicted for that crime, Sir. I have been indicted only for the crime of heresy, to which I have not confessed, and therefore I do not believe I can be tried for the crime of altering the calendar.

This threw the three justices into a deep uproar, and the numerous observers and gentry attending the scene broke into loud laughter and guffaws. For it was now clear to all that the justices had tangled themselves in the cords and folds of their own procedure and that all their combined anger could not disentangle them. It was also clear that they would, in spite of themselves, try me this day, for one crime if not for another, and probably for no better reason than that they were being driven to it by their anger.

Hale: If your name is on the calendar, then we shall indeed try you, Sir! And the crime for which we shall try you is that of having altered the court calendar! As for the crime of heresy, for which you have already been duly indicted and to which you have confessed, it is recorded that you were, by virtue of your recorded confession, condemned in absentia, that is to say, without public trial, and thus you shall still remain ineligible for the pardon occasioned by the solstice, which applies only to those duly convicted at a public trial and now standing at prison. This new trial and the conviction that will doubtless follow shall bring with it the death penalty. And from that there shall be no pardon also! You, Sir, and all your followers, shall learn that the procedures of law exist to protect the rights of the law-abiding. They shall not be abused by those who, like yourself, wish to subvert and destroy justice! (Here he fell into a confused and angry tirade against tax evaders and other petty criminals, wandering in his words, it seemed to me, until at last he tailed off among mumbled phrases and uncompleted sentences.)

Then my brother, my jailor, came forward, and by his intelligence and courage and his love for me, made me crack with shame, for he had discerned what, in my pleasure at having discomfited the several justices, I had not discerned. He had seen that if I were to be tried for having altered the calendar, I would be swiftly convicted, for the justices, even the saintly Hale, were in such a temper as to find no one now before them innocent, and he had seen that they were ready to condemn a man to hard labor for life, if given the chance, for no greater crime than that of misspelling the name of the month. My brother had also seen what I had deliberately allowed myself to be blinded to: he had seen that they would hang me for the crime of altering the calendar. And therefore, he had determined, by virtue of his old life's values, that I would be far better off languishing for numberless years in a cold damp prison cell than hanging from yonder gallows tree. This meant that while he had been sufficiently converted to my teachings and example so as to be able to face death courageously himself, he was not sufficiently freed of his old life's courtship of itself to realize that I would be shamed and heartbroken by his taking my place at the gallows.

For these reasons, he came forward to the justices and declared that it had been he, John Bethel, who had altered the calendar so as to include my name upon it, and that if any man were to be tried and convicted for the said crime, it must be he. Let this interview and this assertion stand as an indictment and confession, said John Bethel, and let the clerk of the court properly add my name and blot out the name of the coffinmaker, and let the trial proceed as ordered by the statutes of procedure.

I cried out in vain that he must not sacrifice himself for the living, that he must only sacrifice himself for the dead, as we have long been taught (*II Carol.*, iv, 34, 35), but it was too late. Judge Hale ordered the sergeant-at-arms to clap the jailor in irons and to present him in the docket, from which I myself was roughly removed. I saw the jailor's peaceful eyes as I was wrenched past him and he took my place, and I uttered these words: My brother, you shall have my own coffin. Though you are in error, you have earned the right to it, and I have not.

This was the most public event in the twelve years of my imprisonment that have so far transpired, and thus it was the most misunderstood and the most slandered. By this brief private account I have tried to make understanding possible and slander libelous. Also by this account have I tried to tender mercy to the beloved dead man, John Bethel, who in life was my jailor and who in death awaits me as a brother.

MY JAILOR WENT forward unto the dead in my stead, and though there sometimes passed through my heart a swift blade of grief, and though I was often, on the occasion of dark and cold afternoons that first autumn of my imprisonment, lashed by regret and shame, I was able to obtain a measure of release from my guilt and comfort for my pain from my having been able to provide him with my own personal coffin for his journey unto the dead, and I was further released and comforted by the sure knowledge that, though he had taken my place among the dead, I was now taking his place among the living. I remembered the old teachings on death, how it must fall to every one of us, and whether it come sooner or later matters not, for time is valueless to the dead. Only the living can be tempted by time; the dead, by their nature, treasure it not at all.

It was during this early period of my imprisonment, when I had not yet obtained a coffin to replace the one I had transferred to my jailor, that I determined to atone for my rashness and stupidity in the matter concerning the alteration of the court calendar. I decided to atone for my life by resisting death. This meant that henceforth I would be compelled to avoid any confrontation that would risk my life. It also meant that I would no longer be able to deny myself any sustenance, any food, rest or medication or other physical comfort that in whatsoever way contributed to the further resistance of death.

I did this, said I to my wife and several friends, all of whom were at first astonished by this change in my behavior, to honor the dead John Bethel and the manner of his dying. My beloved frail wife, who had not yet wholly absorbed the principles and the celestial hugeness of the design that undergirds and guides our faith, was at first inclined to give outward evidence of great pleasure at my determination to avoid all activities and practices that could lead me into a fatal encounter with death. She clasped me to her tender bosom when she first heard of my decision and amid much weeping and wild high laughter exclaimed that now our children would be saved, for, as she saw it, now their father would be saved. And to my surprise and disappointment, she let it out that she now expected me to recant and forswear, as I had been so many times encouraged as well by the justices to do, my life long practice of the making of coffins and the teaching of this skill and the meanings of the skill to others.

No, dear wife, I admonished her. That I will not permit myself to do. For I am now uniquely situated in life, by virtue of my imprisonment, so as to be able to sustain my life and in that way scourge myself for having sinned in the matter of altering the court calendar without, at the same time and by that means, having also to deny the worth and significance of my worship of the dead and my desire to join them. This my life of imprisonment is come to me now as a great opportunity to bless and show mercy to one among them, the man who was my jailor, John Bethel. I cannot, indeed, I must not, let that opportunity slide away. To do so would be to render a meaningful existence meaningless, would be to sow confusion among the brethren, would be to desert my children altogether, and in the end would be to place myself beyond deserving your wifely love, which even now, by my failure to have given you deep enough understanding of my acts, seems to be withdrawing itself from me so as to attach itself back to its source, there to stagnate, a foul perversion of love and not at all the pure spring-like bubbling forth of love that you have carried to me up to now. Sit yourself down here by me in my cell, I said to her, so that I may begin to teach you from the ancient texts the meanings of our movements between life and death, and free me thereby to atone for my prideful oversight and the earlier inadequacy of my teaching, which, even as you exclaim and clasp me to you, reveals itself to us both in the painful form of your thrilled weeping at my new determination not to resist life.

And thereupon did I commence to instruct my young wife from the ancient texts and the myriad examples of death that have come down to us from olden times. And every day she came unto me, often in the company of a relation, to sit for hours and there to listen and reason together and exchange views, until such a time had passed as she did feel that she had fully penetrated my understanding and had taken it unto herself in such a form and thoroughness as to be able to convey it to our children, who, because of the corrupting nature of the prison, were not permitted to visit me during those years. (Later, when the two oldest grew large enough to pass as adults, they were to come unto me, and I will soon describe their visit.)

DURING THE PERIOD of my wife's instruction, there grew within me, in the secret manner of a tumor, a quickly rising desire for fleshly contact with women, that at the start would as quickly, after I had become aware of its presence and had with mild horror rebuked it, weaken and droop back upon itself. This abominable longing would steal upon me and catch me unawares, even as I was deeply immersed in the teachings of the patriarchs and matriarchs or in discussion of theological history with my wife or her cousin (a young woman who sometimes accompanied my wife to the prison), or even when, for we then frequently resorted there, we three would each face a place in the tiny cell where two walls came together and, folding ourselves in our own arms, attempt to pray. These eruptions of lust knew no bounds of decency or decorum, honored no categories of thought, argument or inquiry, nor would they share the stage of my thoughts and sensibilities with any other player. Thus it was only with an enormous effort of will, frequently supplemented by quantities of anger (at my weakness, my own, no demon's strength, no dark deity's), that each time I was able to yank that player off the stage and replace him with the legitimate one.

I cannot deny this depraved interlude, that it existed, that I fought it, to be sure, and that, in the end, I was overcome by it. Nor can I lay the blame at anyone's feet but my own. I confess my transgression against the spirit of the dead, which by its glory and infinitude demands our entire devotional attention. I confess it because I wish to let myself serve as a warning and a lesson to others who may in some future time during a similar period of connubial deprivation find themselves afflicted as was I. Therefore, I beg the reader's indulgence and understanding of the presence, to follow, of certain descriptions that in a less somber, less deliberately instructional work would be reprehensible, if not morally disgusting. And let the prurient minded be warned: there will be nothing of interest for you here, for all that follows is woe and deprivation, and what may appear on the surface to be the glitter of sensual gratification, at bottom is but the enlightening muck and mire of self-disgust.

In those months of her instruction, which was the wintertime of my first year of imprisonment, my wife grew wan and sickly, as a consequence of her sufferings from the birthing of the child born dead the previous spring, and also from the sufferings wrought by the poverty of her life without the presence of a husband able to earn a living in the world. I do also fear that her daily journey to the prison, which was often a damp and chilled place, despite my efforts to warm the cell with the brazier that my new jailor had kindly supplied me, exacerbated her condition somewhat. So that by the middle of December she had gone to a pathetic thinness and her skin had come to be cracked and chafed by the wind and cold, and she was beginning to cough. Even so, each noontime when she arrived at my cell, often bearing freshly baked cakes or bread, she would smile cheerily and fill me with news of our dear children and the lives of our brethren in the faith, most of whom, by having watched me be overwhelmed by the power of the state, had either made their practices of worship invisible to the state or had chosen self-banishment and had gone out of the nation. (This was but one of the reasons why it was then so difficult for me to obtain a new coffin to replace the one I had made over to my saintly jailor, John Bethel.) However, many was the day when, at the arrival of my wife, I peered into her gray eyes and saw the suffering hidden there, and the sight, despite all my efforts against it, often brought me to tears.

After a short time my wife began to see the effect her wretched state was having on me, and so she struggled all the more bravely to disguise it, even to the extreme measure of wearing dresses that exaggerated and pointed with innocent directness to the few remaining curves and rises of her body. She took to wearing a dark blue wool dress that I gathered she had knitted herself during the long evenings alone in our cottage after the children had gone off to bed. This dress, unintentionally provocative, was designed to fit snugly around her hips and buttocks and to lift and round her small breasts so as to make her seem to me more healthy and jocular than in fact she was. I cannot say it forcefully enough, but let it be known to all that my wife in no way was attempting to encourage in me the lust that her presence in that knit dress soon began to provoke. So did I then believe, and so do I believe today. Let this account in no way besmirch her pure and devoted life, her noble death, and the majesty of her present and everlasting existence among the dead. Let it merely serve as a warning to those who, desiring to bring comfort and good cheer to the living, inadvertently wreak havoc and establish depression among them instead. We cannot provide solace for the living, no more than can we avenge ourselves upon the dead. Presence evades attention, absence invites it, and there is no choice, for there is but the acceptance of what is possible, or the denial. (*Trib.*, iv, 13.)

If, then, my dearly beloved wife erred, she erred in this way, and given the brevity of her previous period of instruction in the faith, she was no more to be condemned for her actions than was my jailor John Bethel for his. And to be sure, if anyone is to stand condemned, let me be the one, for I was the only person, in both cases, who could be said to have been responsible for their instruction in the faith, for in both cases did I myself undertake their instruction. Yet I had mistrusted John Bethel's pleas for the name of a coffinmaker, so that he could in life have practiced the uplifting rite of prayer, which would have opened him sufficiently unto the wisdom of the dead so as to have forbidden him from supplanting my death with his own that day in court. The result therefrom must be blamed on me. And I did pridefully assume that my young wife's proximity to me day and night for the two years of our marriage prior to my arrest was sufficient instruction for her to know at once that whatever device she used to provide me with less pity for her, if it awakened in me appetites that drew my attention away from the dead and toward the living, then the device, regardless of her kind intent, was diabolical. No, I am the one who must be blamed for these two errors in faith. I am the one who has failed the terms of his calling and who, therefore, must beg forgiveness of the dead.

It thus happened that one particularly sour and chilled December noontime, when my wife came unto me and entered my cell, and when the jailor had left us alone and had returned to his post below, the close heat of my cell swiftly brought a blush to her face and encouraged her to unwrap her scarf and shawl, which revealed in the glow of the brazier and my reading candle an illusory fullness through her hips and breasts, an illusory healthy roundness to her arms, and great warmth of illusory color in her throat. I declare it illusory simply because I well knew that the woman had long been ill and pinched by pain and that in my absence she had been forced frequently to deprive herself so that the plates of my children, her step-children, could be filled. Further, I declare it illusory so that it may be known abroad that she did in no way provoke me or otherwise draw from me lustful ambitions. They existed prior to her arrival that noontime and they merely used her presence as an occasion to arise and make themselves known to us. The woman lived purely. She wished no more than to let me beget a new child upon her, a child of her own who would be able someday to tender proper mercy to her when she herself had joined the blessed dead. I, I was the one who had no pure thoughts that day, no thoughts of an unborn child coming to life so as to bless me in death, I was the one whose lust had no ambition other than its own satisfaction, a means with no end, a cause with no effect.

Therefore did I reach out and paw her soft body and draw her to me, and then did I wrench her dress from her body and expose her creamy surface to the flick of candle light and the steady glow of the reddened coals in the brazier, and then did I strip my trousers off, and pulling my wife down, did I cover her with my body and swarm over her for a great long time, until at last did I fall away and, exhausted, uncouple from her.

At first, my response to this act was, of all the possible responses then available to me, the weakest one. I strode down the path of least resistance, as it were, by simply refusing to acknowledge this lustful seizure and the seizures that regularly every afternoon followed it, like links in a binding chain, as being anything more than some natural expression of my body, no less natural than the continued growth of the hair of my head or the hair of my beard or the nails of my fingers and toes. This insistance upon the naturalness of my act was, of course, as the reader must know all too well, nothing but a means of construing the situation so as to be better able to repeat the act, over and over, day after day, until it had become a hideous habit and there seemed to be no way of separating the head of it from the tail. Each time after my wife had wrapped herself once again modestly in her scarf and shawl and had left my presence, I would groan aloud and beat my breast with shame, and each time, before long, I would start up with assurances that what I was doing was no more than any man's body, so deprived by imprisonment, would wish him to do. I even contrived a clever guard against shame by wheedling out of my intelligence this argument: that to berate myself for having fallen into lustful copulation was to give an unnatural attention to things and events of this life, which was unnecessarily and sinfully to pull my proper attention away from contemplation of the dead. And like a true sophist, I even used scripture to woo me from self-disgust. Leave off undue fascination with and morbid examination of things of the body, I told myself, quoting the sacred book of *Walter* (x, 42). Thus did I not only debase myself, but I debased the words of the sainted dead as well. And all this in but the very beginnings of my period of transgression! I elaborate on and attend to it here solely that the reader will know that I too have been confronted by the forces of life that would demean and destroy our faith, and I too have walked across the barren desert of my own weakness and have come to the mountains beyond, and I have at last ascended those mountains. I have endured as all men may endure, if they will but will it.

From here my debauch, like a tropical river, broadened and deepened, until it seemed to flow irresistably into a sea of life, a tepid expanse where nothing but teeming forgetfulness and transience may exist, where the permanence of remembered death is denied a place and the singleness of mortal existence, our movement from life to death, has no meaning. For not only did I begin to curtail by an increasing amount of time the period of instruction and prayer each afternoon with my wife, so that I could squirm and roll with her on the mat in the darkened corner of my cell, but I began to vary from one day to the next the modes and positions of our interpenetration. This was, to be sure, a consequence of the regularity of our unbridled comings together, a way of avoiding contact with and recognition of our essential boredom with the act and our deep knowledge of its superfluity and utter gratuitousness, for we had long since removed ourselves from any possible rationalizations such as the begetting of new children. It may also have been the consequence of a newly released idle curiosity. (I credit this motive only to myself; I know that my wife never experienced such a loathsome provocation.) But whatever the cause, before long we were engaged in acts that could only be named beastly, in positions that could only be described as perverse or, if one were inclined toward compassion, as pathetic or, if one were maliciously detached, as comic. And we worked heatedly and furiously, as if we were about to be interrupted and publicly exposed while in the midst of our abominations.

Which, unhappily, is what happened. One afternoon in late December, when my wife and I were feverishly engaged in copulation, from a position that in retrospect now appears grotesque but which at the time functioned on my visual sense so as to draw forward from me a great long surge of erotic attention, my new jailor, a man named Jacob Moon, suddenly appeared at my cell door, which, as was the practice with political and religious prisoners, perpetrators of what were then called crimes of conscience, lay open and unlocked. It was only at night or during a rare emergency or during the visit of some legal dignitary that the cell doors in my section of the prison were closed and locked. This relative freedom of movement was considered a privilege and, more importantly, a tacit acknowledgement of the vague and ambiguous terms of our crimes and the punishments attached thereto, for during those years both the prisoners and the authorities felt that it was to their respective group's advantage to perpetuate for as long as possible the vagueness and ambiguity of the terms of the crimes and punishments. Now, of course, both parties have taken the opposite position, which accounts for all the recent bouts of litigation, the continuous appeals to higher courts, the rising income of attorneys, and the facts that the cell doors are locked at all times and that many other amenities, such as my coal brazier, have been eliminated. For nowadays the prisoners have come to feel that they must be either wholly free or wholly imprisoned. In previous years, however, since they had feared that the only alternative available to them was total imprisonment and that total freedom was out of the question, and since the authorities feared that total freedom was the option and that total imprisonment was out of the question, both groups had struggled to achieve the mid-point between, a compromise that, because it denied both parties' worst fears, satisfied everyone. At present neither party is satisfied. And therefore, one of my several tasks here, as I see it, is to try to show both parties the wisdom of the old way.

Jacob Moon was John Bethel's replacement as chief jailor, but in no other way was he that man's replacement. He was not unfriendly, and he was not unkind to the prisoners, neither was he especially efficient nor especially inefficient as manager of our confinement. He had been, up to this moment of his discovery of my wife and myself in a particularly humiliating circumstance, a man who had struck me by his strikingly ordinary manner of doing his job and by a singular lack of curiosity or interest in the lives and minds of the often quite interesting and enriching individuals under his care. He did seem, however, to come to life that afternoon, and with a forthrightness that surprised me, he asked if he could join me and my wife. His request was tenderly put, and because it came at precisely the moment of my and my wife's greatest sensual arousal, I signalled him impatiently to enter the cell and to join us, which he proceeded to do in quite a matter of fact manner, as if it were his habit or custom so to find himself on an otherwise uneventful mid-winter afternoon.

Naturally, I was afterwards filled with great remorse and shame. Not only had I debauched myself and transgressed the teachings of my faith, but I had also led my wife, my poor trusting wife, into debauchery and transgression likewise, and here I was now, leading yet a third person into debauchery and transgression. The fact that Jacob Moon, or Jake, as we came to call him, was not of our faith in no way lessened his transgression or my responsibility for it. The scriptures say, If you would transport yourself unto the dead, you must also transport others, and if you refuse to transport others thither, the gate shall be closed to you also. (*II Craig.*, xxii, 43.)

My wife and Jake attempted to calm me and tried valiantly to purge me of guilt by asserting that I was not responsible for their participation, and for a brief period I was sufficiently weak and spiritless (in will, for my appetites were extremely strong) to believe them, so that I was then of a mind that the only weakness I was contending with, the only one I had to feel guilty for, was my own, a vain fantasy, I now realize, but one that I clung to during those horrible months with the desperation of a man drowning in a sea of overpowering desire. During this period I turned with embarrassment away from prayer and scripture, and also I gradually gave up attempting to explain the ethics and metaphysics of my faith, upon which I heretofore had expended great energy, time and ingenuity in conversation with my wife and, now and again when she accompanied my wife, her cousin Gina.

I cannot blame any of these three good people for having joined me in my debauch. I blame only myself, for clearly, if I had not permitted it, if I had not given myself over with such foolish abandon to the physical pleasures offered by my wife's body, if I had not permitted Jake that afternoon to enter my cell but had instead reacted with proper horror and self-loathing at his proposal, and if the following week I had not permitted Gina to give herself over to Jake's demands, and then later had not allowed myself to answer her wild cries for satisfaction or my wife's child-like demands for equal attention from Jake, if at the beginning or at any point along this long, satiny, declining path I had stood up and had said, No! and in that humble way had begun again to turn my attention back to the dead, then none of it would have occurred. I here publicly admit my failure and in this way offer to the dead what meager mercy and remembrance I am capable, in such a fallen state, of offering.

My strength did eventually, though only partially, come back to me, yet it came suddenly, like a room filling with darkness when a candle is extinguished. It came back to me in full force much later, however, and only on the day when I finally obtained my coffin again, an event of great magnitude, coming as it did after such sustained desolation. And then once again would it be proved to me that solely by the careful and proper observation of rite and ceremony and the methodical, informed use of artifact may the mind of the living be permitted the transcendent experience of contemplation of the dead, which in turn is the only way to obtain a proper understanding of the meaning of life. All other means, despite the best of intentions, are but approximate and ultimately misleading. And innocence leads nowhere at all. (*The Book of Discipline,* viii, 23-25.)

How it came to pass that I obtained a new coffin will be described near the end of this testament. In the meantime, let the reader imagine me, in the descriptions to follow immediately, as daily, usually in the afternoons, engaging in the awful practices and depravities I have described above, while during the mornings and evenings I passed my time in peaceful argument with my jailor (for we had become brothers of a sort and an exchange of views between us was a natural extension of our new affiliation) and also with diverse other prisoners who were of a religious turn of mind but who were not of my faith. For my purpose now is to reveal how the mind of the fallen man, the man who has allowed his attention to wander off the dead and fix itself onto the living only, swiftly divides itself into segments, boxes of thought, attitude and activity with no necessary or discernible link, consistency or communication between them, resulting inevitably in that pathetic and sorrowful figure, the man of time.

THE MAN OF time is without self-unity. I was now such a man. Every day early in the day, I hailed my jailor Jacob Moon in his office at the bottom of the stone staircase that spined the prison, and upon first catching sight of his grim and wholly pragmatic face, the face of a man who had long ago made of himself a tool to fit what he regarded as the job of life, I instantly arranged my own face into a matching mask, and because he never signalled with a wave or other such greeting gesture, neither would I make any gesture. After I had initially hailed him with the sober utterance of his name, Jacob, I merely entered his office and leaned against the jambs, like a wrench or sledge hammer laid there by a workman, and we commenced to speak, drily and without feeling, of economic and political affairs in foreign lands or the difficulties encountered by certain civil engineering projects or the desirability of a central heating system for the prison.

Gone from me now the glorious, unifying vision that had come to me with my faith when I was but a boy. Gone from me now the work of my calling, which was to make coffins. Gone from me the ways of being used in a process larger than that of my own decaying body's, gone from me the affectionate need of the community. Gone from me now even the need of my brethren in the faith, for not enough of them had followed to where I had been led, and then only a few had known, until this account, my reasons for having forsaken death and clung to imprisonment. And gone from me the urgent presence of my five children, their wonderings, their desires and needs that the incomprehensible be made comprehensible. And now, now, gone the cleaving presence and trust of my wife, for she more than any other person, except for me myself, knew now of my weakness and the state to which I had fallen. And finally, of greatest significance, gone from me the dead, gone timelessness, gone its continuous flow of wisdom, gone its absolute clarity. Gone from me now was I myself, and all that remained were the hard bright surfaces of a self that generated no light but merely reflected back whatever surfaces it met. For once a man loses his connection with whatever looms forever larger than himself, he has lost himself as well. He exists solely as a nexus after that, a mere contingency, a crossroads without a place name.

So it began to appear to me that I was utterly dependent upon the nature and character of whomever I met, before I could reveal any particular nature or character of my own. Unless I could locate clues and hints as to the forms a person used to present himself and deal with other people, which clues and hints would lead me to design appropriate forms for me to present myself back to him, then I trembled all over my body, I whimpered and spoke with an uncontrollable stammer, I fairly well wept with terror. For I had become the man of time. I had lost myself, and lost, I moved in a found world, a very real place that was stuffed to brimming with very real and threatening human beings, animals, plants, powerful objects of all possible descriptions. Nothing there was then that did not fill me with terror and confusion. Though you are seen, you cannot see, and though you are heard, you cannot hear, and though others will walk along with you, you may not walk along with them. For such is the punishment made for the man who has exchanged what is absent for what he cannot avoid. (*The Book of Discipline,* iii, 30-31.)

Every day I left my cell at dawn, and affecting gaiety, strolled to the dining hall, there to sit among my fellow prisoners and exchange views and idle thoughts while eating our usual breakfast of bread and porridge. To be sure, my stance and affect were those of a game man, a courageous fellow full of wit and intelligence, yet all the while I trembled inside, all the while I guessed and hoped and tried on faces and phrases rapidly, one after the other, eagerly awaiting the click of recognition in the eyes of the man sitting at table across from me or the sleepy eyes of the bland steward handing me my meager meal across the counter or the eyes of the guard at the door as I passed out of the dining hall to the corridor and, desperate for confirmation, found myself rushing down the stairs to the office of the man I tried to think of as my brother, for he was a man I had come to know solely by means of and in the terms of my fall from faith, and it had come to me in my moral confusion of that period that if I could love my jailor, I could perhaps learn to love myself, or what at that time claimed to be myself.

Fortunately, however, this feat was not to be accomplished. Jacob Moon was a grim man and also, as I have said, most characteristically a pragmatic man. He did not smile so much as, at moments of gaiety or high mirth, he grimaced. As, for instance, when once a donkey wandered into the prison from the street and soon had lost itself in the maze of corridors and common rooms and stairways, and as it was encountered suddenly and all out of any familiar context by one prisoner after another and one guard after another, discoveries that brought one prisoner and guard after another to the chief jailor's office to report its, the donkey's, presence, soon there had gathered at the office nearly all the prisoners and all the guards and assistant jailors and staff and even a few visitors, and still one or two more prisoners trickling in to file the identical report, that there was a donkey in the prison. The atmosphere of the gathering was jovial and easy, almost that of a holiday (for it was a particularly wintry day and the event was doubtless more diverting than if the prisoners had not felt quite so confined by the snow and cold), when at once the door to the street swung open and the chief of administration for all prisons entered, and he naturally demanded to know why the entire population of the prison had gathered here before him, to which Jacob Moon in all sincerity answered that it was because an ass had come in off the street, which statement caused a long, hearty chorus of laughter from all, even from the chief of administration himself, once it had been given him to trust that no one had intended any slight to his dignity or reputation for excellence, not to say brilliance. I myself, as the wave of laughter commenced to wash over the group, had quickly looked over the sea of faces to that of my jailor, so as to determine how he would express himself, so that I could know how I wished to express myself, and I saw his somber face spread tightly into the grimace of a man who hears laughter but no joke, and immediately I formed my face similarly. Not, I hasten to add, before I had first studied the face of the chief of administration, to be positive that he had heard and accepted the joke good naturedly.

By so great a distance was I by then lost from my old forthright self, the man who once had defied the might of the justices of this land, who had let himself be set up as an example for his brethren, so that they would know how to resist the coming pressure against their faith, by so great a distance had I drifted from that man, that I now slinked invisibly through a crowd of laughing men before I myself dared merely to let even a grimace modelled after my jailor's grimace cross my face and thus allowed myself, disguised, to join them. I was like a jackal lurking at the edge of darkness, just beyond the circle of firelight, sneaking around that edge, always peering in but always taking cowardly care never to be seen itself.

Guilt is not so much the cause of such aberrant obsequious-ness and affectation as it is the result of a prior loss of unity. It is the rip in the fabric of the carefully, deliberately woven spirit of the man of faith that occurs when he misplaces or weakly gives up his faith. Where before there was a whole, a unity, there are suddenly two separated pieces, two distinct cells, and then where there were two, there are suddenly four, then eight, and so on, as the man stumbles through blocks of time, dividing and sub-dividing like an amoeba drifting through a pool of stagnant water. Obsequiousness and affectation, therefore, though they characterized all my different selves at this time, took slightly different forms with each presentation, so that, with my jailor, at least in the mornings and evenings, I was dry, dour, detached, and concerned with the kinds of events that concern engineers and administrators, but with each of the several other prisoners I associated myself with I was, in one case, as giddy and silly as an adolescent fop, even dressing up as a well known actress one morning and walking through the exercise yard presenting forged autographs to some of the simpler men, and in another case, with like-minded men, I was physically tough, stoical, dis-ciplined, and scornful of physical weakness or disability in oth-ers, and in yet another, philosophical, meditative, pursing my mind and time thoughtfully before problems in history, language and mathematics. I was not aware at the time of any particular hierarchy among these personalities, because I was not aware at the time of any hierarchy among the models, but before long I had found myself in a sufficient number of situations where two or more of these models were in dark competition for my slav-ish imitation, so that I could see I was responding indeed to an hierarchy among them. At the bottom were those prisoners who were the least threatening to me physically, the weak and infirm and the principled non-violent ones, and of course my wife and her cousin Gina, and just above that level were the prisoners whose physical violence seemed to be structured on certain principles of self-defense, which made their violence somewhat predictable, and above these figures were the guards, and then the assistant jailors, and at the pinnacle, the dour figure of the chief jailor, Jacob Moon. It was with yet an additional burden of shame, then, that I came to know how utterly devoted to life had I become that I would curry favor most from those who posed the greatest threat to my life and least from those who were the least threatening to my life. I knew then that I was a lost soul, of the type that can no longer save itself but instead must be saved, if at all, by virtue of some will other than its own, which is to say, by the power of grace. I would be saved now only if the dead themselves wished it.

And so it came about that there was given to me at this time a long dream one night late in the first winter of my imprisonment, in which there spoke to me both my father and his brother my uncle, the man who had taught me my skills as a coffin-maker and who, at my father's request, had constructed my own coffin, the very one I had passed on to the saintly John Bethel some seven or eight months before. If in life we are to be touched and directed by a will other than our own, it will most likely happen while we are asleep, for sleep is as like unto death as a footrace resembles flight. Thus, in miming death, I was drawn into a passive openness to the dead and the wisdom thereof and the enactment of their will, so that my father and his brother were able to come and speak to me and I was able to hear. The encounter took place in the kitchen of the house where I had been born and raised to the time when I left and went off to live with my uncle, there to learn from him how to make coffins. My father was as he had been during my earliest childhood, very large and looming, with a broad, almost sarcastic smile, and my uncle was as he had been when I had worked with him later, my own size, solemn, bearded, and infinitely patient. We three were seated at the kitchen table, my mother was somehow present in the room but remained silent and out of sight during the interview. My father towered over my uncle and me, though we were all three seated at table as if after a pleasant meal, with dishes and cups and various implements scattered before us. Here follows the sense and direction and much of the tone of the statements given me by these two men:

Father, in a sarcastic tone signifying disapproval: We hear lately that you have allowed your attention to wander. We suppose that this is a result of some wonderful understanding you have recently come by, an understanding which supercedes our own. Perhaps you believe your new perspective unique, and if not unique, then perhaps you think it valid and ours invalid. For we, after all, are but the dead, and you are the living.

Uncle: My brother wishes to advise you, he loves you, so do not be afraid or abashed before him, merely give him your attention.

Father, angrily: He has no choice but to give me his attention! He is asleep and dreaming, and thus we have taken it from him! That is how bad a pass things have come to!

(Is this what is meant by grace? I wondered.)

Uncle: Listen to the man, he is your father, you are without wisdom, he is dead. Do not be frightened or abashed, he forgives you, he understands, you do not, he is dead and you are among the living. Fear only the living.

Father, more calmly: Fear the living, indeed. And fear even more your loss of contact with the dead. Go, return to your coffin, find yourself a gate, a wicket, and pass through it to the ground of faith that makes life endurable because honorable, honorable because honoring the dead. The coffin is your gateway. There is no other possibility for your return to honor. Expect, without it, to disappear utterly, utterly! If you will not honor the dead while you are among the living, you will be without honor yourself when you are among the dead! This is your last chance for redemption. It is your only chance for redemption.

Uncle, soothingly but with urgency: Believe him, nephew, believe him. Do not resist any longer.

Whereupon the images spun and twirled about before me, and I came awake in my cell to the glistening light of dawn, and I felt freshened in my heart, and I determined that moment to set about that very day to obtain a coffin to replace the one I had given away. I felt joy in my heart for the first time in months, and I could barely keep myself from leaping about my cell.

My first thought was that I would request my wife to search out and deliver a coffin for me, but then I realized that I would end up incriminating her and possibly some others in the crime, for such it was now, a crime. Therefore, I determined to build my own coffin in my cell and to begin the construction that very day. And when I had eaten breakfast in the dining hall, I rushed out and ran down the stairs to the chief jailor's office to request the necessary materials and tools for the building of a coffin.

For the first time in many months, as I spoke to Jacob Moon, I did not consider the manner of my being perceived. I let myself show plenty of cheek and high spirit, just as I felt it, and boldly I asked him to make certain materials and tools available to me as soon as they could be requisitioned and delivered (it was not at all uncommon for the prisoners to request materials and tools not unlike these, for many of them were engaged in such diverse projects as building sailboats, carving furniture and making paneling for their cells, and other items). The list of materials: thirty-two linear feet 1″ by 12″ pine board; 1 pint cow-glue; 2 flat steel hinges & screws for same; 6 sheets misc. grades sandpaper; 3 lbs. cotton batting; 5 yards red velvet cloth, or approx. if not available; 1 box upholsterer's tacks; 1 quart clear varnish. The list of tools: claw hammer; plane; square; handsaw; wood chisel; screwdriver; sablehair paintbrush. I cannot now remember if I listed anything more, but I think this was all.

Jacob Moon, after he had read my list, directly asked me what I wished to do with these materials and tools, for his requisition form was required to show the proposed purpose for all such materials and tools as were requested by prisoners or anyone else. He pointed to a particular paragraph on the lengthy form, which did indeed assert that not to indicate thereon in detailed language the precise use to which any materials or tools requisitioned by the office of the chief jailor from the central supplier for all prisons, whether that use be specifically for the personal deployment of the prisoners or for prison maintenance or for the use, personal or otherwise, of the chief jailor, was to violate the law and to be subject to dismissal and possible prosecution by the office of the chief of prosecution. I saw, therefore, that Jacob was merely doing his job and that he had no personal desire or need to expose or confound me, and in fact, if I had been willing to tell him that I wished to have these materials and tools for the purposes of building a coffin, he would simply have filled out the requisition form appropriately and sent it on, even though he knew as well as did I myself that to request materials for the building of a coffin was to bring upon my head probable banishment from the land and possibly worse as soon as the form were received. In fact, I am sure that Jacob had not even the slightest curiosity or other interest in why I had suddenly asked for these materials and tools; he only wanted the form to be filled out as close to properly as possible.

Therefore I informed him that I did not wish to lie to him or otherwise deceive him, but I wanted to have these materials and tools for the purpose of building myself a coffin so as to pray and contemplate the dead, as I had been trained and given to do since childhood but the which in recent months had been denied me, with certain awful effects on my spirit and mind and, as I saw it, also on my destiny. I did not, however, believe that he, meaning my jailor, ought to declare on his requisition form that my purposes were as I had just described to him, for if he did so, it would doubtless go ill for him as well as for me. The offices of the chief of prosecution would think him joking, and they are not known for their enjoyment of jokes when it comes to such somber matters as the laws against worshipping the dead, and thus they would prosecute him for inappropriate levity, a mild form of heresy, to be sure, but one punishable by law none the less.

When my jailor had come fully to understand my analysis of the situation before him, he informed me that, therefore, he had only one recourse, which was to deny me my request for a requisition, and to warn me that he was by law compelled to restrict and forbid all evidences of worship of the dead, which meant that no coffins were allowed inside the prison, except as required by regulations of the sanitation and medical services administration for the transportation out of the prison of the corpse of any prisoner said to have died by infectious disease. John Bethel, his predecessor, by his example of leniency in these matters, had set a bad example, said Jacob Moon, but in his later trial and punishment, had set a good example. His fate will always stand before the jailors who follow, Jacob told me, as a clear warning of the consequence of leniency in matters concerning the laws against the worship of the dead. For that reason, I will not permit you to build a coffin or to have one brought in here for you by one of your secret brethren or your wife or Gina, and I will not let you use anything as a substitute for a proper coffin, such things as packing crates, wardrobe closets and other such enclosures as you people in your extremities of fervour have been known to employ, unless, of course, you are said to have died of an infectious disease.

There was no more to be said about it. Therefore I returned to my cell, disappointed, certainly, but full of a strength and clarity that I had not enjoyed for months, for now I was properly engaged with the task properly before me, the which I had previously refused to heed, the task of attending to the dead. I was back at the old business of setting up the proper rites, sacraments and artifacts, and the effects on my spirit were immediately felt by me and manifested to everyone, so that no longer was there any demeaning confusion over how I should relate my divided self to the distinct, contrasting realities around me, for no longer was there any contrast between them, or them and me. I had joined them.

WHAT NOW FOLLOWS is a description of how a great many of the imprisoned, both at my prison and at others across the land, who had no coffin came to have a coffin, and also what further was created thereby. It is, in addition, a description which must be taken as a type, revealing a type of worldly process, in the same sense that sacred scriptures are well known to reveal through types the more general events and processes.

It sometimes is forced to come out that the solution to a simple problem cannot but be complex. My problem was surely simple, that of a need to obtain a coffin, so as thereby to have followed the instructions and heeded the warnings of my beloved ancestors, instructions and warnings which, once heard, must be followed hard upon with dedicated acts of obedience. Mere suggestions and hints from the dead must be taken as absolute commands. In spiritual matters such as this, disobedience implies nothing more or less than a lack of understanding. And equally it is assumed that whoever properly understands the commands of the dead will be incapable of disobeying them. This is a necessary closure and must be accepted as such, if what is to follow will not be meaningless.

As said, my problem was a simple one. And though at first I had thought the solution would also be simple, it was not to be so. After considerable pondering upon my problem, it came to me that because Jacob Moon had been compelled to prohibit me from building my own coffin, I was now required to have one brought in to me ready-made. To be sure, he was compelled by law to prohibit me as well from importing any coffin or from utilizing any substitute as I might find among my incidental furnishings, but by disobeying him in these matters I would not, as in the former proposed solution, implicate an innocent man in my crime. I was therefore free to ignore his latter pair of prohibitions, and this thought filled me with jubilation, and I grew impatient for my wife and her cousin to arrive so that I could unfold these thoughts to them.

Upon their arrival at my cell, and after I had explained to them that henceforward I would not compel them to participate with me or with the jailor Jake (as they had come to call him) in the foul acts of sensual gratification, those spirit-soiling celebrations of life to which we had become habituated, I related to the two women the nature of my dream and the warnings and instructions I had received from my father and uncle. They both seemed greatly relieved and pleased with my obvious recovery from the disease of sensuality that had debilitated our wills for so long, and even Jacob Moon, when I had opened my experience of the dream to him, and my consequent resolution, seemed somewhat relieved and in a clear way impatient to get back downstairs to his office where, as I knew, he had a massy pile of paperwork awaiting his attention and signature. My wife's cousin, Gina, indicated that she was already late for a prior appointment in the city, and afterwards, when she had taken her leave, I related to my wife my most recent conclusion, that I was compelled by circumstance and the law to order and have shipped to me a ready-made coffin from some coffin-maker among our brethren outside.

As she is an extremely intelligent woman, she quickly pointed out to me that I would not be free to have a coffin shipped if anyone were able by examining it to determine that it was indeed a coffin, for to manufacture and distribute such items, as I more than any man must know, was a crime. In my excitement at the prospect, I had forgotten this obstacle. After a moment of dismay, however, I started up again with pleasure, for my wife suggested to me that I could surely receive a wooden cabinet or trunk, if one could be made and shipped to me, and especially if it were properly fitted out as a cabinet or trunk, so that any postal authority or prison examiner looking for contraband would, on inspecting it, conclude that the object was nothing more harmful to the common weal than a cabinet or trunk. She imaged such an object for me, pointing out that it could be made according to my specifications for a coffin, with the skin of it hinged and set with brass handles and with short legs attached to the base so as to resemble what is commonly called a hope chest and often used by young women for storing up their dowry of linens and clothing against the day when they marry (for that reason are they called hope chests). She further pointed out that it would be necessary to fill the chest with numerous items of cloth, linens, blankets and garments, &c., or the inspectors and surely my wiley jailor would discover the deceit, for they would know that I, as an impoverished prisoner, could not own sufficient items so as to require such a large chest for their storage.

This last observation by my wife, however, filled me with despair again, for I saw that no one would believe that I, of all prisoners, was the legitimate recipient of such a lavish gift as a large wooden chest filled with expensive items of cloth. My poverty was well known, for my calling had been publicly forbidden to me, and it was also well known that my wife and five children had been forced as a consequence to throw themselves upon the kindness of strangers and the few among the brethren who dared to be seen aiding them. How could a man, people would ask themselves, who cannot afford to feed and clothe and house his own wife and children, suddenly provide himself with a large handmade wooden chest stuffed with blankets, coats, hand towels and warm undergarments?

My dear wife saw my despair and with reluctance conceded that the ruse would not be taken, though at first she had seemed to view the expense of such a gift as not especially dear or difficult to finance, even. By so much was she conscious of my need that she had difficulty making herself aware of the practical considerations. But I had swiftly itemized for her clarification the costs of such a chest and its necessary contents, as I knew any inspector would be able to do immediately upon opening it and examining it for contraband, an itemization, in fact, he would be required by law to make, so as to fix the shipping and delivery charges, and then she realized how incriminating (of me, my presumed poverty) it would be. It would be as if a starving mouse were suddenly revealed to own a cupboard full of cheese, she lightly said to me, in a characteristically generous attempt to dispel my gloom with humor.

It here came to me that the gift of the hope chest would have to be made by someone of means, if it were to be a believable gift, and such a person would have to be a philanthropist who had determined to aid and comfort those who, among society's less fortunate creatures, had been designated by society as its prisoners. Now since there was no way to regard me as worthy of being singled out by such a benefactor, for there were many who were as needy as I and some even more so, then the gift of a hope chest would have to be made to many prisoners equally and at once, enough of them so that I would not seem to have been specially chosen for the gift. The only number of prisoners that seemed appropriate, however, was three hundred eighty-seven, which was the number of prisoners, including me, then inhabiting my particular prison. I very quickly calculated what this would mean, in terms of materials alone, so as to estimate the approximate cost of such a huge undertaking as the manufacture of three hundred eighty-seven hope chests, and to my disappointment, I determined that the project would require over a half-ton of cotton batting (one thousand one hundred sixty-one pounds, to be exact), and also one thousand nine hundred thirty-five yards of red velvet cloth, and over two and one-third linear miles of twelve by one inch pine board.

At my recital of these quantities, my wife gave a high laugh and turned away from me, as if to hide tears of discouragement, for I knew that she could not imagine any benefactor wealthy enough to be willing to pay for such an undertaking. And we both knew that we could not request the gift of these hope chests and their contents from my impoverished brethren, my fellow coffin-makers who were now so scattered in the land as to be hopelessly out of contact with one another and quite incapable of a cooperative endeavor of these proportions, even had we been able to pay for the materials ourselves.

I then resolved that the cost of the hope chests and the contents therein might be borne by those wealthy citizens who seemed frequently to be willing, when properly approached, to finance the causes of the underprivileged among them, a surprisingly large group of ladies and gentlemen who, when they believe that most of the fashionable others in their class are supporting a particular cause, will themselves support that cause without question or stint. What was needed were a group of money collectors, a person able to arrange the appropriate publicity, an accountant or two to attend to the financial details and to keep scrupulous track of all funds, also an attorney, secretaries, an office of some sort, an executive director, and a board of directors. And we would need these people and facilities in the reverse order of their naming, for, once we had invited several prominent philanthropists to serve on our board of directors, which invitation, by the flattery of being singled out, they would eagerly accept, we would then be able to hire an executive director at a salary consistent with his or her responsibilities, and once we had hired an executive director, we would be able to hire the necessary secretarial help to take care of the paperwork that would commence to arrive once the newly hired attorney had filed for the incorporation charter and with it the plea for exemption from taxation, which would not be granted by the tax authority, of course, until we had procured the services of several accountants and clerks so as to keep our records in a satisfactory way, at which point we would be ready to hire the publicist, and as soon as he or she had begun his or her work, we would hire a battalion of collectors to begin calling on the numerous individuals who wished to support our particular cause.

My wife now grew exceedingly excited, and she showed me that the most important link in this chain was the post of executive director, for that person would be required not only to arrange and bear the responsibility for all the contributions coming in, but also for all the expenditures, the half-ton of cotton batting, the two and one-third miles of pine board, the thousands of yards of red velvet cloth, and the purchase of the blankets, linens, clothing, &c., and also that person would bear the responsibility of letting out the contracts to the numerous cabinet makers and woodworkers for the manufacture of our three hundred eighty-seven hope chests, a tedious task and one that could only be performed by someone close to me, so that it could be guaranteed that my specifications for the hope chest would be followed exactly.

Who could such a person be? we asked ourselves. My wife did not think that she would be incapable of the job, but I disagreed, for it did seem to me that, because of her longtime association with me and my heresy, it might be thought by the philanthropists, if she were the titular head of the organization, that they were coming out in support of my particular crime of heresy. No, I told her, they would not wish to have their endorsement of the cause of benevolence towards prisoners in general be construed as supporting any crime or prisoner in particular. And besides, I said to her, you are frail and weakly, and the demands of such a position would be beyond your capacities. She protested nobly, but I was eventually able to convince her of the foolhardiness of her desire to place herself in that position, however well-intended that desire. Next we considered her cousin Gina for the post, but again, I argued persuasively that Gina's association with the crime for which I had been imprisoned was almost as close as my wife's, especially since she had been coming to visit only me and no other prisoner for these last several months. We also considered several among the brethren who had not been imprisoned or who were not in any way known for their past or present practice of the various rites associated with our faith, but these too we had to dismiss, for the obvious reason that to organize and operate a philanthropic organization such as we were proposing would be to rip into shreds the careful fabric of invisibility that the brethren had woven in the last year. And naturally there was no imaginable way for me myself, condemned and immobilized as I then was, to direct the soliciting of funds and the expenditure thereof. And so, by gradual degrees, I began again to slip into despondency.

But I was not to remain despondent, for it shortly occurred to my wife to suggest to me the name of Jacob Moon, and immediately the gloom lifted and all was clear and bright again. For Jacob Moon was the perfect man for the job, and he would think so quite as much as we, I assured my wife. The responsibilities and tasks such a post would place before him would not leave him gaping in awe or trembling with unsureness. Jacob Moon was a man of the world, and though in a certain way, because he was so much a man of the world, I pitied him, still and all, it gave him a definite facility for working efficiently and effectively in the world. He was a living demonstration of the only aspect of being a man of time that could in any way be rationalized as a benefit of that condition, for while it is not true that every man who is able to function efficiently and effectively in the world is, ipso facto, not a man of the eternal dead, it never the less is true that every man of time, if he does not agonize over his condition and fight against it, will turn out eventually to be one of our nation's fine administrators, technicians or government functionaries. These people, because they cannot trust to luck or fate or to any of the various forces that transcend their own mortal lives, are forced thereby early in life to cultivate and refine to an amazing degree their skills and the quality of their attention to the ways of the world, with the result that they often become the men and women who are great in the eyes of the world. Only the dead, and those who worship the dead, do not envy them. The scripture says, Envy not the living. Cast not your eyes with longing upon their heaped up wealth and worldly honors, for they are but the wages of inattention to the dead, the fruits of a season lived as if it were endless. (*I Trib.*, ix, 9.) And (*I Trib.*, xxii, 30): Look unto the heavens, and let your feet fall where they may. Whether the road be smooth or rocky matters not to them, nor should it matter to you.

Thus there got created, one afternoon during the first winter of my confinement, the organization that later became known as the Society Of Prisoners, which now employs thousands of collectors, clerks, attorneys, secretaries, assistant directors and directors, the organization responsible for the physical aid and comfort of millions of our citizens (not just the prisoners, who will soon receive their hope chests, but also the manufacturers of hope chests and the hundreds of purveyors of blankets, linens, and clothing, &c.). It is the organization that has come to own and manage large blocks of real estate and public bonds and which has recently funded chairs in the field of prison administration at several of the most prestigious universities in the land. And presiding over all this vast enterprise is the remarkable man, Mister Jacob Moon, who once was my jailor and, in a sense, my brother. My wife's cousin Gina is also an executive in the Society Of Prisoners, for her special skills were required by Jacob Moon hard upon its founding, and even my wife for a brief period was employed by SOP (as the journalists came to call it), albeit in a relatively menial position. Though her later illness and death, which, along with the spiritual clarities it provided her and our children and provided me as well, I will soon describe, prevented her from remaining at Jacob Moon's and her cousin's sides for long, even so, her salary and later her disability pension were more than adequate for the support of her and our children during the period of their greatest need. So while I do not envy Jacob Moon or any of those men and women whose association with the Society Of Prisoners has brought them wealth and worldly power, nevertheless, because it is not expressly forbidden by the dead, I am grateful to them. And, of course and most importantly, I am grateful to them for their enormous effort to make my coffin available to me at the time of my greatest need. Gratitude is a polite form of inattention, we are taught. It corrupteth not.

I WAS NOT, however, to come to possess my own coffin for a certain lengthy period of time, which delay came as a result of the numerous obstacles to be surmounted before the Society of Prisoners could first be set up to function properly, many of which obstacles had been anticipated by my wife and me in the conversation recorded above, but a small number there remained that we had not anticipated and that were due to shortages and other market fluctuations in the nation during those years, and thus encouraged great delay in the delivery of the actual hope chests to the prisoners. During this period of waiting, I languished in many ways as a man of time, though not so much as before, when I had not yet been visited upon in my dream of my father and my uncle and was slinking hopelessly through my days in wickedness and obsequiousness and affectation. For while it had not been difficult for me to change my behavior, such of it as could be observed by another, the difficulty came when I needed to make changes such as no one but I and the dead could see. And the behavior in particular that I came to have to labor over, in order to change myself from being a man of time to a man of the dead, was the desire that springs from memory.

This desire, sometimes called nostalgia, as such is by many overlooked and is by them regarded as of little significance morally or legally. Also, there are people who even go so far as to cultivate the appetite, to encourage the growth of those desires that have set their tap root in the soil of the remembered past. The man who worships the timeless dead, however, cannot be one of these people. He cannot condone the desire called nostalgia, and he cannot regard it as of little significance, for its presence is a sign of his fallen state. Nor can he under any circumstances actually cultivate that kind of attention. But be warned: the desire that springs from memory can trap all but the most wary of believers, and whosoever finds himself trapped, he is no longer a believer. (*The Book of Discipline,* ii, 23.)

Nostalgia comes upon a man's spirit in as many forms as the weather, blithely as a summer breeze that opens his mind to an afternoon one summer long ago when he felt at deep peace with himself, or stormily, as when a sudden violent awareness of the meaning of death sweeps over him and his mind gets crudely yanked back to another moment in time some years ago when he experienced a similarly violent awareness of the meaning of death. Or it can come like the fog, in silence and almost without his knowing, for then it will not come forthrightly as a form of memory but as something else, as a pure and particularized desire, a direct and focused appetite.

Few of us cannot recognize nostalgia in its blithe form, as simply itself, easy to dismiss as being of little consequence morally or legally. It appears innocent, to be sure, but it is not, so it is providential that what is easy to dismiss is also easy to identify, and for this reason it is only the common mind that gets tripped and trapped here. More difficult to recognize as nostalgia might be the more stormy of the two forms, but to encourage it, one must first determine whether the memory is of a pleasant sort or not, and the pause such a decision requires often exposes the trap. But many even among the most wary do not recognize nostalgia when it comes in like the fog, auguring a clear day but in fact leading in a month of rain. That is desire disguised as pure desire and not itself, which is the desire that springs from memory and which characterizes the man of time. There came a time in my imprisonment when I myself was so entrapped, when I mistook one desire for another and thus was unable to break free of time. Here is how it happened to me.

It began when I grew weary of the stale and flat food that was served up to the prisoners who had not the means to purchase their own victuals from caterers outside the prison. This daily fare of porridge and hard bread in the morning, potato soup at midday, and chickenbacks and rice in the evening, served up relentlessly without variety in the menu, soon caused me to gripe among the other prisoners, for it was a favorite topic of conversation with them, and since I wished to engage in cheerful and sociable talk with them, I was drawn to talk in a similarly complaining manner about the food. I had not noticed that the food was especially worthy of complaint until I had begun to complain of it, when, as if to confirm the reality that my words seemed to describe, I began to peer skeptically into the porridge pot in the morning and groan aloud or to smell the potato soup being prepared and shake my head and mutter bitterly, or in the evening to look to the ceiling with dismay when the attendant shoved my plate of rice and chickenback across the counter to me.

So it was that my complaint about the food, though it had commenced as a social activity, soon had validated itself against the physical surround, and thus strengthened, had taken on an obsessive and energetic quality that was matched by the complaints of only the most disgruntled and epicurean among my fellow prisoners. I was not at this time aware of my having joined these fellows in their distraction, of course, but even if I had been, I do not think I would have resisted, for a process had been set in motion that would not be ended until I had been able to turn my attention back once more to the proper contemplation of the eternal dead, who never hunger after variety or epicurean delight. The reason for this persistence of mine in complaining about the food, I then believed, was my desire, pure and simple, for varied and delightful food, and often at night while I lay in my cot and listened to the coughing, wheezing, murmuring sounds of my fellow prisoners in the darkness, I would image to myself a breakfast of fresh chilled melon, followed by a platter of shad roe and poached eggs, with hot crusty cloverleaf rolls and a pot of pure mountain-grown coffee, or a lunch of delicately flavored conch soup, fresh broiled trout and chilled white wine, with a key lime pie for dessert, or an evening meal that began with cold split pea soup with mint, cabbage in white wine, wild rice with mushrooms, a deep green spinach salad with vinegar and oil and subtle herbs, and a crown roast of pork with sausage-apple stuffing, and a cold orange souffle as a dessert. My mouth would fill with water at these images as they paraded past, one exquisitely arranged meal after another, glistening and aromatic, but soon I would topple from this pinnacle of wavering, transparent and transitory delight and would fall into a contracting pit that began with dissatisfaction, passed through resentment, and ended with gloom.

Night followed night, and so too did my longings continue unabated, evoking each night a fresh cycle of foods that I could not have, leaving me, as a result, gnashing and groveling at the bottom of my pit in frustration and gloom. Sometimes I imaged to myself only light and delicate, pastel-hued meals, fresh fruits and vegetables and thinly sliced meats, and the next night would come a menu of heavy, succulent, roughly flavored foods, to be followed the next night by a variety of casseroles and sauces, and so on, with all the accompanying greens, appetizers, desserts, breads and pastries, with all the appropriate wines, and lingering after-dinner platters of cheeses and chilled fruit and clarifying liqueurs. My desire seemed to me endless, bottomless, infinite. But so too seemed my frustration, and thus there came those moments at the gray beginnings of dawn when, questioning the legitimacy of my desire, I dragged it out before me and tried to upbraid it for causing me such sleepless frustration and gloom, and I would find myself unexpectedly defending my desire, arguing that it was endless, bottomless, eternal, asserting that thus my attachment to it was but an expression of a growing freedom from time.

This was a cruel rationalization that was but a subtle means of sustaining my desire, of feeding it like some kind of parasite that had attached itself to the interior wall of my gut. But I did not understand this at the time, because I was weak and out of contact with the voices of the dead, for I had not my coffin at this time. My dreams were silent, and I had no voice but my own to advise me, and whatever construction I could put upon the scriptures that yet rang in my head, and while my own voice told me in consoling terms that my desire was a natural one for a man who had been cast away in prison, the scriptures, or so did I construe them, told me that the appetite that cannot be sated, the longing that knows no end, the desire that feeds only on itself, these are but a few of the many paths out of time. Anywhere, so long as it is out of this world! cries the prophet Walter (vi, 12). So I reminded myself, and thus, at the bottom of my pit of longing, would I raise up my head and listen, and soon a consoling peace would come over me, and I would sleep.

For several months did this circle turn in me, of complaint followed by longings which evoked glittering images followed in turn by gloom which I nightly escaped by rationalization and misconstrued scripture. It was in the early spring, when I had been imprisoned for almost a full year, which at that time seemed a great long while to me, that several unexpected events occurred. Most men and women who are not of our faith would not regard them as events, but that is of no importance here. For events are what they were, and what follows is how I understood them then. Though I will reveal shortly how I eventually came to understand them, through the guidance of the dead, for now, so that my trials and tribulation can be better grasped by the reader, let me withhold my later comprehension until I come to describe its fortunate arrival.

The first event was simply that I noticed one night while I lay in my cot and conjured images of loaded boards of steaming food, before I had come to the part in my nightly sequence when I began the quick slide into despair, I realized that the feast set before me was one I had already imagined, was a meal I had conjured several months earlier. This came upon me first as a surprise, for I had thought the menu could be infinitely varied, and then as a disappointment, for immediately the image of the meal seemed less succulent, less attractive, less necessary than before, and my mouth did not fill with water quite as before. I did not understand this diminishment of my desire, and somewhat fuddled, I tried again, and I sent the broiled trout back to the kitchen, as it were, as if the waiter had made a terrible mistake, and ordered again, this time a crispy roast pig stuffed with apples and sausage. But this meal too was familiar to me, for it too had I earlier brought forth from my imagination (for there did I then believe these images to emanate from). Again I returned the meal to the kitchen and called for another, barbecued swordfish, but this too, when it appeared steaming in its juices before me, I saw I had already ordered once, and thus it went sailing back to the chef, who by now must have been close to despair himself. On it went, one after another, until I began to grow shrill and wild, ordering rapidly and without care.

Suddenly, as if to quiet me for a moment while the poor harried chef struggled to assemble his masterpiece, there was set before me a glass and a dark bottle of twenty year old port wine. I poured a glassful, raised it and with my eyes praised the regal hue of the wine, sniffed it with pleasure, and let it into my mouth. This was the second event. For it was as if the wine had replaced the banquet of before, and instantly my earlier endless desire for delicious and various foods had been replaced by a new endless desire, this one for fine wines, hearty whiskeys, froth-topped ales and sharp tangy liqueurs and brandies that heat the chest. In my mind I drank off the bottle of port wine, and as soon as it was emptied, I tumbled as before into my pit of despondency, where I nursed myself with consoling rationalizations concerning the spiritual quality of my desire and with scripture appropriated and translated for my own greedy use.

The next night I requested a brilliant beaujolais, and then the following night a chablis from an obscure but old and honorable vineyard, and then, one night after another, one excellent old wine after another, until it occurred to me that a peaty ten year old whiskey from the north would be pleasant, and then a bottle of cognac, a coffee brandy from the tropics, a rice wine from the orient, a powerful honey liqueur, a pale and breathtaking rum, and on and on, long careful solitary nights at table as I raised glass after glass to the light, admired the color and texture, brought the glass to my lips, and while it still quivered there, suddenly plummeted into the pit of frustration, resentment, gloom, there to anesthetize my pain with specious argument and misapplied scripture.

So it was that I did also complain as before among my fellow prisoners when at leisure or at table, except that now I whined about the prohibitions against alcoholic beverages and other intoxicants, and that now the prisoners among whom I gathered to complain were the swollen-bellied addicts of alcohol, the slaves to gin, the nervous red-nosed lovers of whiskey and rum, the bleary-eyed connoisseurs of wine. No longer were my consorts the epicureans with their jowls and gout, the feasters and thick-lipped lovers of dripping chunks of flesh and all the fastidious gourmets of my small society. To exchange one group of complainers for another, however, was merely to rattle the chain that bound me, though I did not realize that then. I believed instead that I had moved from a dull group of misanthropic associates to a group more responsive and sensitive to my spiritual quest. Such was the extent of my delusion, the degree of my depravity. And so it was that by night I conjured images that eased my hungers and slaked my thirst without releasing me from either, while by day I sourly studied and discussed prohibitions and limits without attempting to transcend or overleap them.

I do not know how long, as my condition, this would have gone on, or if in the end I would have profaned myself utterly and turned irreconcilably away from the dead, had I not one night exhausted the inventory of wines, whiskeys, brandies, liqueurs and ales that were available to me and had I not, while wildly sending back each new bottle as it appeared to me, suddenly been distracted by the image of money. Be not astonished by this, for someday you too may find yourself in a similar trap, and then may you recall that after the desire for food comes the desire for drink, and after the desire for drink comes the desire for money, cash, coins, currencies of all nations, bullion, personal checks, bank checks, refunds, all forms of money, one after the other, in bound stacks, in high trembling columns, in glimmering solid bricks, in all the forms that you have ever seen. Oh, what chests of money I had hauled out, what safe deposit boxes, what caches and stashes I rifled and gloated over during those long summer nights! What great good fortune suddenly would shower me with riches, coins of all realms falling through my fingers, bills stuffed into all my pockets, my wallet bulging like a thick mackerel in my hand, while I lay there in my cot in the darkness of my cell, counting on into the night, tens, hundreds, thousands, millions of dollars and cents, pounds, pesos, francs, marks, pesetas, reals, ruples, yen, lira, and on and on, as if the numbers were able to run endlessly on all the way to infinity.

Precisely as I had before, I moved to a new link in the chain that bound me, turning my backside to my former friends, the lovers of drink, so that I could complain alongside those who were poor, those who resented the wealth of certain individuals among us or the wealth of the jailor and his assistants, who, by bribery and other emoluments, had managed to supplement their salaries quite handsomely, and even resented the wealth of the citizens who remained outside the prison and whom we never saw but still remembered. Thus, as before, my days were spent with all my attention directed bitterly to the limits that bound me, and my nights were spent in vain fantasies that those limits did not exist, with the inevitable collapse against the unavoidable knowledge that they did truly exist, and the last self-solacing whimpers at dawn that this terrible cycle somehow expanded my spirit.

Oh, foolish, deluded, self-profaning man of time! What will save you from yourself? What will turn you away from this pathetic ferreting about? Must you count all the money in the world, all the dollars and all the cents, all the bills and coins ever issued by all the treasuries in the histories of nations, before you can see the truth? Must you exhaust all the finite inventories in the universe, and still go on longing, before you realize what it is that you long for? Do you not know that while you are counting, still counting, long before you have neared the end even of this finite set, death will come and take you, and everything will have been for nought, for zero, as if you had never counted the monad that all along stared you in the face?

These are the questions that came to me, then, one slow word at a time, until it appeared to me that the chain I was forging was itself endless and that it could go on longer than I could. For while it is the chain of delusion itself that is infinite, my own delusion was that each finite link was infinite. Had I possessed my coffin during those months of my vain desires, I surely would have seen that each set of desires was a finite set, for I would have seen, as I see now, that each set depended on my personal memories of food and drink and monies in order for me to image any particular member of that set. And when I had seen, by virtue of the grace sacrament provides, that I had been all along experiencing nothing more than the desire that springs from memory, no twisting of scripture would have worked for me to excuse myself. Thus armed, I would have steeled myself against the desire by denigrating the memory and then by turning all my attention to the further contemplation of the dead, who have no memory.

But without my coffin, without access thereby to the sacrament that could have provided grace with ease, I was forced to lengthen the cycle, to add link to link, until at last, no matter how I squirmed and wriggled, I could not deny the evidence that all the links would be the same and endlessly, and that all I was about during these complaining days and dreaming nights was the business of binding myself into time. It was a discovery made possible by intellect, rather than by rite, but it was no less gratuitous for that and thus no less an aspect of the grace that flows from the dead. I fell on my knees, as I do now, and I thanked the unruffled, objective, endlessly uninvolved dead for the freedom to think clearly and thereby to free myself from the bondage of the finite, the chain of life, the links of the desire that springs from memory.

This episode in my spiritual growth marked the end of my weakness for nostalgia. By cleansing myself of my desires for varieties of food, for varieties of drink, and for endless numbers of money, I cleansed myself of the taint of nostalgia. And thus was my growth allowed to continue, where before it had been impeded and had even been thrown backwards so to create a diminishment. It was a painful period in my life, and often a bewildering one, but all that was to make my ultimate freedom from it the more victorious and exemplary.

FOR REASONS AT first unknown to me, when I was falling regularly into disputes with those prisoners who previously had joined me daily in my complainings, I felt compelled to blame myself. Later I saw that my reasons were natural if not well-founded, for as much as I had made myself come forward after months, even up to a year or possibly more, of complaining and then dreaming and then making specious argument, by that same distance as I had come forward was I regarded by my old associates with mistrust. Now, this is in the nature of things, that when a companion comes forward and leaves you behind, you will bridle at him when he speaks to you and attempts to bring you forward also to stand beside him. You will try to argue that he has fallen away, and he will argue that he has come forward, and so the two of you will fall into dispute.

It was not wholly a legitimate thing for me to do, then, when I proceeded so quickly to blame myself for the disputes, but after all, I was the one who had moved out of step, and I could not think of my movement except as a forward one, and so naturally I could not help but attempt to convince my fellow prisoners to follow me to that place, which place I knew was no more than a quickstep nearer to death. Yet all the same, I knew that if I had not tried so diligently to bring my fellow prisoners to a deeper understanding of the worship of the dead, there would not have been those painful, sometimes frightening disputes and arguments and the numerous sudden flights of irritation. My companions did not want me to leave them, whether by means of a step forward or of a falling away, but once I had done so, they did not want me to try to take them with me.

Yet I had no choice in the matter. It was my calling to make coffins to aid in the further worship of the dead, and in the absence of conditions which would make that activity possible, in order still to practice my calling I was obliged to draw others unto the dead in whatever ways there were available to me, and in this case, at this time, the only means available to me was argument. And so, whenever possible, I met my fellow prisoners with argument and deep reasoning, with intent talk and formal challenge and with careful discussion, bringing my own most complicated and subtle thoughts to bear on the question of the proper place for a human being's attention, and in the process drawing forth from my fellows their most complicated and subtle thoughts on the question. Thus, if I could not make my fellows a coffin, I would make them some deep and thrilling argument instead. If I could not work for the dead in one way, I would do it in another.

The first of my previous companions to grow weary of my company and to show it to me were those who in the previous winter had got me to dress myself up as a famous actress and go about in the exercise yard where there were many of the simpler prisoners and offer them my autograph, which they excitedly accepted and soon were squabbling over amongst themselves, to the lasting amusement of my companions and also to me at that time, although later it seemed to me a pointless and even slightly cruel thing to do, and I was ashamed of myself for having done it. But after I had gone through my long winter and spring of complaining and griping and fantasizing and rationalizing, and eventually had come to know myself in this matter, then I could no longer join these fellows in their play and their jokes on the other prisoners. I was forced to refuse them on several occasions, first when they came to me and invited me to join them in their attempt to trick up some of the exercise equipment in the gymnasium so that the bigger, athletic men would be likely to fall and hurt themselves when they began to exercise, and then a few weeks later when they wanted me to help them decorate the dining hall for a Mayday masquerade party. I thought both activities wrong headed, the first because it would cause unnecessary anger and possible injury and the second because the celebration of the first day of the month of May was a deliberate carry over from the days when it had not yet been thought of to worship the dead and men and women went around year after year making holidays out of seasonal and celestial cycles and changes which they foolishly associated with the patterns and needs of their own mortal lives. The amnesty associated with the solstice and applied every year to the short-term prisoners and the tried and convicted political and religious offenders willing to sue out a pardon, as they called it, was a celebration of this type. Possibly this amnesty was one of the reasons why Mayday, too, was regarded as such a significant holiday in the prison. I could not say for sure, but when I offered my reasons, as described above, for not wishing to participate in the preparations for the masquerade party associated with the holiday, I was told by one of the celebrants that soon the amnesty would be made, and then all the prisoners in his group, and here he waved his hand in a circle to indicate to me his many friends, would be gone out of prison and would be lost to one another forever. Some of them even had wives, he said to me, as if this were a sad thing, and many of them would be obliged to go back and make their residences far from one another all across the nation. Thus, he said, Mayday was an important holiday for them.

I could feel a certain sympathy for them. It was true that most of this particular group of prisoners would indeed be affected by the workings of the amnesty at the solstice, for most of them, as it turned out, had been confined for political reasons, in so far as the manner of their affection for men and their preference for the company of a man to the company of a woman were to be understood as crimes against the state. For indeed, when the continued good health of the state is economically dependent upon the family and upon sexual unions therein between a man and a woman, to withhold oneself from participating with eagerness in such a union is to undermine the very foundations of the state. Though I myself was not guilty of this particular crime, I was, however, guilty of a crime similarly identified, and for that reason I felt a special kinship with these surprisingly good-natured fellows. I say surprisingly because I knew how much they had suffered for their predilections and derelictions, and it would have been a reasonable thing for them to have been far more bitter and belligerent towards those of us who were not of their particular persuasion as regards the family or as regards copulation with women. (Many of them, in confidence, did tell me that they often had copulated with women and in fact were very fond of the company of women, even more than was I myself. I found this hard to understand. Actually, I found it hard to believe, and that is what I found hard to understand, for why should I not believe what I am told by a man I do not hold to be a liar?)

They made no particular protest to my refusal to join them in their tricking out the exercise machines, even when I volunteered my reasons for not wishing to join them, which were, as I said, because I feared it would cause unnecessary anger and possible injury. I added that the taking of one's pleasure from any increase in the quantity of anger in this already steaming world was inattentive to the teachings of the dead, and here I showed them from *The Book of Tribulations* (xi, 13) that the man who cultivates anger cultivates a desert. But they heard me not, and heard not the words of the dead, and instead went laughing away from me and set about to arrange the exercise machines so that several of the machines did indeed break with malicious force as soon as they were used, and as I had predicted, this caused a significant amount of anger, which did not seem to dismay my friends in the least, and also caused one rather cruel injury to the groin of one of the men caught in a tricked-out machine, which injury did not sadden any of my friends, at least in no way that I could determine.

When a few weeks later they came back to me and tried to convince me to join them in making their decorations of the dining hall for the purposes of the masquerade party associated with Mayday, they were more persistent than before, the which persistence I credited to the fact that as a coffin-maker I was known to be a clever man with tools and certain of their plans were sufficiently elaborate that they required the aid of people who were clever with tools. So when I refused them and gave them my reasons, which I have already described and will not say over again here, they were irritated with me and fell into arguing heatedly with me, some of them, while others tried cajoling me, while yet others promised rewards and certain unnameable services in return for my help. But I resisted them all. To their arguments I responded with counterarguments, which I fortified and validated with scripture, so that before long it was clear to everyone that all they had to present on their side was merely the argument of justification by sentiment, whereas mine was the argument of justification by metaphysic, and when I had pointed this out and had reminded them of the hierarchy among forms of argument, they were silenced, though I fear they were not convinced. To those who tried cajoling me with their high spirits and jokes and the promise of hearty fellowship, urging me to go along with the group because not to do so would leave me in a solitary way, I responded that without the dead I am forever in a solitary way and with the dead I am never alone. This also was successful in silencing them, and their cajoling ceased directly, and they too went off from me, leaving only those few who were making promises of unnameable services to me in return for my helping with the decorations, which help involved the construction of a garlanded and festooned temple in the middle of the dining hall, along with some machinery and stages for certain proposed theatrical and musical productions. To these last among my former companions, I said that I had turned my attention away from the living and toward the dead and that I was therefore striving mightily not to be a man of time any longer, which meant that such sensual pleasures as they promised were meaningless to me at best and corrupting to me at worst. Therefore, said I, to offer me a meaningless pleasure is to offer me no pleasure at all. It is to offer only confusion, guilt and fretfulness, for which I would not be able to thank you, for which, in fact, I would virtually resent you. No, said I, the service shall be mine, and that service is to refuse you, so that I will not resent you. But this did not please them as I had hoped it would, and with several blatant shows of their disgust and incomprehension, they departed from me.

Another group of men with whom I fell frequently into dispute were the athletic men, most of whom were committed to violence, I admit, but who only opened themselves to its use in a principled way, in comparison with the several madmen and the dozen or so youths who saw violence more or less as a symbol for something else (rather than the more usual opposite way of regarding it). These the madmen and the flightly youths with knives and other honed bits of metal that they secreted in divers parts of their bodies and clothing, these were a type I did not dare dispute with. I confess it now, even though I know that had I then my own coffin to which I could have resorted for strength and wisdom every evening, I surely would have dared to confront these madmen and youths who are, every time they are seen, in a wild chase for anyone who would obstruct or hinder them, and the one who would do so would get mashed up by them, for it is the mashing that they love. They often chased after me to obstruct or hinder them, but I would not, despite their attempts to force me by making outrageous demands upon me. For without my coffin, no matter how elevated and rigorous my attempts to transcend the limits of my mortal structure, I was never the less in this respect, in the respect of my physical cowardice when faced by a madman, or a gang of wild-eyed youths trying to make themselves secure by committing acts of violence, still a man of time.

It was not so difficult for me to stand and bring forth argument with the athletes, though, those hulky, bulky men who lifted enormous weights and exercised for long hours every day and even at night, for I knew that, regardless of their commitment to and enjoyment of certain acts of violence against other human beings, it was under the guidance of principles of self-defense and was thus predictable. They relished and told long stories of mighty bouts, recounted great bone-crunching episodes of violence, but all their stories and accounts were guided by the wish to point up the principle of self-defense, its necessity, utility and justification, almost as if they were telling little fables or parables designed to say the virtue of their authors' lives of heavy discipline, their lives of contrived restraint. And of course, because they tended to be much larger than most men and much stronger and more skilled in the ways of breaking bones and tearing muscle and rupturing organs and various membranes, they also tended to regard the granting of protection as closer to the act of grace than they did the actual perpetrating of violence on the body of someone smaller, weaker or less skilled than they. Instinctively, almost, they knew that if they withheld their great power, they would be exercising the greater power, for grace, which is always gratuitous, functions essentially to dignify and glorify the dispenser. It is self-redounding, and for that reason whether it is utilized by the recipient or not matters not a whit to the dispenser.

Over the course of my first year of imprisonment I had often been placed under the protection of one or more of these men, a pure act of grace on their part, awarded to me regardless of my need or particular qualities and given out solely because they were huge and I was not, because they were skilled at various of the martial arts and I knew nothing of these, and because they were extremely strong, especially through the upper body, and I was no stronger through the upper body than any man who has spent his adolescence and young manhood as a builder of coffins. I welcomed this dispensation, naturally, for it meant a distinct falling off of the number of mean and nasty occasions during a day when I would be accosted by one of the madmen or the gangs of flighty youths out looking for someone unable to keep himself from obstructing or hindering them. I also enjoyed the companionship of these large, soberly disciplined, methodical men, and many were the mornings and late afternoons when I would descend the stairs to the exercise room, where they moved about like enormous beasts of burden in the cool, dim light, lifting barbells and cast iron weights, pulling rhythmically on thick rubber belts attached to the walls, studying their development in the mirrors that lined the room. Sometimes a pair of them would meet together on a mat and wrestle for a while; under strict rules and heavy manners, so that they would not injure one another by accident. It pleased me to stand and observe while they went through their numerous exercise programs and afterwards to listen to their conversations about bodies and physical tests of all kinds and even sometimes, especially after the spring, to discuss matters with them, such as the need to worship the dead.

Ordinarily they tolerated my argument with them, which necessarily took the form of disagreement followed by a presentation of my view only, for they did not seem to think the situation warranted their presenting their argument or point of view, and to be sure, they were not always as easy with speech as I doubtless seemed to be, for their response to my argument was usually to throw themselves grunting back into a series of exercises or to whack against the large sandbag several hundred times with their fists.

Once, however, they came to me and urged me to accept an exercise program for myself, one of their own design, and when I declined, with lengthily explained reasons, all of which were of course religious, they became quite angry and heated about it. This surprised me, but it soon came out that a particular pair of them had decided to experiment with my body because it was so approximate to the shape and condition of the body of the average citizen outside the prison, and they felt that if they could design an exercise and conditioning program which was capable of converting my somewhat flabby structure into an iron-hard, machine-like, impeccably muscled structure like theirs, then they would be able to sell their program, like a recipe for a cake to the hungry, once they were released and let back outside again. I did not see anything amiss with their plan, and I even told them this, for if indeed they had been allowed to employ my body in this testing out of their exercise program, I was sure that in time they would have come up with a series of diets, exercises, activities and sports that would have converted my structure into the kind of organism that would have evoked deep envy and marvelling from among practically all men who do not worship the dead. Then they could have come forth with descriptions and measurements of my rapid progress to physical perfection, and their program would have been eagerly purchased by untold numbers of citizens outside. It might have made my two bulky companions into rich men.

But no, I would not allow it. The body is not the temple of the worship of the dead; it is the priest's vestment, no more. To attend with any great part of one's time, energy and treasure to the care of this vestment is to leave off the proper use of it, which is merely to signify the office. For we have been granted ordination at birth, and only death can properly remove the vestment and the obligation that adheres to it. Tending to it ourselves, I told them, cultivating it, treating it as if it were some object of worship itself, is to fall into a subtle yet dangerous form of blasphemy. Said the prophet Dirk, We wear our bodies. They do not wear us. For while we can ignore them, they can never ignore us. In life, it is crucial to learn what can be ignored, and then to ignore it. For what cannot be ignored, must be worshipped. (*Dirk*, xxiii, 12-15.)

As it happened, then, the two who had asked it of me that I let them use my body to exemplify the bodies of the future purchasers of their program, these two had up to then been my most consistent protectors against the raids against me by the madmen and the marauding gangs of youths, who spent much of their idle time accosting the prisoners who often walked about without any clannish loyalty from among the principled violent ones. Unfortunately, my argument against my protectors' plan for my body was such that it smouldered them angrily against me, so that they withdrew their protection and talked bitterly against me among their brethren, until there was no other protection from any of them forthcoming.

And thus in a short time I was accosted by one of the gangs of knife boys, and to punish me for my cowardice, which let them pitch me around one to the other while they laughed at me and urged me to stand and fight any one amongst them, the leader of the group cut my skin with his knife, not deeply enough to injure me in any debilitating way, but sufficiently to indicate his capacity for killing me and his deliberate withholding of that capacity. The cuts were also deep enough to create the scars on my face which have caused so much rumor and confusion among my brethren. I hope now that there will be no more wild and exaggerated tales to soar about the countryside concerning the sufferings of my imprisonment. To be sure, there followed numerous other encounters with violence which were equally characterized by their unavoidability, now that my protection from the athletes and body builders had been withdrawn, and even though several of them indeed left me with injuries, none of the injuries have given rise to the type of rumor and outright lie as have done the scars on my face, so for that reason I will not ennumerate and describe them here.

Excepting the company I kept with those men among the prisoners who could be called the philosophic ones, I was now more alone than I had been since my arrival in prison the year before. This did not so much depress me as it frustrated me, for I had, in my enjoyment of the daily company of these various fellows, sought to work amongst them for their conversion to the wisdom and the ultimate salvation of the worth of a life that lay in keeping my faith and observing its sacraments. I was not capable of expressing this ambition in my dealings with the philosophic ones, however, for their conversion is not normally accomplished by their coming to know the texture and the quality of the life of a believer. No, the philosophers, though they may indeed adhere to a set of beliefs for no other reason than that they themselves once, when youthful and less taught in argument, came to know the texture and quality of the life of a man they admired, once they learn how to philosophize with those beliefs will brook no further conversions to be similarly accomplished. Thus they are seldom seekers of belief so much as they are defenders of it, and therefore, if you would attempt to work conversion on them, you must first destroy their present set of beliefs, and this, according to scripture, would be in defiance of the dead. Shatter not any man's faith if you would have him as your brother. Let him love your faith and with his love shatter his own. Make not a man naked before you present him with a cloak. (*I Craig.*, vii, 18.) In addition, I was not as clever and schooled as they generally were, and often, in explaining the nature and the principles that defined my own mode of worship and the very necessity of worship itself, I made a poor case for myself and my brethren, and I sometimes glumly conceded that I was making no sense.

So it came about that, even though these men were then my only companions among the prisoners, as I was compelled by my love of the dead and my wish to obey scripture, I left off attempting to work conversion among the philosophic ones, with the immediate result of their no longer desiring me to come among them. As long as I had been willing to argue against the faith they defended, I had been welcomed as one of their fraternity. But when I determined that by my own faith I must not attack theirs (and by that means also no longer to be forced into glum concessions of making no sense), the philosophic ones no longer found me of interest. This was to become a considerable deprivation for me, for I had learned to value the companionship of the philosophers above all others and for reasons that had nothing to do with the disputation they themselves valued so highly, and when I was no longer able to sit with them at table or in the prison reading rooms or even to play dominoes with them (for when I left off arguing against them, they no longer were able to respect my intelligence), I sat alone in my cell and wondered what they were doing at that moment, what they were saying to each other, what they were analyzing, discussing and evaluating together, for these were men who talked with feeling and intelligence about many of the things that interested me.

I did not complain then, nor do I now, even though I had fallen into a deep solitude that was broken only by the sporadic visits of my wife, who was growing more weakly, and, for a brief period, the occasional conversations I had with Jacob Moon prior to his departure from his post as jailor, which also took place that second summer of my imprisonment, when he assumed the directorship of the Society Of Prisoners. I did not complain of my solitude, first, because there was no one but my wife to hear it and I did not wish to increase her sufferings by a relation of my own, but also because I knew that my solitude had been achieved by me in the service of the dead, and so I saw my sufferings as yet another way to tender mercy to the dead, and this made me glad.

I CANNOT NOW say with certainty when it was that I reached this period of my deep solitude, which goes on even to today, except to notice that it occurred sometime long before the death of my beloved wife, which means that it probably took place during the early part of the first eleven years of my imprisonment, for I am told that her death took place only a year ago this last winter. Regardless, my experience of the passage of time for those years had become over the years such that I could recall the most distant parts with great clarity and detail, almost as if they were events of barely a month ago. But as the events came nearer in time to the present moment, I found myself unable to recall them very clearly and sometimes not at all. I do not know for sure why this should be so. It is more usual that the opposite should be the case, that I should remember events of ten and twelve years ago only vaguely and with great gaps of forgotten days, with even months and whole seasons missing, and that I should remember the more recently transpired events of my imprisonment with a more reliable continuity and in much sharper and more plentiful detail.

I have studied this seeming paradox with care, especially in the absence of my coffin, to which ordinarily I would have repaired for meditation and access to a higher intelligence than my own, and I have devised a theory to explain the phenomenon. Here it is. In as much as all my efforts during my imprisonment after the loss of my coffin were bent singlemindedly toward freeing me from being the man of time who moves through tiny segmented cells of experience in time, and in so far as I did succeed in those efforts, by that much would I be freed of the burden and the incriminating stain of memory. And in so far as my success in this undertaking was marked by gradual degrees, so too would my freedom from memory be gradual and relative.

This made sense to me, and on the several occasions when I related my theory to my wife, it made sense to her as well. I had no one else to confirm or deny or even to question the validity of my theory, for, as I have described, my fellow prisoners had removed themselves from my company, setting the kind of precedent which in prison life does not easily get broken, regardless of the regular movement in and out of that society, and when my jailor Jacob Moon had departed from his post, there was no one even among the staff who was willing to associate with me either. According to my wife there were many of our brethren who wished often to visit me in my confinement, but because to do so would bring upon them certain exposure and possible prosecution, they were forced with reluctance to stay away. And even if they had wished to take such a risk, I would not have allowed it, for my best use to them was as an example, not as a companion nor even as an object for their sympathies. Also, as I mentioned, my wife's cousin Gina, who in the beginning of my imprisonment would visit me frequently, after my having been brought to my senses by the words spoken to me in my dream by my father and his brother, feared that I would only be reminded by her presence of that for which I felt considerable guilt. This I took to be an unintended but precise description of how she herself doubtless felt, and thus I urged my wife to assure her cousin that she need not visit me anymore, that in fact I would consider it unbecoming of her to do so, for I would take it as an indication that she did not herself feel any guilt for the nature of our carnal activities together in those early days of my imprisonment. My wife told me that her cousin accepted this message with her usual placid understanding, and this pleased me and gave me hope that the entire experience had enlarged her spiritual understanding of the nature of carnality and the dead as much as it had my own.

But with regard to my theory about the paradoxical way in which my memory had come to function and not to function, almost as if it had come partially to withhold itself, because there was no one against whom I could test it with argument, except my wife, of course, who agreed fully with me on most things of a theoretical nature anyhow, I was not able to be sure that I was not merely constructing an elaborate disguise so as to hide some painful truth from myself. Whenever one is unsure in this way, if he cannot resort to his coffin and there obtain his confirmation or denial, he has little choice, indeed, he is obliged to do nothing else, than to turn to scripture and hope that his confirmation or denial can be obtained there. For as the scriptures themselves say, Certainty eludes him who will not read deeply into the language of the dead. (*Craig.*, xiv, 22.) And truly, there amongst the scriptures did I find confirmation of my theory, concerning my memory's increasing ability (as I extricated myself from time and came slowly back into the proper and fitting worship of the dead) to withhold itself.

Now this my reader may think odd, for it may seem to him that I was testing and confirming a theory about the gradual loss of memory with scriptures that I had access to only by means of memory (for the possession of scripture in any printed form was strictly illegal, then as now). May it here be pointed out that my memory was not flawed or imperfect with regard to what it described to me, whether of scripture or of the nature of my experience, as much as it was increasingly absent altogether and increasingly, therefore, reported nothing to me of my experience. My memory of scripture, which I had learned when a mere child, was not affected. But whole days went by without leaving a word in my mind's report to me on myself, then whole weeks, and then months and seasons, until it was no longer my memory that told me how long I had been imprisoned or precisely when particular events had occurred, as much as it was a tattered calendar on the wall of the dining hall or a casual conversation between two prisoners overheard in the exercise yard or a newspaper in the reading room.

Thus I gradually lost my old ability to move easily among sequences of events, public and private, and my old ability to relate the two chains so that I could immediately know what public events had transpired at the same time as a given private event. There was a morning, for example, when, upon looking into the mirror over my wash basin, I realized that my hair had gone all to white, where before it had been dark brown, and I cannot now say whether I made that discovery mere days before I learned of my wife's death or seven whole years before. And there was the period of several months when the prisoners were talking amongst themselves of the war that the nation was evidently prosecuting abroad, and I cannot say whether this period was before or after my hair had turned white. And though I can remember the evening of resignation when I decided that I would no longer every ninety days file an appeal for a trial at the upcoming quarter-sessions, so that I could be tried and properly convicted and thus be made eligible for amnesty at the following solstice, a decision I knew was based on the fact that I had been refused such a trial by peremptory notice a hopelessly repeated number of times, I cannot now say how many times I had been refused. That is to say, I cannot now say on what numerical basis I made such a momentous decision.

Doubtless there are some among the brethren who would say that this seeming dysfunction of the memory, even if it indeed was a direct result of my attempt to remove myself from the life of a man of time, was a deprivation and a kind of suffering. But I cannot agree. For the prophet Walter says, There will come a day that will not differ from night, and a night that will not differ from day. (vii, 7.) No, this was not a dysfunction of the memory. It was a more and more frequent withholding of itself, and thus it was another of the many kinds of grace that get granted to those who worship the dead. And grace, as I have said, is the gift that redounds to the greater glory of the giver, and in that way does it serve its purpose. By this gift, therefore, was I permitted to see the true and overwhelming nature of the dead all the more clearly. To hear the voice of the dead is to obey it, and to see its everlastingness is to honor it. To obey death and to honor it, then, are to make the life of a man overflow with meaning. If the gradual loss of my memory, properly understood as grace, served to make my life gradually more meaningful to me, how could I call it a dysfunction? Or even more absurd, how could I call it a deprivation or a kind of suffering?

THERE CAME TO me a slowly dawning realization, like the spread of a thick silvery light, that my wife had left off coming to visit me in my imprisonment. For a long time her visits to my cell, where we would sometimes converse and more often would sit comfortably together for hours in affectionate silence broken only by some one or another of my thoughts or memories that I felt would be of use in her instruction, had been less and less frequent. Or so it then seemed to me, for whenever she did appear to me there, it did seem to me that I had not been in her company for a long while. As I look back now to that period of my imprisonment when I first began to notice the infrequency of her visits to my cell, I picture her as being somewhat distracted and erratic in her words, but I did not then notice that her behavior was anything out of the ordinary. I had noticed, naturally, from the very beginning of my imprisonment, even from the day of my arrest, when, because of the tumult and frenzy of those days she had been delivered too soon of the child she was then carrying and which as a consequence had died, that her health was precarious and that she was often in pain and would fall to coughing and wincing from it. Her condition worsened, and I did notice that and did advise her on how to medicate herself as

best I knew how, and I did direct her to those among the brethren who I knew could provide her, out of their love for me, with
aid and comfort and who would also stand forth in the support
of our children. For this support my wife expressed often to me
her large gratitude, for she as well as I knew how dangerous
it was for them to make any show of public sympathy for my
dependents.

During those early years of my confinement, my wife and
I were at deep peace with one another and were in continuous
agreement on all the questions, quandaries and tribulations that
beset us and the numerous ways by which we tried to answer
and alleviate them. But there came at last a season when it was
known to me that no longer was I capable of advising or otherwise aiding her in her attempts to contend with the obstacles she
faced in the world outside my prison as she struggled to care for
herself and our children. Her knowledge of the outside world
had grown to be superior to mine. And thus I gave off attempting to provide more than a generalized and abstract reassurance,
which I am sure must at times have led her to believe or to fear
that I no longer cared very deeply about the welfare of my family
and that I no longer held for my wife the same passionate devotion as when before I had been imprisoned. It is to this belief or
fear, then, that I credit her increasingly distracted and erratic
behavior, which I did not notice at the time but from which, if I
had noticed it, I would have drawn the same conclusions as now,
and I would have tenderly remonstrated with her so as to show
her the constancy of my caring about the welfare of my family
and the continuity of my devotion to her person.

This was not of course the cause of her death, any more than
it was the cause of the death of my first wife, the mother of my
five children, even though, according to the physicians who
attended the women during their last days, they both died from
the same affliction, a congenitally distressed heart, the physicians called it, worsened by the depredations of poverty and the

stress of life and time. My chiefest grief is that I could not be in attendance when these two precious women passed over from their sufferings in life to their comfort in death and that, therefore, my last memories of both my wives are sombered to such a huge degree by the character and intensity of their tribulation in life rather than of their bliss in death. Thus it had been with a certain amount of envy that I had heard my first wife's father tell me how his daughter had joined the dead, for during the months of her dying I had been compelled by my calling to provide crucial training to the many in the north who wished to become coffin-makers. And it was with a similar envy that I heard my sons tell me of the dying of my second wife, their stepmother, during the winter of the eleventh year of my confinement. Here is how it came about.

My wife had not come to visit me for a long time. I could not say exactly how long, nor could I even be approximate, but I had concluded never the less that she had left off coming to the prison, and the conclusion had filled me with a kind of releasement that I did not at first understand. Since that time I have come to view that releasement, which felt to me like a thick silvery light spreading across my mind, as, first, a secret awareness that my wife at last had more satisfying things to do with her time than to sit in a tiny damp cell with me, and this gladdened and relieved me, and, secondly, as a quiet harbinger of her death. At the time, however, I did not view the presence of that light in either of these ways, I merely opened myself to it, and it was only after my two oldest sons had come and had presented themselves to me that I went back to that light and attempted to interpret it.

One of the assistant jailors, a man whose name I do not know, brought the two boys to me. The older of the pair, my firstborn, had grown into his young manhood, and I did not recognize him. The second so closely resembled his mother that at first I took him to be her in fact, and I gloried in her presence, for I knew her to have been among the dead for many years. But soon they had told me their names and had led me to understand that they were indeed my two oldest children, and we sat down together side by side on my cot and began to speak fondly to one another, albeit somewhat tensely, it seemed, for many years had passed since we had been in each other's company and we were all three not sure of how best to make ourselves known to one another.

They told me straight out that my wife had died, calling her that, my wife rather than their stepmother. This was due, I am sure, solely to the fact that I had not recognized them at first when they had come in to me and thus I might not have known to whom they were referring if they had said only that their stepmother had died. I asked them if she had died without great pain, and they answered that she had died with eagerness, and I expressed my relief at that, for she had lived with great pain for many years, and they said that their knowledge of her life confirmed this observation.

The older of the two was the spokesman, it seemed, for his younger brother remained mostly silent throughout our interview, except now and again to interject a word or two for emphasis or clarification, such as, when the older brother had told me that the physician attending my wife had pronounced her dead of a congenitally distressed heart exacerbated by the depredations of poverty and a life of stress, the younger added the information that this was also how my first wife had died. That was how he referred to her, as my first wife, rather than as his mother, again doubtless because I had not recognized them when they had first appeared to me and thus I might not know who he was talking about if he had said, My mother.

Here a slight misunderstanding between us arose, for we were as yet unused to each other's company and our respective ways of expressing ourselves. I wished to know if my wife had died in her coffin, which of course is one of the rites which would have characterized her life and would have lent it meaning, if it had been followed properly, and which thereby would have provided us, her survivors in life, with the greater occasion to praise her, thus lending to our lives also a quantity of meaning they otherwise would lack. This circle is crucial to the maintenance of faith, as are all the rites, for no practice can evolve successfully into the sacred function of rite if it cannot stand the test of circularity. My sons, still boys, of course, probably had not yet arrived at the kind of informed worship of the dead (the faith that sustains itself by knowing itself) that would have let them know immediately my purpose in asking so quickly after being informed of her death if my wife had died in her coffin, because the older of the boys upbraided me with considerable feeling for my lack of feeling, as he saw it, and his brother grew stern.

But I was able to calm and smooth over their bristled words and glowerings against me by elaborating on the texts of several scriptural passages which prescribe the meaningful use of coffins during our life times, such as *The Book of Discipline*, xxxii, 12: Let the coffin serve up wisdom to the foolish, let it be a buckler for the timorous. For wise is the man who lies down in his coffin early in the day of his life time, and victorious is he who arms himself thereby. Also, xxiii, 4-5: This doth the dead hate, that a man come unto them naked and pretending like a babe that he was surprised by death.

My sons seemed pleased and enlarged by my explication and also by the rigor of my application of the said texts to the particularities of the death of my wife, their stepmother, so that in a short while we were all three quite at ease and hearty together in our praise of the dead, for they had admired their stepmother, my wife, quite as much as I, and it took no puffing up of our imaginations and language for us to tender mercy unto her. I was greatly relieved, needless to say, that my sons were able to give such abundant evidence of my wife's intellectual capacity and her dauntless energy for teaching them the basic articles of our faith, despite their lack of adult comprehension, for in the modern world where children are so cleverly and constantly cajoled into seeking transient pleasures and relations, it is not an easy or simple thing to drive them to the path of righteousness and meaning, and having got them there, to keep them from wandering off that path and getting all lost among the living.

HERE I SHALL enter into a description of certain afflictions which have characterized my recent months and have sorely tested me in divers ways. Know, however, that it has not been my belief in the worth of worshipping the dead and the eternal benefits that accrue thereby that has been tested, but my old decision, described early in this relation, not to resist life. I refer to my atonement for having failed my first jailor, John Bethel, so that he went unto death in my stead and bore with him my own coffin. He had not fully comprehended my teachings, even though he had become converted by me to my faith in certain of its aspects, and for that he had willed himself to sacrifice himself for the living, not yet realizing that the only worthwhile and meaningful sacrifice of one's life is for the dead. (*II Carol*. iv, 34-35.) In atonement for the cursoriness of my instruction and the stupidity of my plan to alter the court calendar, thus incriminating another in my crime, I had made over to my jailor my own coffin, and as he wished, he was executed while in it, praise the dead. But that was not yet sufficient atonement, I felt, and so I determined to sacrifice myself also. But because of the nature of my offense, and my desire not to make my sacrifice a way of life, which would have been reprehensible to the dead, for my penance thus would have been eternal, as was John Bethel's sacrifice of himself, I chose instead to limit my penance by a certain measure of time, the which was the natural extension of my life time. Therefore, I moved henceforward to avoid all such activities and practices that could lead me into a fatal encounter with death. It meant that I should not deny myself any sustenance, any food, rest or medication or other physical comfort that in whatsoever way contributed to the further resistence of death. To be sure, I would not chase obsequiously after these substances like some life-clinging wretch, but I could not permit myself to deny them when they were necessary or when they were imposed on me.

For many years this penance was easily made. Prison food and prison medication, required only rarely, were more than adequate, and my cell and few furnishings therein provided me with adequate comfort, and on the few occasions when my life was threatened by the violence of certain prisoners, my cowardice, though it shamed me, also made it so that I was making my penance, for it kept me from foolhardiness and forms of reckless behavior. Too, I was rarely ill during the early years of my imprisonment, partly because of my constitution and partly because of the generally benign physical conditions of the prison. Also, until her death, I was tenderly looked after by my wife, despite her own failing health, so that whenever I showed any slight sign of illness, no matter how insignificant, she would hurry to me with medications and kindness and would quickly cure me.

After her death, however, and following hard upon the visit from my sons, there commenced my period of illness. It introduced itself to me modestly enough, so that, unawares, I did not protect myself against it, because, as yet a man of time is inevitably inclined, I saw each new affliction as separate and independent from the other and saw not at all any sequence or heaping up, and surely I did not suspect that I was entering upon a whole and lengthy period of illness. Therefore, when there came into the corners of my mouth and upon the bridge of my nose a small number of boils and hard chancres, I was not alarmed or even especially discomfited by them, and so I merely waited for them to leave as they had come, silently and in the night and without apparent cause.

They did not leave, however, although individual boils and chancres did sometimes soften so that the pus beneath could break through and drain from the sore, which sore, when it had fled, would seem to reappear in another part of my mouth or nose. During this time I also contracted the disease called favus, which is characterized by small yellowish crusts on the scalp with raised edges and depressed centers. The crusts have a peculiar odor, like that of a mouse nest, and the hairs in the encrusted areas become brittle, loosen, break and fall out, so that when the inflammation has passed, there are left blotches of baldness across the scalp. This condition did not seem to me a disease at the time, for while I had the disease I was aware only of the itching, which was irregular, and I did not discover the bald patches until sometime later. The peculiar odor, because it was indeed so like unto that of a mouse nest, I simply attributed to the presence in my cell somewhere of a mouse nest. Furthermore, I was also then suffering for the first time from a condition known as dry seborrhea, which affects the foreskin of the penis and is characterized by itching caused by an accumulation of a cheesy material consisting of body oils mixed with dead cells and other tissue debris, and thus I was somewhat distracted from the favus infection on my scalp.

The reader should keep in mind that I did not at this time know what was yet to come, and therefore each new affliction I regarded as the last in a series. When I had developed boils, I did not know that favus would follow and that dry seborrhea would follow the favus. Nor did I know, when the dry seborrhea had cleared somewhat, that I would soon be afflicted by neuralgia, the chief symptom of which is extreme pain that comes on in paroxysms and severe twitching of the muscles of the affected part, in my case the cheeks of my face and the muscles surrounding my mouth. These symptoms took expression as a sudden grimace, practically an openmouthed but silent laugh, despite the pain, and thus I was often thought to be enjoying some private hilarity, when in fact I was not. To further confuse people, one of the boils from my mouth had relocated in my right ear, to be followed by another in my left, and soon the swelling in the canals had become sufficiently extensive to cause a temporary but total deafness, so that I could not know what was being said to me and thus could not answer questions with regard to the incongruity between my facial expression and the absence of anything particularly humorous in my immediate situation or surroundings.

Along about this time I began to reason that there was a connection between my various afflictions, however tenuous, and I grew fearful, yet none of my diseases were such that they could be cured by any treatment other than rest and cleanliness, which were my habits to encourage anyhow. Unavoidably, one affliction seemed to lead to another, so that one night during my sleep, the neuralgic twitching of the muscles surrounding my mouth caused me to bite into the meat of my tongue accidentally, which in a short time became inflamed, swelling the tongue exceedingly and leading to an ulcerated and very tender condition and also several abcesses there. This condition brought on a constant and copious flow of saliva and also made it difficult and very painful to speak. In a few days I observed that my gums as well had become infected, for they had grown spongy and tender and had puffed out and sometimes bled and from time to time oozed pus from between my teeth. And still there was little I could do to cure myself, except to provide myself with rest and cleanliness.

Here I became sufficiently ill that the jailor at last brought a physician unto me, for there had appeared on the skin of my chest several large thickly encrusted areas of a purplish color. These masses of granulated tissue and tiny abcesses, bathed in a thin film of pus, had come from within my lungs, the physi-

cian thought, and indicated a condition he named blastomyco-
sis, which he speculated had been caused by some type of yeast
infection somewhere in my body. When I had told him of my
dry seborrhea, he chuckled and said that it surely explained the
cause but gave not a hint for the cure, for there was no cure,
except to treat the affected areas of the skin with certain chem-
ical solutions, which he dispensed to me and which I assidu-
ously applied, bringing about a small measure of relief. I was
left, however, with a painful cough and more or less difficulty
with breathing, and with chills and sweats in alternation, and an
indisputably foul-smelling sputum, these all coming as a result
of the lung infection, which the physician told me might in time
abate of its own volition.

I lay in my cot for most of my days now as well as the nights
and no longer moved outside my cell. The pain from my lungs
and from the boils and divers other sores as had appeared across
my body and from the neuralgia and the diseases that filled my
mouth and stopped up my ears, and the continuous itching in
the various parts of my body, made me shrink inside myself like
some dumb animal cowering in a corner, and I began to fear that
I might be compelled, by my commitment to my life time's period
of penance, to live this way for a long time, and this brought
me to conclude that my will to atone was being tested by the
dead. I believed that the dead were trying me because there had
come into my spirit during these weeks a longing to join them
that was exceedingly strong and that was not altogether spiritual. Against this longing I brought forth numerous scriptures
and remembered teachings from my youth and all my powers of
reason, for this was now a clash that rang out continuously in my
mind with all the noisesome fury of a great clash between armies.
I know that I often wept and groaned aloud and thrashed helplessly through the long nights.

It was now that the physician began to attend to me daily,
as if he did not expect me to live, and it was in that way that I

learned of how the abcess in my lungs, when it had somewhat
subsided, had created a certain amount of scar tissue adhering to
the walls of the entry to my stomach, causing these walls to pull
away and form a sac, which he called a diverticulum and which
unavoidably, as the sac increased in size, filled with slivers of
food. And when the particles of food decomposed there, the sac
expanded still further until it had grown to the size of a tobacco
pouch and had caused a foul odor and much pain and vomiting.
As a joke, the physician told me that the best cure was starvation,
for no matter how little I ate or what I ate, there was bound to
be some small particle that would be drawn into this ever enlarg-
ing pouch. For several days thereafter I did indeed wrestle with
the temptation to cure myself by starvation, but after a while I
was able to overcome this test also and thus agreed to follow the
physician's instructions and attempted to keep food from entering the sac by laying myself in such a position as to place the sac
at a level higher than the entry to my stomach, with the mouth
of the sac pointed downward, which is to say, by lying on my
right side with my head and shoulders on the floor and my hips
and legs on the cot. Thus I was able to take a small amount of
nourishment, mainly in the form of dry crumbly cereals so that
the few grains which, despite these precautions, nevertheless got
into the sac, could be drawn out daily by the physician with his
rubber tube and pump.

But the cure for one affliction is frequently the cause of
another, and because my diet was now restricted wholly to sips
of water and bits of dry cereal, I soon developed the symptoms
that accompany the absence of acid in the stomach, abdominal
pain, headache, ringing in the ears, and constant drowsiness,
a condition which additionally led quickly to pernicious anemia, which brought with it extreme weakness, breathlessness
and heart palpitations. My skin all over my body, such of it as
was not inflamed with boils and various sores, was a lemonish
color, and my feet and hands had puffed out grotesquely. It now

seemed to me that I would surely succumb to the temptation to die, for to live meant only to contract yet another, more nearly fatal disease whose cure seemed to be a still worse disease. When I slept, which was only in brief spasms, I had furious dreams, and though I wished for those among the dead to appear to me there and to advise me and I often cried out the name of my wife or of John Bethel or of my parents, none from the dead came to me then. Only the living appeared to me, in my sleep as much as when I was awake, my physician, my jailor, occasionally a curious prisoner who might have heard my groans, until I was no longer able to tell when I was not sleeping from when I was not awake, for in both states did these people appear to me in wildly threatening postures with their faces horribly distorted, as if they themselves had contracted all my diseases and had grown as grotesque to look upon as had I myself.

Now there came upon my body a great fever, which lasted for about ten days and nights and brought with it profuse night sweats and continuous headache, and when it had abated, left me weaker even than before, with certain of my other afflictions somewhat worsened, such as the neuralgic pains in my face and the coughing and the various symptoms of the pernicious anemia. The physician who had taken a sort of scientific interest in my case, for it presented him with many ongoing puzzles, could not at first diagnose this fever, until there had followed several more episodes of about ten days each, coming as if in waves, each one leaving me afterwards weaker than before. These waves, he said, were characteristic of undulant fever, an uncommon disease among the population as a whole but not uncommon among those who are known to deal with the dead, for it is contracted and spread chiefly by having come into contact with a similarly infected body or carcass, but because the germ often lies dormant for years, it is very difficult to trace the path of contagion. Thus, since my calling long ago had been as a coffin-maker, the physician had swiftly concluded that I doubtless at some time long before my imprisonment had dealt with an infected corpse, and it was only now, in my weakened condition, that the disease had made itself known to me. There was no cure for the disease that the physician knew of, but the symptoms could be treated as they appeared, and because he was interested in the course of the disease and in containing its spread, he determined to stay close to me and treat me as kindly as he could. He thought that he might thereby learn something about the disease so as to be able to devise preventive measures against its future occurrence, especially among the prison population.

From my own perspective, that of the sufferer rather than that of the detached observer and attendant, the wave-like ebbs and flows of the fever created in my life a paradoxical series of troughs of easefulness, for when my body temperature rose, the numerous pains I had been experiencing throughout my body would seem to diminish, so that the higher the fever went and the longer it lasted, by that much was I released from the pain of my boils and other skin afflictions and the neuralgia and the lung abcess and the pain of hunger caused by the diverticulum and the several other related agonies of that time, so that I came to welcome the approach of each new wave, each new undulation, of the fever. Though afterwards I was left each time as weak as a newborn babe, I was able for a few hours to experience considerable clarity of mind, and despite the inflammation of my tongue and my infected gums and teeth, I was able to speak with a remarkable clarity.

During the attacks of fever, however, I was not aware of anyone who happened to be in my presence, nor was I aware of the passage of time, so that I had to be shown with a calendar how long each wave had lasted and told, with notes from the physician, for I could not understand his speech due to my deafness, who had attended me and what had been done for my comfort, information I desired so as to be able, during my periods of lucidity following the wave, to show my gratitude. In this way

I learned of the physician's sustained efforts to cool my body by applying alcohol soaked sponges and the regular baths he provided for the removal of the stools and urine that I emitted while feverish and unable to care for such functions myself. I also learned that my jailor, too, and even his superior officers had taken an interest in my condition and had posted an assistant jailor to keep watch over me, so that at no time was I without someone keeping vigil.

During the first few onslaughts of fever, I felt as if I were in a dream, although I knew I was not sleeping, and there came to me numerous faces from among the dead, and they would speak soothingly to me, as if to strengthen me in my resolve not to resist life so as to keep my penance. In this way I was encouraged by my father and my uncle, and also my first wife and on another occasion my second wife, both of whom knew from their own lives how difficult and painful it often is not to resist living. There also came to me Justice Hale, who had died during the second year of my imprisonment and who now appreciated the wisdom of a faith that in his life time he had merely been willing to tolerate (which raised him above his brother judges, however, for none there were among them, except Justice Hale, who had been willing even to tolerate dissenters), and he too encouraged me in my resolve to exchange my life for John Bethel's death, for he reminded me of the foolishness of my desire in the beginning of my imprisonment to bring my case to a legal point.

Then there followed several more waves of fever, and no longer were the dead presenting themselves to me. In their stead came the faces of the living. First there came my second jailor Jacob Moon, who was wearing now a handsome pin-striped business suit instead of his old gray uniform, and he too tried to comfort me, but his words were of a different order than had been those of the dead, for he kept telling me that I should not fall into despair, for soon I would no longer be among the living. And my wife's cousin Gina, in the company of my five children, all of whom looked upon me with great sympathy and said that I had suffered enough and should give myself over from this penance. Mingled with these were the faces of my present jailor, and sometimes his assistants, and even sometimes that of my physician, and they were all saying to me the same thing, that I should let myself die now, for my sufferings had gone on long enough for many normal life times. There even came to me one of my own brethren in the faith, my friend of long ago who had counseled me to leave off the making of coffins and turn my skills to the manufacture of glass-fronted cabinets, and he once again gave me his sympathetic counsel, because of his love for me, and again it was counsel that denied my understanding of my own love of the dead, for he urged me to leave off my determination not to resist life.

Until there came at last the waves of fever in which there appeared to me the faces of both the living and the dead, and I could not tell one from the other, the living from the dead, although I knew them all, and they all counseled me and cajoled me and showed me great sympathy, and I loved them all for it and was grateful to them, even to those among them who said nothing, some living and some dead, who merely with their presence showed a concern for me, the Justices Bester and Twisdom of long ago, and certain of my brethren, and the infant born dead to my second wife, and many of my fellow prisoners, the party boys and the athletes and the philosophers, and even the knife boys and madmen who had wanted to do so much violence. Some among these were dead, and some were yet living, and the dead among them urged me not to come among them, to hold fast to my penance, and the living among them urged me to depart from them now, to join the eternal dead. And their voices were like a chorus that harmonized their differences and sent up a song of such precise beauty that I wept uncontrollably, for I loved them all so very much.

THOUGH MY IMPRISONMENT continues, my relation of it cannot. I must bring it to a close. I have composed it during the interludes between the attacks of the undulant fever. My strength for this composition, despite the effects of my illnesses, has been given to me by my coffin, which was presented to me at last by the prison authorities when it seemed to them that I would soon die of a disease that could be spread chiefly by handling an infected corpse. For this reason, they came into my cell during one of my attacks, when I was not aware of their presence, and placed my body into a simple but adequate wood coffin, so that when the wave of fever had passed over me and I knew again where I was, I found myself lying in my coffin. My joy was great at this, and to the astonishment of my physician and the jailor, I was immediately given sufficient strength to use the periods of lucidity that followed each new attack of fever for the purpose of composing this relation. I asked for pen and paper that very day, and also a board to prop against the sides of my coffin, and as I lay there, I began to write. In no other way during my life time have I been able to tender this much mercy to the dead, as I do now, with this relation of my imprisonment, for it has been composed expressly for the use of the living, to whom I must now say Farewell.

About the author

About the book

Read on

Insights,
Interviews
& More . . .

Meet Russell Banks

"Russell Banks has now become . . . the most important living white male American on the official literary map, a writer we, as readers and writers, can actually learn from, whose books help and urge us to change."

—VILLAGE VOICE

RUSSELL BANKS was born in New Hampshire, in 1940, to a blue-collar family. His tumultuous relationship with his father led him to steal a car and briefly run away from home at age sixteen. He later enrolled in Colgate College on a full scholarship, the first in his family to attain higher education, but dropped out a few months later in a case of what he calls "turbulence." He headed south, resolving to join Castro's Cuban revolution. "It seemed like a noble thing to do. In the late 1950s we had very

© Ileana Florescu

few political heroes, us young folk, us kids. . . . We could project romantic, altruistic, idealistic, political feelings onto [Castro and Che Guevara]. I was running off to try to make it real." He hitchhiked as far as Florida, but soon ran out of money. "Then I'm moving furniture in a hotel and trying to survive, and pretty soon I forget about Castro." Banks later ended up dressing mannequins at a Maas Brothers department store.

By age nineteen he had married, and by twenty he had fathered a child. By age twenty-one, he was already divorced. Living in a trailer park in Florida in the 1960s, pumping gas and doing odd jobs, Banks, inspired by Walt Whitman and Mark Twain, first contemplated being a painter. "Writing isn't one of those things, in a literate culture, like music or painting, where the gift is obvious at a young age. My obvious gift as a boy was in painting. I could draw well; I had the gift genetically. I didn't know whether I had any particular writing talent at all. I set out to be a painter in my late teens and gradually discovered that I was writing, as one discovers one is breathing—and so you feel you must be alive! The discovery, the definition, came after the activity." But his new identity didn't come easily. "I was doing something that seemed a self-destructive kind of compulsion. Wanting to be a writer seemed to be a terrible waste of a life to my family and to me." At a writers' conference, he met migrant worker-turned-novelist Nelson Algren, who "gave me permission. He never told me how to write. But he said, 'You can do it, kid, and it's worth doing.'"

For a time, Banks returned to New Hampshire and followed in his father's and grandfather's footsteps: he became a plumber. A few years later, he attended the University of North Carolina and graduated Phi Beta Kappa at age twenty-seven. He taught writing at the University of New Hampshire and had several short stories published in literary reviews, but it was not until age thirty-five that he published his first book, a story collection titled *Searching for Survivors*.

His pursuit of literature removed from Banks a nasty appetite for barroom brawls. "There are certain things that writing has done for me that if I hadn't had them, I probably would have killed myself or somebody else," he told Salon. "Some magazine was asking writers what they would have become if they hadn't become a writer, and I said what would have happened to me is that I would have been stabbed to death in the parking lot outside a ▶

Meet Russell Banks *(continued)*

bar in Florida at twenty-four, or something like that. I really believe that, actually. I think writing saved my life. I was so self-destructive, so angry and turbulent, that I don't think I could have become a useful citizen in any other way. So I don't think it worked as exorcism, or therapy, but I think it saved my life."

During his thirties, Banks developed a passionate interest in Jamaica. "I had been to the Caribbean, like most Americans who can swing it, a week here, a week there in the wintertime. I became deeply attracted to the culture, the people, and fell in love with the place." When awarded a Guggenheim Fellowship to write a book, he took his family to Jamaica and stayed there a year and a half. He spent much of his time "up in the back country" of the island, absorbing the local traditions and idiom. Drawing on his experiences in both Jamaica and Florida, Banks next published *Trailerpark*, a collection of short stories, and *The Book of Jamaica*, a novel.

But it was not until the publication of his eighth book, *Continental Drift*, in 1985, that Banks first achieved critical success. The novel is the story of Bob Dubois, a burned-out oil-burner repairman from New Hampshire struggling to escape mediocrity, and Vanise Dorsinville, a refugee struggling to escape Haiti for the promised land of America, and the tragedy that ensues when they become involved in each other's destiny. The novel's title refers to the theory that the earth's continents were once a united land mass that broke up and continues to drift slowly apart. Banks, however, is referring to demographic, not geologic, drifting, as people all over the world flee their homes in search of new lives. He is also describing the drift that occurs

66 I think writing saved my life. I was so self-destructive, so angry and turbulent, that I don't think I could have become a useful citizen in any other way. 99

between human hearts, leaving an unbridgeable gap between husbands and wives, families and friends.

In order to capture a narrative voice capable of encompassing the disparate worlds of blue-collar New England and Caribbean voodoo, Banks invokes the Haitian *loa*, or mouth-man, the spirit of the dead that speaks through the mouth of the living, to help tell the story. "I'm really interested in reinventing the narrator. It's a convention that went out the window in the twentieth century. I want to feel I have my arm around a shoulder of this reader and I'm explaining, narrating, telling a wonderful story to this person that I've stopped, like the wedding guest in Coleridge's 'Rime of the Ancient Mariner.' I'm like the ancient mariner stopping the wedding guest in his rush to tell this wonder to him. And I want to have that sense of intimacy, a face-to-face, arm-around-the-shoulder contact." *Continental Drift*, a finalist for the Pulitzer Prize, won the John Dos Passos Award and an American Academy of Arts and Letters Award. James Atlas, writing in *Atlantic Monthly*, hailed the book as "a great American novel . . . a lesson in history. . . . It is the most convincing portrait I know of contemporary America."

Writing also helped Banks come to terms with his past. Though he made peace with his father before the older man's death in 1979, the theme of troubled father-son relationships continues to play a large role in Banks's novels. In *Affliction*, he explores the terrible legacy that an alcoholic and abusive father, Wade Whitehouse, has upon his son. "Writing *Affliction*, and dealing with Wade Whitehouse, gave me a kind of mercy and certainly forgiveness and understanding of my father that if I had just turned my back on him and walked away and acted bruised and ▶

66 I want to feel I have my arm around a shoulder of this reader and I'm explaining, narrating, telling a wonderful story to this person that I've stopped, like the wedding guest in Coleridge's 'Rime of the Ancient Mariner.' 99

hurt the rest of my life, I never would have obtained."

In *The Sweet Hereafter*, Banks again explores the world of troubled blue-collar families. The novel takes as its central event the fatal crash of a school bus and the devastating effect it has on a small town's emotional life. Banks was initially inspired by a newspaper clipping of a similar crash, as well as the tragic early death of his younger brother. The freight train his seventeen-year-old brother hopped onto was caught in a mudslide in Santa Barbara. "It was an inexplicable event. It was a mystery, finally." The novel wrestles with issues of blame and causation in cases of accidents.

Rule of the Bone returns to the author's twin obsession with Jamaica and dysfunctional American families. The novel tells the story of a teenage misfit's flight from an unhappy home in an upstate New York trailer park and the series of adventures he embarks upon until his final redemption in Jamaica. Banks borrows from *Huckleberry Finn* in order to create a contemporary American odyssey of race relations and alienation of youth.

Buoyed by the success of these novels, as well as the film adaptations of *The Sweet Hereafter* and *Affliction*, Banks retired from teaching and gave up his professorship at Princeton. "A funny thing happened when I quit Princeton," he recalled in *The Irish Times*. "My attention shifted. I immediately forgot opinions I had on things like deconstruction. And I started noticing things like: 'Why is the television set on in my neighbor's house at five in the morning? Is that woman really unhappy? Or has the old man got drunk again and passed out?' I sat in on a murder trial in the next town. I read the local paper instead of the *TLS*."

Banks and his fourth wife, poet Chase Twichell, bought a second home in Keene,

> **❝** [In *Rule of the Bone*], Banks borrows from *Huckleberry Finn* in order to create a contemporary American odyssey of race relations and alienation of youth. **❞**

New York, not far from the abolitionist John Brown's old farm. The move inspired his thirteenth novel, *Cloudsplitter*, a finalist for the Pulitzer Prize and winner of the Anisfield-Wolf Book Award. Seven years in the making, *Cloudsplitter* is the story of the firebrand John Brown and the events leading to his disastrous raid on Harpers Ferry, as told through the eyes of his son, Owen. Banks began thinking about his legendary neighbor and realized John Brown's story has all the themes "I've been concerned with, some would say obsessed with, for twenty years—the relationships between parents and children, particularly fathers and sons, and the interconnections between politics and religion and race."

The Darling (selected by the *New York Times Book Review* as a Notable Book of 2004), is set in late twentieth-century Liberia. The work spans topics of civil and political upheaval, and strained loyalties to country and family.

His latest novel, *The Reserve*, is a national bestseller. Set in the rugged beauty of the Adirondacks, *The Reserve* explores the intersections of class, politics, art, love, and madness that occur when two powerful personalities come together on the eve of the Second World War.

The father of four daughters, Banks continues to write in a converted sugar shack just down the road from John Brown's grave. ❧

From the Russell Banks Papers

The following letters, manuscript pages, and other curiosities are printed by permission of the Harry Ransom Humanities Research Center, University of Texas at Austin.

Letter to Elliott Anderson, editor of *TriQuarterly*

Sept. 21, 1973

Dear Elliott:

Well, okay, if you think chapter ten from FAMILY LIFE works that effectively on its own--as a sympathetic parody--then I'll take your word for it and agree to have it printed alone. The only request I would make is that you preface the chapter with a note: "Remember Me to Camelot" is a novel written by a character in a novel, FAMILY LIFE, written by Russell Banks.

I wish I could add that the novel will be published in _____ by _____, but I haven't placed it with anyone yet. Mike Anania had promised me early this summer that he wanted to publish it at Swallow, but this morning I got a long letter from Mike explaining how Swallow was out of money and was now forced to go back on all its commitments for new books for 1973-4, but he still wanted to publish FAMILY LIFE, etc., etc., etc. Too bad for me. I had pretty much given myself over to the assumption that Swallow would be bringing the book out in the next year sometime and was setting about some other tasks. Now I've got to go back and start sending the ms. out again. Ech. Know of any publishers looking for a weird little novel? Of course not. No one has ever heard of such a thing.

When will you be running chapter ten, by the way? Just so I can tell my mother.

All the best,
Russell Banks
Northwood Narrows, N.H. ▶

Front of a postcard from Kenward Elmslie, editor and publisher of Z Magazine.

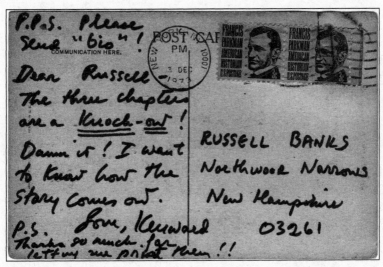

Back of postcard: "Dear Russell—The three chapters (of Family Life*) are a knock out (double-underscore)! Damn it! I want to know how the story comes out. Love Kenward / P.S. Thanks so much for letting me print them. / P.P.S. Please send bio."*

From the Russell Banks Papers *(continued)*

Letter to James Tate

The following excerpt is taken from a four-page letter to James Tate dated March 10, 1977. Russell Banks notes: "We were both on Guggenheims that year, he in Portugal, I think, and I in Jamaica, both of us somewhat isolated and writing lots of letters back and forth."

. . . Meanwhile our daily life plods happily along in the sunshine, surrounded by blossoming trees and birdsong. I spend a lot of idle time down the road in the neighborhood tavern drinking with the locals and playing dominoes--a national male pastime played with incredible fervor, very complicated the way they play it, like the Arabs, and I've gotten pretty good at it, much to their surprise, because very few white men and almost no foreigners ever learn the game well enough to play competitively, but you know me, Al, I learn fast and I'm very competitive, and besides, it's the best way to get into their incredibly foreign heads and it's the only time they talk in patois un-selfconsciously with me. Also, I've learned to dance pretty good, if I do say so myself--in fact, my nickname (Jamaicans are very fond of nicknames-- my pals are named Juke, Skinhead, Speedy, Stammer, and Bush) is Starboy. Johnny Starboy. Nashville Glitter King.

So it turns out after 5 months that I'm deeply relieved I decided to come back here--for its being tropical, of course, during this the worst winter in the history of New England's bad winters, for its being a "third world" nation (which to me makes the place endlessly fascinating--I'm learning about political realities in the field, as it were, which is frustrating and even depressing sometimes as one by one my political theories fall away), and for its being a black country (which has forced me to face all my darkest sexual and violence fantasies and fears as a white American "liberal," something the racial politics at home make impossible). [Editor's note: at this point in the letter, the typeface undergoes a noticeable change.] (I can't fucking believe it--my typewriter started humming during the last sentence, then clatter-clatter BANG and stopped. Have you any idea how hard it's going to be to get it fixed? I'm now typing on Mary's Olivetti, which is fine except that she works with it pretty much the same hours of the day I use mine. Oh woe.) I'm sorry I came to a non-industrialized country. If only I were in Germany or Japan. This is not a calamity, but it's going to become one hell of a headache. Shit shit shit.

I finished the novel, by the way, ended up calling it THE PLUMBER. I think I told you about my dealings with Houghton on the first half of the ms. and my plan to dump the whole of it on them again in spring, if my agent hasn't sold it by then, with grateful assurances that I'd made the suggested revisions, which revisions of course I will never make. But those fuckers are so intimidated and bewildered by what's going on in the book they'll never know the difference. Of course they may turn it down again anyhow, but this time they'll have to come up with another excuse or else they'll have to come right out and say they don't understand it. So anyhow, I'm in the position of having two completed book mss. floating around out there in publishers' row, looking for a home. And last week I got a Dear Russ sorry about next year but budget cuts . . . letter from the chairman at UNH [University of New Hampshire], so it looks like I don't have a job for the fall. I honestly don't know what I'm going to do about that one. Charlie had given Mary excited assurances when she was up there that I'd be hired full-time as a fiction teacher in Sept. and not to worry about a thing, then this letter comes from the chairman. Either Charlie's got his head up his ass or ▶

From the Russell Banks Papers *(continued)*

else the Chairman is trying to cover all
his bases in case it turns out in April
that he can't hire me back as he'd
promised last summer. In any case,
I've dashed off letters to BU, Emerson
and New England College, asking for a
position for the fall, but I have no hopes
for anything coming through at any of
those places. Know of any possibilities
in the Boston area? I'm afraid I may
end up teaching remedial reading to
night students at Concord High School.
Seriously. Bill told me that unless
I've made real enemies among the lit
panel I'll surely get an NEA in January,
but I've got to pick up $5 grand somehow
for the first half of the year--and
I really can't count on the NEA,
all assurances to the contrary.

Listen, I know I haven't responded to
all the wonderful information about your
life that you gave me in your long letter;
I'm sorry to sound so self-concerned
here, but I figured you'd want to hear
how things were going here first. Suffice
it to say, old friend, that I'm relieved
and very happy to be back in touch with
you, especially during this strange and
enlightening time for us both. I think of
you regularly and affectionately, with a
genuine longing to talk on and on into the
dawn with you. I often try to imagine how
you would handle this or that situation,
how you would understand this or that
absurdity or profundity. So you are on
my mind a lot, maybe more so than when
I'm in New Hampshire. You and Charlie are
the two people I most wish could visit me
here who have been unable to make it. Bill
Matthews would've been the other, and he
made it, for a great visit, incidentally.

Take care, and give my love to Lisa.
Mary sends hers to you both. And pray that
I'll be able to get my typewriter fixed
swiftly and cheaply. All love,

[Editor's note: the author signs off under the
nickname Starboy, beneath which he draws a star.]

a second step.

I was terrified-- the sight of one of the most
stable creatures I had ever known, one of the most admirably predictable and rational women I had ever met,
standing wild-eyed before me with a high-powered rifle
zeroed in on my thundering heart, so upset my notion of
the real and expected world, that anything could happen,
anything, and it would have seemed appropriate. [Rochelle
could have broken into a Cole Porter song and started
tap-dancing her way down the road, using the rifle as a
cane, waving over her shoulder at me as she pranced out
of sight, the end of a musical comedy based on the exciting
life of a girl revolutionary. Or she could have suddenly
opened her mouth wide, as if to eat a pear, and shoving
the tip of the barrel in, jammed her thumb against the
trigger and blown the top of her lovely head away. Or
she could have simply squeezed one finger, nothing more
than that, just wrinkled her trigger finger one-sixteenth
of an inch, and I would have heard the explosion, possibly
would have smelled the fire and smoke, seen a shred of
the narrow belt of blue sky fall into my face as I was
blown back against the side of my car, my chest an erupting
volcano for no more than a split second, and then Nothing, unimaginable Nothing.]

With a shudder, I decided it didn't matter what happened,
so long as anything could happen. ~~and Especially~~, I took ⊙
another step, then yet another, and gradually, as I neared ⊙

RB. I'd cut this section. It's a long book and these digressions really slow things down. DAE.

Page 22, typescript manuscript of Hamilton Stark. The editor's note, from
Daphne A. Ehrlich of Houghton Mifflin, reads: "RB. I'd cut this section.
It's a long book and these digressions really slow things down. DAE." The
offending section lived to tell the tale. ▶

From the Russell Banks Papers *(continued)*

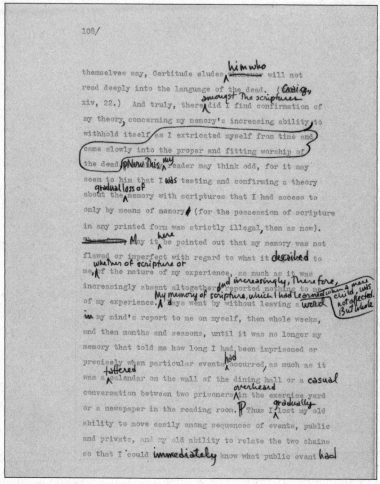

Marked-up typescript of The Relation of My Imprisonment. *Russell Banks notes: "A little, stapled-together mimeo-mag called* United Artists, *edited by Lewis Warsh and Bernadette Mayer on the Lower East Side, serialized the whole of* The Relation of My Imprisonment *over about six issues. Now very rare and probably worth a pretty penny on eBay. That was how Douglas Messerli first saw it and then asked to publish it at his small press, Sun & Moon, in a handsome hardcover edition. Then later on it went to Ballantine, and then HarperCollins."* ～

Have You Read?
More by Russell Banks

THE RESERVE

Part love story, part murder mystery, set on the
cusp of the Second World War, Russell Banks's
sharp-witted and deeply engaging new novel
raises dangerous questions about class, politics,
art, love, and madness—and explores what
happens when two powerful personalities,
trapped at opposite ends of a social divide,
begin to break the rules.

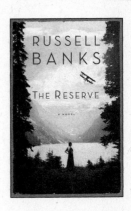

Twenty-nine-year-old Vanessa Cole is a wild,
stunningly beautiful heiress, the adopted only
child of a highly regarded New York brain
surgeon and his socialite wife. Twice married
already, Vanessa has been scandalously linked
to any number of rich and famous men. But
on the night of July 4, 1936, at her parents'
country home in a remote Adirondack
Mountain enclave known as the Reserve, two
events coincide to permanently alter the course
of Vanessa's callow life: her father dies suddenly
of a heart attack, and a mysteriously seductive
local artist, Jordan Groves, blithely lands his
Waco biplane in the pristine waters of the
forbidden Upper Lake. . . .

Jordan's reputation has preceded him; he
is internationally known as much for his
exploits and conquests as for his paintings
themselves, and, here in the midst of the Great
Depression, his leftist political loyalties seem
suspiciously undercut by his wealth and elite
clientele. But for all his worldly swagger, Jordon
is as staggered by Vanessa's beauty and charm as
she is by his defiant independence. He falls easy
prey to her electrifying personality, but it is not
long before he discovers that the heiress carries

Have You Read? *(continued)*

a dark, deeply scarring family secret. Emotionally unstable from the start, and further unhinged by her father's unexpected death, Vanessa begins to spin wildly out of control, manipulating and destroying the lives of all who cross her path.

Moving from the secluded beauty of the Adirondack wilderness to the skies above war-torn Spain and fascist Germany, *The Reserve* is a clever, incisive, and passionately romantic novel of suspense that adds a new dimension to this acclaimed author's extraordinary repertoire.

"A vividly imagined book. It has the romantic atmosphere of those great thirties tales in film and prose, and it speeds the reader along from its first pages. . . . Banks's talents are so large—and the novel so fundamentally engaging. . . . *The Reserve* is a pleasure well worth savoring."

—Scott Turow, *Publishers Weekly*

"Of the many writers working in the great tradition today, one of the best is Russell Banks." —*New York Times Book Review*

CONTINENTAL DRIFT

A powerful literary classic, *Continental Drift* is a major novel about uprootedness, migration, and exploitation in contemporary America. Russell Banks has brought together two of the dominant realms of his fiction—New England and the Caribbean—by skillfully braiding into one taut narrative the story of a young blue-collar worker and family man who abandons his broken dreams in New Hampshire and the story of a young Haitian woman who with her nephew and baby flees the brutal injustice and poverty of her homeland.

Hailed by James Atlas in *Atlantic Monthly* as "the most convincing portrait I know of contemporary America . . . a great American novel," Banks's 1985 novel is one of the most celebrated works of fiction of the last twenty-five years.

"A vigorous and original novel."
                                    —*New York Review of Books*

"An excellent novel . . . An important novel because of the precise manner in which it reflects the spiritual yearning and materialistic frenzy of our contemporary life. It is also an extremely skillful book, both in its writing, which is impeccable, and in the way it unfolds. . . . Always, Banks writes with tremendous knowledge, convictions, and authenticity."   —*Chicago Tribune*

Have You Read? *(continued)*

THE DARLING

The Darling is Hannah Musgrave's story, told emotionally and convincingly years later by Hannah herself. A political radical and member of the Weather Underground, Hannah has fled America to West Africa, where she and her Liberian husband become friends and colleagues of Charles Taylor, the notorious warlord and now ex-president of Liberia. When Taylor leaves for the United States in an effort to escape embezzlement charges, he's immediately placed in prison. Hannah's encounter with Taylor in America ultimately triggers a series of events whose momentum catches Hannah's family in its grip and forces her to make a heartrending choice.

Set in Liberia and the United States from 1975 through 1991, *The Darling* is a political/historical thriller—reminiscent of Graham Greene and Joseph Conrad—that explodes the genre, raising serious philosophical questions about terrorism, political violence, and the clash of races and cultures.

"In The Darling, [Banks] is working at full strength, and his readers are in his debt."
                    —*Washington Post Book World*

THE ANGEL ON THE ROOF:
THE STORIES OF RUSSELL BANKS

With *The Angel on the Roof*, Russell Banks offers readers an astonishing collection of thirty years of his short fiction, revised especially for this volume and highlighted by the inclusion of nine new stories that are among the finest he has ever written. As is characteristic of all of Banks's works, these stories resonate with irony and compassion, honesty and insight, extending into the vast territory of the heart and the world, from working-class New England to Florida and the Caribbean and Africa. Broad in scope and rich in imagination, *The Angel on the Roof* affirms Russell Banks's place as one of the masters of American storytelling.

"A beautifully lucid, frequently wrenching collection. . . . What elevates these stories far above their tacitly heartbreaking events are the vast reserves of compassion and wisdom that Mr. Banks brings to framing tragedy."
—Janet Maslin, *New York Times*

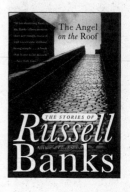

Have You Read? *(continued)*

CLOUDSPLITTER

Cloudsplitter is narrated by the enigmatic Owen Brown, last surviving son of America's most famous and still controversial political terrorist and martyr, John Brown. Deeply researched, brilliantly plotted, and peopled with a cast of unforgettable characters both historical and wholly invented, *Cloudsplitter* is dazzling in its re-creation of the political and social landscape of our history during the years before the Civil War, when slavery was tearing the country apart. But within this broader scope, Russell Banks has given us a riveting, suspenseful, heartbreaking narrative filled with intimate scenes of domestic life, of violence and action in battle, of romance and familial life and death that make the reader feel in astonishing ways what it was like to be alive in that time.

"A huge and thunderously good book."
—*Chicago Tribune*

When we first meet him, Chappie is a punked-out teenager living with his mother and abusive stepfather in an upstate New York trailer park. During this time, he slips into drugs and petty crime. Rejected by his parents, out of school and in trouble with the police, he claims for himself a new identity as a permanent outsider; he gets a cross-bones tattoo on his arm, and takes the name "Bone."

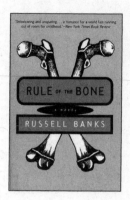

He finds dangerous refuge with a group of biker-thieves, and then hides in the boarded-up summer house of a professor and his wife. He finally settles in an abandoned school bus with Rose, a child he rescues from a fast-talking pedophile. There Bone meets I-Man, an exiled Rastafarian, and together they begin a second adventure that takes the reader from Middle America to the ganja-growing mountains of Jamaica. It is an amazing journey of self-discovery through a world of magic, violence, betrayal, and redemption.

"[O]ne finishes the book with indelible sympathy for tough-guy Bone, touched by his loneliness, fear and desperation, and having absorbed Banks's message: that (as he said recently) society's failure to save its children is 'the main unrecognized tragedy of our time.'"
—*Publishers Weekly*

THE SWEET HEREAFTER

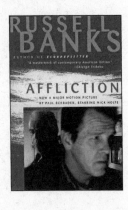

When fourteen children from the small town of Sam Dent are lost in a tragic accident, its citizens are confronted with one of life's most difficult and disturbing questions: When the worst happens, whom do you blame, and how do you cope? Masterfully written, *The Sweet Hereafter* is a large-hearted novel that brings to life a cast of unforgettable small-town characters and illuminates the mysteries and realities of love as well as grief.

"The characters are rendered with such clear-eyed affection, the central tragedy handled with such unsentimental artistry, the wonderfully named mountain hamlet of Sam Dent described in such precise (and often funny) detail, *The Sweet Hereafter* is not only Banks's most accomplished book to date, but his most accessible and ultimately affirmative. Russell Banks knows everything worth knowing . . . and much, much more."

—*Washington Post Book World*

AFFLICTION

Wade Whitehouse is an improbable protagonist for a tragedy. A well-digger and policeman in a bleak New Hampshire town, he is a former high-school star gone to beer fat, a loner with a mean streak. It is a mark of Russell Banks's artistry and understanding that Wade comes to loom in one's mind as a blue-collar American Everyman afflicted by the dark secret of the macho tradition. Told by his articulate, equally scarred younger brother, Wade's story becomes as spellbinding and inexorable as a fuse burning its way to the dynamite.

"Magnificently convincing . . . beautifully sustained, suspenseful."

—*New York Times Book Review*

HAMILTON STARK

Hamilton Stark is a New Hampshire pipe fitter and the sole inhabitant of the house from which he evicted his own mother. He is the villain of five marriages and the father of a daughter so obsessed that she has been writing a book about him for years. Hamilton Stark is a boor, a misanthrope, a handsome man: funny, passionately honest, and a good dancer. The narrator, a middle-aged writer, decides to write about Stark as a hero whose anger and solitude represent passion and wisdom. At the same time that he tells Hamilton Stark's story, he describes the process of writing the novel and the complicated connections between truth and fiction. As Stark slips in and out of focus, maddeningly elusive and fascinatingly complex, this beguiling novel becomes at once a compelling meditation on identity and a thoroughly engaging story of life on the cold edge of New England.

"Banks has skillfully used his repertoire of contemporary techniques to write a novel that is classically American—a dark, but sometimes funny, romance with echoes of Poe and Melville." —*Washington Post*

SUCCESS STORIES: STORIES

In *Success Stories,* an exceptionally varied yet coherent collection, Russell Banks proves himself one of the most astute and forceful writers in America today. "Queen for a Day," "Success Story," and "Adultery" trace the fortunes of the Painter family in their pursuit of and retreat from the American dream. Banks also explores the ethos of rampant materialism in a group of contemporary moral fables. "The Fish" is an evocative parable of faith and greed set in a Southeast Asian village, "The Gully" tells of the profitability of violence and the ironies of upward mobility in a Latin American shantytown, and "Children's Story" explores the repressed rage that boils beneath the surface of relationships between parents and children and between citizens of the first and third worlds.

"Each story is uncommonly good . . . surprising, lively writing and believably human characters. . . . Banks has a terrific eye, mordant yet affectionate, for the bric-a-brac and the pathos of the American dream."

—*Washington Post Book World*

THE BOOK OF JAMAICA

In *The Book of Jamaica*, Russell Banks explores
the complexities of political life in the
Caribbean and its ever-present racial conflicts.
His narrator, a thirty-five-year-old college
professor from New Hampshire, goes to Jamaica
to write a novel and soon becomes embroiled
in the struggles between whites and blacks. He
is especially interested in an ancient tribe called
the Maroons, descendants of the Ashanti, who
had been enslaved by the Spanish and then
fought the British in a hundred-year war.
Despite this history of oppression, the
Maroons have managed to maintain a relatively
autonomous existence in Jamaica. Partly out
of guilt and an intellectual sense of social
responsibility, Banks's narrator gets involved in
reuniting two clans who have been feuding for
generations. Unfortunately, his attempt ends in
disaster, and the narrator must deal with his
feelings of alienation, isolation, and failure.

"A compelling novel. . . . Banks achieves effects
at once beautiful and brutal. A virtuoso
performance."   —*Publishers Weekly*

TRAILERPARK

In *Trailerpark*, Russell Banks introduces a colorful cast of characters at the Granite State Trailerpark, where Flora, in number 11, keeps more than a hundred guinea pigs and screams at people to stay away from her babies; Claudel, in number 5, thinks he is lucky until his wife burns down their trailer and runs off with Howie Leeke; and Noni, in number 7, has telephone conversations with Jesus and tells the police about them. In this series of related short stories, Russell Banks offers gripping, realistic portrayals of individual Americans and paints a portrait of New England life that is at once dark, witty, and revealing.

"Mesmerizing. . . . There are times when Banks's prose fairly dazzles." —*Publishers Weekly*

THE RELATION OF MY IMPRISONMENT

The Relation of My Imprisonment is a work of fiction utilizing a form invented in the seventeenth century by imprisoned Puritan divines. Designed to be exemplary, works of this type were aimed at brethren outside the prison walls and functioned primarily as figurative dramatizations of the tests of faith all true believers must endure. These "relations," framed by scripture and by a sermon explicating the text, were usually read aloud in weekly or monthly installments during religious services. Utterly sincere and detailed accounts of suffering, they were nonetheless highly artificial. To use the form self-consciously, as Russell Banks has done, is not to parody it so much as to argue good-humoredly with the mind it embodies, to explore and, if possible, to map the limits of that mind, the more intelligently to love it.

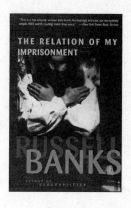

"This is a marvelously written little book, fascinatingly intricate, yet deceptively simple. Well worth reading more than once."
—*New York Times Book Review*

Have You Read? *(continued)*

FAMILY LIFE

Family Life, Russell Banks's first novel, transforms the dramas of domesticity into the story of a royal family in a mythical contemporary kingdom. Life inside this kingdom includes the king (dubbed "the Hearty" or "the Bluff"), who squeals angrily as is his wont; the queen, who, while pondering the mirror in her chambers, decides to write a book; three adolescent princes who are, respectively, a superb wrestler, a fanatical sports car driver, and a sullen drunk. Then there are the mysterious Green Man with a thing for princes; the Loon, who lives in a tree house designed by Christopher Wren; and a whole slew of murders, mayhem, coups, debauches, world tours, and love and loss and laughter.

"Banks writes with trembling knowledge, conviction, and authenticity."

—*Chicago Tribune*

Don't miss the next book by your favorite author. Sign up now for AuthorTracker by visiting www.AuthorTracker.com.